Heathen

By
Paul Webster

1

The first thing he can define, as he surfaces from the abyss of unconsciousness, is the solitary sound of a bird crying in the distance. It's cry is a high pitched squeal that pierces sharply into his muddy mind. The pain that it brings is the first sure sign that he is once more awake.

The second thing he can define is the aching pain on the back of his head, making his head throb in time with every beat of his pounding heart. His heart is beating rebelliously with more of an aggressive thud, than a calm, smooth beat.

He slowly starts to open his eyes and immediately squeezes them shut again as a white hot glare of purest sunlight burns directly into his retinas. Instinctively, he raises a heavy arm to block out the light, freeing his mind from the additional pain and allowing it to focus on his environment and to take stock of where he is.

Passing squinting eyes over his surroundings, he is met with rusty metal walls, ceiling and flooring. Other than the beginnings of puddles that have started to gather in the corners of the room and the thin veins of water running down the walls that feed them, the room is completely empty.

Fuck, he thinks, *I'm still alive.*

With a sigh, Kerrigan dropped his arm back to his side, shut his eyes and allowed his head to droop forward so that his chin rested against his chest. His raven black, shoulder length hair hung flaccid over his face. Sunshine warmed the exposed nape of his neck. It might have been a welcome feeling in any other situation, but he was in too much pain and discomfort to take any pleasure from the small feeling of warmth.

After a few moments of doing nothing more than taking a couple of shallow raspy breaths, Kerrigan, with a tremendous effort, raised his head again to rest against the hard metal wall to which his back was leant. He inhaled sharply as the contact of the sore spot on the back of his head connected with the wall sending a sharp bolt of pain into his skull. The throbbing area at the back of his skull, which he'd noticed upon his awakening, was still very tender and fresh. He knew that he must have been dealt a mighty blow there recently.

He cautiously risked opening his eyes again, this time deliberately doing so by only the tiniest of amounts.

Like a trapped bird's wings, his eyes fluttered reflexively against the brightness that attacked them, but after a couple of seconds of forcing his eyes to remain open, they adjusted to the light and he was able to keep his eyelids under control.

He found himself sat in a column of light on the floor of an empty, square room, barely big enough for a man to lie down in. Apart from the omnipresent rust that covered all of room's surfaces, and the thin film of brown puddles that were collected in the small room's corners, the only other feature of any worthy note was a small hole about the size of an adult's fist, through which fresh air and the agonizingly bright sunlight annoyingly shone.

The heat was incredible. It seemed to push against Kerrigan's mind's attempt to try and wake himself up. The sun light acted as a weight on his sleepy mind, keeping him in a state of semi-hypnosis that was impossible to fight against.

His entire body was covered in a slimy film of sweat, making his clothes stick uncomfortably to his skin and his hair group together in thick, greasy strands that hung heavy from his brow. He licked his lips to no effect. He thought he heard the sound of two sandstones grinding together as he did so, but wasn't sure if it was just his imagination. He wondered which was drier: his lips or his tongue.

For a long while he just sat there in a state of drowsiness, not doing anything and not thinking any thoughts. He wanted to go back to sleep but he found himself unable to do so. Finally, his mind reached the conclusion that he had to do something, anything,

other than sit there brain dead while he marinated in his own sweat. So, in an attempt to get away from the column of sunlight burning his face, and in the hope of gaining some slight degree of comfort, Kerrigan tried to push himself to his feet.
The physical effort of gaining a vertical stature proved too much in his current, sleepy condition and after clearing his bottom off the floor by only a couple of inches, he bumped back down sending a dizzying bolt of pain straight up his spine and into his groggy mind. Before he had time to control himself, the jolt had unbalanced him from his sitting position and he slid side ways down the wall to land heavily on his shoulder.
He was not yet alert enough to prevent his head from hitting the floor with a low, metallic thud.
I deserve all this, he thought and drifted back into unconsciousness.

An unknown length of time had passed when Kerrigan started to drift slowly back into the world, but he knew it must have been several hours as his favourite, annoying column of light which had caused him so much discomfort earlier, was now shining on the wall opposite him.
The bird that had awoken him earlier was still crying to itself outside of the room.
The heat, Kerrigan realized, had somehow gone up several notches. The room wasn't just hot any more but sweltering. Every breath he took filled his lungs with hot dry air, burning his lungs, making the entire process of breathing into a one of mild self-torture. Each exhale of breath seemed to carry a little bit more of his strength with it. The weight of the heat sat heavy on his entire body like a giant lead blanket, smothering out what little motivation might have remained within him.
As if he needed further proof of how long he'd been out, the arm that he had fallen asleep on was now completely numb.
He lay with his face pressed into the metal floor for a long time.
Taking several hot breaths, Kerrigan prepared himself as best as he could to raise himself up off the floor.

With a grimace, using his one still waking arm, he pushed himself back to a sitting position. His sense of balance and vision swam as blood gushed back into his head causing him to feel sickeningly dizzy.

Focusing on his boots helped his mind to settle and he gradually fought off the urge to throw up. He wasn't even certain he'd have the strength to move if his stomach lost the battle. The last thing he needed right now was to vomit all over himself.

He briefly considered taking off his clothes to help his body cool down, even just his ankle length leather coat which seemed to have doubled in weight, but as quickly as the thought occurred he dismissed it. For one thing, it would be just too much effort to remove them. He felt like he was smothered in quick setting amber. Every movement was too slow, too heavy and too much effort to be worth the potential rewards.

He found it hard to keep his eyes open, wanting only to succumb to the temptation of sleep being forced upon him by the oppressive heat.

Taking his eyes off his boots, he raised his eyes to the wall opposite. Once a dark green, the paint had peeled away over many years exposing the metal underneath which had then rusted over creating hectic, brown patterns everywhere he looked.

It reminded him of sunburnt, peeling skin.

As Kerrigan stared, his tired mind started to make images out of the random patterns and slowly, faces started to dissolve themselves out of the chaos, like stones seen at the bottom of a shallow pool. The faces were wicked looking with long pointy noses, beady little eyes and sneering mouths filled with too many long, razor sharp teeth. They looked like little laughing demons with bony skulls made entirely from rust. The more Kerrigan stared at the faces the more he became convinced they were laughing.

No, not just laughing. Taunting. Taunting, because their laughter was directed at him. He could swear he could almost hear their wicked little cackles inside his skull…

To avoid driving himself mad with his own illusions, he looked to

the wall to his right and with a sudden flash of hope, he realized that he'd been completely stupid and sloppy with his initial examination of his surroundings: He hadn't even checked the wall against which he sat!
Maybe there would be a window he could smash, or a shaft down which he could crawl. Maybe even the handle of the door that led into this oven, after all, he had to have been placed in this room somehow. If he could find it maybe he could grab hold of it, and with a quick twist, pass out of this metallic prison and back into the cool air of freedom!
With an uncomfortable twist of his neck to look over his shoulder his hopes were dashed just as quickly as they'd been raised. Just more mocking rust met his searching eyes. There was no window, no shaft and certainly no handle.
He sighed and settled back into his previous slouching position, thinking himself stupid to place such high hopes on an unrealistic optimism. However he had ended up in here, he was sure that it was not of his own choice and so his release would not be so easily gained.
It seemed to Kerrigan, that the room was specifically designed as some kind of holding pen. The small hole was presumably meant for ventilation meaning it was not a storage room, not that it was big enough to be considered a practical storage room anyway. Little more than a few crates could be stored in the room before it would have became full.
He took this as a sign for the purpose for his incarceration - He was at least meant to live, otherwise why else place him in here? If he was to be killed, why not have done it while he was out cold? He must at least be being held by someone for something.
Unless, his sceptical mind countered, the idea was to draw out his death into as long and as agonizing torture as possible, with only his unanswered questions, his stench of sweat and the mocking rust demons for company.
It wasn't a pleasant thought and so with a numb arm lying at his side like a dead snake, a pounding headache from some unremembered blow, and his body currently stewing in it's own

juices, Kerrigan tried to recall exactly what circumstances had happened to him to place him in this current situation. Maybe if he could remember that, it might help him to interpret this predicament better and figure a way out of it.
Something about a fight…
He couldn't keep his mind focused on the thought for long enough to determine any thing more helpful; The blistering heat was ruining any kind of concentration he might have been able to muster on the memory.
He slowly raised his heavy eyes to the wall opposite. It felt like he was having to lift weights with his eyeballs. Out of the chaos, his mind instantly drew out the demons from the rust he had noticed earlier, who laughed at him from the safe distance of the wall opposite. Although only six feet away, if he was asked to reach out and touch it, it might as well have been on the other side of the moon.
He stared back at the rust demons who laughed cruelly at him. He knew deep down in his mind that they weren't actually real, but that didn't mean he'd let these little monsters have their fun. He'd stare back at them to show them he wasn't afraid.
Their laughter appeared to grow louder, more lucid…
It also strangely appeared to be coming from outside the small ventilation hole.
The more he focused on the laughter the more he became convinced that not only was the laughter coming from outside, not only was it getting louder, but it was definitely getting closer.
Somebody was outside of the room!
Despite a huge effort to shout for help, the best his dry lungs and depleted energy could muster was a small wheeze of a cry as he tried to hail the disembodied laughter. If only he could gain their attention, they might help free him from this impenetrable oven.
Again he tried to suck in a lung full of air to yell for help, but achieved little more than a wheeze for his efforts.
The laughter had stopped anyway. In fact, he was already doubting that he had heard it originally in the first place, at first thinking, and then knowing that it must have been a hallucination brought on

by his boiling brain.
The rust demons grinned and laughed at his futile efforts. God how he hated those bastards.
He needed water, and his thirst grew when he stared at the baby puddles which lay in the corners of the room on the opposite wall, on the other side of the world. They seemed to taunt him with possibility. If only the baby puddles were full grown adults bursting with life saving liquid. He wouldn't have cared if it was brown and the pieces of rust that floated in it would have cut his throat to shreds… it would be worth it, and it would be the sweetest, most refreshing drink of his life.
Suddenly, he couldn't keep his eyes open any longer and as sleep enveloped him, it took his thirst with him for company, and the laughter started again…

2

…A loud bang awoke him briefly…
…He was lying on his back and felt fresh air brush over his face. It was a moment of purest relief…
…He could feel movement below himself and knew he was being moved, dragged by his ankles but did not know by who, where or why…
…He heard voices but could not hear the words...
...and always, there was the mocking laughter…

A feeling of smoothest cool silk awakened Kerrigan as it flowed over his lips and down his chin. It splashed down onto his shirt cooling his chest, and as it flowed into his mouth and over his dry tongue it immediately awoke his mind to the realization that here was water! Precious, beautiful, life giving water was being poured into his mouth!
He greedily gulped down two huge mouthfuls relishing the cool sensation it brought to his barren throat. From here it burst outwards in a cold explosion originating in his stomach, spreading and rejuvenating his entire body.

Like a hungry chick, he stretched his neck out for more, but there was none to be had. The hand that had pursed his mouth open to pour in the water thrust Kerrigan's searching head back with a sharp unkindly push.
"That's enough for now" the voice that owned the hand growled, "Don't want ya throwing up all over the God damn floor."
Kerrigan opened his eyes on the most familiar four walls in his life. Although three of the walls were just more rusting metal, unlike the ones in his previous surroundings, these three walls held no laughing rust demons. They were still rusty of course, but the rust was to a pattern that Kerrigan was so familiar with seeing, he could have drew the design from memory with as much detail as a Cartographer's map. He had been seeing these walls every single day for as long back as he could remember. The fourth wall was made up of inch wide vertical metal bars.
He was back in his cell.
"I'll leave the rest here" said the guard who had forced the water into him. He dropped the pitcher of water against the opposite wall from Kerrigan's bunk. "You can get the rest yourself when you get your strength back."
The guard, who Kerrigan could not quite place the name to despite his familiar face, let himself out of the cell and locked it behind himself. He grabbed hold of the vertical bars and address Kerrigan once more, "You better hurry up and get better before the supplies come in, for your sake". He looked Kerrigan up and down with a look of disgust, "Your one sick fucker you know that?"
Despite his spinning head and exhausted body, Kerrigan grinned wildly showing all of his teeth at once.
"Sick fucker" commented the guard once more, spat on the floor, and left.

The next hour passed in a kind of haze for Kerrigan. He started by allowing the water that the guard had forced into him to spread throughout, and reinvigorate his body until he had the strength to rise from his bunk and drink the pitcher of water for himself.
Ignoring the guard's earlier advice, and instead listening to his

stomach's crying plea for more, Kerrigan quaffed back half the water in the jug in one sitting. Despite the water's now warmth, it was the sweetest feeling he could possibly have imagined. The water cascaded gently down his throat, applying soothing kisses to the inside of his throat as it journeyed onward and into his stomach where it's soothing embrace would continue.

However, thirty seconds after drinking the water, his stomach convulsed with having too much liquid forced upon it after such a long status without, and most of the water ended up back on the floor.

Despite his continued thirst, Kerrigan forced himself to sip the remainder of the water for the next hour, knowing that if he wasted it, the guards would not be kind enough to bring him any more.

Slowly, his headache faded and he was at last able to focus his thoughts coherently.

He was back in his cell. No change here that he could see. Same bare walls, bars and uncomfortably hard bed. Home sweet home.

So where had he been?

He remembered being dragged along on his back. If not for the protection provided from his ankle length leather coat, he could have had some nasty cuts and infections to deal with. The floors around here were hardly known for their cleanliness.

So that was how he had ended up back here in his cell. But what else?

He found it hard to focus on what had come previous to this memory. Perhaps because he had been in a semi-catatonic state throughout most of it brought on by the dehydration he had been suffering...

Dehydration...

That brought back a patch of memory. He could remember being inside a swelteringly hot oven with, bizarrely, little demons laughing at him. No, that wasn't quite right. There were demons sure, but what was it about the demons that stirred his curiosity?? What was it about them that made them capture his attention?? Was it their beady little eyes? Their mouths that were over packed with thin, razor sharp teeth? All that he could remember was that

they were brown in colour like bronze or rust....
Rust demons! That's right! Suddenly his mind seized upon the thought. That's what he'd called the faces he had seen in the rust encrusted walls of the oven... but it wasn't an oven, it was... it was a sweat box!
He'd been sent to the sweat box!
Now his mind was racing, hurtling along at a pace he could barely grasp. Just how long had he been in there for? Why did he have a sore spot on the back of his head? Had he been struck as he suspected? And if so, who had dealt the blow? And why?
He didn't want to lose his current mental momentum and so started to focus his attention on the most important question of all, something that might aid his recollection and fill in the blank in his memory; what had sent him to the sweat box in the first place?
Reluctantly, the memory resurfaced itself, revealing it's details bit by bit like how an image glimpsed amongst clouds might slowly take form and substance once the initial image was realized, slowly taking form until it was more detailed and more elaborate than had originally been conceived...
He remembered he'd been in the mess hall at lunch time, waiting silently in line for his regulation slop that was supposedly a decent meal. As usual, the fellow inmates that surrounded him talked, moaned, bickered and insulted one another with anal conversation and crude remarks.
Kerrigan often spent these moments trying to block out the mundane racket that constituted as conversation among his fellow inmates. He found the conversation of the scum to which he lived with, annoying, insulting and to be of such a meaningless quality as to be not worth even the slightest bit of his attention. The only conversation among the inmates that was not grumbles of how shit their lives were, of how they had been falsely or unjustly imprisoned (sure), or how one prisoner was going to kill another in as slow and excruciating manor as possible, was talk of how good it would be to feel the wind of freedom once more caressing their pocked faces.
That, and women of course.

Some particularly foolish inmates even spoke aloud plans of how they intended to escape from the prison and live a life of heavenly bliss. For Kerrigan, it was almost laughable how they clung to this impossible idea. No-one had ever left the prison alive. It was pathetic that they clung to a dream that would never come to fruition.

All their meaningless talk made Kerrigan's head ache if he paid too much attention to it and so he often chose to eat his meal alone, rather than listen to their banal chatter.

At a call from the guard at the front of the lunch queue, who's job it was to ensure that the procession proceeded smoothly, Kerrigan reached the front of the line and waited to be served up his regulation dollop of grey slop. It was supposedly designed to give a man all the proteins and energy he needed to support him and keep him strong throughout the day.

It was definitely not designed to be tasty or aesthetically pleasing, and was it affectionately known as The Grey Snot among the inmates.

In Kerrigan's experience, it tasted even worse than it looked and left you hungry well before your next meal entitlement.

Not that he cared. He felt he deserved everything he got.

The assistant who was in charge of serving up the grey delicacy, scooped up a ladle full of the thick mucus and ungracefully slopped it down in the general vicinity of Kerrigan's withheld bowl. The vast majority of it missed and spilt over Kerrigan's hands and dripped down onto his boots.

Kerrigan looked down at the spillage then, slowly, raised his head and scowled at the kitchen assistant in front of him. It was Duncan, a regular kitchen assistant with a wide smile that showed too many dirty teeth and narrow shifty eyes.

"Oh, sorry about that." grinned Duncan. It was a grin which clearly portraying that he had deliberately intended to cause the accident, and was taking great amusement in seeing Kerrigan's displeasure. He had a reputation amongst the other inmates and guards for being a trouble maker and enjoying it.

He was not the only inmate with a reputation for trouble. Kerrigan was known as a loner, never attempting to make conversation and spent most of his time frowning angrily back at anyone who met his gaze. He got into trouble with the guards so often that it was widely believed that he enjoyed breaking the rules and being punished for it, however this was simply not true… he just didn't take shit from anyone was all, regardless of the consequences.

It was a bizarre attitude that no one could fully understand, except for Kerrigan himself, for it was only he who fully accepted that his imprisonment was completely and totally justified. He deserved it and he knew it. Yet he also knew that he deserved worse. He deserved to be beaten, tortured, burned, broken, lashed, cut and many more agonizing acts... but he did not deserve death. Death would be a relief. Death would bring an end to the suffering that he knew he must endure for as long as possible for his terrible, heinous crimes…

Clenching his jaw and grinding his teeth, scowling at the kitchen assistant and his stupid grin, Kerrigan could feel the anger swelling up inside of him ready to explode out like a hot geyser. And very much like how a hot water geyser spewed out it's contents until it's internal pressure had receded, Kerrigan would be unable to stop his tirade of violence until his body was drained of the rage within.

"Move along, Kerrigan" ordered the guard at the front of the queue. Like most of the guards, he was taller and broader than the average man. No doubt this was a job requirement when living, dealing and controlling the scum of humanity. In his hand he brandished a two foot long metal pole, and was rhythmically smacking it into the palm of his left hand.

Kerrigan continued to glare back at the kitchen assistant, his gaze never faulting.

"What?" provoked Duncan with the same cocky grin, "You wanna piece of me you fucking mute?"

"Alright," intruded the large guard stepping between the two men and meeting Kerrigan's glare, "You know the consequences for fighting around here." His focus indicated that it was Kerrigan who would be liable to start any trouble, not Duncan, despite the kitchen assistant's blatant provocation.

Kerrigan knew the consequences of getting into yet another fight alright. Not that he cared.

"Now," commanded the guard, stepping a little closer to Kerrigan, almost blocking Duncan entirely from the smaller man's view, "Move...", another step, "along." He said each word slowly, forcefully.

Not noticing the guard's intimidating proximity, and after a moment of fighting off the anger threatening to burst out from within him, Kerrigan finally tore his focus off Duncan, briefly met the unflinching eyes of the guard, and turned away towards the eating tables.

"That's white whittle baby," cried Duncan to Kerrigan's back in a mocking baby voice, "move awoooong"

"Alright that's enough!" snapped the guard in response, turning towards Duncan and pointing his baton to his face, "Keep your fucking big mouth shut!"

"What?!" cried Duncan in faked innocence, "it's not my fault he's a fucking freak."

Kerrigan stopped in his tracks.

"I said THAT'S ENOUGH!" boomed the guard so loud that all the chatter in the mess hall abruptly stopped, and everyone sat at the meal tables turned their heads towards the source of the commotion. The guards who normally patrolled the perimeter of the hall also stopped and turned their attention towards the meal service area.

Observing the scene, one might have been mistaken in thinking that Kerrigan had not heard the commotion behind him for he stood motionless, facing in the opposite direction. However he had heard, and he took one deep shuddering breath. The rage he had worked so hard to suppress had returned full force and was ready to overflow.

Slowly, Kerrigan first turned his head to peer over the upturned collar of his blood red leather coat then followed the move by turning his shoulders and finally waist to face the kitchen assistant. The turn was performed as smoothly and as gracefully as a swan.

Kerrigan's eyes blazed beneath his furrowed brow, his lips were squeezed into a tight straight line and his shoulder-length black hair hung limply over his face, obscuring most of his twisted face beneath.

If looks could kill, Duncan wouldn't have known what hit him.

"What did you call me?" snarled Kerrigan. He didn't separate his clenched jaw when he spoke as if his teeth were the bars of a prison that barely kept his anger contained within. His voice was deep and husky, growling like how a wolf might sound if one could talk.

"Ha ha!, so the fucking mute can talk!" mocked Duncan with obvious pleasure at having provoked a response from Kerrigan.

"Right! That's it!" snapped the guard, "you and your big fucking mouth need to learn when to shut the fuck up!" The guard raised his metallic baton high into the air and brought his arm down in a rapid arc directly towards Duncan's face.

Duncan raised his arms in self defence.

If the baton had still been in the guard's hand, Duncan would have been knocked to the floor unconscious or worse, with the force of the guard's blow. Certainly, his face would have taken on interesting new angles that it hadn't previously worn.

As it happened, it took a moment for both Duncan and the prison guard to realize that the baton had vanished. The guard's clenched fist swung down in an arc that passed harmlessly before Duncan's shocked face.

Once the harmless strike was complete, the guard looked at his clenched fist with a look of disbelief. Slowly, the guard opened his clenched fist as if he expected to see that the baton had somehow managed to shrink itself and hide itself amongst the folds of his open palm.

The baton had gone.

Just as soon as the guard accepted that his weapon had vanished, he was thrust aside and fell clumsily onto a table which was being used to stack the used, dirty meal bowls from lunch. The table over turned from his weight, sending bowls clattering to the floor, each making a hollow, wooden plop as it struck the metallic surface.

Some bowls went rolling off under other tables in a wide arc as they rolled along on their brims.
Through arms which had been raised instinctively in defence of the guard's attack, Duncan watched the officer's tumble and looked up to see Kerrigan standing where the guard had previously been.
The guard's baton was held high above his head.
With one quick swoop, Kerrigan brought the baton down to smash directly into Duncan's mouth, his raised arms doing nothing to slow the attack down. Kerrigan felt a deep satisfaction as he heard and felt Duncan's teeth shatter beneath his blow.
Blood and bone flew from Duncan's mouth in a wide arc as his body twisted, spun and fell sprawling to contribute to the mess on the hall's floor.
Luckily for Duncan, although he was no longer conscious to appreciate it, Kerrigan was restrained from delivering any further blows by the guards who had patrolled the outer perimeter of the mess hall. Having seen Duncan's taunting from a distance, and knowing his reputation for not knowing when to be quiet, the guards had discreetly closed the gap between themselves and the brewing trouble without any of the involved party realizing.

It took three men to restrain the struggling Kerrigan, one on each arm, and one at his kicking legs, but only one to punch him twice in the face and then once in the solar plexus, knocking the wind out of him. Kerrigan didn't remember what happened next, but knew what this blank in his memory must mean - he had been struck on the back of the head knocking him unconscious.
During his restraint, there was one thing that Kerrigan later recalled noticing - not one of the other prisoners had dared to move a muscle either in support, or rebellion…

Kerrigan brought the pitcher of water down from his lips as his recollection reached it's violent conclusion.
Fucker had it comin' thought Kerrigan, as he caressed the spot on the back of his head where he had been struck.
He was glad he had done it.

3

"OK dickhead, time to go."

Flanked on both sides by two guards, Kerrigan saw that it was Warden Ashe who had spoken to him beyond the bars of his cell. He was, and always had been, Kerrigan's guard for his section of the prison, and like all the other prison guards, he lacked any kind of emotion reminiscent of being human.

Dressed in his regulation blue and silver uniform he said, "Supply's are just arriving."

He was also, Kerrigan realised, the guard who had brought him his water earlier - he'd just been too dehydrated at the time to remember his name.

He rose to his feet slowly using the cell wall as a balance point.

Standing over six feet tall, Kerrigan was not strikingly tall nor particularly broad across the shoulders, however beneath his deep, red leather coat which hung down to his ankles and which he wore with the collar up, his formerly white shirt clung tightly to a sinew of highly defined muscles. Kerrigan's belief was that the human body was no different than that of an animal's and should be kept in peak condition at all times. There was no excuse for being flabby or overweight. It was a sign of weakness to be so, a sign of poor self control and no will power. It was a display of greed, and it sickened Kerrigan to his, very defined, stomach.

Life in prison was not hard for the inmates, not on the body anyway. It was meant to be gruelling on the mind intended to break the will of inmates and, it was said, break their sanity to the point where they ultimately killed themselves. Except for the daily exercises that were mandatory for all inmates to keep them strong for the occasional work they were assigned to do, the vast majority of inmate's time was spent inside their locked cells with no entertainment, luxuries or anything mentally stimulating. Only the bland, peeling walls of their respective cells kept the prisoners company during these long, tedious hours alone.

Whereas most inmates would spend their solitary time sleeping or

wanking off to whatever perverted thoughts gave them their jollys, Kerrigan would spend his time doing press ups - both one armed and two armed - sit ups and leg crunches. He would not allow both his mind and his body to decay or go lazy just because he was confined to an eight foot by eight foot cell for hours at a time.
More days than not, he would often do this crude exercise regime five times a day. He would only do less than this if the opportunity did not arise due to working a particular chore, or, more likely, he was confined to the sweat box where the heat was so strong that exercising was an impossibility.
For Kerrigan, he felt most alive when his muscles were literally tearing themselves from his bones as he pushed them to the extreme. He took a satisfaction in the knowledge that his muscles were damaged and his body would need to expend energy to repair and rebuild the damaged tissue. It made him feel powerful, dangerous. He hated to think that he would ever become an obese, lazy slob like some of the other prison occupants.
But it was not just that. He also believed that this physical self destruction was a part of his endless journey of punishment.
After a couple of shaky steps, Kerrigan was able to leave his cell, which Ashe had opened, and stood in the corridor a moment while Ashe closed the cell door behind him. He wobbled slightly while this was happening, still feeling completely drained from his time spent in the sweat box. The two guards that flanked Ashe offered no support to prevent him from falling down.
Not that he would have accepted their help anyway.
"Follow me" said Ashe leading Kerrigan down the corridor while the two other guards flanked Kerrigan from the rear.
It was a route he had walked many, many times before and, like a musician can play a piece of music instinctively, Kerrigan could recount their passage from memory even before it happened.
After passing ten cells - five cells either side, Kerrigan reached the base of a set of stairs twelve steps high.
After ascending the steps he reached another corridor which ran perpendicular to the corridor which ran amongst the cells.
Passing another set of stairs that fed into their windowless corridor,

the trio turned left into Warden Ashe's office.

The cells of each prison wing were laid out much like the prongs of a fork. Each of the five 'prongs' was a corridor of twenty cells, and each set of cells ultimately converged into one corridor which led to the only way in or out. This exit was reached only by passing through each wing's Warden's office. In this case, Warden Ashes. The offices were locked on both sides to ensure that all comings and goings to the cells were properly monitored and audited. If the Warden did not approve it, then nobody was allowed to enter or leave.

After passing through Warden Ashe's office, ensuring that each set of doors was locked securely behind them, there was another brief rise consisting of ten steps which led them to the final door on their journey out of the West Wing. Some fantastically witty guard had placed a sign on this red door reading, "There are no walls! Your welcome to leave whenever you like! PLEASE!"

Ha ha. Hilarious.

Ashe opened the door and led Kerrigan out.

After passing through the door, there was a moment were an inmate of the prison could almost believe they actually were a free man.

There was a cool wind that tickled Kerrigan's face and ruffled his hair as it blew from all directions at once, the sun shone brightly in a cloudless sky which made his skin feel like it was instantly burning... and the sign on the exit side of the West Wing was correct in it's promise: there were no walls. Nor were there any watch towers, patrolling guards, mines, traps or any other means of preventing escape. But there was also no where to run to either. In all directions all that could be seen was where the deep blue of the sea, met the light pastel blue of the cloudless sky.

The red door led onto the deck of the prison ship, Chimera.

4

The Chimera.

Two kilometres long and half a kilometre wide, it was designed and built to contain within it's hulk up to four hundred of societies worst criminals. It's cells were rarely empty and housed a permanent guard of one hundred dedicated men. It also included a crew of thirty seven skilled personnel including navigators, maintenance, kitchen personnel and cleaning staff.

If the Chimera could talk, much like an elderly grandmother, it would ask you to pull up a chair, settle down and ask if you were comfy as it began a long and woeful tail of it's rise to glory, a magnificent career and then it's slow, unfortunate fall from grace.

Once a proud sandstone yellow, the Chimera had stood on the horizon with it's impressive array of towers and antennas thrusting mightily into the sky: A golden beacon of pride, justice and authority. It's bow stood higher than it's stern giving it a muscular, confident look, like how a knight of old walked with his chest thrust. To look at the once powerful ship was to see a graceful, majestic creature proud of it's important role in service to civilized folk.

At the time of it's construction, the ship was powered by the latest in engine designs. The entire ship was primarily powered by hundreds of efficient solar panels housed atop the various structures on deck that fed down into Chimera, powering all of her systems, computers, radars and engines meaning Chimera could potentially remain at sea almost indefinitely, never having to expose it's unsavoury cargo to the innocent land dwellers. It's primary engine was, at the time it was created, an almost soundless electrical wonder, admired by all mechanics and technicians who were privileged enough to view it and adored by those who had designed and built it. In addition to this, the main engine was supported by five huge batteries which were also fed by the solar panels and always remained fully charged. In case of bad weather, the batteries would automatically take over powering the engine enabling the ship to continue sailing for a further month - plenty of time for any poor weather to subside or if absolutely necessary, return to any port in case of emergencies.

In the unlikely event of the primary engine failing, the ship also came supplied with a second back up engine powered by more conventional means - coal. This engine was much smaller than the first and produced only enough power to thrust the engines. What little additional electricity it produced was directed solely to the bridge and it's vast array of delicate navigational equipment, meaning the entire ship would be kept in darkness until the main engine could be restarted, or a port could be reached.

This did not prove to be a problem in regards to keeping the prisoners locked away, as their cells were locked securely with reliable locks and keys, however it would make the living conditions for the officers and guards of Chimera a little less comfortable.

Luckily, this had never happened.

For countless years Chimera was a testament to how criminals would be confined to an inescapable prison and safely kept away from civilized society, only needing to return to land for supplies, and this was seldom done. Upon it's creation, it was hailed as being a triumph of good sense and reason and work begun immediately on creating additional prison ships.

Now however, those glorious days had long since passed. No one alive could remember those majestic days, nor could any one state for certain just how long Chimera had been in service, although it was generally known that it had served much longer than was originally intended.

Chimera was now barely a shadow of it's former self. It's finest moments in it's long arduous life were long forgotten, along with the knowledge of her maintenance and understanding of her delicate interior workings.

None of the lights, radar's, sonar's and other "ar's" worked anymore and probably never would again - the parts needed to repair or replace them were simply not available anymore. Even if any of the broken systems were repaired, barely enough power was supplied by the mostly broken solar panels to power the engine, never mind any such luxuries like navigation.

Only two of the five original back up batteries still worked, and these were seldom ever above a third of full charge each. Too many long years of draining the batteries and recharging them had

left their efficiency of the past something that could only be imagined. Were once it was a pessimistic notion to consider the use of the coal engine, now it was used almost as much as the electric one.
Although nothing to be proud of, the prison cells aboard Chimera remained full – a sign that although time may corrupt and change many things, the human soul remained as reliably corrupt as ever.
It's once smooth hull had been fixed up with an ugly patchwork of repairs which too closely resembled dried scabs on it's side. Time had ravaged the golden paintwork leaving it peeling and flaky like sun burnt skin.
At some point during it's tragic fall from grace, Chimera had also been modified in a clumsy, undignified manner so that it's deck was now dotted with spindly, ungainly cranes and other insect like appendages.
Were once Chimera looked like a magnificent lioness of the ocean, it now looked more like an ugly spiked fossil, barely capable of keeping itself afloat.

Without further encouragement from Warden Ashe, Kerrigan headed towards one of the mandible claws to take up his customary position during the process of loading supplies onto the ship.
Supplies were brought direct to the ship by a small flock of rowing boats from a small fishing village that could barely be seen upon the horizon. A lot of prisoners often took this opportunity to stare at the slither of land on the horizon with their mouths agape in wonder and longing, dreaming of returning there. Not Kerrigan, he couldn't remember what it was like to be free to miss it.
Besides, he knew that being on the prison ship was where he belonged.
Once the row boats had reached the sides of Chimera, it was the prisoner's job to use the assortment of cranes, winches and pulleys (along with a considerable amount of man power) to load Chimera with the huge number of resources it consumed and used in it's general running.

In addition to all the food needed to keep over five hundred men healthy, or in the cases of the prisoners, alive, there was water, coal for the back up engine, basic spare parts along with the removal of materials that needed to be sent back to shore.

As each row boat was only large enough to be powered by ten rowers, five on either side, each boat was restricted by how much it could transport in one trip. Therefore, there was literally hundreds of crates, sacks and bags of supplies to be loaded onto and off of Chimera.

It was a huge operation which took several hours of hard labour. Every prisoner had to take part in the operation, and each was given a specific role to try and co-ordinate the transfers in as smooth and efficient manner as possible.

All prisoners that is, except those who had recently had their mouths destroyed in a recent mess hall scuffle.

Kerrigan took up his usual role on one of the manual cranes. Previously, these cranes used to be electrical and could have been operated at a control board by a single man. A simple flick of levers and the press of a few buttons would have been enough to operate the huge crane.

Unfortunately, like everything else, the ship's cranes had become broken over the years and, lacking the knowledge to repair the old technology, the cranes had to be stripped down of most of their pistons and gears to allow them to be moved and operated physically. They were clumsy and gruelling in operation, however the reloading process would have been nearly impossible without them.

Also, it was no secret that this operation was also partly based on the fact that if the prisoners didn't use the cranes manually, then those prisoners would have no other role to play in the transportation process. These prisoners might then use this time to orchestrate some kind of mutiny amongst themselves whilst the guards on deck were busy supervising the operation.

It was well known that Captain William Bronco, Captain of Chimera for sixteen years, was paranoid that any such rebellion might take place.

As such, despite the cranes criminally cumbersome operation, and the wasting of human strength, Captain Bronco insisted that they still be used.

Kerrigan was joined to his left by a relatively new prisoner, a small, thin man barely old enough to grow a respectable growth of stubble, by the name of Eddie. He was shorter than Kerrigan with a gaunt face and two black, beady little eyes peering out from below one long mono-brow.

Gossip was that this small, wiry man had came home one day to find his pregnant girlfriend in bed with another man. Apparently he had literally punched the other man to death with his bare fists. He had then turned his fury on his girlfriend and had tried to do the same to her. Whether mercy had finally stayed his hand before he could kill her, or whether she was simply lucky, Eddie's girlfriend survived his beating and subsequently had him arrested.

The unborn child within her, had not been so lucky.

He looked up at Kerrigan with a barely concealed look of fear in his eyes. No doubt he had seen Kerrigan quiet Duncan's never ending mouth earlier and had heard about his reputation.

"Hey." he ventured.

Kerrigan stared back at him. Eddie met his gaze for barely a second before turning away and bracing himself for the operation ahead.

It was a critical time for the guards of Chimera. Every prisoner was now taking his place on the deck in their respective positions. Thankfully, the assorted transportation tools were scattered around on both sides of the deck with considerable distance between the various cranes to allow them to swing their cargo around on deck. This meant, to the crews unstated relief, that there was never too large a group of prisoners congregating together. In the past, foolish pockets of uncoordinated resistance had arisen during this hectic time hoping to overthrow the guards and control Chimera for themselves. None of the mutineers were still alive to recount their futile rebellion, but plenty of witnesses were still onboard who had quickly learnt the swift justice rebellion would bring. As such, during the supply transport, the guards were outfitted with a more serious means of defending themselves: guns and rechargeable electric stun guns were the standard issue.

As the first of the supply boats came along side the hull of Chimera, Kerrigan and his fellow prisoners heaved and strained the huge crane down to water level so that the boat men below could load up their supplies onto the crane.

Absolutely no-one was ever allowed to leave the row boats to board Chimera. Those who tried would be shot.

Prisoners who tried to leave via the row boats would also be shot.

They were easy rules to co-operate with.

When the men below had finished loading their goods, they hailed the men above to begin the back breaking effort of re-raising the crane and cargo up onto the deck.

It was phenomenally hard work. The weight of the crane itself weighed as much as several adult men, most of this weight being in the arm that extended to the boats below. As the crane's pivot was deck side, and with very little leverage to push on to raise the crane up again, the crane's weight was ridiculously unbalanced needing the strength of many men just to re-raise it. It worked much like a misbalanced see-saw. Once the cargo was added at the bottom, the shift in weight became even more unbalanced resulting in a total of twelve men or more needed per crane when in use. Most men choose not to wear upper body clothing during this routine in an effort to minimize overheating themselves, however as a result, the sun blazed down on their exposed skin leaving many of the prisoners with a deep red burn to show for all their hard work. This wasn't a problem for Kerrigan; his thick coat shielded his skin from the directness of the sun, but did nothing to help keep his straining body cool.

"FuuuuuuuUUUUCK!" hissed Eddie through clenched teeth and he pushed against the crane, raising it back onto deck. It was his first time helping with the re-supply process. Pumping veins and strained tendons stood out on his neck to the point where they threatened to rip themselves away from the bone. The sun sparkled off a hundred beads of sweat that covered his brow.

After a lot of heaves, grunts and straining from the twelve

prisoners, the first of the cargo crates was safely brought aboard the ship. It was a huge crate of Grey Snot.
"Fuck..." Eddie panted, "me..." he finished. He was taking a moment to lean himself against the crane while other prisoners removed the crate from the crane's secure housing.
Kerrigan's crane loaded a further two more crates of food and a mysterious unlabelled box that sloshed and made strange banging noises when it was placed on deck. Much straining and sweating later, Eddie asked, "Just how many.... more of these things... are there?". He was folded forward, supported his aching back by placing his arms on his knees. He spat a mouth full of thick mucus onto the floor.
"Fuckin loads kid" replied a huge burly man who was also helping with the operation of the crane.
"If you didn't eat so much of the Grey Snot, Ward we'd have been finished two hours ago!" joked another in response.
"The only thing ah bin' eatin too much of is your momma's pussy".
This was met with laughter by the other men stationed around the crane.
Sweating, but not out of breath, Kerrigan actually kind of liked the huge physical efforts needed during the transportation process. For him, it was a beautiful mixture of exercise and self torture. He would never admit it if asked, he would never admit it even to himself, but he took a slight satisfaction in exerting his muscles to breaking point. It made him feel powerful, like a wild animal.
He looked briefly over the side of the ship to see the row boats below. Ward was right, there was plenty of cargo still to be boarded. Much more than usual.
In Kerrigan's experience this could mean only one thing, but before he had time to dwell upon it, a shout from one of the guards meant he was about to start working again. The latest crate had been unloaded and the crane was ready to be used again.
With a quick intake of breath, Kerrigan pushed, strained and heaved in time with everyone else.
Once the crane was lowered to the boats below, the crane operators

were given another brief rest whilst the next cargo crate was attached to the rigging.

Eddie took this moment to ask between pants of breath, "Why don't we… just sail to port… to load the cargo directly… on board?" He swallowed another deep breath, "It's gotta be easier than this!"

It was a fair question, and a one that had been asked by every inmate the first time they went through this rigorous routine.

"B'cause me lad," it was Ward again, "this 'ere ship is 'aunted." He said it with pure conviction, not displaying any embarrassment at giving such a ridiculous answer.

Ward was a huge stocky man, nearly seven feet in height who carried an impressive, wobbly belly before him. His gut was often a basis for much bemused mocking among other inmates as it was often wondered just how Ward was able to keep his rotund physique on such an unsubstantial diet. With short blonde hair and beard, he was often perceived as a kind of fatherly figure. He wouldn't look out of place with two kids bouncing on his knees whilst reading them a bed time story.

Perhaps it was because of this image, or due to how long he had been incarcerated upon Chimera, that Ward was often considered an informal head figure amongst the other inmates.

"What?!" Eddie snapped, "Look, don't fuck with me.", his attitude was quickly turning sour, "I may not look as old as everyone else but that doesn't give you the right to take the fucking piss out of me!"

"I'm tellin ya lad…" Ward replied in his deep baritone voice. He was looking Eddie directly in the eye "…it's 'aunted."

Eddie, with one eye brow slightly raised, looked back at Ward trying to read any signs of jest on the bigger man's face.

After a few seconds of not finding any give away signs, he looked away shaking his head. "Fuck off." he said but with out any real menace.

Kerrigan couldn't agree more. Haunted? He knew the story that Ward no doubt based this belief on, but under no circumstances did Kerrigan believe it had anything to do with ghosts, witchcraft or any other superstitious bullshit. It was just bad luck what had happened that's all. Considering the poor condition the ship was in, he was surprised it didn't happen more often.

Haunted? Rubbish! In Kerrigan's opinion it was only a side step from believing in the supernatural to believing in Gods and religion.

Then you were really fucking screwy.

With a signal from below, the next load of cargo had been loaded and was ready to be hoisted up. This shipment was five drums of water.

Once on deck, and with the crane currently not in use, Ward took this brief rest to recount his tale and to convince the new lad of his beliefs.

"It was many years ago…" he began.

Fuckin' hell, Kerrigan thought. Normally he would have just ignored this drivel, but the heat, combined with his exhaustion from the labour, had made him irritable. Might as well have started with "Once upon a time"… Shut the fuck up for fuck's sake!

Kerrigan leaned against their crane with his arms folded across his chest, head down. He was exhausted but would not show the slightest sign of weakness in front of anyone.

"..and the old Captin', Captin' Armaine 'is name was, 'ad just been replaced by fuckin' Billy Bronco up there." Ward nodded in the general direction of the bridge were the Captain was no doubt over seeing everything from behind glass windows. "Anyway's, ee comes onboard and ee doesn't believe the story that the ship's 'aunted either. So anyway, the time comes when we needs to load up the ship an' instead of mooring up 'ere as we are now, ee decides to 'ead into port directly." He mopped some sweat off his face by stretching up the bottom of his already sweat soaked shirt to wipe his face.

"Sweatin' like fuck 'ere" he grumbled beneath his big hands.

After he'd succeeded in rubbing the sweat around his face a little more rather than actually drying it, he continued, "Anyways, no sooner does we get close enough to see the 'ouses of the town, do the engines cut out. Just like that." He clicked his fingers to emphasis just how quickly the engines had failed, "No explosion to show summit else 'ad bust, no smoke comin' from where it shouldn't, no alarms, nuthin'… it just went off." Ward's tone was one of awed fascination.

Eddie stared sceptically back at the larger man. Chimera was old and rusty and was getting older and rustier everyday. It was hardly surprising that it's engines might fail on occasion. Eddie's look conveyed both boredom and pity that the older man was spooked by such ordinary, and expected, circumstances.

Ward didn't seem to notice the smaller man's look or was too enraptured in his own storytelling to realize that he was being humoured, and so he continued, "Anyway's all 'ell breaks loose on deck as we realize that we're currently coastin' into a town with no means of slowin' ourselves down. So all the guards are rushin' round tryin' to ignite the second engine and tryin' to keep all us scabs under control at the same time, ya see? To tell ya the truth," Ward leaned in a little closer and lowered his voice to a conspiratorial tone, "we was all hopin that we'd crash into the town so we could jump off this 'ell 'ole and run off into God know's where." He straightened back up "Remember Kerrigan?, you was there weren't ya?" He looked at Kerrigan with a slight smile of nostalgia.

Kerrigan looked at Ward, then at Eddie, then back at the ship's decking again without responding.

"Well maybe ee wouldn't 'ave" indicated Ward, cocking a thumb at Kerrigan, "but the rest of use sure as 'ell would of."

"Reeeeeeally?" said Eddie bored, "So go on, what happened next?"

"Whaddya think happened?! We're all still 'ere aint we??" Ward had his arms spread wide, "Bronco got the coal engine up and runnin' just in time and managed to slow us down. Scared the shit out of 'im though. Thought ee might loose 'is job I 'eard. Anyway's to make sure that none of us tried to swim for the shore anyway, which would definitely have cost 'im his job… or more, ee backed up to where we is now and continued the cargo transport as normal."

"So what's that gotta do with this ship being apparently haunted?" Eddie's frustration was beginning to show.
"Because you slow shit, as soon as we got far enough away from port, the electric engine started workin again!" he said this as if this conclusion to the story was obvious in it's meaning, "Story goes that this 'ere ship is afraid of the land, son. She was built to be at sea and that's just where she likes it." He patted the crane of the ship in a fatherly gesture.
Eddie, clearly unconvinced that such a mundane story could be proof of the supernatural, was interrupted from arguing further as three guards approached the group.
"Kerrigan, you're to come with us" ordered the lead officer.
Kerrigan looked up at the guard who'd addressed him. It was the same guard who's baton he had stolen to break Duncan's face with. He appeared to be slightly bruised around the face himself, something which Kerrigan hadn't noticed on the guard earlier. He wondered if this bruising had happened when he had pushed him sprawling onto the kitchen table, or whether Captain Bronco had punished the guard personally for the incident in the mess hall, "Captain Bronco would like to see you. Now." The last word, a command.
Ward, Eddie and the other prisoners turned to look at Kerrigan to see what he would do. He was known not to take orders well.
Still, he'd had been expecting this one. They all had.
With a slight rebellious pause, just enough to give the guards an unspoken message of how much he respected their authority, Kerrigan pushed himself off the crane and followed the guards.

5

Captain Bronco watched Officer Barrington, the fool who's baton had been snatched away and used to injure an inmate in the mess hall yesterday, and two other officers approach Kerrigan from the bridge of Chimera. How had Barrington allowed a prisoner to acquire his baton? Such sloppy behaviour simply could not be tolerated. These were the absolute bottom of society they were living with here and were already dangerous enough without the benefit of weapons. What if it had been a gun instead? The possibility was simply unthinkable.

Barrington's shamefully negligent behaviour had potentially endangered them all.

After hearing Barrington's side of the incident, insisting that he could not have foreseen or prevented what had happened, Bronco had become so frustrated and angry at his officer's lack of self awareness that he had dealt out Barrington's punishment personally.

He rubbed his still aching knuckles as he stood upon Chimera's bridge, watching the activity below. From this view point, he was able to watch over the transferral of the supplies and ensure that every prisoner and officer was where they should be.

He did not want anything else to go wrong.

A middle aged man, Captain William Bronco had been Captain of Chimera now for over a decade and a half and had hated practically every minute of it.

The hatred came from how he was literally his own boss. Most people would view this as a pleasure, as Bronco himself had when he had initially taken the post, but as Chimera was at sea for such prolonged periods of time, everyday life became something of a bore for Bronco.

He felt very much like one of Chimera's inmates in some ways. For him, everyday was the same routine of waking, supervising, eating and sleeping.

In all the time that he had been Captain of Chimera, he had only left the ship a handful of times, and even then, his visits to the main land were business related. He longed for the day when he could simply walk off the ship and go wherever his feet led him. What natural beauties are out there waiting to be appreciated? he wondered.

In his opinion, the only privilege he held over the prisoners he supervised was that he could choose when to sleep and what to eat. That, and his toilet was somewhat more presentable.

Despite his years of service, and his depleted love for the job, he still demanded that his officers behave correctly, enthusiastically and with dedication - even if he himself was not so passionate about the job anymore. If he allowed standards to slip, then potentially their already uncomfortable lives could become dangerously vulnerable to the never ending conspiracy's of the prisoners. That, or he would loose the respect of his officers, which could be equally just as dangerous.

He wondered when the day might arrive when he could earn his freedom.

Maybe next time...? he mused.

Without the pressure of any kind of functional tracking equipment on board, his only communication with his superiors was during the transportation of supplies. Even then, all he had to do was file a report with any kind of disturbances, deaths or suspicious behaviours and hand over and log any harvested goods that needed to be transported back to the main land.

Rarely did he receive any communication or orders in response.

Today however, was one of the rare occasions when he did. He just hoped it would be something different, something more... exciting, than his previous orders.

Judging by the size of some of the crates waiting patiently to board the ship, Bronco already knew the order he was about to receive and felt a familiar wave of disappointment wash over himself – it would not be something exciting as he had hoped.

Unless...

Watching the straining prisoners below, Bronco stood straight backed with his hands clasped behind himself, waiting for his Communications Officer to return and confirm his suspicions.

The conventional uniform worn by all Officer's and Wardens of Chimera was a predominantly blue uniform. The jacket's breast was an upside down silver triangle, with the base reaching across the shoulders, and the tip touching down to the waist band. It was designed to look like it accentuated the wearer's shoulders and chest. With black polished boots and leather belt accessories, the uniform was complete. Rank was distinguished by coloured emblems emblazed upon the left breast.

Bronco's authority was displayed by how his was the only dark green uniform on the entire ship.

Below, Kerrigan was being escorted to the bridge and had nearly vanished from Bronco's view when he heard footsteps approaching from behind him. He did not turn to greet the approaching steps, knowing to whom they belonged. Instead, he kept his focus on the operation below as Communications Officer Dack approached and stood to the left of Bronco. He saluted smartly, although Bronco barely noticed, and waited to be acknowledged.

Without averting his gaze from the scuttling deck below him, Bronco addressed the patiently waiting Communications Officer, "Officer Dack"

Dack replied, "Captain Bronco sir, we have received orders to excavate Site B once the loading of the supplies is complete."

Just as he had expected.

"Very good. Was there anything else?"

"No Captain Bronco sir."

"Thank you Officer, that will be all."

With another crisp salute, Dack turned and strode away.

Kerrigan had vanished completely from Bronco's view now. In a few moments he would arrive on the bridge and Bronco could enjoy a rare moment of pleasure as he gave him the unpleasant news.

Kerrigan was pushed heavily down into a metallic seat that was firmly attached to the deck of the bridge with a number of bolts at the base of each leg. Whilst heavy hands pressed down on his shoulders to prevent him from rising, big hands worked to secure his hands and feet with handcuffs. His arms were bound, twisted behind the back of the chair and his feet were secured underneath. Both sets of cuffs were then joined together with a metal chain. Once complete, Kerrigan was safely
secured to the chair by his own limbs, and the chair itself was secured to the deck floor.

There would be no hope of escape.

During his restraint, Bronco kept his back turned to Kerrigan.

"Have a seat Kerrigan." offered Bronco, as though he was oblivious of Kerrigan's binding taking place behind him. He continued to observe the supply loading operation still taking place outside the glass.

Hilarious.

The hands doing the binding felt huge compared to Kerrigan's own, able to move his limbs with the ease that an adult could manipulate a rag doll.

He would not have resisted anyway. If he was going to do that he would have done so on deck where at least maybe some other crazy inmates might have joined in.

Then again, no one had attempted to help him yesterday in the mess hall.

It was the same recollection of yesterday's incident that had prompted Bronco into making sure Kerrigan was securely restrained in his presence.

In Bronco's experience, it was almost impossible to judge how a prisoner might react to any given situation. Their bored, tired, and often failing minds were much more susceptible to violent, unpredictable reactions when presented with stressful situations.

Take Kerrigan's case as an example: It was only yesterday when Kerrigan had attempted to kill the kitchen assistant Duncan and all that Duncan had done to provoke the reaction was to call Kerrigan a few harmless names. It was really quite sad.

In Bronco's opinion, Kerrigan's mind was on the verge of snapping. Another successful product of Chimera's justice.

Once the handcuffs were securely attached a bit too tightly, the guards who bound Kerrigan stepped back to stand behind him. Just in case he tried something. About the only thing Kerrigan could have hit Bronco with from within his restraints were words, and perhaps a particularly well aimed glob of phlegm.

He waited.

"That was a pretty interesting injury you caused to Duncan yesterday, Kerrigan" spoke Bronco quietly, still without turning his back. With his formal working career background, Bronco believed he was conveying a sense of authority, and also an insult to Kerrigan as he refused to turn and acknowledge the bound man. Kerrigan just thought he was a pompous arsehole.

"Poor man lost all but four of what few teeth he already had," he snorted through his nose, "Good job all your food is already mushed up eh? He wouldn't be able to eat other wise, poor chap."

Kerrigan was bored already and began to look around the bridge. In front of him was a chunky looking control panel crammed full of multi-coloured buttons, blank screens and levers. He had absolutely no idea what any of the switches could mean or what they were ever used for, which, he believed, was probably the extent of the crews knowledge as-well. That, or like most things, it was broken - either way it was clearly never used; the console was covered in a thick carpet of grey dust.

Looking further around the room, the entire length of the opposite wall was one long window, through which Bronco's gaze was currently directed. The window was smeared with dirt on the outside, but still allowed the intense light of the sun to shine through in thick bars which sparkled from floating dust particles. Below the window, also running the length of the wall were more mysterious consoles and controls.

Some of these at least appeared functional as the occasion light winked at Kerrigan, and a computer screen displayed data that was unreadable from his current vantage point.

At the far right of the room was what appeared to be a metallic filling cabinet with a file of some sort perched on top of it.

He started to turn his head to see what else might be in the room. A quick blow to the side of the head, which started a high pitched squealing in his ear, told him that this too was out of the question, and to keep his head and attention facing forward.

Bronco must have heard the blow as it was only then that he turned his head to the side allowing Kerrigan to see his profile.

"Are you listening to me Kerrigan?" asked Bronco, turning around completely to look directly at him. Short wavy white hair and a neatly trimmed white beard grew around a craggy, lined face. He looked older than his age, his face ageing harsher than it should have from a life lived mostly at sea. Direct sunlight and salty winds were not a good combination for one's complexion.

His body, which clearly used to be of a muscular physic, was now holding up a growing gut which had just started to hang over his leather belt. Whether this was caused by middle age, or from a rich diet denied to inmates, was not clear. Either way, it disgusted Kerrigan. Anyone overweight did. Being middle aged was not an excuse for being overweight, it was quite possible to grow old without growing a belly. To grow old gracefully, proudly.

He stared back at Bronco from beneath his untidy hair.

After a moment of holding his stare, Bronco smiled slightly. In his experience with dealing with Kerrigan, this was typical behaviour, "Same old silent Kerrigan" he stated.

He began to pace the bridge, "Do you know how long I've been Captain of Chimera?"

Here we go... thought Kerrigan. If Bronco had been looking at him he would have seen him roll his eyes. As it was, Bronco was watching his shoes as he strode back and forth.

Kerrigan shifted uncomfortably in his chair, making the cuffs on his wrists bite in painfully.

"Sixteen years" answered Bronco. It had been a rhetorical question. Even if it hadn't have been, he'd have continued anyway knowing that Kerrigan would have remained as silent as the radar console he was sat behind. "Sixteen long years" he repeated with disbelief. "During my time here, I've come to take certain things for granted.

Take the sound of the ocean for example. Every time I wake up and every time I go to sleep, there is always the sound of the ocean. When I first came here it was one of the first things that I noticed. In fact, it used to irritate me. Gradually though, you get used to it and without even realizing it's happened, you stop noticing it. It blends into the background and becomes a part of your life."

Kerrigan had no idea why he was being told all this. Whenever he had heard Bronco speak in the past, which was seldom, he was usually pretty direct with his message.

This pointless waffle seemed somewhat out of character.
"The ocean breeze when I step out on deck is another example. At first the salty tasting air hurts the back of your throat and burns your lungs, but gradually you become used to it. The stale taste of water which was fresh months ago is another example. The bland taste of food designed to remain edible for months, the broken navigation equipment, the colour of the walls..." Bronco stopped his pacing and finally looked at Kerrigan, "and you."
Where was he going with this? Wondered Kerrigan suspiciously.
"Tell me, just how long have you been here?"
Kerrigan didn't like this line of questioning. He'd been here as long as he could remember. He wouldn't have been able to say just how long even if he had tried to recall the exact figure. If Bronco had been here sixteen years, then he'd been here...?
Longer, he thought.
As if reading his thoughts, Bronco continued "Longer than my decade and a halves worth of service of course, you were here before my arrival. Not that it really matters, like everyone else onboard, you're here for the rest of your life. What does interest me though, is just what did you do?"
Kerrigan's permanent frown grew deeper at this line of questioning and he leaned forward in his chair until his shoulder muscles were straining from the twist they were in. It was none of this fat man's business why he was here.
"What despicable act did you do to end up here?"
Kerrigan continued to scowl.
Bronco smiled, "I didn't expect an answer." He resumed his previous pacing. "When I finally leave here, I've no doubt that I will miss the sounds of the ocean when I try to sleep. The crash of the sea is almost a part of Chimera herself. Much like you." He stopped and turned to Kerrigan once more, "I wonder... will I miss you when you're gone?"
Kerrigan's frown didn't faulter, however his bottom eye lids did raise up slightly giving him a slightly curious, yet angry scorn.
Bronco kept looking at Kerrigan. He wanted to savour the moment Kerrigan lost his composure, "We're going to Site B, or more

accurately, you are."

Kerrigan didn't react. He'd been expecting this news anyway and wouldn't give old, fat man, Billy Bastard Bronco the pleasure of seeing him react. In fact he only distantly heard him, he was still seething at the fat man's attempt to pry into his past.

"You see, every time there's an accident, or a lack of discipline, I have to report this to my superiors. I also have to show them that I am taking action to resolve the issue, or reprimand it. I cannot be seen to allow unruly behaviour in the eyes of those I report to after all. Your little incident with Duncan is the latest in a series of unruly and violent behaviour exhibited by yourself. My superiors want to know what I am doing about it. Hence, Site B"

Bronco leaned forward at Kerrigan as if trying to see beneath his icy exterior shell, trying to see the outburst he hoped to provoke. Referring to Kerrigan's lack of response, he said "I guess you expected this. After all, your not the first prisoner who's continued behaviour has resulted in this punishment. However, I'd have thought you'd have shown more emotion than your usual pout. It's pathetic. Do you think that you scare me? Or that somehow your silence earns you respect?"

If only he wasn't restrained, Kerrigan would bust Bronco's mouth as surely as he had bust Duncan's, "I thought you had more respect for your own life than that."

Kerrigan's only response was his continued scowl.

Disappointed at Kerrigan's lack of emotion, Bronco straightened back up displaying a stature that said he was bringing the conversation to an end, "We'll be leaving once the cargo is finished loading. In the mean time you'll be confined to your cell. In case you decide you'd like to go for a long walk." He smiled slightly at what he thought was a charming suicide euphemism.

Turning to the guards who were stood behind Kerrigan for the first time he said, "Take him away."

Again the heavy hands came down on Kerrigan's shoulders to prevent him rising whilst his shackles were unfastened. Kerrigan's eyes never strayed from the man who had just signed his death warrant. He hardly noticed the relief to his aching muscles and

swollen wrists as the metal restraints were removed.
Once the binding was clear, the guards gripped his upper forearms in a vice like grip to lift him from his chair.
Using the upwards momentum given to him by the guards, Kerrigan pushed out with his legs, lunging towards the Captain.
He didn't gain much distance, the guards were too well prepared for him to gain much more than a few inches between himself and Bronco before the restraint of the guards held him back.
What he did gain though, was the pleasure of seeing Bronco flinch back reflexively at his sudden advance.
Grinning his feral smile, showing all of his teeth in one wide smirk, Kerrigan was dragged roughly from the bridge by his escort to be taken back to his cell.

Bronco watched him leave feeling mildly unsettled.
Although he had prompted the brief attempt at attacking him, he found no pleasure in the reaction as he had hoped he might.
There was just something so…feral about Kerrigan that stood him apart from the other prisoners.
When Kerrigan was gone from sight, Bronco cleared his throat and straightened his uniform jacket. All of a sudden it felt too tight, hot and sweaty.
A moment later, Communications Officer Dack strode back onto deck. With another smart salute, he waited to be address by his Captain.
"Yes what is it Officer?" asked Bronco. He hoped it was nothing important. He wanted to get back to his quarters and shower off the sweat his body was seeping out at an alarming speed.
"Captain Bronco sir, the cargo has finished being loaded onto ship. Including the specialist equipment needed for our latest excursion."
"Good, good. Thank you Officer. See to it that it is collected at the stern." he turned to leave the bridge.
"Excuse me, Captain Bronco sir"
"Yes what is it Dack?" asked Bronco turning back to face him.
"Umm" he seemed uncomfortable, "I need the report to give back

to the land crew."

"Oh right, of course." In his haste to leave the bridge he'd forgotten to give the file to Dack, "how foolish of me". He hoped he sounded merely forgetful, rather than flustered.

Crossing the room Bronco picked up the file from on top of the filing cabinet, and handed it to Dack. Sweating even more from the embarrassment he now felt, Bronco left for his quarters and to the shower that beckoned.

6

Back in his cell, Kerrigan was furious.

After his meeting with Bronco, he had been dragged off of the bridge scrapping his boots along the floor as he went. He did not attempt to try and walk with the guards, making it as difficult as possible for them to return him to his cell. He didn't owe these people any favours, so why help them out?

Once back at his cell, he was thrown unceremoniously to the floor were one guard spat on him while the other locked the door. No doubt they had wanted to beat him to a pulp for being so uncooperative, but they knew that they'd be lucky to land a single blow.

Over a year ago, although he could not remember exactly when, Kerrigan had been helping stoke the fires of the second engine in the furnace room. The primary engine had being inoperable at the time due to poor weather conditions that had lasted several weeks. The heavy rain that fell soaked through the rusting bulkhead into Chimera's intestines and the strong winds caused the ship's weakened framework to snap and groan, threatening to rip itself apart.

The furnace room was essentially one huge oven with a pile of fuel for burning in one corner, and a large burning hole through which the fuel was supplied in another.

The heat had been unbearable, the air was thick and heavy with coarse, black smoke and visibility was down to only the intense orange glow supplied by the roaring furnace. They were terrible conditions to work in, and when combined with the irritation and frustration that the prisoners who were forced to work it felt, the frustration would often turn into an anger as heated as the furnace they stoked.

Somehow, Kerrigan had gotten himself into a fight with another inmate. He could not recall why he had gotten into the fight anymore than he could remember his opponent's name.

Having easily defeated the other prisoner, the other men in the vicinity had stepped in to pull Kerrigan off his downed adversary as he continued to punch him in his unconscious, bloody face.

Those who had stepped in to help, were attacked so quickly and savagely, that the remaining bystanders either looked on horrified, unable to move, or were too afraid to risk their own health.

A smart decision.

None the less, some men did step forward in an attempt to stop Kerrigan who seemed intent on killing the other man, and any one who tried to stop him. He sat on top of the defeated prisoner and repeatedly raised and smashed their face into concrete floor. Each connection made a deep, muted wet thud. The blood that poured from their face and nose mixed with the soot on the floor and plastered itself back onto their ruined face. It later transpired that the poor man's cheek bone had been completely shattered. He spent several weeks with his face patched and bandaged but without the necessary tools onboard to aid a full recovery, the left hand side of his face healed looking like it had collapsed inwards.

Kerrigan had continued to fight prisoners until a particularly large guard named Dower had stepped.

Dower was not just big, but huge, even by Chimera's guard's standards. He easily stood seven feet tall, and seemed almost as broad. His dark skin and shaven head glistened in the glow of the furnace. He took particular pleasure in taking a very hands-on approach with inmates who failed to abide by Chimera's very simple rules.

He bent over and picked Kerrigan up by one half of his coat's collar as effortlessly as if he were weightless. It gave Kerrigan an unbalanced, lopsided feeling as if he were a painting hanging crooked on a wall. Dower raised his meaty fist to punch Kerrigan straight in the face.

If the blow had of connected, it would have easily broken Kerrigan's nose and squashed it flat into his face. It could quite as easily have sent splinters of bone up into his brain killing him instantly.

But the blow hadn't connected. Kerrigan blocked the incoming boulder sized fist with lightning reflexes. Dower's fist stopped as suddenly as a bird hitting a wall. Kerrigan's arm barely quivered with the connection.

Dower let go of his collar and attempted another heavy blow with his other fist. It was blocked as surely as the first.

Growing increasingly frustrated of failing to land a blow, Dower attempted another strike, however his frustration hampered his skill and the blow was made with more power in mind than accuracy. He grunted with exertion as he put all of his weight into the next deadly strike.

Using both his hands this time, again Kerrigan blocked the blow.

Not once did Kerrigan attempt to strike back at Dower. Despite his earlier rage, he still had the sense to know that to strike one of Chimera's guards would result in him being shot dead on the spot.

Only he would decide his own death, and only he would be the one to choose when it happened. Getting shot fighting in the backup engine's furnace room against this ungraceful brute was not the time, nor the place. He was not yet ready to die.

The fight was eventually disbanded when Warden Ashe arrived in the room accompanied by two armed guards.

After ordering the two men to separate or be shot, Kerrigan was eventually sent to the sweat box for several days with nothing to survive on but only the minimum amount of water and nutrition his body had needed to survive.

He emerged looking weak and starved even by Chimera's low standards.

Back in his cell, Kerrigan was throwing himself into his press up exercises with anger infused gusto. His triceps and pectoral muscles burned from the continual strain placed upon them as he relentlessly pushed himself up off the floor. They had become strained quicker than they might normally due to the exercise they had already received from operating the loading crane not long previous.

Kerrigan could feel the pain, but instead of it slowing him down, he focused on it, relished in it, giving him extra enthusiasm to keep pushing himself up just one more time.

Sweat was soaking out of his pores, beading on his brow. The droplets grouped together, ran down his face, tickled his nose, and dripped onto his cell floor. Some droplets ran into his eyes making them sting harshly.

Again, Kerrigan focused on this added discomfort giving him the extra will to keep pushing himself just a little further.

Only when he muscles were so weak that they literally could not raise him back off the floor would he give up.

Down he went again, until his chest touched the floor and pushed. Every used muscle in his back and arms stood out and strained as he put all of his strength into pushing himself back up.

He focused on the ache in his shoulders, the sting in his eyes, the metal grinding into the palm of his hands, the strain of the exercise on his wrists - he focused on the pain.

Grunting with exertion, his muscles were quivering with the effort of raising himself off of the filthy cell floor. It felt like the tendons were about to snap off his bones making the same metallic twang as a snapped metal cable.

Down he went and attempted just... one... more.

It was no good, his muscles had done all they could and he rolled onto his back gasping for breath.

In a few moments, once he had gotten his breath back, he would place his legs up onto his bunk and start doing sit ups. They were a particular favourite of his as the harsh metal floor would grind into the skin of his lower back with each stomach crunch. Often, by the time he had finished, he would have a blood spotted graze there.

Fucking Bronco, thought Kerrigan, *who the fuck does he think he is?*

He was still seething at the Captain's attempt to pry into his past. For Kerrigan, it was no-one's business but his own.

Having gained a normal breathing rate once more, he placed his legs up onto his bed and moved his leather coat out from underneath his bottom and away from his lower back. He didn't want his exercises to wear a hole in the coat.

With this done he placed his hands behind his head and started to do his sit-ups.

Nosey fat bastard.

One.

Focus.

Ugly fucking cunt.

Two.

Focus on the burn.

Prying little shit.

Three.

Focus!

Personal details of all inmates and the reason for their imprisonment were handed over upon each new prisoner's arrival. It was common knowledge however, that despite this being a prison, a lot of the prisoner's personal details were missing.

It was the riot that had cost the previous Captain, Captain Armaine, his job that had resulted in the majority of this personal information being lost. The rioting prisoners had discovered the files and burned them with much glee not realizing that just because their files were now destroyed, this did not gain them the freedom they so desired. After all, they were still stuck on a ship in the middle of the ocean. Burning a file of paper did not change that.

Despite Armaine's best efforts to subdue and ultimately control the mutineers, as soon as Chimera's superiors had learnt of the riots, Captain Armaine had been removed immediately from office and Captain Bronco had been appointed to the post. Without any kind of formal handover, this meant that Captain Bronco only had the information in a few surviving files to know why some of the inmates were imprisoned.

Kerrigan's file was one of the files burnt during the riot.
That was fine by him. It meant that no one could ask any questions they had no right to be asking about his past. Questions, he didn't have the answers to.
He deserved to be here and that was all.
He continued with his exercises.
Ten.
Nosey fucking arsehole!
Focus on the pain!

7

That night, Kerrigan experienced a bizarre and somehow, disturbing, dream.
He blamed the vision on his gruelling exercises he had performed in his cell earlier in the day. Exercises that were even more gruelling than normal due to the rage Bronco had awakened within him. He blamed Bronco.
He dreamt that he was stood in a field of sickly black grass which extended on to the horizon in all directions. The grass and his coat ruffled slightly as a warm wind flitted gracefully at his ankles. The sky was a dark red that seemed to hang lower in the sky than it should, giving him the feeling that he was actually stood in a room with a black floor, a red ceiling and no walls, rather than outside.
He stood in the field and stared at the grass dancing at his feet. It sparkled with crimson high lights as it reflected the deep red of the low sky. It was as if the grass was made from a flexible polished metal. He wondered if it might cut his hands if he tried to reach down and grab some, slicing through his fingers without resistance, but noticed at the same time that it made no damage to his boots as it brushed against them.
The wind made a soft thumping noise in his ears as it changed it's direction in a rapid marionette of motion.
He raised his head away from the grass to look at the horizon but the black grass remained forever in his vision. Still raising his head, he expected the horizon to appear at any moment until it

seemed he was looking straight up, but the grass still remained in his vision, it seemed to go on forever as if he was encased in a giant sphere of oily black grass.

He felt dizzy and disorientated from the exaggerated movement.

Just as he thought he couldn't lift his head any further, that his neck would break if he lifted it any more, the horizon snapped into his vision. Only when this happened did he observe that his head was not looking straight upwards, as he had expected, but instead looked horizontally across to the horizon as normal.

The wind continued it's occasional whisper into his ear.

The horizon was a perfect line of black grass meeting burgundy sky. No foliage or land contours blotted the perfect meeting of colours.

He turned in what he thought was a complete circle. It was difficult to tell when he had completed his revolution with no point of reference to know where he had started from, and observed nothing that was neither grass nor sky.

The wind's whisper was growing into a growl as the noise continued to batter into his ear. It was not a natural sound for the wind to be taking on. It felt like the wind was being beaten into him.

He looked straight up, expected to see a giant bird fifty feet long throwing the wind at him with leathery wings as it hovered above.

Instead, all he saw was perfect blood red of the sky.

CAW!

He was startled by the sound which had originated from next to his left ear.

Reflexively taking a step to his right and looking to the left at the same time, a back bird had somehow managed to land on his left shoulder without him being aware.

It didn't fly off at his sudden movement, nor did it beat it's wings to keep it's balance.

The wind had lowered it's voice back to a gentle whisper.

Looking at the black bird, it refused to meet his gaze, instead it's perfectly black eyes looked straight forward at the contrasting horizon.

It did not blink.

It did not stir.

In fact, it gave no signs of life at all. It could have been a puppet for all Kerrigan knew, but something about it's eyes told Kerrigan that it definitely was not as dead as it's frozen image suggested.

It almost looked like it wanted him to look at something on the horizon.

Not wanting to take his eyes off the creepy, motionless bird, Kerrigan chanced a look to the horizon and saw only what he had seen before, an endless stream of shimmering liquid grass flowing ever onwards.

He turned back to the bird and was shocked once more to see that it's face had changed in the brief moment it had left his vision. It had become that of a rust demon from the sweat box's walls.

It grinned it's familiar wicked grin at him. The same long nose, the sharp teeth, the pointy ears… but there was something different about the face aswell.

It's eyes were the colour of brightest green. Kind and gentle, they looked out of place in the demons face, not at all wicked. The demon's face continued to smirk, but the smile did not reach it's new, sombre eye's. The effect only served to add to the overall creepiness of the demon's face rather than soften it.

It looked straight at him with it's penetrating green eyes, eye's that appeared strangely human, and Kerrigan felt it's gaze going through his eyes, into his head, and down into his very soul.

Although it's mouth did not move, it started to laugh it's high, wicked cackle at him.

Disturbed by it's laughter and it's proximity, Kerrigan raised his right arm to brush the bizarre crow/rust demon creature off of his shoulder. As his fingers made contact with it's body, it exploded with the sound of a lover's sigh, turning same oily grass at his feet, and danced away on the breeze…

He awoke panting and sweating. His eyes darted around him, trying to find anything that was not black grass and not red sky. His shirt was plastered to his torso from perspiration, bonding

itself to him as a second skin. His heart was hammering at his ribs as if it was so scared by the dream that it wanted to burst out of his chest and run away never seeing Kerrigan again.
After a few dizzying gasps of air, his disorientation subsided and he knew that he had been dreaming.
He rubbed a hand down his dripping face.
He tried to replay the dream hoping to make sense out of what seemed like nonsense, or to find some hidden meaning in it all, but even as he started to recollect the nightmare, the dream broke up and floated away out of his grasp, like grass on the wind.

8

The next few days for Kerrigan, were spent no different from normal.
Like how a snake slithers through grass, leaving unrest and anxiety in it's wake for all those creatures afraid of the scaled predator, rumours had started to spread throughout the inmates that Chimera was heading to Site B.
The newer prisoners were eager to learn any snippets of information as to what exactly this ambiguous sounding location could be. The sought information was keenly given, often by those who enjoyed making other people nervous or uncomfortable - Duncan was still unable to talk at this point, much to his disappointment - but the stories changed from individual to individual making it hard to filter out what was fact and what was fiction.
Stories varied from the plausible, if not mysterious, talk of how it was some kind of cave or tunnel, to the fantastically ridiculous of how it was giant man-eating machine.
Other's merely spoke in ominous riddles of how it was a "dark place not of this Earth."
Eddie, having heard the news of Site B, and knowing Ward's comfortable belief in the supernatural, decided to ask the larger man for his opinion. He replied with unfaltering confidence that, "Site B is an 'aunted graveyard filled with the lost souls of the

underworld son, and they is charged with the duty of seekin' revenge upon the livin' for the crimes and sins of the past."

Eddie had expected nothing less of the blonde giant.

The reason why the stories varied so much was due to the one element of the story that remained consistent. No-one had ever returned from Site B alive to explain exactly what it was.

Kerrigan had heard all these tales previously and had allowed them to wash over him as easily as the wind passed over him on deck. What was the point in listening to them? None of the stories were based on anything substantive. Indeed, listening to them would only cause your fear of the unknown to increase and nothing of use could be gained from listening to a variety of increasingly bizarre stories.

He would find out soon enough for himself. Although this was not the first time that Chimera had been to Site B during his imprisonment, he had never actually seen the location for himself. Those not involved in Site B were kept within their cells.

Despite the prisoner's constant daily, grumblings and often miserable lives, they did not accept the thought of a looming inevitable death easily.

Which gave rise to a second slithering snake. A snake of fear and unease. Who was it who would be sent there?

The most likely suspects were noticeable by their absence over the following days. These were the unlucky few. These quarantined prisoners could not be trusted to not attempt some kind of desperate revolt or escape attempt knowing that their time had been drastically cut shorter than they might like.

However, not everyone who would be sent to Site B would be told in advance. Only those that the Captain particularly disliked would be told their death was only four days away. Captain Bronco himself would give the news hoping to see the men crumble at his feet and beg for mercy over the coming days.

The rest he would announce upon their arrival.

This had two beneficiary results: It provided a co-operation amongst those who had not been quarantined to the point were they rivalled even the most disciplined military, not wanting to

focus their Captain's attention, or wrath, upon them. Secondly, it spread a tangible fear amongst the men.
This, again, was for the Captain's perverse amusement
It was quickly known that Kerrigan was one of the doomed individuals who had been picked out by Captain Bronco. He remained confined to his cell where he continued his increased exercise regime.

9

A jangling of keys awoke Kerrigan from his doze.
"We're here." announced Warden Ashe as Kerrigan turned his attention to his cell door.
He rose and was handcuffed by Warden Ashe's ever present, guard accompaniment. Silently, Kerrigan followed Warden Ashe past the remaining cells of his wing where silent inmates stared back at his passage. Any prisoners not involved in the coming task were never allowed out of their cells. There was nothing for them to do but watch and conspire against the crew. It would be foolish to allow so many scared, unsettled and often deranged prisoners to gather together in one place with only a sick, disturbing show to occupy their attention. Without question, if just one prisoner started to cause trouble, the hysteria would spread to all the other inmates quicker than wild fire. One or two sympathetic inmates wished Kerrigan "Good Luck" or said "Goodbye", but they were in the minority, most of the prisoners merely stared at the condemned man with wide, terrified eyes. Along the multitude of dark corridors, through Warden Ashe's office, past the hysterically witty sign, "There are no walls!", Kerrigan and Ashe emerged onto Chimera's deck.
He'd come to accept that it was very likely that he would not return from this trip alive, and if that was to be the case, so be it.
However, he would not accept this fate without putting up a tremendous fight. Not with the guards of Chimera, that would result in a needless death of being shot dead instantly for his revolt, but with what ever it was that had killed those who had gone

before him. Whether it was predatory animals, impassable terrain, un-breathable air or anything else, he would make sure that his death would not come easily.

And if somehow he did manage to survive whatever hardships he encountered at Site B, then he would continue his punishment on board Chimera without expecting anything in return. He would continue his punishment as he always had: with a deep sense of acceptance, knowing that a lifetime spent aboard Chimera would not be enough punishment for his heinous crime.

Besides, the Captain and his crew were never so generous as to offer some kind of reward for good behaviour.

He stepped out onto deck and instantly felt the burning directness of the sun's glare blaze down upon his skin and smelt the salty freshness of the blowing wind.

It was a crisp, beautifully warm day.

He gave himself a brief moment of standing just outside his wing's door while Warden Ashe locked it behind them both, savouring what would surely be his one last moment of simple pleasure.

He allowed the moment to soak into him, calming him and soothing his muscles as the pleasant warmth seeped down into his core. He was actually looking forward to the task ahead. He would embrace death when it finally came.

Looking across the deck, the first thing that captured his eye was how the horizon had changed. Whereas previously, whenever he had stepped out on deck, all that could be seen was sea, sky and clouds, now there was a huge green blotch starting from the sea and swelling up into the pastel blue sky.

It took Kerrigan a brief second to realize what this growth was.

It was a mountain. Rich greens of a thousand different shades splashed themselves up and down the mountain, from the bushy base right up to the grey, cobbled band that marked the peak of the mountain. The greens shimmered and flowed as the same wind that licked Kerrigan's hair brushed through and swayed the lush foliage that enveloped the mountain side.

Site B.

Lowering his gaze, Kerrigan saw, on the opposite side of

Chimera's deck, there stood a row of doomed fellow inmates. A smattering of blue uniformed guards stood at either end of the line and around the condemned men, and at the closet point to Kerrigan, stood directly in the middle, in front of the line of prisoners, stood a solitary dark green uniform - Captain Bronco.
On the periphery of the scene stood several steel drums and a pile of scrap metal sparkling in the light of the sun.
Ashe had finished locking West Wing's door and beckoned for his guards to escort Kerrigan over to the waiting group.
A space was cleared for Kerrigan at the end of the line next to one of the guards.
Standing in line, he turned to look at Bronco who was waiting to address his audience.
"Good Morning gentlemen" he started, "I trust you all slept well?" Another witty remark disguised as politeness behind a charming smile. Kerrigan had a brief recollection of "Have a seat Kerrigan" from four days previous.
"Take a deep breath and savour it gentlemen, for this will be the last time that you breath the sea air." He closed his eyes and took a deep breath to show them how it was done. He let the breath back out as a sigh through his nostrils.
"Invigorating isn't it?"
A bird of some breed Kerrigan was not familiar with landed on the decking near Bronco and started pruning itself.
Ignoring Bronco and his self indulgent speech, Kerrigan watched the bird's carefree attitude of self grooming. Oblivious to the macabre scene that was beginning here in front of it, the bird tucked it's small head underneath it's wing and started to comb unseen insects and parasites out of it's slick white feathers.
The bird looked ill as patches of pink flesh peeped out from beneath the gaps in it's coat, as it if had been crudely plucked by aggressive hands. It had a long beak that looked unnaturally bent out of shape
Kerrigan wondered briefly about the fight the bird must have been in to sustain the injuries. If the bird was as perfectly honed as he himself was, maybe it would have won the fight. Maybe it had, and

it's opponent lay floating in the sea, bobbing up and down in the ocean's flow.

Unlike the other prisoners who also watched the bird, Kerrigan did not envy it's freedom.

"Welcome to Site B. You all know why you are here," Bronco continued. He had placed his hands behind his back and started to pace up and down the line up of men, "Everyone of you has, in some way, wasted the gift of life that the Gods have blessed upon you. You have all either killed, raped, beaten, sodomized, or in some way, hurt the free and innocent people of this world. As such, you were deemed unfit for civilised society and that is how you ended up here. Unfortunately, you cannot even co-operate to our very basic rules. You were given the opportunity to keep on living here aboard Chimera for the rest of your lives, but due to your repeated failure to live by the rules, in both society, and here aboard Chimera, you have been deemed unworthy to carry on abusing the gift of life. As such, you are all to be disposed off." He turned to start walking back up the line of men, "However, you may have one more use before you die. Which, I assure you gentlemen, you will die."

He stopped his pacing and turned to the men he was addressing, "Now before we begin, it is probably best that I explain why it is that you should all listen to me. After all, I should have thought that even now most of you will be thinking of attempting to kill me and as many of my fine officers as possible without attempting the task ahead. It's a fair thought, why bother trying to help us out if your going to die anyway. Right?" No one answered.

"Well, let me make you a little bit more co-operative. If any of you has the huge fortune of being successful with what we ask, you will be given your freedom."

No-one said anything but a few prisoners looked to one another as if hoping to read the truth of the Captain's words in their fellow inmate's faces.

"That's correct" he continued, addressing their doubt, "You will gain your freedom. Not only that, all of your past crimes will be forgiven and forgotten. You may go back to the real world and either attempt to live a normal, happy life or, as I suspect most of you will no doubt succumb to, return to your evil ways. The choice will be entirely yours.

But only for one of you. If any of you should attempt to board Chimera without being successful, I will take great pleasure in shooting you myself," he looked every man in line in the eye. It seemed to Kerrigan that he was focused on the longest. Bronco smiled at the group, "and I do hope that at least one of you gives me that pleasure.

So, let me explain what it is that you will be doing today in order to earn this most prestigious of gifts." Once again his pacing resumed. "You will be venturing into Site B with the aid of the specialized equipment that you will be provided with. Once there, you will begin your search for a certain item. This item gentlemen, should you return with it, will gain you your freedom". With each revelation came a dramatic pause and observation of the gathered crew. He was clearly enjoying his own theatrics. "The ticket to your freedom lies not on the island that you can see behind you, but at the bottom of the ocean, where Site B itself lies." Another dramatic pause, wanting to gain as much shock value and pleasure from his speech as possible.

It was working. No-one had said a word since his address had started. "Once there, I want you to find a small black box no bigger than this." He indicated with his hands the dimensions of a box approximately the size of a man's forearm and about half as thick, "Once, or should I say, IF the object is discovered, you may climb back up to Chimera using the chain attached to the anchor. With this object, gentlemen, you will gain your freedom and life back."

He paused once more, "It is as simple as that." He spread his arms wide to show his honesty.

"Now, let us get you prepared" he walked over to the small collection of open drums that Kerrigan had noticed upon his arrival. Bronco arrived at the first of these steel drums, rolled up the sleeve of his uniform and dipped his arm inside. He withdrew a small squirming creature just big enough to be held in his clenched fist.

The creature was a dark grey or green in colour, with five tentacles about twice the length of a man's middle finger dangling below. The tentacles quivered slightly as the frightened creature attempted to escape, or attack it's captor. It's bulbous head, which Bronco held in his hand, was smooth and shiny in the afternoon sun. If the creature had any eyes, Kerrigan assumed that they must be hidden beneath the folds of flesh that stacked from the base of it's tentacles, to the top of it's head.
None of the gathered prisoners had ever seen such an animal before.
Bronco looked at the dripping creature and then addressed the men once more, "This fascinating little creature, for those who do not know, is what we like to call an Oxypus. It will help you breathe underwater as easily as you are stood on deck now." Everyone observed the bizarre wriggling creature for a moment longer before Bronco dropped it back into the steel drum with a small splash.
"I trust there are no more questions?" concluded Bronco as he rolled the sleeve of his uniform back down over his arm.
"What... Is that it?!?!?!" dared ask a prisoner three down to Kerrigan's right. All eye's turned to him as he voiced his concern into the still air, "I mean, that all sounds a little vague... and what the do we do with that thing anyway?" he pointed to the steel drums nearby.
"All will become clear upon your descent to Site B. Just remember to breathe normally and not to return without the black box."
"What the fuck's so important about a little black box that we should risk out lives?"
"That is none of your concern. I would have thought that the promise of freedom should be motivation enough. Now, since there are no more questions," he gave them no opportunity to ask any more, "my Officers will help you prepare for the search." He glanced briefly among his blue uniformed crew. "If you will please, Officers"
Twenty condemned men stood on the deck of Chimera waiting to be sent to their deaths, and twenty blue clothed guards moved at Bronco's command to approach each prisoner. A further ten armed

guards watched over the prisoners incase any of them tried to do something. Each of the armed guard only had to observe two men. They were not good odds for a retaliation, and so each prisoner stood his ground preferring to risk the astronomical odds of succeeding in Bronco's search, rather then face the guaranteed death by attempting an escape.

As the guards approached each of their prisoners, Bronco explained what was happening, "To aid you in your descent, weights will be attached to your ankles. Once on the ocean floor, you can pick these anchors up and carry them with you to keep rooted on the sea bed."

Each prisoner's guard approached the pile of metal heaped up against the steel drums. As each guard picked up a piece of metal, it became obvious that the pile was not just scrap. Heavy pieces of metal were attached by chains to shackles. These shackles were then attached to the ankles of the prisoners using a simple pin clasp.

"Also, to aid you in under water manoeuvrability, your shirts and coats will be removed. I'd like you to have every advantage possible." He smiled.

The sound of ripping material filled the air as each man was ungracefully de-clothed.

Kerrigan's guard advanced towards him. It was Dower from the furnace room fight and he smiled unfriendly as he approached.

He grabbed the collar of Kerrigan's shirt.

With a yank he started to rip the material downwards. He was stopped after only an inch or so as his wrist was grabbed tightly by Kerrigan.

The move was so quick that Dower had to look at his hand to see why it wasn't still moving downwards. As he did so, he noticed a small black mark on the part of Kerrigan's chest that had been exposed. It looked too intricate to be a natural birth mark. As he stared at the mark, Kerrigan's grip tightened painfully causing Dower to lift his eyes to meet the fury of Kerrigan's glare.

"Is there a problem here Officer?" Bronco asked politely as he came over to the locked pair - Dower's hand gripped on Kerrigan's torn shirt and Kerrigan's hand gripped on Dower's wrist. He looked at the men's interlocking and then at Kerrigan who hadn't acknowledged the Captain's arrival. He was still glowering at Dower.

"If Mr Kerrigan does not want our help, so be it" stated Bronco. At his Captain's suggestion, Dower released his grip and after a brief moment, Kerrigan did likewise.

Dower was visibly angered by the embarrassment Kerrigan had caused him in front of his colleagues.

"Now," Bronco was striding back to his previous position in front of all of the gathered men, "Each guard will attach an Oxypus to your face. Do not be alarmed, it will only cover your mouth so breathe normally through your nose for now and then through your mouth once under water."

Some prisoners looked warily at the mysterious creature in the guard's hands, unsure if this 'attachment' would be painful but more concerned that it would be revolting. The idea of having a living creature attached to your face was not an attractive one.

Dower strode purposefully towards Kerrigan with an Oxypus swinging in his grip. He grabbed Kerrigan roughly by the upper arm and thrust the Oxypus onto Kerrigan's face.

It felt like he had been punched. His head snapped backwards from the impact and he felt warm liquid oozing down his jaw from his nose and mouth.

It took Kerrigan a second to realise that this warm sensation was not his blood, but instead was the secretion of the Oxypus which was now gripping to his lower face. It's grip was so hard that it felt like his lips were being sucked from his skull. The flesh of his cheek bones stretched down and pulled his lower eye lids slightly with it.

Muffled shouts of rejection and disgust were heard up and down the line as the men attempted to object to the uncomfortable marriage that had been thrust upon them. Finger tips were gently brushing the folded heads of the Oxypus that were now a part of their skulls. They were all feeling their new facial attachment like how blind men feel the faces of their friends to try and envisage their looks.

Bronco watched the prisoners discomfort with pleasure. Thankfully, none of the prisoners tried to rip the Oxypus off their face, he didn't want to have to start shooting people before the mission ahead had even started.

"Finally, amongst our latest cargo loading, were included some depth charges that we will drop to…scare off the local's." Bronco smiled slightly at his own wit, "Now that your equipped and ready, I wish you all the very best of luck. Goodbye gentlemen."

The prisoners were still in a state of discomfort and their attention focused on the Oxypus', rather than on Bronco. Using this vulnerability, each prisoner's guard gave them an incredible push to the shoulders sending them reeling over the guard rail of Chimera to splash down into the waters below.

With a smile, Dower took great pleasure in pushing Kerrigan over the edge with the others.

10

For a moment, there was the horrible sensation that he was falling too far. His mind seemed to think that he should have hit the water by now. His vision was a spinning kaleidoscope of sky blue, mountain green, sea blue, brown hull, sky blue, mountain green… The wind rushed past his ears in a deep, whooping growl. A nauseating sense of vertigo arose within him as his fall continued.

Just as Kerrigan started to think that somehow something had gone wrong with his fall, and that he was going to spend eternity flipping end over end never reaching the sea below, Kerrigan struck the sea below.

With an abrupt crash, he landed heavily in the water, back first. The impact sent a shuddering bolt throughout his spine which spread throughout his whole body leaving a tickling sensation in his fingers and hands.

He briefly thought that the water had always looked a lot softer on the deck of Chimera than it actually felt.

His vision was filled with a million scurrying bubbles which raced against one another to reach the surface. His ears were still filled with a deep growl, but it had changed, replaced instead with the muffled sounds of the ocean.

The impact had knocked the air out of him and his lungs were already burning with an immediate lust for oxygen. Despite the initial disorientation of his new environment, Kerrigan was still aware of the disgusting sucking sensation to his lower face from the attached Oxypus. Bronco had said that the creature would help him breath underwater. He would test it out when he had no other option, instead he decided that he would take the safe option and catch his breath when he bobbed to the surface

He barely had time to start swimming upwards, when the weight that was attached to him grabbed his ankle and started to heave him downwards.

He'd forgotten it was there.

As he was pulled below the bubbles that he had brought underwater with him, his vision cleared and he could see the other prisoners who were also thrown over board. They too were all floating dreamily downwards. If not for the surface of water rising away from them as they descended, it almost looked like they were flying.

Kerrigan's lungs were now on fire from the lack of oxygen, the edges of his vision were starting to flicker with the black squiggles of unconsciousness. He could no longer refrain from breathing in. In a moment, his lungs would reflexively force him to inhale which, he realised, could be through his nose. If that happened he would be guaranteed to drown here, only moments after being thrown over board.

He made a decision that he had to risk breathing through the Oxypus and hope that he had not been lied to. Even if he had, he conceded, the worst that would happen would be that he would die a few moments sooner, but maybe in a more interesting fashion should the Oxypus use his open airways to somehow enter his body.

He opened his mouth as much as he could. He could feel the resistance placed upon his lower jaw from the Oxypus's grip. He managed to open his mouth a little ways, maybe as much as a finger's width, and inhaled.

It felt like he was forced to suck the air into his lungs through a thin tube. The air came, but it came reluctantly. It tasted warm and moist and slightly fishy, but it was certainly breathable and his lungs cooled with relief.

After a few deliberate breaths, Kerrigan knew that breathing through the Oxypus was not going to happen unconsciously, naturally, as normal breathing does, but would require a small amount of concentration devoted to it.

Looking up, Kerrigan could see the bottom of Chimera lazily drifting up and away from him. It looked like a huge black disc as it was silhouetted from the sun above.

Kerrigan could still see the ugly patch work of repairs that spotted it's skin, but knew that as he sunk further down, light would fade as it was unable to penetrate so deep and his vision would become darker and less defined.

Bringing his vision back down, passing the ghostly shapes of his descending colleagues, Kerrigan looked below himself to see if he could see just how deep his descent would be.

Never one to be easily shocked, Kerrigan was more curious by what he saw than startled.

Being anchored so close to land, Kerrigan knew that the descent would not be far, but he was none the less impressed by just how shallow the waters here were. Despite the murky green of the ocean, he could easily see the bottom of the sea below him, in fact, descending at his current speed he would reach the bottom very quickly indeed. The sun's light still penetrated to that depth making visibility low, but certainly not dark.

While he still floated above the sea floor, he had an aerial view of where he would be arriving at in a few moments.

In the middle of the ocean floor amidst the smattering of coral or weeds, he saw something that should not be found at the bottom of the sea.

There was a building.

From this distance the building emerged out of the bluey green gloom slowly, fading into existence like a huge concrete monster lumbering towards him, bringing with it more clarity and definition as it emerged.

Just what the hell was a building doing under water?

Upon first glance the building appeared to be no bigger than the bridge of the Chimera. As Kerrigan progressed down through his lazy descent, still focusing on breathing through the Oxypus, the surrounding area around the building also started to creep out of the murk.

Snuggled against one side of the building was the second biggest feature of the scene. At first it appeared to be a dark mound of dirt, almost as tall as the building it rested against, but as the mound became clearer, it's definition showed that it was actually a pile of rubble and debris.

Both the main building and the pile of rubble were positioned in a field of other, smaller piles of rubble and building foundations that grew less dense as they expanded out from the main site. It was once a town, or section of a city that had been all but destroyed. Only the main building that Kerrigan had noticed first remained erect.

It was clear where their destination lay.

Kerrigan was nearing the bottom of the sea now. He was roughly in line with the top windows of the main building, which he could now see stood at an unnatural lean. The base of the building was also clear and it was evident that what was now the ground floor was once a floor higher up - the base of the building was jagged and destroyed as if the top of a hundred story building had been ripped off by a giant and flung into the ocean.

Kerrigan wondered if the huge pile of rubble to the side of the building was perhaps it's destroyed foundations.

The weight attached to Kerrigan's ankles hit the sea bed before he himself did, causing his descent to suddenly stop, floating above the weight like a human balloon.

Bending down Kerrigan used the small piece of chain that connected his ankle to the weight to pull himself down to the sea bed were he could pick up the scrap metal to which it was attached. Once the weight was cradled in his arms he was able to stand vertical upon the sea bed.

Before striding foolishly off into the unknown, Kerrigan took a moment to observe his immediate surroundings.

He had landed in an underwater forest of weeds and coral. He could see the building where his destination no doubt lay a short distance off in the distance. It was hard to judge exactly how far away it was, and how long it would take for him to reach it in the slow moving conditions incurred from underwater movement.

Had the distance been on land, it might have taken him only a few minutes to cover the distance, but with the water resistance that tugged and pulled invisibly at his billowing leather jacket, the weight of the scrap metal cradled in his hands, and the constant struggle of breathing all working against him, Kerrigan surmised that it would take him more than treble this and that he would no doubt be out of breath when he arrived.

He saw the other prisoners doing the ungainly manoeuvre of pulling themselves down to lift the weight so that they too could walk vertically across the sea bed.

Behind him, he saw the anchor of Chimera and hoped that he would still be able to see it as it sunk into the green murkiness of the ocean as he headed towards the destroyed buildings.

He might be able to see the building from this distance but a building had a lot more substance than an anchor and chain.

Above, he heard muffled explosions as the depth charges Bronco had mentioned were released and detonated.

"Scare off the locals" he'd said. Just what did that mean?

Kerrigan took his first careful step forward. It was an awkward, slow movement requiring much more effort and co-ordination than he imagined. It gave him the impression of how it must be like to walk through sludge.

Or like walking through a vat of the Grey Snot.

For one moment, Kerrigan thought that he would not get his leg out in front of him and back on the sand before he toppled over sideways, but just as he felt he was about to over balance, his foot reconnected with the sea bed.

After a couple more of these unbalancing steps he tried to increase his pace to something more natural, but found that the harder he pushed, the more he was resisted by the water. The extra effort didn't seem to gain him any more speed and only tired himself out more, so he continued his journey in the slow, nearly unbalancing walk he had first conducted.

He soon found himself walking amongst sea weeds of bizarre formations, never seeming to be repeated by others that he passed. He saw weeds that grew to the height of his waist which had strands of thin white reeds that flowed and waved dreamily as they were brushed gently by the sea's current. It reminded Kerrigan of Bronco's thick white hair as it drifted lazily about him.

Another weed was twice as tall as he was and was made of flat purple slithers that were stiff at the base and exploded out into soft flowing purple tentacles at the top, much like a tree might if it's highest branches grew out soft and slack instead of hard and firm.

Tall, short, white, purple, brown, green, fat, thin, with protrusions, without protrusions, the sheer variation was as exotic and varying as cloud formations in the sky, never repeating.

Kerrigan saw some weeds that looked quite menacing in nature and wondered briefly why weeds would need sharp looking thorns. Were they needed to protect themselves from "the locals"? wondered Kerrigan.

Luckily, from what Kerrigan could tell, none of these menacing looking weeds lay directly in his path. If any should come up, he thought it would be best to try and avoid them, it would not be wise to risk walking into a creature that was designed for killing when he was unarmed, out of his natural environment and carrying a heavy lump of scrap metal in his arms.

Not that he was afraid of what these mysterious looking weeds might be or what they might do to him, but he was not foolish enough to risk finding out either.

As he walked through the wavering underwater forest, he focused his mind on the task ahead. He would relish the break in the tedious life he had lived for the last… how many years? He tried to focus on the question but his mind shut his prying thoughts out as effectively and as quickly as a slammed steel door.

Instead he turned his thoughts back a little to focus back on what lay ahead of him, in the task laid out by Bronco. A black box he had said. Logic dictated that this must be found in or around the main building that loomed like a half risen moon in the distance. He would start his search there. If anyone should happen to find the box before him he would kill them without hesitation. Same went for anyone who might attempt to take the box from him. He felt no disgust at knowing he could kill so casually. It was a kill or be killed situation. The other men no doubt felt the same and would attempt to kill anyone who stood in their way of the freedom the successful retrieval of the Black Box promised.

Freedom, he mused, is that what he really wanted? He knew that that was what the box would gain him if he could find it, and if Bronco was true to his word, but was that what he wanted? He had lived his life up until this point knowing that he deserved his imprisonment, for what he had done. He had done terrible things, he had… and again this thought was halted by the slamming of his mental steel door.

It didn't matter, he was not even surprised to find that he couldn't remember certain things given the pressure applied to his mind from the thousands of tons of water that flowed lazily above his head.

So if freedom was not what he sought, why was he doing this?

The answer was that he had two choices, and neither of which gave him anything he wanted. The first choice was to not obtain the box and either die of exposure down here or board Chimera without the box and be shot by the guards. Neither of which was an honourable way to die and so was not even a consideration.

The other choice was to find the box and continue his life and his self punishment. It was entirely possible that Bronco may well simply throw him back in jail having used the freedom promise as bait to lure the explorers into co-operation. If so, Kerrigan would not consider himself betrayed. Even if he was set free, he would continue his punishment on his own until he felt he had paid enough and was ready to die.

That time, was not yet upon him.

He looked ahead and saw that the main building was visibly emerging out of the murky blue sea water and was starting to take on it's own colouring; a dirty splattering of mixed greens and grey.

Although he had not walked a great distance, the strain of walking through the ocean's resilience and having to breath through a reduced airway had made his breathing become noticeably more ragged. He wondered how the other explorers were coping with the environment, knowing that his own physical fitness was far greater than theirs.

He walked past yet another new species of sea weed. This one was sickly yellow and appeared to be dead or dying as it's thick tentacles lay lifeless on the sea bed. They quivered slightly to the flow of the invisible under water breeze.

As he looked at the limp weed, an eel-like creature about the length of an adults arm swam out from the centre of it.

Kerrigan stopped to observe it's passage. Like a delayed after image, a moment after Kerrigan himself had stopped, the tail of his coat also stopped it's progress and slowly sunk to meet his ankles.

The head of the creature was flatter and wider than it's long cylindrical body, as if someone had made a tube out of wax and pinched one end to create a head. Two entirely black eyes were perched on either side of it's flat skull.

It's body was completely transparent. Through it's skin, Kerrigan could see the intricate wiring of it's tiny intestines and thought he might even have saw the pumping of it's little heart.

Tiny, see-through limbs ran the length of it's see-through body which ended in an long arrow of tail.

Swishing it's body from side to side, the creature silently rose up out of the dying weed and swam slowly away towards the building in the distance.

Having never seen a creature like it before, it was possible for Kerrigan to know if it was hostile or not. It appeared harmless, but Kerrigan waited until he was sure it would not turn around again before continuing on. It could have a defence mechanism that he had not noticed upon first observation; a toxic bite or some kind of hostile discharge.

He did not want to die down here at the mercy of a creature he had assumed was as harmless as it's gentle appearance suggested.

This thought got his mind up and running again, just why hadn't the previous explorers returned? So far the most dangerous things he had seen had been a spiked sea weed and a benign looking transparent eel. Surely these were not the cause of the previous failed missions? Which would suggest that there would be worse dangers further ahead.

He wondered what they might be.

After a few more moments of nothing more exciting than passing more alien foliage, Kerrigan emerged onto the periphery of Site B.

Before him, dominating his view, lay the dormant sleeping giant that was the building where he knew he must go. Covered in green moss and algae, it looked almost organic in appearance, like it might start to swell with an intake of breath any minute. The heaped pile of rubble that lay snuggled against the side of the main building was similarly covered in algae giving it a hill like appearance. Kerrigan's earlier estimation as to the height of the building had been greatly underestimated. Counting the rows of windows that ringed it's exterior, it was ten floors high.

An untidy landscape of further ruination and building foundations lay between Kerrigan and these two dominant structures.

Empty streets wove between the destroyed husks of former buildings. It was as if there used to be a town here and a giant sword and lopped the roofs off all the buildings.

Upon first observations, as he had descended to the sea bed, these ruined foundations appeared to have been only a foot or two in height.

Now stood amongst them, Kerrigan realized that his impression of these ruins was as misjudged as his impression of the size of the central building.

The foundations were twice the height he was. They were only the shells of former buildings, no internal structure remained as if the house that had once lived here had grown too big and had needed to abandon this shell in search of a newer, larger shell. Random piles of rubble, twists of rusting metal and odd metallic husks dotted the streets that lay between Kerrigan and his goal.

Struggling over these obstacles was not easily accomplished. Many times his footing would slip on the slimy surface of moss that coated each obstruction. Tucking the anchor he held under his left arm, he used his right arm for balance and purchase. He imagined briefly the damage that could be caused to himself if he were to slip and fall landing on the sharp angles of the scrap metal anchor he held tightly against his rib cage.

After clearing and passing several more slippery green boulders, Kerrigan arrived at the base of the main building. He was not the first to arrive, but, like the others, he stood a respectable distance away from the building to observe it before going charging in. To outside observes, they may have looked like pilgrims idolising a glorious statue devoted to their God.

At such a close distance the damage caused to the base of the structure was much more evident. The jagged tear from where the current lowest floor had once been attached to others below it, was a violent rip that pierced into the sea bed in places, and allowed access to it's interior in others. Harsh cracks on the building exterior clawed their way up from the base like lightning bolts. It seemed impressive that what remained of the former building was still held together at all. Had this piece of building been on land, Kerrigan doubted that it would have held it's structure and would have collapsed long ago.

Observing the pile of rubble to the left of the main building, Kerrigan's earlier musing was confirmed - this also used to be a building. Large sections of wall which contained the shape of long destroyed windows were discernible amongst the ruin. The colour and design of the material, and the similar amount of destroyed material as the main building, told Kerrigan that this was once the lower half of the other piece of building. As the pile of rubble was almost as high as what remained of the total structure, the entire building itself must have at one time been approximately twenty floors high.

He hoped that the Black Box he was searching for would not be located in the pile of rubble. If it was, it could be situated right at the heart of the destruction covered in hundreds of tons of impenetrable steel and concrete. If that was the case, it might explain why no one had yet discovered the box.
Hoping to take advantage of Kerrigan and the other stricken prisoner's awed observations, a couple of explorers set off again in hopes of reaching the main building first. No one appeared to be heading towards the pile of rubble, no doubt having already reached the conclusion Kerrigan had of the folly of searching there.
Joining the procession, Kerrigan also headed off towards the main building.
As the base of what remained of the building was not flat, and was instead jagged like a broken egg shell, there were many entrances to be used to gain access to the interior. Not one prisoner used the same entrance as another, wanting to gain access to their own private search area for themselves.
Mentally deciding on which access point to take, Kerrigan started his own approach towards the looming concrete giant.

He arrived at his chosen entry point and ducked down beneath protruding metal stakes, careful not to snag his jacket as he did so, and entered the main building of Site B. As he did so, he had the strangest sensation that he was passing between the broken teeth of a long dead giant sea monster.
Once inside, he straightened up and looked around.
The light was dimmer than it had been outside - the light from the surface could only penetrate through the empty windows and crumbled holes that had broken through the exterior. As such, the light shone through in patches, illuminating only individual sections of the floor at a time, like small, mucky spot lights. Tiny creatures floated lazily in the columns of light.
Looking around, Kerrigan found himself inside a room strewn with debris. The floor was covered with fallen chunks of concrete which had fell from either the ceiling above or from the walls that

segmented his current floor into individual rooms. Holes in both the walls and ceiling gave him sneaky peeks into the rooms that lie ahead, and into the floor above.

Much like the exterior, an omnipresent green algae coated almost every exposed area, from the corroded concrete walling, to the debris that coated the floor. Beneath the furry growth, a treasure trove of unknown, rusting objects lay waiting to be discovered.

Kerrigan dreaded the thought of searching through such a cacophony of mysterious items, but knew that it would be through these objects that his search might eventually have to take place if the Black Box did not present itself in an obvious declaration.

Smaller versions of the weeds he had passed through on his arrival to this also place dotted the room, having penetrated the formidable concrete exterior.

Moving to the first pile of salvage that he could see, Kerrigan began to lift and remove the various items that he found. Most were slimy and greasy to the touch from the thick coating of algae that had accumulated over the long time that they had rested here.

As to how long that was, was impossible for Kerrigan to determine but it was evident by the substantial growth that it had been a very long time indeed.

He picked up the first item on the top of the nearest pile. Although it was clearly not the Black Box that he was looking for, being as how it was not the right size or colour, he none the less took a brief moment to view each item that he discarded, intrigued by the intricate, unknown design and possible function of the separate objects. The item that he held in his hand was obviously designed for a specific function, but each item that he examined remained as unknown to him as the various species of weed he had passed on his way here, yet he found their design fascinating. Clearly each item had a specific function, but what ever that may be remained as much a mystery to Kerrigan to why he had become imprisoned upon Chimera originally...

He wondered what the items might be, what they might have been created for...

Realizing that he had no time for trivialities, he scanned the pile to

see if there were any objects resembling the Black Box. As he thought, there wasn't. He was not going to be fortunate enough to stumble across the Black Box in the first pile of the first room that he entered. If it was going to be that easy, then someone would surely have retrieved the item long ago.
Abandoning the pile, he moved on. There was a door to his left that led outside of the room and this was where he headed.
After exiting the room with the unfamiliar objects, Kerrigan found himself in a near pitch black corridor - there were no windows or gaps broken into the wall to allow light to pass through and illuminate the surroundings. Progressing by touch alone, Kerrigan continued his progress into the heart of the building. The impossibly dark corridor worried him more than any confrontation he might have had with one of the other submerged convicts. At least with an all out fight, he would be able to see his enemy. As it was, he was unable to see even the hand that stretched out in front of him, feeling it's way along the eternally dark corridor that lay ahead.
Despite his mind's paranoid precognitions, as Kerrigan progressed down the corridor, his vision gradually adjusted to the light and he was finally able to make out the dimensions of the pitch black, abandoned corridor. He was not able to see further than the distance his arms could reach, but he could at least see the walls of the corridor on either side.
He could see where he was, but not where he was going.
It gave him an ominous impression of the destiny his life's path was taking him.
Taking each step as slowly as he deemed reasonable, ever aware of his time restraints, the corridor eventually reached an end turning a right angle to his left.
Turning the corner to follow down this new route, he soon discovered that this ended abruptly after taking only a few steps.
Looking around himself once more, he noticed light coming from above and to the left of him through a small hole that had crumbled in the building's exterior. The light shone down illuminating the individual steps of a stairway that lead to the floor above.

With no where else to go but back from where he had came, Kerrigan climbed the stairs.

As the building was resting at an angle that was not flush with the horizon, neither were the stairs that he climbed. It was an uncomfortable sensation climbing stairs that were not parallel to a natural sense of balance. As such, it gave Kerrigan the impression that the building was toppling even as he climbed the stairs - albeit without the continued motion of a collapsing building.

At the top of the stairs Kerrigan once more took a moment to survey his surroundings. He once again found himself in a corridor, but this one at least benefited from the source of light provided by a window that had once gave viewing to the surrounding area. It may have been that the building once looked out upon flowing fields of glorious golden flowers, or a wild meadow where innocent minded animals grazed in the quiet ignorance of their simple lives. Now, it looked out upon a mucky blue canvass with the occasional blemish of unknown weeds dusting across the landscape.

Following down the corridor, Kerrigan noticed several doorways branching off from his own, each of which led to a separate cubicle of varying size.

Peering inside each new room, Kerrigan saw that some cubicles had additional doorways which led to further rooms of slightly different dimensions. The rooms gave Kerrigan a faint sense of deja-vu reminding him of Warden Ashe's office on Chimera - he could make out the familiar shapes of what were once desks, chairs and storage cabinets, however due to the prolonged exposure to the erosion of the sea, the furniture had become distorted, twisted with the algae that grew upon them and the hundreds of tones of pressure that had pressed down upon them for tens, maybe hundreds of years.

To ensure that nothing was missed, Kerrigan explored each room which he encountered first before moving on to the next. If the searched room had an adjacent room, he would explore that next before ultimately returning to the main corridor and continuing on. He continued in this same manner until he finally reached the corridor's end and met another stairwell that led up into another level.

By the end of the first floor, Kerrigan had unconsciously adjusted to the stale, resistant air provided by the Oxypus and the slow-motion movements of his unbalanced body as he traversed along the sloping corridor. He no longer focused his mind on the difficult breaths he was forced to take.

Kerrigan arrived at a new room and peered inside. Within was one of the fellow prisoners who had been forced into this scavenger hunt along with himself. The other man was busily thrusting aside rotting tables and throwing away anything that was not held down causing thick clouds of dirt to bloom about him, slowly obscuring him from view. His actions, although flowing in slow motion, conveyed the sense that this man was in a terrible rush to find their treasure before everyone else. So pre-occupied was he with finding the key to his freedom that Kerrigan was able to observe his hectic search for some time without ever being noticed.

Once he accepted that the Black Box was not to be found within the room to which he had further demolished, the other man turned to leave and at last noticed Kerrigan who stood blocking the exit to which he headed.

During the man's ransacking of the room, Kerrigan had not moved a muscle. This had no doubt added to his stealth-like observation of the other man.

Once he noticed Kerrigan, the other man stopped briefly in his exit, clearly stunned to find Kerrigan blocking his departure.

The other man was shorter than Kerrigan with a balding head. He was approximately twice the age of Kerrigan, around middle age, and had a disgusting looking growth attached to his lower face. This, of course, was the Oxypus that Kerrigan himself also wore, but it took a moment for Kerrigan to understand the artificial growth for what it was.

Looking at the man, Kerrigan saw two things that disgusted him. The first was the Oxypus which he understood he himself had the misfortune of also wearing. It bloated out from the other man's face like a hideous, throbbing growth. The second thing that disgusted him, and disgusted him more than the Oxypus ever could, was the man's pot belly. It offended Kerrigan to think that anyone would allow themself to become so lazy and disrespectful of their own body that they would allow themselves to become such a disgusting, flabby individual.

The fat man looked Kerrigan up and down recognizing who Kerrigan was.

The two men faced each other through the murky waters without moving and, much to the fat man's frustration, without being able to say anything to one another.

Reluctant to allow the man to exit the room by the corridor in which he stood, Kerrigan remained where he was. Fat Man had not entered the room in which Kerrigan had found him by the stairs or corridor down which he himself had already explored - he was the only man to enter the building by the entrance he had chosen, and he was reluctant to allow Fat Man to progress further down the corridor he had not yet fully explored for himself. The risk being that Fat Man might find the Black Box before Kerrigan himself could. Therefore, Fat Man could have only entered the room by the doorway on the other side of the room. and that what ever lay beyond and through the other doorway did not, presumably, contain the Black Box. Assuming of course, that Fat Man had searched the other rooms and passages thoroughly.

After a few moments of eye balling one another, Fat Man took a tentative step backwards and exited the room by the doorway in which he had entered, deciding that he was no match for the ferocious, violent intensity that Kerrigan had a reputation for.

That, or there were other rooms on his side of the floor that he had not yet explored.

Either of which was fine by Kerrigan, he still had plenty to explore for himself.

Turning from the room, he continued in his own exploration.

At every opportunity, Kerrigan would look out of the holes in the wall that were once pained with glass, to observe the sea-weed field below, looking to see if there might be somebody else heading back towards Chimera's anchor which would obviously mean that someone else had beaten him to the Black Box. It would not gain him any advantage knowing that someone else had beaten him, as he doubted that he would be able to catch up with anyone who might have beaten him to the Black Box when he himself was stuck on the second floor of a building and still rising. That said, he would still have liked to have known when the race was over.

He could just make out the thin fuzzy line of Chimera's anchor chain in the distance. At least he would not be too disorientated to find his way back should the need arise.

Floors three and four proved to be of similar design as the ones below, a corridor ran the length of the floor branching out into individual rooms. After searching through these, he discovered that, as he had suspected upon his first encounter with Fat Man, another corridor ran the length of the floor parallel to his own. This corridor also branched into additional rooms with further doorways leaving Kerrigan to wonder just how many rooms and corridors filled each floor, and how many of these he might have missed. It must be a lot more than he first assumed as he had yet to encounter any other explorers but Fat Man.

Suddenly, Kerrigan saw Fat Man's shadow slide along a wall of a room off Fat Man's corridor.

It was at this point that Kerrigan made a mental decision to always keep in mind Fat Man's location in respect of his own. If Fat Man was only searching the rooms that branched off from his own corridor, which he appeared to be doing, given how they had not encountered each other since the second floor, then Kerrigan would know that the Black Box was not contained in any of Fat Man's rooms. Combined with his own search, he would effectively be covering twice the area than if he ran on ahead.

Also, if Fat Man did find the Black Box, Kerrigan would know instantly and could kill the glutton and claim the Black Box for himself.

Easy. What was all the fuss about?

Upon reaching the fifth floor, things started to change slightly. Kerrigan arrived in his corridor and could see that the wall at the far end of the corridor was missing. At first, he had assumed it to be just another crumbled hole in the outer wall, like how he had seen on previous levels. When he had finally finished searching the rooms on this level, while keeping a watch on Fat Man's location, Kerrigan reached the end of the corridor and looked out of the crumbled hole. He realized that his initial impression was wrong.

The side of the building he was currently on, was on the opposite side of where he had approached and where Chimera's anchor lay. The view itself wasn't much different from anything else he had seen; the same mixture of unknown sea-weeds waved at him languidly in the underwater currents below and scattered piles of rubble dusted the sea floor.

However, his attention was drawn to a particularly large boulder beneath which lay a human skeleton. How the deceased had ended up beneath the boulder, Kerrigan could not imagine. Surely, who ever it was, must have noticed a boulder of such huge dimensions falling upon him/her and would have taken appropriate action to avoid being squashed?

Still staring out of the crumbled hole, Kerrigan tore his gaze-and thoughts-away from the crushed cadaver and looked up to see just how much more of the wall had collapsed. He expected to see the top of the hole that he was peering through arching only a few feet above him. Instead, what he saw, was the blue waves of the sea sparkling the sun's rays above him in a silent firework display.

The hole which he had at first assumed to be only a few feet in diameter, continued up the rest of the side of the building. Looking from side to side to follow the sides of the hole, he was able to see that they too continued up the building's roof, never converging as a circle should.

The outer wall of this side of the building had been destroyed from the fifth floor up, along with increasing amounts of the up flooring itself.

It was as if something had taken a giant sized bite out of the top of the building.

He had not been able to see this devastation upon his approach to the building as the route he had taken had been from the opposite

side, completely hiding the damage from view.
The damage was obviously not caused by natural erosion, clearly there was a story to be told about what had happened here.
Kerrigan had an ominous feeling that both the damage and the reason why the previous expeditions had failed were somehow linked, and that the answer to both of these mysteries would soon reveal itself and become known to him.

Arriving at the sixth floor, the layout of the building changed. Where once each floor was a series of rooms running off parallel corridors, the sixth floor was open plan.
Cresting the stairs that led to the floor, it came as a relief to Kerrigan to be emerging out of such previously confining spaces. The room itself was easily a hundred square meters in size, making the farthest walls appear hazy and hard to look at as they faded into the murk of the water. If not for the ceiling above his head, it was hardly like standing in a room at all.
There were two sets of stairs that gave access to this floor, but only one that led any higher. In the centre of the room, rose a wide set of stairs giving access to the floor above.
Looking around the room was like looking around a sea creature's home who lived a particularly slob-like life style. Every where Kerrigan looked there was the never ending green growth of algae covering every available surface. Thick glistening weeds dangled from the ceiling and the myriad of objects that scattered the floor were either broken or toppled. Kerrigan could make out the familiar shapes of chairs and tables that had long ago rotted away to the metal skeleton underneath. Against some walls were rusted shapes of filing cabinets and what appeared to be rusting equipment similar to that used on the bridge of Chimera.
The farthest wall, and part of the floor, was missing as the devastation he had noticed earlier continued it's expansion upwards, towards the building's roof.
He was not alone in his new surroundings for long. Fat Man had ascended the stairs that were at the end of his own corridor and he too arrived on the sixth floor. It would not be long before other's

joined them both.

Looking at each other's disfigured faces briefly, the two men started to explore the new surroundings with an unsounded treaty.

As Kerrigan moved aside tables and chairs, lifted metallic boxes which had metallic lids that swung open on their rusting hinges as he lifted them, he wondered as to what purpose this floor with it's distinctive style could have served, and by extension, the building as a whole.

It was the appearance of the rusting consoles, so much like those used aboard Chimera, that provoked this thought within Kerrigan. He had a very limited knowledge as to the workings of any technology, the only technology he had ever had contact with was that which was placed aboard Chimera, and the vast majority of that was broken. The small amount that did work was operated, manned and serviced by the guards and serviceman of Chimera, so any knowledge as to their workings was irrelevant to himself. Besides, being a prisoner he was only allowed to operate the most basic of manual machinery anyway. The technical equipment that decorated the bridge was strictly off limits to all prisoners. He had been told however, that those consoles on Chimera's bridge, when it was still a fully functional and impressive prison machine, were used to plan out their courses and return them to any given destination quickly and accurately. They were also used to communicate to the main land from across large distances, foresee weather conditions and many other practical applications. Some even said that no one onboard knew what the purpose of every machine served anymore, and that there were whole rooms of abandoned machines that no one knew how to operate. Apparently it was a Captain even well before Armaine's service that had sealed off these rooms, as he had feared the machines being tampered with by inquisitive minds and therefore further crippling Chimera's already dilapidated service even further.

Assuming that these consoles within the sunken building served the same function as those aboard Chimera, and Kerrigan had no reason to think otherwise, what could they have been used to calculate? And who were they used to talk to? This was a building, not a ship.

As Kerrigan finished looking inside a line of cabinets, he noticed that he and Fat Man had been joined by another two prisoners. Very soon, Kerrigan understood, this scavenger hunt was going to turn ugly as the desperate men would fight and kill one another to obtain the Black Box, the very key to their freedom.

No sooner had he had this thought, when Fat Man, who's face was transfixed to the floor, strayed near one of the newer men who had arrived. The newcomer grabbed Fat Man and, with a great heave, ripped the Oxypus from his face in a violent burst of bubbles. Fat Man reached out desperately for the Oxypus, waving his arms around in the air like he was trying to catch a feather on a breeze.

Kerrigan thought he recognised the newcomer, but it was hard for him to be sure viewing him through the murk of the water and with an Oxypus obscuring the lower part of his face. The newcomer held Fat Man at bay with one straight arm, his hand clenched tightly around Fat Man's throat. He turned his head away from Fat Man and held the Oxypus out in his other arm well out of Fat Man's reach.

Fat Man desperately flailed for the Oxypus that had been ripped from his face. His strength was already fading and, too late, he attempted to remove the newcomer's own Oxypus. His finger's merely tickled the oxygen giving creature of his captor before, slowly, his own life drained out of him. He dropped the weight that kept him anchored and he floated gently to the ceiling. He touched the roof and floated there, rooted to the spot where the anchor lay, like a macabre balloon.

The newcomer dropped Fat Man's Oxypus, which also appeared to have died, and looked around the room, glaring at the others, warning them against stopping him. He then started to search the floor of his immediate vicinity.

Kerrigan watched this scene without emotion. He had expected this to happen and knew that he would do the same if the situation arose. It was kill or be killed.

Simple.

Leaving the sixth floor and the other men behind, Kerrigan headed up the stairwell to the seventh floor.

The seventh floor was devastated. Where the sixth floor had been a mess and only partially destroyed, the seventh was in ruins. There was more rock and rubble scattered across the floor than there was human furnishings. The same wall that had been destroyed on the sixth was also completely missing here. The flooring of the eighth level only covered half of the ceiling, the other half of the flooring had been destroyed and lay scattered across the seventh level. The stairs that would have led up to the eighth level were only partially still erect, destroyed midway preventing access to the level above.
Kerrigan hoped that the Black Box was not to be found anywhere higher than the seventh floor. If it was, a dangerous climb up onto the exterior of the building would be needed.
As Kerrigan observed his surroundings, he noticed what appeared to have once been a picture, a map, or at least some kind of visual image filling the middle segment of one wall. Rotted beyond repair, the image was impossible to discern. Ragged flaps of soggy canvas fluttered silently in the unseen currents. The square frame of the picture had once been of such an intricate gold design that it itself would have, at one time, been considered a work of art in its own right.
It was now rotted to a sickly green.
The frame, and what was left of the picture, came as no surprise to Kerrigan. The building had clearly been something important at one time and so he found it not surprising that it would be furnished with occasional luxuries. The picture and frame seemed to fit here, it seemed right somehow.
Starting his excavation towards the rear of the room, where flooring, walls and ceiling were still intact, Kerrigan continued the tedious act of lifting, moving and searching copies of identical tables, cabinets and chairs that he had searched through from the floors below.
As he progressed from one side of the room to the next, his coat caught on protruding fingers of rusted metal which poked out from

fallen chunks of ceiling or wall. He frequently had to stop to unsnag his coat.

As had happened on previous floors, Kerrigan's searching was not done solo for very long. The newcomer who had killed Fat Man arrived soon after Kerrigan, fearing that Kerrigan may gain an advantage in the search over him. Newcomer was then followed shortly by another man who, seeing the other two men ascend the stairs so urgently, feared he may also be missing out.

Arriving in the corner of the room furthest from the destroyed wall, Kerrigan found a desk that had been over spilled and lay on it's back, it's drawers facing up towards the roof, like a dog waiting to have it's belly scratched.

He knelt beside the desk and, with a quick jolt, that was not easy to muster with only one arm and being under water, Kerrigan prized the drawers open one by one to study the contents. He found only more mysterious, broken equipment. Who ever had once run this building was clearly using equipment that Kerrigan himself had no understanding of.

It made him think once more about what the purpose of the building had been.

After studying a particularly baffling object, Kerrigan's attention was drawn to the newcomer who had killed Fat Man on the level below, who was currently engaged in searching the most devastated part of the room. This was the area immediately in front of the destroyed outer wall and ceiling.

The other man was staggering backwards, holding his hand to his mouth as if to suppress a gag reflex. It was a useless gesture as all his hand encountered was the slippery warm texture of the Oxypus which still clung to his lower face.

If he had thrown up, it was likely that the other man would have drowned in his own vomit, with thin streams of stomach bile forcing itself out of the Oxypus's embrace.

His eyes were transfixed wide on the area he had been searching. After a moment of standing still with his hand still held uselessly at his face, Fat Man's killer took a tentative step forward, back towards the area where he had recoiled.

Considering how he had just killed another man with his own hands not ten minutes previous, Kerrigan found it odd to observe the other man reacting with such clear revulsion.

Knowing that he must have uncovered something of interest, Kerrigan put aside the small device he had been studying, rose from his crouching position, and strode over to where the other man was now kneeling. He was reinvestigating the sight which had just caused him so much disgust.

Kerrigan arrived behind the kneeling man, without him being aware of his arrival. He peered over Fat Man's killer's shoulder.

In front of him and scattered across a large area, were the remains of a man.

Or, more accurately, men.

Rotting skeletal arms thrust upwards from the debris as if they were still alive, trapped beneath the destruction. It was as if they were reaching up desperately for someone to take their pleading hands, to pull them free from the entrapment that had claimed their lives…

Dotting the area were legs, hands and other unrecognisable body parts. All the limbs were rotted to some extent, and the flesh that still clung to the bones wafted gently in the water's under-current streams. The white skeletal bones of decomposed fingers pointed accusingly towards the ocean surface.

Closing in on the kneeling man, Kerrigan peered over his shoulder to see what it was that he cradled in his hands. It was the decapitated head of an unfortunate individual who had been killed here.

The head's skin was a sickly pale white with light green tinges at the edges. The hair was brown and flowed lazily in the water like an organic fire. The eyes were wide open and bloodshot and seemed to stare through the man that held it, through Kerrigan, and through the building they stood in, on into the never ending depths of the sea.

For Kerrigan, the most prominent feature about the head was the way the mouth hung open in an eternal grimace of terror, fear and shock.

Just what the hell had happened here, Kerrigan couldn't imagine. Several of the bodies had literally been torn apart. What remained of the ligaments had deep lacerations down the length of remaining flesh.
Dropping the head which he held, the other man hopped into the middle of this sick pile of scattered limbs.
Kerrigan hung back watching him, there was no where the other man could go unless he chose to leap out of the building via the destroyed wall, or attempt to climb to the level above by the same means.
His progress into the destruction was almost comical as he lifted and bounded his legs in an exaggerated manner, as if he were trying to traverse the scattering of limbs with as little contact as possible, like how a man might cross a path of blazing coals.
Arriving in the middle of the rubble, silhouetted by the blue of the ocean visible through the missing wall, Fat Man's killer knelt down and grabbed at something Kerrigan could not see.
He froze a moment and then rose.
In his hand, he held a disembodied arm. Still held in this detached arm, in a death grip, was a small rectangular object. Although the item remain in silhouette, it was obvious to Kerrigan that it could be only one thing.
The Black Box.
As the other man lifted the arm from where it lay, another of those see-through snake creatures Kerrigan had seen amongst the sea weed field rose from where it had been laying, spiralling up and into the room.
The other man held the dead arm at arms length as if it disgusted him, despite holding a dead man's head in his hands only moments ago, and ripped the Black Box from out of it's grip.
He dropped the dead arm and turned to face Kerrigan.
The transparent snake creature ignorantly swam in front of the other man's face. Suddenly, dropping the Black Box, Fat Man's killer grabbed the eel around it's flank and squeezed.
Issuing a high pitched squeal, the creature squirmed in pain and tried to turn it's head to bite at the hands of the man who was

crushing the life out of it.

Thin squiggles of red blood squeezed out from between the killer's fingers as he continued his crushing of the defenceless creature.

It was an act that said he was not to be messed with. He was not to be stopped, or he would crush anyone who tried, as quickly as he had off-handedly killed the transparent snake.

Twisting it's head and tail upwards, the eel let out a final, ear splitting squeal that rose in pitch until finally it's body went limp and it died. The other man dropped the carcass and it floated lazily to lie amongst the scattering of human appendages. It's crushed body left a red ribbon of blood behind itself as it coasted gently to the building's floor.

As soon as it touched the building's ruined flooring, a deep rumble issued throughout the entire building as if, somehow, the dead snake weighed an incredible amount, thousands of times greater than it actually weighed.

Silt and dirt dislodged from the ceiling above causing the silhouette of Fat Man's killer to look about himself.

When the rumble wasn't repeated, Fat Man's killer picked up the Black Box again, smearing the intestines of the dead eel over the handle in the process. He started to side step around Kerrigan in a vast arc, never breaking the eye contact that they shared, as if the two men were kept apart at a set distance by an invisible barrier.

Kerrigan took a step in the direction that the other man was heading.

Fat Man's killer hesitated. He had not expected Kerrigan to attempt to stop him.

He found himself in an awkward position: He held the anchor to keep him erect under one arm, as did Kerrigan, but in his other hand was the Black Box - he couldn't defend himself from any attacks Kerrigan might make with objects in both hands. He would be killed for sure. The only option he had was to drop the Black Box, kill Kerrigan and then continue on. He believed he could do it too being as how Kerrigan was still fully clothed in his boots, leather trousers, shirt and thick leather jacket. The entire ensemble looked incredibly heavy and cumbersome underwater. He himself

was only dressed in boots and jeans being as how he was stripped aboard Chimera's deck.
Seeing no other option and without dropping his gaze from Kerrigan's, Fat Man's killer placed the Black Box gently on the floor and rose back to his full height.

It was clear what the other man's intentions were, and Kerrigan prepared himself for the battle ahead. He dropped the weight which he still cradled in his arm, wrapping his leg within the chain to keep from floating away and in doing so freed both of his arms for the coming assault.
Fat Man's killer strode towards him with one fist clenched, and the other still hugging the weight to his side. As soon as he was within reach of Kerrigan he dropped the weight, bent over and lunged his shoulder into Kerrigan's midsection.
Kerrigan, braced for the conflict that he had expected, did not topple beneath the charge.
He braced a leg behind himself to prevent being thrust backwards which could potentially overspill him, or have him trip on some unseen rubble, and tried to land a blow to the other man's exposed kidneys.
It was extremely hard to land a harmful blow to someone whilst underwater. It felt like his arms were being held back by some unseen guardian force, protector of the man who found the Black Box first. It was his and no-one elses.
Of course, Kerrigan knew that it wasn't anything so stupid, he didn't believe in ghosts, spooks or guardian spirits, it was just the natural resistance of the water.
His fist struck the other man's flesh with no more force than a hard push would produce, and so failed to bring the other man to his knees as he had hoped.
Fat Man's killer continued his thrust, reached out behind Kerrigan's knees in an attempt to topple him over onto his back. Should that happen, he could straddle Kerrigan and choked him to death, or rip the Oxypus from his face as he had the man before.
Seeing as how blows of any kind were clearly not going to hurt the

man who was currently trying to burrow his way into his navel, Kerrigan instead reached down and started to prize the Oxypus's tentacles off the rear of the other man's head.

Feeling what Kerrigan was doing, and realizing his stupidity at having exposed such an obvious weakness to his adversary, Fat Man's killer immediately withdrew from Kerrigan and placed his hands behind his head, forcing the Oxypus to keep it's life giving grip on his face.

Suddenly, the entire building started to shake once more. It was an instantly violent shake, as if the building itself was collapsing whilst they were still in it. The rumble was felt through Kerrigan's boots and shook all the way up his skeleton into his skull, causing his vision to blur slightly.

Dust bloomed from cracks in the ceiling and floated lazily to the floor below.

Looking around himself and fearing being buried alive, Fat Man's killer picked up the Black Box and his anchor, abandoning the fight, with the intention of trying to out run Kerrigan.

He took a few steps towards the central staircase noticing Kerrigan was matching him step for step.

Hesitating briefly in his escape, Fat Man's killer tried to figure out what would be his best course of action. He could either stay and fight in a building that was collapsing all around them both, or try and out run Kerrigan with no means of defending himself as both of his arms would be in use.

Before he had time to make his choice, just as Kerrigan was striding towards him to make the decision for him, an almighty roar filled both men's ears, immensely deep, it compressed the water in Kerrigan's ears and caused the very water to vibrate, their vision blurring worse than it previously had.

At first, Kerrigan interpreted the roar as the sound of the building's collapse. The crumbling walls which held up this half of the building had finally given up the strain of having to support so many new, moving bodies at once, and were now collapsing beneath their feet.

But the roar took on a different tone, increasing in pitch instead of remaining a deep, continuous grumble.

It strained Kerrigan's ears listening to the noise. If he could have shut it off, he would have. The sound felt like daggers pressing into, and ultimately, puncturing his ear drums. It rose to such a high piercing level that it felt the noise was going to not only burst his ear drums, but to pierce on through, directly into his brain.

His vision became nothing but a blur as the roar rattled the very matter around and within him.

Despite the discomfort the roar caused him, Kerrigan knew that the sound was not caused by the collapse of the building. The sound had a distinct organic quality to it, sounding more like a distressed animal, rather than bricks and cement falling and grating against one another.

Huge bubbles were flooding up and past the segment of collapsed wall. They filled the empty window, rushing past the gap in a desperate rush to out race one another to the surface.

They were pursued by their creator.

Upon seeing the sight that confronted him, Kerrigan's mind immediately dismissed the appearance as being impossible. For several moments, Kerrigan viewed the arrival with a mixture of awe, rapture and disbelief. Surely what he was seeing was beyond the realms of conceivability? He almost believed, however briefly, that his mind had become unhinged from the strain and stress that it had endured for so long, and was now conjuring up it's own images as a result.

He was wrong.

However comforting it may be to believe that he had gone mad, Kerrigan knew that what he was seeing was, unfortunately, reality. Suddenly he knew, despite there being no empirical evidence to justify his belief, that this was what had caused the noise he had mistaken for the building's collapse.

A giant, monstrous head loomed into view, obscuring all but the very edges of the panoramic view provided by the collapsed wall.

A deep blue and green in colour, the head was a flat disc coated in shiny hard plates of armour which extended from the back of the creatures neck, over it's scalp, and down to the middle of it's face.

A mouth as wide as the skull itself was set along the rim of it's disk shaped head and was filled with too many needle thin, razor sharp teeth. Some of the teeth were either broken off half way, missing completely, or hung onto the creature's gum line with a tentative grip, like a monkey swinging from a branch one-handed, giving the mouth a crazy broken leer.

The beast had a long flowing moustache; scaly flagella sprung out from above it's mouth, waving gently as the bubbles it produced from it's gaping maw bumped against it.

Two yellow, intelligent eyes were placed not on top of it's head, but on opposite sides of it's flat, wide skull.

It had a huge neck which was covered in the same armoured scales as it's head. Disproportionately small arms or legs ran down both sides of it's body, rising and falling in a smooth, coordinated wave motion.

On and on it's neck went until Kerrigan understood that it's neck was so long because it had no body to connect to.

The beast was some kind of nightmarish eel creature, complete with multitudes of quivering little arms and just as many sharpened teeth.

It was suddenly all too obvious to Kerrigan that this mammoth creature before him was the mother of the eel that had just been crushed to death by Fat Man's killer, and he felt his stomach fall as if the building had finally collapsed, taking Kerrigan's stomach with it.

The monstrous sea-snake peered in at the two shocked men, twisting it's head in an inquisitive manor as if to assess if the men were alive or as dead and as lifeless as their motionless, stunned appearance suggested.

Undecided, the monster reared back it's huge head and roared it's ear piercingly high pitched squeal once more. Both Kerrigan and Fat Man's killer reflexively snapped up their hands to their ears to block out the deafening sound.

Abruptly, the creature's roar stopped.

There was a horribly still moment that seemed to last several moments, but in fact only lasted a second or two, when both men realized their mistake.
The creature lunged.

With a huge explosion, Kerrigan was knocked from his feet. Dust, rubble and steel rained down upon him. He closed his eyes tightly and turned his back towards the rain of debris. He heard and felt a deep impact nearby that shook his entire world, turning it from a once stable, defined environment into a blurred, distorted chaos. The impact was immediately followed by a long scrape that prolonged the world's distortion. At some point he fell, but he could not define at which moment amidst the carnage.
Around him, the water turned brown as the loosened dirt was shaken loose and mixed into the water.
Kerrigan lay where he had fell with his arm's covering his eyes. He felt, rather than saw, the settling of the debris and dust around himself.
After a moment of allowing the murk in the water to diffuse, Kerrigan cautiously risked opening his eyes.
There was now a huge pile of rubble where Fat Man's killer had once been, the roof above had noticeable withdrawn even further away from the building's exterior. The giant eel had rammed it's head through the floor above to grab Fat Man's killer.
As the brown water started to fade back to murky blue, Kerrigan was able to see the monster's head through the newly retracted flooring above. It's jaw was chomping up and down as it ate. Blood and bit's of Fat Man's killer rained from it's masticating jaw in a horrid red shower.
Knowing it would not take long before the eel's attention would return to the rest of the food trapped inside the building, Kerrigan looked around, desperately hoping to find the Black Box. He was all too aware that it was entirely possible that the Black Box could now be in a place that was unreachable, except by the unacceptable route that Fat Man's torso was now taking.
Shocked by his good luck, Kerrigan saw the Black Box lying

amongst the fresh destruction that lay beside the junk metal that Fat Man's killer had used as an anchor. The chain that had attached the metal to his ankle had a strained stretched look like melted toffee, were it had been snapped.

Fat Man's killer must have dropped the Black Box in his fear.

Moving as slowly as possible, without removing his gaze from the eel above, the eel's eyes were focused on some point in the distance, and not on the building, as it continued to eat it's meal, Kerrigan approached the Black Box. If he could reach the Black Box before the eel's attention returned, he might be able to slink back into the shadows and, hopefully, out of the eel's attention and away into freedom. He moved as quickly as he dared, which seemed terribly slow even in the water's reduced maneuverability. He dared not risk moving anything quicker than a slow walk incase a sudden movement were noticed by the, currently occupied, eel.

Without removing his eyes from the eel, Kerrigan reached for the Black Box. As he grasped it's handle, he felt a soft squish beneath his hand, leading him to think that perhaps Fat Man's killer hadn't dropped the Black Box at all, perhaps his hand and been sliced off leaving behind pieces of his flesh attached to the artificial casing.

With the Box firmly in hand, he cautiously stepped slowly backwards, seeking safety in the shelter of the depth of the room.

He had almost made it so that he was out of the eel's vision when it looked down and met his fixed gaze. It jerked it's head upwards in two quick motions as if scenting the air, and roared.

Fearing the worst and knowing that the time for caution had passed, Kerrigan turned and ran. The water's resistance pushed against him with an agonizing dedication.

He had gone no further than two, slowly advanced steps, when the eel one more thrust it's giant head through the flooring of the level above. It came down only meters behind where he had been, the force of which picked him up and tossed him away from the eel's deadly puncture, as if he weighed no more than a leaf in a breeze.

He fell clumsily on his side, smashing the anchor he carried into his ribs and crushing the hand that carried it into the rough concrete beneath. The flesh on the back of his hand tore open and the exposed the bones beneath, grated them along the gritty concrete surface.

Not daring to take even a moment to recover, Kerrigan rose back to his feet and ventured a look over his shoulder.

The eel had barely missed him and was frantically twisting it's head around in the hole it had created, striving to find it's prey. It caught a glimpse of Kerrigan through the dust cloud that it had created and snapped frantically at him with it's wild, thin teeth.

Kerrigan was just out of it's reach. With the eel's neck stuck in the whole, it was unable to stretch out further to grab a hold of it's target.

Before the eel could attempt to withdraw and strike down upon him once more, Kerrigan ran for the stairs that would lead him to the floor below.

It was not a quick escape. The water's betrayal of his movements continued, seeming to make an actual effort to slow his departure.

From behind him, Kerrigan could hear the agonised howls of the eel's frustration. The noises rung through every bone in Kerrigan's body, making them vibrate and hum in harmony with the eel's anguish.

Descending the stairwell, Kerrigan reached the sixth level and continued downwards. As he did so he noticed some of the other men who had been sent down to Site B along with him. They were stood still, looking upwards at the ceiling, towards the origin of the horrific screaming they could hear. Every one of them wore the same slack, wide eyed faces of those who were afraid of the dark, afraid of an unseen danger.

Above Kerrigan, the screaming continued, but moved away as it withdrew it's head from the level it had punctured into.

As the sound moved, so too did the heads of the motionless men, as if the two were connected by some unseen force.

Kerrigan looked for the stairs that would lead him down to the level below, and as he did so his vision passed the missing wall. Outside, the eel had brought it's head down to gaze upon himself and the terrified men that were gathered in the vicinity. Only then, when the danger was seen rather than heard, did any of the grouped men remember the use of their legs and made a clumsy retreat, unable to remove their eyes from the ponderous beast outside.

This time, instead of stabbing down from above, the eel pulled it's head back and thrust itself into the side of the building, like a high velocity dart.

One unfortunate man, who was near the already devastated wall, was crushed to death by the eel's colossal head. His legs were trapped by the momentum of the creature's driving skull. He beat futilely at the beast for a moment before the eel's continued forward motion ground his torso, and then head, into the concrete.

Gradually, the squeeze of forcing itself in-between two floors of the building slowed the eel's progress until it slowed and finally stopped completely. As soon as it had stopped, it swept it's head from side to side, gnashing it's demented jaws, destroying anything that could be broken and sweeping aside those objects that could not. A small plume of red blood bloomed from beneath it's neck as the sweeping motion rubbed the crushed man beneath it into a mushy paste.

Without wanting to watch further, Kerrigan raced down the stairs into the floor below. His breathing had quickened, yet he found it hard to catch his breath through the resisting filter of the Oxypus. He hoped that the little animal wouldn't give up on him and die through stress or over use.

He reached the fifth floor and his surroundings returned back to the corridor scenario that he had traversed once more. The close confines of the corridors seemed claustrophobic in comparison to the open floor plan of the levels above.

He ran as quickly as he could knowing that he would have to pass the small section of outer wall that had also been destroyed on this level in order to reach the safety of the undamaged level below. From what he could remember, the gap on this level would not be big enough to allow the eel's head to penetrate into the floor.... yet this came as no comfort. The eel had already smashed itself through plenty of concrete and steel framework to tell Kerrigan that the fifth level's wall would not be sufficient to suppress an attack should the eel wish to continue it's assault.

Running in slow-motion, which was as fast as the sea would allow him to run, Kerrigan approached the broken segment of wall. As he approached it, he could see that the eel had withdrawn it's head from the level above and was peering down into his level, directly at him.

It was definitely following him.

But why? What was it about him that the eel had targeted? He felt that he was being paranoid, but at the same time he KNEW that he was not. It's attacks were too direct and it's visuals too focused upon him to be nothing else but a pursuit. As to why that might be, remained a mystery to Kerrigan.

With an sharp upward curl of it's neck, the eel brought it's head down like a fist. It's lower jaw and nose slammed down onto the ledge created by the hole in the wall. The force of the blow sent violent shakes throughout the entire structure. The hole that already existed in the exterior of the building became noticeably wider with the impact: It was, Kerrigan realized, trying to hammer itself a bigger entry onto Kerrigan's level so that it might reach in and grab him directly with it's sword-like teeth...

Raising it's mighty head once more, which seemed to have barely sustained a scratch from the repeated attacks it was inflicting, the eel prepared to hit down again at the increasing entry it was making for itself.

Seizing the opportunity, Kerrigan ran past the hole and further into the bowels of the building. Feeling incredibly exposed during the brief moment when he was directly in front of the hole, hoping that the eel would not be able to whip it's head back down as suddenly as his frantic mind suggested it might.

Just as Kerrigan passed the gap, what he had feared happened. and the eel brought it's head down with incredible force, shaking Kerrigan's vision and balance and further expanding the destroyed wall. It hadn't quite made a gap large enough for it's head to fit through yet, but it pushed and ground it's head anyway, desperately trying to burrow it's head into the too small gap.

Without looking back at the devastation behind him, Kerrigan

reached the stairs to the level below and descended them.
He had a moment's relief upon reaching the fourth floor. This floor was entirely enclosed, the devastation of the floors above did not reach this far down and so the eel could not gain access to him. Even if it did continue it's hammering of the hole above, it's progress would not be quick enough to catch his steady decent.
A howling cry of frustration issued from the floor above which pierced Kerrigan's ears and made his head throb deep within.
Every action the eel took seemed to hurt Kerrigan, and shake the environment around it.
As he ran down the corridors of the fourth floor, Kerrigan glanced briefly into each room that branched off from it. He saw other prisoners either rushing to leave or leaning out of the shattered windows, staring in awe at the giant eel that attacked from above.
Suddenly, Kerrigan was grabbed from behind. A strong arm wrapped around his throat as another gripped hold of the precious, oxygen supplying Oxypus attached to his face.
For a brief moment, Kerrigan was unable to breath from the applied pressure of the choke hold.
The hand that gripped the Oxypus squeezed.
With no other option, Kerrigan dropped both the Black Box and his anchor to free both his hands in an attempt to remove the arm encircling his throat.
Almost as suddenly as the choke hold had been applied to his neck, was it released.
Straining for breath, Kerrigan turned to face his attacker.
The man who had attacked him had both arms wrapped around his right leg's thigh, and was desperately trying to pull it with him.
Kerrigan's anchor had landed on the other man's foot. A blooming red cloud of blood was spreading from beneath the anchor as the sharp metal cut deep into the other man's flesh.
Smiling at his good fortune, Kerrigan reached out for his attacker's throat and gripped his windpipe beneath his strong right hand. As his fist squeezed upon his opponent, the other man's eyes bulged from his head. Using his free hand, Kerrigan gripped the Oxypus that was wrapped around the other man's face and squeezed that

too. Thick black blood issued from the holes where Kerrigan's fingers sunk into the Oxypus's tender flesh.

The other man raised his arms to grab Kerrigan's wrists but to no avail.

Kerrigan felt a deep pleasure at seeing the panic in the other man's eyes as he killed the Oxypus that supplied precious oxygen to his victim's lungs. After only a few moments, Kerrigan succeeded in killing the other's Oxypus where his opponent had failed.

As the Oxypus died, it's tentacles gave up their grip on the other man's face and Kerrigan was easily able to remove the creature off the other man's head.

He dropped the dead breathing apparatus to the corridor floor.

Kerrigan stared into the dying man's eyes as he struggled desperately against him. His eyes had grown so large, so round… so scared. It was hypnotic, beautiful to see such pure, perfect fear.

After a moment of beating desperately at Kerrigan's clenched fist, the man who had attacked Kerrigan also sunk to the floor to lie beside his dead Oxypus, looking like how a small child would cuddle up to an item of comfort when they wanted to sleep.

A thought suddenly occurred to Kerrigan: Was this the first time he had killed someone? True, he hadn't killed the man before him with his bare hands; he hadn't stabbed him in the heart or anything so direct, but he had removed his Oxypus, therefore removing his source of oxygen, which was, ultimately, the cause of his death.

Following this thought, were a barrage of other question's, so sudden in their rapid intensity that he was unable to focus upon one for long enough to give it a definite answer.

He knew that he had been placed a prisoner aboard Chimera for some reason…. Was this it? Had he somehow forgotten that he was a murderer? If so, how many had he killed before? He sure didn't feel like a murderer, but how does a murderer feel? and why was he not repulsed by his actions as he knew, deep down, that he should be? Why was he not upset? Disgusted? Scared? Remorseful?

He wasn't entirely sure he could answer the question… HAD he killed before? Nor, he realized, was this the time or place to dwell upon the question. But there was one thing he was sure about, he felt no guilt for what he had done.

It was kill or be killed.

Picking up the Black Box, Kerrigan realised that it was too dangerous to continue carrying the object around in plain view of the other prisoners.

He stuffed the box down his shirt hoping it's rigid shape could not be seen beneath.

He picked up his anchor, finally releasing the dead man's foot, turned back in the direction he had been travelling, and continued his decent.

As he went, Kerrigan continued to look out of each window that he passed. The eel had stopped it's violent attacking of the building and was now swimming in circles around it instead. It's body was huge, approximately two hundred to three hundred metres in length, covered in reflective green and blue scaling. The disproportionately small arms that ran the length of it's body rushed past the building in a blur as it continued it's orbit.

It was now, as the eel's full body was revealed, that Kerrigan realised that this was definitely an adult of the see-through eel creatures he had seen during his arrival at Site B. The same breed Fat Man's Killer had crushed.

Kerrigan had a bizarre thought that the behemoth outside was the mother of the baby eel that Fat Man's Killer had crushed. There was no evidence for him to believe such a thought, however the attacks did seem to have been provoked by the little one's death.

But Kerrigan himself hadn't killed the eel, Fat Man's killer had. So why was it attacking him??

Obviously, for some reason, the eel felt that Kerrigan was responsible for it's babies untimely death. Was this, in some way, connected to his current possession of the Black Box?

FUCK! He thought, hitting upon the explanation. When he had first picked up the Black Box, he had felt a soft fleshy sensation beneath his skin. When Fat Man's killer had killed the baby eel, he had then picked up the Black Box for himself. The dead babies

crushed intestine's had then been smeared onto the Black Box's handle.
Smelling the scent of her babies death on Kerrigan, the mother eel was now seeking revenge for it's dead babies execution.
He looked down and noticed the small pink patch that had bloomed on his shirt. The baby eel's crushed intestines had already stained the inside of his shirt, transferring the smell of their death from the handle, onto his person.
Kerrigan grabbed the cloth and rubbed it briskly between his hands, hoping to remove the scent and stain in the water, but to little effect. The stain hardly seemed to lighten in colour.
Continuing on, Kerrigan ran down the remaining corridors and stairways without further incident.

In no time at all, Kerrigan found himself back at the lowest level. He braced himself against the final section of wall and cautiously risked looking out at the waters above. The eel was still spiralling the building, awaiting the emergence of it's babies executioner. It let out an occasional cry that sounded strangely birdlike, mournful in the otherwise quiet waters.
He considered waiting out the situation. Eventually, Kerrigan presumed, the eel would tire of it's circling and leave to mourn it's loss back in it's nest or cave or where ever it had came from.
However, judging by the eel's dedication so far; thrusting it's head through concrete and steel, injuring itself in the process of attempting to kill it's babies killer, the eel's dedication seemed more than capable of sustaining a prolonged stake out.
Also, Kerrigan's breathing, where previously it had been restricted yet natural, had become a gruelling task. His Oxypus had been hurt when he was attacked from behind and he doubted if it's life was going to continue on for much longer. He had to force air into his lungs now, air that had taken on a metallic, bloody taste. His Oxypus was dying, he was sure of it.
So his choices were simple: stay here and drown like a coward, or go outside and either live or die trying.
It was an easy choice to make. Never would he allow himself to

die like a coward, without even trying.

He watched the eel for a moment longer. His best chance would be to wait until the eel had made it's pass above him. As it circled to the other side of the building out of sight, he would run out of his cover and...

He looked around. The mine field of desolation before him didn't seem to hold many hiding places. Most of the it was the ruins of destroyed buildings. Only the foundations and small segments of walling remained erect.

Directly in front of him and slightly to the right, Kerrigan saw the base of a building with a corner of wall still intact. If he could reach that, he could hunker down inside it and hopefully evade the eel's sight.

From the locations that he might be able to reach in the short space of time that he would be out of the eel's sight, it was the only option he had.

Looking up, the eel was just about to pass round to the other side of the building.

He ran.

Moving as quickly as he could through the water, Kerrigan immediately knew that he was not going to make it in time. Crossing the distance on land would not have been a problem. Underwater it was another matter entirely.

The distance between himself and the wall foundations seemed impossibly far. It was as if the distance between it and himself had some how grown in size and that he was making no progress at all.

The situation had a dream like quality, like one of those dreams where no matter how hard you run you can never reach or catch the thing in front of you, the thing that you most desire.

To contradict this, the wall had grown in size as it grew closer to him. It no longer seemed to be only a few feet tall in size, but seemed tall enough to easily hide his frame should he reach the ruined structure and crouch beside it.

Despite this positive development, Kerrigan was still convinced that he would not reach the safety of the foundation in time. Surely

the eel would have completed it's pass by now and would be returning to the side of the building which gave full view of himself.
He felt that he had been exposed far too long.
He could almost sense the eel darting towards him now, it's jaw yawning open to reveal a mouth filled with rows of needle sharp, dagger like teeth, it's forked tongue snaking in the water's current, flicking in anticipation of it's next meal…
And what if the wall provided no shelter from the eel's higher perspective anyway? Surely it would be able to peer over the broken wall to see his soft defenceless body, cowering feebly in the foundation's crude security.
It was a stupid idea, stupid. And he would pay the ultimate price for his naivety.
The wall was right in front of him, but even the small distance that remained was too much. The eel was going to grab him, any second…
Without expecting to do so, Kerrigan reached the wall, ran around it, and huddled up into a ball as tightly as he could in the corner formed by the two meeting walls.
He panted through the straw like supply of oxygen he was being provided with, and hoped that he had been quick enough. He might not have been plucked off in the open, but the eel could still have seen him, could already be charging in to consume both him and the flimsy thin wall he hid behind.
He braced himself, certain that the eel and seen him and was about to come crashing down from above or through the walls against his back.
He did not want to risk further exposure by peering over the wall to see if his paranoia was true. If the eel hadn't completed it's cycle, then it surely would have been very close to. If he looked around the wall straight away, then the eel would notice him for certain.
He waited.
After a moment or two, enough time for the eel to have discovered and eaten him, Kerrigan knew that he was, for now at least, safe.

Unfurling himself, he glanced nervously around the wall to view the eel. His progress back to Chimera's anchor was going to have to be a series of carefully timed bursts from one destroyed building to the next.

The eel was still circling the main building, oblivious to his escape. Looking at the building, he could see other prisoners looking out from various windows throughout the building, each watching the eel from their own relative safety.

If the mother eel was hungry, then there were plenty of men to choose from. They made no particular effort to hide themselves from the eel's vision, curiosity at the mysterious creature being stronger than thoughts for their own safety. However, the eel was not attacking them and it continued it's steady surveillance.

It was this behaviour that confirmed to Kerrigan once again, that he was the beast's sole target.

Looking around himself, Kerrigan saw the next base to which he must run to if he wished to escape the eel's surveillance; another growth of intersecting foundations lay thirty feet away.

He waited for himself to once more pass out of the eel's line of sight.

Just as the eel went around the side of the building, another prisoner emerged from out of the base of the main building. Having seen Kerrigan's example, this other man was trying the same manoeuvre.

He was a short, stocky man who ran with his one free arm swinging around his chest in a wide arc at a right angle to his body. He was old, fat, stupid and about to die. He was simply not fit enough to make the short trip quick enough.

Worst of all, he was approaching the exact same spot where Kerrigan himself lay.

You fucking cunt! Kerrigan thought. If the stupid git were caught, and he surely would be, it would lure the eel almost directly to where Kerrigan lay.

He looked around his immediate surroundings hoping to find another shelter close by that he could run to before the eel reappeared, but there was nothing he could safely reach in time.

Turning back, he knew what was about to happen.
The eel had completed it's pass and saw the running man immediately. It's former passive glide turned into a straight dart of attack as it zoomed in on the doomed man.
Swooping down and twisting it's head to the side, the eel bit into the man, biting into the entire length of his body. Teeth puncturing into his skull, crushing and warping it into an ugly deflated ball. His eyes popped out, pulling with them their optic nerves and blooming explosions of brain tissue. Onwards down his body, the eel's teeth bit into the fat, ugly flesh sending out roses of blood at every penetration.
Once it had the man in it's mouth, it started to rise back to it's former altitude chewing the man as it went, spreading chucks of the dead man throughout the long dead streets of Site B.
The swoop had taken the eel a considerable distance from it's cycle of the building and the eel had to turn in a wide arc to re-approach the building. The arc started to Kerrigan's left, and just as it reached it's apex, it brought the eel directly out and in front of Kerrigan.
The eel spotted him immediately.
As before, the eel straightened out it's flexible body and lunged straight towards Kerrigan.
He braced his arms and legs and just as the eel was about to snatch hold of him in it's giant maw, bursting through and out the wall he huddled against, he pushed off the wall and leapt to the side.
The eel, moving as fast and as powerful as a locomotive, was moving too quickly to change direction suddenly. It missed Kerrigan and smashed through the wall where he had just been sat in a slowly blooming cloud of brown dust.
Continuing it's attack, the eel swooped up, covering a great distance in very little time, and turned gracefully for another try at getting it's babies killer. It's shadow-black silhouette filled the sky like a giant wingless bird.
Only briefly watching the graceful movement to assure himself that the eel was definitely readying itself for another attack, Kerrigan turned and ran down the ruined street in which he now

found himself.

The eel pursued.

He had to risk fleeting glances over his shoulder. He needed to gauge the eel's approach exactly or his life would be taken and crushed as quickly as the eel could bust through concrete walls.

It covered the distance with phenomenal speed. It charged down the abandoned street filling the space with it's huge armoured body. It's tiny arms stroked the tumbled walls of what structures remained on either side of the street.

Turning to face the beast, Kerrigan had stopped his fleeing and prepared himself for the eel's arrival. An alley lay to his immediate right.

The eel launched itself towards Kerrigan with startling ferocity.

With a powerful kick of his legs, Kerrigan leapt. The eel shot past where he had been only a moment ago. He could feel the tugging of rushing water in his legs and clothing as the huge animal roared by.

Again he had evaded the eel's attack.

Standing up, he could once again see the eel arching up and circling around for another approach.

Looking around, Kerrigan's options for escape were even more limited.

He had leapt into an alleyway where the only exits were either by the way in which he had entered (which was no option as that was the direction that the eel would now be approaching from), or the exit at the other end of the alley - too far to run to in time.

A couple of doorways led from the alley into half destroyed buildings.

The eel had completed it's turn and was already starting it's third approach.

With no time to give serious consideration to which direction or option to choose, Kerrigan simply chose the nearest way off the street available. He ran through a doorway set into the side of dilapidated building. Large, ragged holes in the wall gave multiple access choices to the interior.

The building in which he found himself was as destroyed as all the others he had seen at Site B - Debris, weeds and algae were the standard decoration of choice it would seem.

The ceiling was almost completely destroyed giving Kerrigan a patchwork view of the sparkling sky. He could see the rippling of sunlight on the surface of the water high above.

Other doorways led from the room into additional sections of the building.

Sidling over to the next doorway, Kerrigan kept his eyes on the missing patch of roof, desperately searching for any sign of the eel's attack that he knew must be approaching, surely must only be moments away...

With an enormous crash, the eel burst through the wall of the building he had only seconds ago been hugging, surprising Kerrigan by the violence of it's attack. He had expected the eel to lunge downwards from above as it had in the upper levels of the building where he had found the Black Box.

Instead, it had burst through the wall and charged into the room, as easily as a man could punch through sodden paper.

Luckily, Kerrigan had progressed further into the room than the eel had estimated. The lunge narrowly missed Kerrigan but the speed and force behind it knocked him splaying onto his back.

The eel didn't slow in it's charge and smashed out of the opposite wall as easily as it had the first. As the body rocketed past in front of Kerrigan, he had the image of a giant, organic steam train passing before him.

Once outside the building, the eel stopped it's charge and reared up onto it's tail in a posture similar to that of a rattle snake. Once the dust settled, and it's vision had cleared, Kerrigan knew that it would stab down at him devouring him with ease.

Before that could happen, Kerrigan scuttling backwards on all fours, stumbled to his feet and ran to the doorway that led to the next room. As he reached the archway, the eel's arrow shaped head stabbed down behind him, hitting the point were he, moments ago, had been knocked off his feet.

Entering the next room, he saw the usual messy surroundings and without taking a pause, headed straight for the next doorway in an indirect line.

The eel stabbed down again only a few feet from where he was running. It was having trouble judging exactly where he was at any given time as it could only catch glimpses of him through the patchy roof.

Jumping and leaping in sideways bounds, Kerrigan crossed the room as the eel continued to stab down behind him, puncturing roof and wall as it went. With each stab, the ground beneath Kerrigan's feet shook from the blow. The eel's face was becoming bloody and cut from the damage it was inflicting to itself, it's former grin had sever gaps in it as teeth fell out and others swung on the gum line in a tentative grip.

Kerrigan was desperately trying to think of a plan. He could not rely on there being an endless stream of rooms in the building, at best he guessed there could be no more than a few rooms remaining. As soon as the rooms ran out and he was exposed to the eel's unfiltered observation of the open streets, he would be doomed.

What to do, what to do?!

Gaining extra momentum by pushing himself off rocks and concrete, Kerrigan crossed the second room and entered a welcomed third. Unable to stop, Kerrigan looked about himself for anything that might help.

So far the eel had been pretty accurate with being able to stab down in places where he had just been. If there was something in the room that might injure the creature, anything at all, then he could maybe pass by it and with a little luck or skill on his behalf, hopefully the eel might do itself an injury.

Quickly scanning the room, Kerrigan saw a fallen pipe. It's purpose, when the building was intact, was a mystery to him, but it's jagged edge would serve his purpose.

Crossing the room in a zig-zag fashion, he reached the pipe and erected it at the same time as using it as a level for his next underwater bound.

Seconds later, the eel stabbed down as it had before.

The pipe missed it's intended target area, but not the target itself.

Instead of piercing the eel in the throat as Kerrigan had hoped it might, thus ending it's rain of tyranny, it instead pierced the eel in the soft flesh of it's exposed gum line, directly above it's teeth.

The eel reared back it's head and emitted an agonizingly high pitched squeal that seemed impossibly loud in the underwater conditions. The pipe that had pierced it's gum line sticking out at an unnatural right angle from it's face.

Taking only a moment to view the injury, Kerrigan ran from the room.

Finally his luck had ran out and he emerged onto the empty ruined street he had dreaded entering. Frantically looking about himself, he could either run directly for Chimera's anchor, which still lay far away, hazily floating past the field of seaweed, or skulk inside another ruined building.

Believing that the eel's physical pain would be only temporary, and that the emotional pain for it's lost loved one would be greater than any injury that might otherwise have caused an animalistic retreat, Kerrigan ran briefly down the street and entered the closest property with what appeared to be a mostly intact room.

Also, the eel was now gonna be pissed.

Pissed and angry.

Pissed, angry, in pain and a mother in mourning, to be precise.

Once inside, he found the area with the least visibility, huddled down, and listened to the eel's agonising cries, hoping to determine where it might go next.

It's agony pierced the heart and reached out across the sea. The water's conductivity carried the eel's agony farther than any normal anguish, seeming to stretch out forever.

Listening to the eel's pain, Kerrigan could tell that the eel was holding it's location. Taking advantage of it's stationary position, Kerrigan skulked out from his hiding place.

He kept close to the walls, always trying to remain beneath any roofing that still held. Using as many buildings as possible, he wove his way slowly back towards Chimera's anchor.

At one point, the eel's screaming stopped. Peering out of his current hiding place, Kerrigan was at first surprised by how much distance he had put between himself and the eel. It was snapping it's head back and forth in search of him and was randomly striking down at the area immediately surrounding itself in a desperate hope of crushing him.

Again, it's actions reminded Kerrigan of a coiled snake.

For the time being, Kerrigan knew that it had lost him.

Turning from the sight, Kerrigan continued his progress with relative ease occasionally stopping to check on the eel, to make sure his trail had not been re-established.

Why isn't it following me? Wondered Kerrigan, *it could smell it's babies blood on me before, what's changed?*

He looked down at the pink patch of blood on his shirt and was shocked to see bloody hand prints covering the area.

At some point he had cut his hands – no doubt at one of the times he had been blown from his feet, and as he ran from the eel clutching the Black Box beneath his shirt to prevent it from falling out, his own blood had spread over that of the baby eels.

He was pleasantly amused with his good fortune.

He arrived at the out most building of Site B. All that lay between himself and Chimera's anchor was the field of sea-weeds. Unfortunately the problem was that the field did not provide any hiding places should he be spotted by the eel.

Looking back at the eel, it's attention was focused back towards the main building where another man had been caught by the eel's quick movements. It was tossing the man's body about in it's mouth with violent shakes of it's head. A red ribbon of blood trailed from it's mouth and slowly rose in the water.

Seizing the opportunity, Kerrigan ran.

Passing a rainbow of multi coloured weeds, Kerrigan headed directly for Chimera's anchor. He leapt over bushes and coral, and skirted around a nasty looking weed that seemed to reach out and try to grab him. As adrenaline surged through his body, his breathing became even harder through the dying Oxypus.

With shocked amazement, Kerrigan reached Chimera's anchor quicker than he could have possibly hoped. For a brief moment he wondered if he was actually stood at the giant anchor at all, as if

somehow his hope at reaching the metallic chain to his salvation was so great that his mind was teasing him with a hallucination, a vision of the impossible.
Looking back from where he had came, the main building had faded back into the hazy blue/green of the sea and had become a shadow once more. Above the building, was a living halo as the eel resumed it's previous observations. Whether the eel had forgotten about him, or whether it thought he might have returned to the main building, Kerrigan did not know and did not care.
Reaching down, Kerrigan released the pin that kept his portable anchor attached to his ankle, allowing him to rise back to the surface quicker.
Just as he was bending down, a movement to his left caught his eye.
With his fingers on the pin, he turned to see another baby eel swimming happily close by, it's attention focused on something other than him. He watched it a moment, hoping that it's attention remained else where.
It let out a soft mewling sound that sent a jolt of adrenaline through Kerrigan's body. He hoped that this was not a cry to it's mother.
Was it possible that this was just a natural noise that it made as it scanned it's surroundings? a kind of sonar?
It swam closer to Kerrigan and purred once again. It came right up to his face and looked him in the eye.
Kerrigan was unnerved by how the animal looked directly at him. There was something more behind it's tiny black pupil, something more than just a basic animalistic consciousness... there was something... intelligent...
Surely he was just being paranoid, nervous at failing so close to Chimera's safety, but he could swear he could see sentience in it's beady, little eyes. It wasn't just looking at him, it was studying him... suspecting him.
The eel broke their mutual observation of one another and looked to his chest, to where the imprint of his own blood lay across that of it's fallen brethren.
Reminiscent of it's mother, the eel jerked it's head back twice,

smelling the air.

Oh shit!

At such close range, the scent of Kerrigan's own blood was not enough to mask that of the dead eels.

The dead eel's brethren screamed.

Unlike the mother eel's deep voice, the babies high pitched scream did not make Kerrigan's bones vibrate, but instead it pierced into his head feeling like some one was pushing two thin pins directly into his ear drums.

He jerked his head up to see the swimming halo that was the mother eel, turn and become an arrow of death, heading straight towards him with frightening speed.

Pulling the pin and releasing his anchor, Kerrigan grabbed Chimera's chain and started to pull himself upwards, hand over hand, towards the surface as quickly as his arms would pull him and as quickly as his kicking legs could push him.

Bursting onto the surface, Kerrigan tried to swallow a deep breath for his burning lungs. For a brief moment, he was horrified to realize that he was unable to do so, until he realised that the Oxypus was still attached to his face. As it only worked underwater, he instead took a deep breath through his nose. The air that he inhaled had never felt so good, so refreshing, so good.

With out pausing, he grabbed hold of the anchor chain and heaved his soaked body out of the water.

He could hear raised voices from above but took no notice of what they were saying, focusing only on climbing the chain.

He reached the top and flopped down onto the deck. He lay on his back with his eyes closed, dripping with water and panting heavily through his nose. He never thought it would have been possible to feel relieved to be back on Chimera's deck. For one precious moment, all the stress and panic that had coursed through his body for the last hour was swept away by the sea breeze and warming sun on his skin. The air was so quiet, so peaceful…

A metallic click.

Kerrigan opened his eyes into the black barrel of a cocked gun.

Behind the gun grinned Bronco, "Please tell me you have come back empty handed."

Before Kerrigan could answer, a deep but subtle rumble shook the ship, more felt than heard.

"What the…?" muttered Bronco.

For awhile, no one spoke and no one moved. It was as if the vibration served to silence all audible communication.

Bronco and his guards looked about themselves in all directions trying to see anything that was out of the ordinary, anything that might explain the vibration they had felt. Some guards started asking questions to one another, but their replies were of matched confusion.

Suddenly, as the men on deck started to discard the rumble, a second shake spread throughout the ship. This time, the ship tilted to one side and the guards had to use their arms to balance themselves.

Bronco glared down at Kerrigan who was still laying on his back, and re-pointed his gun at him, "What the fuck have you done???". His eyes blazed with accusation.

Even if Kerrigan had chosen to explain himself, which was unlikely, a thunderous roar filled the air and tilted the ship violently to one side.

The eel had risen out of the water on the port side of Chimera, unfurling like a plant towards the sun,

At first, it's body was hidden beneath the torrent of sea water that cascaded down it's body in a deafening waterfall. It raised it's giant, pointed head to the sky and roared it's bone vibrating call to the heavens.

It's huge body shimmered in the light of the sun, a thousand sparkles of sunlight glittered down the length of it's gem-like chitinous body, as if it wore a coat of diamonds. It's teeth were snapped and broken, and it's arrow shaped head oozed a dark blood from a multitude of punctures and lacerations.

A steel pipe poked out from it's gum line to point in the same direction that the eel turned it's head.

It swung it's head back and forth as it screamed at the skies, as if the very air itself was harming it.

During the eel's magnificent surface, no one moved on deck. Too stunned by the sight before them, they had not the sense to move from where they found themselves and instead remained where they stood, watching the eel's entrance with slack jawed disbelief.
The eel lowered it's head to look at it's gathered audience aboard Chimera's deck. It turned it's head inquisitively as it observed the collection of stationary men.
Kerrigan slowly got to his feet, hoping not to draw the eel's attention back to himself.
He had known that the eel was big, but to see it up close, in his own environment, re-enforced just how big the beast before him really was. It held hold of Chimera's hull like how a man might hold a small guard rail.
Without averting their eyes, Chimera's crew, including Kerrigan, began to walk backwards away from the beast towards the starboard railing.
"By the Gods..." whispered Bronco.
The eel twisted it's head, as if it was straining it's unseen ears to hear the Captain.
"Well don't just stand there," said Bronco grabbing an armoured guard by the upper arm. His was the only voice in the silent air, and his voice rung out across the deck, "Shoot the damn thing!"
The guard looked at his Captain, assessing his superior's judgement.
After a moment's hesitation, the guard turned back to the eel, raised his weapon, and shot.
Normally the sound of a gun being fired is a huge deafening noise that fills the air. In comparison to the giant that was stationed on Chimera's port side, the report of the gun sounded pathetic and weak.
After a couple of lonely shots, other guards joined in adding their own fire to the scene, turning a lonely pop into a mere crackle.
Initially, the guards wondered if their aim was true. Their assault did not seem to be harming the beast in the slightest, nor was it

responding to the assault. It simply kept it's head cocked at the interesting insects before it. The guards only knew that they had struck the eel as little bursts of water jetted of it's armoured hide with each bullet's contact.
There was no blood to indicate that the eel was being harmed by the barrage.
Having retreated as far to starboard as they could go, gathered against the railing, the guards stood their ground and continued to fire as Bronco shouted orders for them to keep firing.
Suddenly, the eel bent it's head back completely, until it almost dunked it's upside down head back into the ocean, and whipped the entire force of it's head and upper body down upon Chimera's deck.
It struck with a tremendous force that shook the entire ship, threatening to rip the ship in half, and made it lean heavily to port, towards the eel.
The men shouted and grabbed onto the railing of Chimera's starboard side as the ship continued to lean further to port as the eel pressed it's weight down on the decking.
It was pushing itself downwards, trying to flip the ship over. As it did so, the crane equipment stationed on deck rolled and tumbled towards it, pelting it in the face as they fell off the ship.
Some unlucky men who had either failed to grab onto the guard rail, or who had lost their grip, also tumbled down and into the sea below. One man fell too close to the eel and it snapped at him as he fell. It caught him neatly around the waist, slicing him in two, allowing only his legs to continue their fall alone into the sea below.
Slowly, unable to keep the majority of it's body on Chimera's steep, slippery deck, the eel slid slowly back into the ocean. With a huge stomach-churning crash, Chimera righted itself once more and rocked back and forth as it stabilised.
Once the ship had settled, the guards hesitantly removed themselves from the life saving grip they held on the guard rail. A nervous silence filled the air.
The destruction the beast had caused to the ship in one hit was

colossal. A huge runnel, at least the depth of a man, ran from the middle of the decking across to the port side where the majority of the guard railing was missing.

Breathing heavily through his nose, Kerrigan suddenly realised that the Oxypus was still attached to his face. With surprising ease, he removed the creature and dropped it to the decking where it struck the metal surface with a wet slap.

The crew looked around themselves, hoping to spy the eel in advance should another attack occur.

"Raise the anchor and get us the hell outta here!" growled Bronco to a nearby officer.

Despite the recent bizarre occurrence, the officer acknowledged the order with a smart salute and marched off towards the bridge to convey the Captain's message.

Bronco walked forward to the edge of the impression that had been carved by the eels hulk, and peered down. At the edges of the canal, bent and twisted steel sheets protruded up, pointing at the sky.

"Shit," he mumbled under his breath. Abruptly turning on his heel, he stamped over to Kerrigan pointing his finger accusingly in his face, "Just what the hell did you do down there?!?!", he pointed his finger to the glistening water below.

Before the interrogation could continue further, a second rocking shook the ship. Peering over Chimera's railing, Bronco saw a long, dark shadow flow from underneath the ship.

"Get those engines started…" commanded Bronco to another officer, "NOW!" he barked.

The shadow stretched out towards the horizon and doubled back on itself. As it passed beneath Chimera, another shudder shook the ship.

As the shudder continued, Bronco turned back to Kerrigan, drawing his gun from his holster in one smooth movement, "You'll pay for this" he snarled jabbing the barrel of the gun into Kerrigan's gut.

It connected not with a soft, fleshy thump, but with a hard, tough bang.

"What the..?" muttered Bronco taking a step back and noticing for the first time, the outline of the Black Box beneath Kerrigan's shirt.

"You... you found it?" a look of disbelief covered Bronco's face, his eyes wide open.

Another rocking thrashed the ship, tilting it so wildly that some men fell to their knees.

"Why the hell aren't we moving yet?!" demanded Bronco to no-one in particular, temporarily forgetting Kerrigan.

Just then, the officer who had been sent to start the engines appeared at Bronco's side. Gasping for breathe, he snapped a saluted and said, "Sir, we're having trouble starting the primary engine."

"What kind of problem?" asked Bronco.

"Sir, were not entirely sure yet. Everything appears in order and the batteries are at full charge, yet it simply wont start."

"Fascinating." Bronco responded sarcastically, "Thank you so much for that fascinating report, officer." Turning serious, he continued, "Start the secondary engine." He was referring to the coal powered engine.

"Sir, yes sir," replied the addressing officer. Despite his previous professionalism, he looked nervous to be addressing his superior. Especially when his Captain was in such a foul mood, "I... I've already given the command and we're starting it now, but it will take some time for the furnace to create adequate pressure to get us moving."

"How long?"

"It could take as long as thirty minutes sir." Replied the officer, squinting as if he expected to be punched.

"If this thing keeps it's attack up we don't have thirty minutes!"

Another violent lurch rocked the ship.

Once his balance was regained, Bronco turned back to his officer, "Hurry up and get back to the engine room and speed things up. Take as many officers with you as you need to get us moving again. Now MOVE!"

"Sir, yes sir" said the guard, and with a final smart salute, the officer left.

"Now," said Bronco, returning his attention back towards Kerrigan. He still held the muzzle of the gun to Kerrigan's torso, "Where were we?" he asked conversationally, as if the ship were not under attack from some kind of monstrous creature.

Suddenly, at the stern of the ship, the giant eel rose out of the water in a deafening roar. As it broke the water it emitted it's deep, bone shaking, yet high pitched scream, towards the heavens. Water rose into the air as it surfaced and rained down upon Chimera's deck in a heavy downpour, saturating the gathered men in an instant. Once it had fully surfaced, it gripped hold of the guard rails and edges of the stern with it's small, feeble looking arms.

"Holy shit…" murmured Bronco above the crashing of the water, falling from the eel and back into the sea, "..well don't just stand there," he shouted to the nearest guard to him, "Shoot it!"

With the order given, the previously stunned guards sprang into action and, once again, started to pelt the eel with a barrage of bullets that sounded weak despite their ferocity. One or two additional guards even raised their electric stun guns, normally used to knock out unruly prisoners, but failed to fire.

Perhaps this was in the guard's favour, mused Kerrigan, being as how the guards and the decking were completely sodden.

As before, the bullets seemed to cause the eel more irritation than pain. It continued to hold onto the ship causing the bow to rise out of the water. The eel's grip was weighing the ship down causing it to drift backwards towards the island they were stationed near.

It howled at the annoyance it was being subjected to and smashed it's head down onto the closest collection of men who were stood firing pathetically at the eel.

They were crushed and flattened into Chimera's decking. The decking buckled beneath the eel's attack thrusting the dead men's crushed bodies deeper into Chimera's heart.

Temporarily forgotten, Kerrigan took advantage of the situation and sneaked away behind Bronco, keeping his back bent to remain as low and as unnoticeable as possible amongst the carnage.

It was clear to him that Bronco's stubborn command to shoot

directly at the eel would be to no avail. It's armoured hide was clearly much too tough for bullet's to penetrate. If the electric engine wasn't working, then by the time the secondary coal engine was operational they could all be dead.
A different approach was needed.
Grabbing a gun that had been discarded by a crushed officer when the eel had slapped it's gigantic head down onto the decking, Kerrigan ran towards the stern with the intention of approaching the eel from the port side. Thankfully, the gun that he picked up was not one of the electric stun guns which Chimera's guards also carried. An electric stunner would not be powerful enough for what he had in mind.

He hoped that the eel's attention would remain focused on the opposite side of the stern.
Kerrigan knew that he risked his life by confronting the eel. If he was seen with a weapon of any kind by any of Chimera's crew he would be shot dead on the spot, despite the enormity of the attacks that the eel had already presented to Chimera and her crew.
He didn't care. He could either allow Chimera's guards to follow the useless orders of a stubborn, close minded leader and allow them all to die, or he could risk his own life to save them everyone. He didn't truly care about everyone else, but he himself would not go down without a fight.
Some might say he was selfish. Kerrigan just believed it was survival.
Survival of the fittest.

The eel had risen even further up onto Chimera's deck. It continued to grip the stern guard rails with it's small stubby arms, but no longer with it's upper body arms. Instead, the arms at the mid-point of it's body gripped the railing, and it's upper body arms now gripped hold of the tower of the bridge as it smashed into the structure with it's massive head.
It's under belly passed over the decking like a tarpaulin sheet as it's body stretched from the guard rails up to the top of the bridge

creating a huge shadow underneath.
The shadow passed over the pile of depth charges that had been previously been used to scare off the very creature that now draped over them, stacked up against the rear railing.
Kerrigan knew that he was foolishly close to the pile, and he was quite aware that, at this distance, he would not be prevented from being hurt in some manor should the charges happen to be ignited in some way or other…
Kerrigan raised his gun, took aim at the depth charges, and fired.

A huge explosion filled and rumbled on, into the air, spewing with it a rain of debris that smashed into Kerrigan's heat blasted body as he was thrown violently away from the blooming flames.
The gun he had used fell from his grip as his head hit hard against the decking. It went spinning away towards the railing and fell over board, although Kerrigan was not able to follow it's progress as he shielded his head from the falling debris.
The explosion was a deafening, all consuming, thunderous roar that obliterated all of the other of Kerrigan's sensory input with it's booming ferocity, yet the piercing scream of pain that erupted from the eel was louder yet, and could be heard even above the exploding depth charges cacophony.
His ear's instantly rung from the intensity of the noise being thrust upon them.
The force of the explosion thrust the stern of Chimera deeper into the water, pushing them forward, away from the island where the weight of the eel had been dragging them.
As the roar of the explosion started to subside, Kerrigan lowered his arms to view the result's of his actions.
What he saw, despite his knowledge to the contrary, appeared to be moving in slow motion.
The blooming, impossibly bright explosion was turning into a thick cloud of black, purple edged smoke that rose smoothly into the air.
His ears were still ringing from the explosion.
The eel, which had been draped above the explosion, was still

alive. It's underbelly however, had sustained a deep, serious injury. The puncture in the eel's belly was considerable; a thick, gaping hole, easily twice as long as Kerrigan was tall, glistened with dark blood in the afternoon sun. Think clots of singed flesh dripped from the opening to splatter upon Chimera's decking.

The eel screamed in pain and slithered off Chimera to splash back into the waters from which it came. The metal pipe that protruded from it's gum line was the last part of it to disappear into the water. As it re-entered the water, it left behind a large spume of foam which slowly floated away from Chimera, as the ship continued it's forward momentum.

Looking at the area of the decking where the explosion had originated, Kerrigan saw a huge ugly hole. It extended deeply into Chimera's hull, exposing rooms and machinery below. Bits of girders and metal plating pointed crudely in all directions like a mouthful of broken teeth.

Rising slowly to his shaking feet, Kerrigan heard foot steps behind him; not running steps, but slow, normal paced steps.

He did not feel inclined to turn to whom ever approached.

In his peripheral vision, Kerrigan saw Bronco appear to his left, his mouth agape, as he stared at the destruction Kerrigan had caused to his ship. His mouth hung open almost to his collar bone.

"What the fuck did you do...?" he whispered.

The entire ship started to hum subtly. The vibration was not as violent as it had been previously, and for a moment, Kerrigan believed that they were once more under attack. It took him a moment to realize that the vibration in this instance was much more gentle and familiar... it was the engines suddenly igniting. Judging by the subtle, smooth shudder, it was the primary, electric engines rather than the crude coal ones.

"Sir... the engines have started." stated another officer who had also appeared to Kerrigan's left. His voice carried with it a tone of disbelief rather than conviction as if he was stating what he suspected, rather than what he knew.

"Yes... thank you." Bronco replied, still staring at the destruction that had been caused to his beloved ship.

Abruptly shaking himself out of his staring with a visible shake, Bronco rounded on Kerrigan.

"YOU!" his fury was instantaneous, "YOU... fucker! Look what you did to my ship! Do you know what this is going to cost me!?!?" He raised his fist and punched Kerrigan in the face. Kerrigan felt the blow before he knew it was coming. His head was still swimming and ringing from his proximity to the explosion.

Another blow hit him, in the gut this time, knocking the wind out of him. Different to the one that had connected with his jaw, the blow to his gut covered a larger area and he heard a hollow metallic thump.

Bronco had struck the Black Box that still hung beneath Kerrigan's shirt.

"Argh!" shouted Bronco angrily, shaking his stinging fist. It took him a moment to process what had just happened to him, and it was then that Kerrigan knew that Bronco understood about the Black Box, "You gimme that!" he growled.

Bronco was now surrounded by a collection of armed guards, all with their weapons aimed and pointed at Kerrigan.

Reluctantly, slowly, Kerrigan placed his arm below his shirt and withdrew the Black Box.

Bronco snatched it away from him like a baby wanting it's favourite toy back.

"I suppose you think this earns you your freedom?" Bronco said, referring to the Black Box, "Ha! If you think I'm gonna let you get away with this," now referring to Chimera's damage, "then your more of a fool than you look!"

Bronco withdrew his gun and pointed it unflinching Kerrigan.

He did not move.

He did not react.

He had done everything he possibly could, and now there was no choice.

It was finally his time to die.

He closed his eyes.

"Captain Bronco sir!" shouted an officer, his voice was too distant to be any of the guards surrounding Kerrigan, "Captain sir!"

"What is it?" Bronco spat. Kerrigan reopened his eyes.
A guard was running across the ruined decking holding an item that swung in his grip as he ran.
"Sir, I think perhaps you might want to see this" he said remaining just outside the circle of guards.
"It can wait"
"Sir…" he said, "With the greatest respect, I really don't think it can."
Tearing his murderous eyes away from Kerrigan's, Bronco turned and strode away to the officer who had dared to interrupt him. As they spoke, Kerrigan could hear their voices, but not what they were saying. Bronco's body language and restrained voice conveyed a sense of annoyance at the interruption.
The other officer showed Bronco what he held in his hand and then explained something. During the explanation, Bronco remained silent and his hunched shoulders drooped back into their normal shape.
Bronco came striding back to Kerrigan, looked him up and down, and said, "I'm not finished with you yet."
He nodded to an unseen officer and Kerrigan fell to the floor, convulsing as he was shot from behind with an electric stun gun.
Smiling as Kerrigan thrashed around on the floor, Bronco allowed the shock to continue much longer than necessary.
Finally nodding to the officer with the gun, Bronco ordered the guard to cease the electricity that coursed through Kerrigan's body. He bent over Kerrigan's curled up body to get a better look. Burnt vomit was matted to his face and clumped in his hair. The
hot, rancid smell of it drifted up to sting Bronco's nostrils.
"Take him away." he smiled.

11

He awoke in his cell with a pounding headache. It seemed to be becoming a common occurrence.
Groaning, Kerrigan raised his arm to cover his eyes from the dull, but none the less painful, light that filtered into his cell. He felt

some thing hard and crispy crackle on his face beneath his arm. He peeled a bit off and saw that it was dried vomit.

Hoping to return to the comfort of unconsciousness, Kerrigan remained where he was, willing his body and mind back to sleep.

After awhile, he realised that his efforts would not succeed. His body and mind were in too much discomfort to allow him to drift off.

He was both ravenously hungry and immensely thirsty. His lips were dry, his head pounded, it hurt his throat to swallow and a deep twisting and stabbing pain convulsed in his stomach and lower intestines.

He observed his room, but no pitcher of water had been considerately left behind to quench his thirst on this occasion. No doubt at Bronco's request.

Despite his knowledge that he would not drift back to sleep, he none the less remained on his bunk with his eyes closed and an arm resting across his face. He did not have the strength or the motivation to rise from his bunk. There was nothing he could do, and no where for him to go anyway.

He might have dozed for awhile, he could not be sure.

He heard the sound of approaching feet. They clapped down the corridor and stopped outside of his cell.

Kerrigan squinted at his visitor. It was Bronco.

He did not rise from his bed as the Captain entered his cell.

Accompanied by two particularly large looking guards, Bronco stood above Kerrigan with his hands clasped behind his back.

"How are you feeling, Mr Kerrigan?"

He did not reply.

"I've came here to tell you that I am a man of my word: I am granting you your freedom."

Kerrigan removed the arm from his eyes and looked inquisitively at Bronco. What was going on here? Hadn't he wanted to kill him not long back?

"You will remain here in your cell from now, until we reach our destination… can't have you causing any more destruction now can we? Once there, you will be escorted from this ship back to the main land.

"However, your recent actions will need to be reported, and I'm very sure that my superiors will be interested in what I have to tell them.

"So although you are free from Chimera Kerrigan, do not yet consider yourself a free man."

With that said he strode from the room. Another guard entered briefly to place some food and water in his cell, then he too left locking the cell behind him, leaving Kerrigan on his own once more.

His head was pounding. It could have just been the after effects of his recent electro-shock treatment, but he seemed to be suffering more and more with headaches. Sometimes they would just start off as a subtle niggle that started at the very top of his head. This niggle would then either last for several hours until it was hardly noticeable anymore, or swell to a booming thought-consuming series of explosions, that blasted in beat with his heart.

He wondered which this would turn out to be.

He gently rose from his bunk, hoping blood wouldn't rush into his skull and strengthen his head ache, and with great gentleness picked his food and water up to consume them on his bed.

The Grey Snot slipped down his throat leaving behind a thick greasy sensation in his mouth and throat like he had just swallowed a slug. He washed it away with room temperature water that did little to quench his thirst.

After finishing his meal, he lay back on his bed and felt his head ache starting to swell. If the headache was indeed the after effects of the stun gun, then the pain should have been going away rather than swelling.

No doubt it was his body reacting to the recent exertions it had been subjected to. He had gone for years with nothing more exciting than the occasional fight, and now this: underwater explorations of a ruined town beneath thousands of tons of water, chased through said ruined town by some kind of freakishly maternal eel, attacked to the point of death by said motherly eel, barely avoided being blown apart by an explosion that he had caused, shocked unconscious by electricity...

As his thoughts drifted back through the nightmarish predicaments he had barely lived through, his mind flooded him with a torrent of questions, the first of which was perhaps the most important of all: Just what *was* so special about the Black Box? He had no understanding of how even the most basic of technology worked, but he knew (although he could not recall how he knew? Had he overheard it sometime?) that if the Black Box could be connected to a working computer, the information that was stored within it could be extracted.

So what was the information?

He recalled seeing some form of inscription on the side of the Box when he had first obtained it. Whether it had been writing or some kind of picture or logo he could not recall. Circumstances had called for his attention to be focused on more important issues.

Just what useful information could be gained from a box found under the sea in a destroyed building, was beyond Kerrigan.

And that was another thing, the building. What was a building doing underwater? And the eel! What a creature! Never before had he seen or heard of such a beast. So huge and powerful, it was, by Kerrigan's opinion, a magnificent animal indeed, well worthy of one's awe and respect. No fat covered it's body like most of the humans he co-existed with, no laziness tainted it's mind.

It was beautiful.

Perfect.

And he had killed a man. Curiously, this thought did not cause him to feel sorrow, shame or guilt as he knew it should. Instead his mind simply acknowledged the thought as being the truth, as if somehow it wasn't he who had killed at all. As if it had been someone else.

In a sense, this disturbed Kerrigan more than remorse itself ever could. How could it be that his mind accepted that he was a murderer with such ease? Was he suffering from shock and the blow would occur to him at a later time? Perhaps, yet he didn't find this to be likely.

His head ache was growing still, but sleep took him before the steel talons of pain could get a firm grip and dig their pointed fingers into his brain.

The trip back to the main land took much longer than it might normally have. The electric engines had remained running from the moment they had reignited at Site B. However, several hours later, they began to stutter and power decreased to the point were by the secondary engine would have to be ignited in it's place. This was done, but the coal driven engine must have also been damaged in the recent assault as it too was also running at less than optimum efficiency, although still better than the electric ones.

Once it arrived at the main land, Chimera was, as always, anchored far away from the shore and a small row boat was sent to the main land so that Officer Dack could deliver the report of Chimera's latest excursion, and to order the extraordinary amount of replacement parts needed to restore Chimera.

While the boat was away, Bronco spent too many hours fretting over what his superior's reactions might be to the report they received. He tried to divert his worrying by drinking a particularly fine alcoholic drink that he had cherished for some time in his drinks cabinet, and by reading one of his favourite novels. However, he could not concentrate on the story and when he suddenly realised that he had read over twenty pages and had not absorbed any of the text, he felt compelled to place it back in it's place upon his shelf

He did not feel the same compulsion to return his drink to his cabinet.

He knew that he should have felt happy, relieved perhaps. He had good - no, GREAT - news of the Black Box's discovery that his superiors had searched for, for so long, well before he himself had became Captain of Chimera. Surely they would be overjoyed by the news, which would hopefully far outweigh the news of the damage that had been caused as a result.

The damage that had been caused to the ship...

The possibility that his superiors would focus more upon the bad news rather than the good weighed heavily upon his mind, and it became harder and harder for him to focus upon the positives for himself…

The following day, Bronco awoke with a fierce hang over and to the news that the messenger ship they had dispatched had returned. Communications Officer Dack had then delivered an ominous message that Bronco's superiors wished to visit the ship personally.

Upon hearing this update, Bronco was immediately apprehensive, a feeling that was not helped by the raging thumping in his still sobering mind.

As suddenly as a lightning bolt strike, his worries from the night before returned with startling clarity.

One thing was for sure; He would be sure emphasize Kerrigan's role in all of this.

Dusk came and the sleepy sun dipped it's feet into the horizon's ocean. The deep light it cast made the decking of Chimera glow a fierce burnt orange as the sun rested in the calm, black waters of the lazy ocean.

The sky was a deep endless purple were only the strongest of stars had started to show their sparkle.

The moon had not yet risen. It lay hidden beyond the horizon opposite the sun, waiting for it's time to spring out from it's hiding place like a lunar version of cat and mouse.

A small contingency of boats grew from black specks on the horizon, to bloom into the shadowy profile of boats as they approached Chimera. These boats were not of the simple, basic design of those used to transport supplies to and from the ship. Instead, these ships looked brand new, with a fresh coat of paint that shimmered in the fading suns light. Wording and insignias were inscribed on the side identified them as not being of Chimera's property, but the identification remained unreadable in the shadows cast by the fading sun.

The deep orange sun was knee deep in the horizon as the first of the main land visitors arrived at Chimera.

As all prisoners were safely locked in their cells in preparation for the visit, those guards that had not been killed in the attack at Site B begrudgingly operated the few remaining cranes to lift the visitors up onto deck.

Bronco observed this operation as he stood proudly on the deck. He was self consciously aware of the runnel of destruction that crossed the deck to his side. He was thankful for the sunset; the damaged decking sparkled in the sun's warm light misleading the ship's image into looking like a proud, damaged heroine of the sea, rather than the nearly decimated mess that it actually was.

The first boarding of visitors were safely lifted onto deck. As the men strode off the crude lifting platform, they walked immediately and purposefully towards Bronco.

The design of their uniforms was the same as Chimera's crew but their uniforms were a spotless white or silver colour (Bronco could not tell in the amber glow of the setting sun) that made his own crew's uniform look old and shabby. Every crease and angle of their suits was perfectly crisp, as if the uniform was made not of cloth, but of a flexible steel.

It made Bronco feel untidy and embarrassed to be stood awaiting their arrival.

The lead man approached Bronco. Where as Bronco's uniform was mainly green with an inverted silver triangle, this man's uniform was the complete contrast to his: mainly silver with an inverted green triangle, yet somehow it seemed… more…

He reached Bronco and the Captain addressed the newcomer first, "Welcome to the S.O. Prison Ship, Chimera. I am Captain William James Bronco at your service." he snapped the salute that he had been practicing all day in front of his quarter's mirror. He had not had to address a superior officer directly in some time.

"Captain Bronco, on behalf of myself, my guards and S.O, itself, I thank you" replied the clean, younger man in front of him. He seemed bemused by Bronco's formality, "I don't believe we have met, I am Regional Director Durrant". His short brown hair waved slightly in the light breeze.

Bronco eagerly held out his hand and Durrant politely shook it in return. "We have much to discuss."

"Yes…yes we do." agreed Bronco, "Are we expecting any more company?" he asked, glancing briefly past the younger man's shoulder. He desperately hoped that there wouldn't be more. If there was just Durrant, then that was definitely a sign that he was not in as much trouble as he had dreaded all the previous day.
"Not today I'm afraid Captain. Just myself and my personal guards."
Excellent!
"Excellent" replied Bronco, clearly brightening to the shorter man before him, "Please, if you will follow me, we will confer within my office."
With their shadows stretched out behind them, the two men left the decking with an accompaniment of silver and blue officers following in their wake.

The passage from deck to his own personal office was uncomfortable for Bronco. Much rode on the outcome of the meeting and so he refrained from making small talk during their short walk, not wishing to appear incompetent or nervous in front of his superior officer.
Arriving at Bronco's office, Bronco indicated for Durrant to be seated in the chair opposite his own. Without being told or permitted to do so, Durrant's personal entourage accompanied them both, and filed in behind the two men to flank the only door in and out of the room.
Once seated, Bronco offered his superior a drink. He looked at the bottle and was shocked by how much it had shrunk from yesterday's indulgence.
"No thank you" replied Durrant, waving away the offer with a swat of his hand. He looked around the office with a look of petty amusement.
Bronco's office was small, filled with objects of both sentimental and navigational value. A huge oak table filled the room, atop of which lay photographs of Bronco's loved ones and a pile of folders and papers.
A huge window filled the entire wall behind the desk. Beyond it,

the sun burned it's final glow of the day, casting long shadows across the office's sparse furnishings.

Bronco replaced the goblets and drink bottle, which he had been holding in expectation of acceptance, back into his drinks cabinet. He sat down behind his desk to return to the business at hand.

He faced the younger man opposite himself with a touch of envy. Before him sat a man surely no older than thirty in a pristine uniform with short, neatly cut brown hair, a smooth chin that barely looked like it had even *seen* a razor, never mind felt one, who enjoyed all the benefits and luxuries of the free world which he no doubt took for granted. Bronco, on the other hand, was a middle aged man with whispy white hair who felt as imprisoned as the men he was in charge of.

He suddenly felt very old.

Had Durrant ever experienced the hardships of mutiny?, wondered Bronco, had he ever had to send a man - or men - to what he knew would be their certain deaths??? Or had he been lucky enough to be born into a family already so integrated into the powers of the world, that he never had to face reality and instead had the privilege of being given his current stature, rather than earning it.

"Captain Bronco" addressed Durrant, breaking Bronco out of his musings and beginning the formalities, "as you know I am here as a representative of SigmaOmega in response to your personal account of what happened at Site B as delivered by Communications Officer Dack." His eyes never left Bronco's, "We have a few questions that concern us and felt it best that they be addressed in person."

"Of course" replied Bronco professionally. He could feel himself breaking into a nervous sweat.

Here they come, thought Bronco anticipating the awkward questions about Chimera's sustained damage.

"Firstly, we would like to know how the damage to Chimera was caused."

Although he had been expecting being questioned about this subject, Bronco was none the less a little stunned by the directness of the question. He had been expecting something more along the lines of, *"Can you explain why you did not anticipate, and therefore minimise, the damage caused to Chimera?"...*

"Did Officer Dack not explain the attack at Site B?" asked Bronco.

"Of course, however we would like to hear it directly from yourself." There was a note of accusation in the final word, as if Durrant and those that he reported to, held Bronco personally responsible.

"Well," started Bronco already feeling as though his sweat were permeating through his uniform to leave large dark, accusing circles beneath his armpits and throat, "The situation is as was reported, sir. A member of the submersion team sent to investigate Site B returned from their search and re-boarded Chimera. Moments later a giant snake appeared out of the water and started to attack the ship, no doubt having pursued the surviving convict. The individual's name is Kerrigan by the way, who is a particularly reckless man with no respect for authority, I might add."

"I see" replied Durrant, "and why would this... snake attack Chimera and your crew, considering how, according to your report, this ship out-sizes the snake five to one?"

"I... I don't know." replied Bronco. His office suddenly felt too confined. "But what I do know is that it followed Kerrigan here, and so there is no doubt that this is his fault that it surfaced in the first place." He realised that he was avoiding his superior's question and was instead trying to blame the damage to Chimera upon one of his inmates.

He felt foolish and embarrassed to do so. Instead, he returned to and tried to answer Durrant's question, but had no explanation. Feebly, he replied, "Perhaps it was trying to eat us? Maybe it was hungry?"

"Yet this creature, despite previous excursions to Site B, has never attacked Chimera before?"

"Well... no." The answer, although no elaboration could have been given, sounded short and weak even to his own ears.

Bronco was self consciously aware of how foolish he sounded...

Was the room shrinking????

Durrant stared back at Bronco and scratched his cheek, "Do you have any idea what the damage that has been caused to Chimera is going to cost us to repair?" It was asked politely, almost conversationally, but Kerrigan could feel the hidden menace beneath the question.

"I understand that it is going to cost a lot but…"

"But nothing," interrupted Durrant, "It is going to cost us a fortune!" For the first time, emotion started to seep into his voice, "and it is a cost that could well have easily been avoided."

"With all due respect Director, this is not an incident that could have been avoided."

"Oh really? It has never occurred before. What is it that changed this time? Why is it that it could not have been avoided this time also?"

"Well… I don't know. Like I say perhaps it was hungry this time…" He was starting to repeat himself and he felt embarrassed to be doing so, "It followed Kerrigan up from the sea!" Despite his earlier conviction that he would emphasise Kerrigan's blame in the incident, he suddenly felt pathetic as he continued to attempt to shift the blame onto a lowly prisoner.

He was a Captain, by the Gods, and he had a responsibility to bare. He was well aware that he was presenting himself to be the weak, old man he had been hoping to avoid.

"And who," replied Durrant as calmly as he had before, "was it who choose to send this man on the excavation in the first place?"

"It… it was myself."

"Precisely", responded Durrant, "If you chose the man, then you are responsible for his actions." Durrant pointed a finger at him on the second "you". Durrant had just put voice to Bronco's own thoughts. Durrant continued, "It is lucky for you Captain, that this… Kerrigan" he said the name as if Kerrigan could be relied upon more so than Bronco, "discovered what we have been looking for for so long."

Feeling the conversation beginning to turn to more positive matters, Bronco straightened in his chair. "That is correct Director.

I have not failed you in this matter at least."

"It is a shame you have not succeeded elsewhere" replied Durrant, reminding Bronco that, despite his success, his failings would not be forgotten. "So…" he cleared his throat and straightened his posture, regaining his cool composure once more, "may I see it?"

"Of course" replied Bronco trying not to sound too keen to impress. He signalled to one of his officers who brought the Black Box to the desk. He set it down with a wooden snap upon Bronco's desk. It's exterior glowed slightly in the warm light cast by the setting sun through the office window.

For a long moment the Box rested between the two men. Durrant stared at the Box without moving for some time. He raised an arm as if to reach out to the Box, but then held it steady and rolled his fingers. He licked his lips hungering to take hold of the Box, yet reluctant to do so.

Finally, Durrant gently grabbed hold of the box with both hands and pulled it towards himself. It made a subtle scraping noise as he did so. He tilted it in the fading light and rubbed away a light coating of dried algae that covered the exterior markings.

He smiled briefly at the box and looked back up towards Bronco, "You have done well Captain." He laid the Box beside his chair, "I will be most interested to discover if it's contents are as believed."

"And if it is as you hope…?" asked Bronco.

"Then you will be rewarded justly" replied Durrant with an acknowledging nod.

"Now," continued Durrant, shifting in his seat, "let us turn to more… interesting matters."

More interesting matters? Wondered Bronco. What could be more interesting than retrieving the Black Box? The same Black Box that had been pursued by the S.O. even before he had become Captain of Chimera? Yet he knew what Durrant was about to say even before it was put into words...

"Let us talk about this, Kerrigan…"

Kerrigan was in his cell performing press-ups when Warden Ashe unlocked his cell door. He had been locked away inside his cell ever since the incident at Site B and, not wanting to just sit on his bunk and allow his mind and body to rot from lack of stimulation, he had resumed his daily regime of exhausting exercises.

He found the routine comforting, but not comfortable. He would always push his body to the absolute limit of it's physical endurance before allowing himself any rest. He took comfort in knowing that he was not growing podgy and weak like all those around him.

The very idea disgusted him.

"Time to go Kerrigan."

Kerrigan stopped his exercises, not in response to Warden Ashe's command, but because he had reached his limit for the day. He sat on his haunches a moment to catch his breath, sweat coursing down his face.

He rose, was handcuffed, and was then immediately escorted from his cell by the familiar faces of West Wing's guards.

As he passed the other prisoner's cells, they stared at him with jealousy in their eyes. Other's scowled with what was no doubt jealousy also. Some reached out, begging to be taken with him. Others simply watched him go.

Kerrigan didn't really care for how the other inmates reacted. He was nothing special, and had done nothing special to be proud of.

Passing through Warden Ashe's office, he read the sign, "There are no walls! Your welcome to leave whenever your ready! PLEASE!", for what would be the last time.

The sign's meaning had a whole new context for him.

He emerged onto a deck with long black shadows, the sun had nearly finished tucking itself below the horizon, turning itself in for the night and allowing the moon to take it's turn at illuminating the world.

The gathered committee that would be his escort back to the main land, were gathered on the opposite side of the deck. Initially, they appeared as black silhouettes against the setting sun, but as he approached them, Kerrigan saw that they were dressed in silver uniforms, which was something Kerrigan had not seen before, nor expected. They were armed however, which was something he had. He may have earned his freedom but that did not mean he was considered to be a sane, civilized man.

Joining the committee, Kerrigan was addressed by Bronco, "Kerrigan, as you know, your recent heroic efforts have earned you a passage off this ship." He was clearly acting up the role of gratitude he wished to display, "These men are here to do that just for you." He waved to the silent waiting figures behind him. Kerrigan could only see half of their faces in the sun's final light, casting the remaining half in shadow.

"Director Durrant here…"

Director? Wondered Kerrigan, *Bronco's immediate superior? Here in person? What the hell?* Bronco indicated the man stood to his right. The other man was perhaps half the age of Bronco with a smooth, shaven face. His uniform looked much neater and smarter, the colour of which was the visa versa of Bronco's.

It was as if this new man stood for everything Bronco wasn't.

Bronco continued, "… would like to discuss in detail the admirable role you played in returning our precious item."

Durrant nodded once. He held in his hand the Black Box.

"So," said Bronco turning to face Kerrigan once again, "you will go with these men and once they have finished with you, you will be a free man once more." The speech was clearly constructed to sound formal and polite, but the look in Bronco's eyes and the tone of his voice conveyed to Kerrigan that he was anything from happy about his release.

"Follow me" ordered Durrant, and with a harsh shove to the spine, Kerrigan was forced to follow the man and his entourage onto the waiting crane.

Once aboard, the crane was lifted with a rickety rise, to be lowered down onto the waiting row boat below.

It was a strange sensation for Kerrigan, he could not remember the last time he had set foot aboard another ship other than Chimera. Come to think of it, he could not remember setting foot *anywhere* other than Chimera… other then the sea bed and Site B that is, but that hardly counted.

He stepped off of the crane, and watched as the recently emptied

cage rose back up onto Chimera's decking. From his lowered altitude, Chimera looked enormous.
Breaking Kerrigan's revere, Durrant said, "Magnificent isn't she?" he was referring to Chimera of course, "A beautiful testament to times long since past." He joined Kerrigan in his viewing of the ship. The last rays of the vanished sun hung in the air and twinkled upon the sharp angles of the bow. The sky was a deep, dark violet that beautifully framed the dark hulking shadow that was Chimera. Her patchwork exterior was hardly noticeable.
"Now," said Durrant. He turned to face Kerrigan, "let us not risk any unpleasantness."
And then blackness.

12

He awoke in unfamiliar surroundings.
Once more, Kerrigan knew that he had been somehow knocked unconscious and felt a moments disorientation as his new surrounds were absorbed. One of his familiar headaches had settled deep within his head making his mind pound fiercely in time with the beating of his heart. It was as if someone was pounding a thick iron nail into his brain to the tempo of his heartbeat. His body felt sticky and sweaty from the long hot days of not being able to bathe upon Chimera. It gave him a horrible dirty sensation that disgusted himself. His palms felt waxy and greasy to the touch, and he knew that if he were able to somehow touch the rest of his body, he would be met with the same oily sensation. If he were anyone else, he would not want to be anywhere near himself. His hair was thick and matted from grease, hanging in front of his face like dark, dead snakes. He could smell his own perspiration. It smelt harsh and feral. It stung his own nostrils to smell himself and he wished for a long relaxing shower to wash away his headache, his greasy skin and his smell, yet he knew that this would forever remain a dream out of his reach whilst his current circumstances remained.
The first thing that his throbbing head determined, was that he was

completely unable to move. He was hung vertically by his wrists to some sort of metal board, with his feet also manacled below him.

Looking around himself, his first impression was that he was back aboard Chimera's bridge. He was surrounded by a multitude of technology and computer equipment that remained a mystery to him.

This moment of false recognition remained only briefly, as the differences between his current surroundings, and Chimera's bridge, became apparent.

Firstly and most obviously, the layout of the room was entirely different. Chimera's bridge had only a couple of long consoles, and the far wall was curved slightly with a window that covered the entire wall, giving the viewer an unobstructed view of all in front, around and below the bridge. Here, there was indeed several long consoles, yet the opposite wall was instead filled with a long mirror.

Secondly, the consoles, flooring, ceiling and smell were much more…cleaner than that of Chimera. Where as Chimera was old and rusty, everything here appeared to be well maintained. Whatever the vaguely reminiscent room's function was, it was much more important and more regularly maintained than anything aboard Chimera was.

A soft humming filled the air. Kerrigan recognised it for the sound of machinery, but it was a sound that had not been present upon Chimera's dead bridge. Instead, the only sound that Kerrigan could recall hearing upon his visit to Chimera's bridge, was the sound of Bronco's voice.

He tried to break free from his restraints. He pulled his wrists away from the metal boarding, trying with all of his might to break the metal bracelets which kept him constrained. The sharp angles of the bracelets bit into his wrists as he strained against them, but to no avail. They were made from a very strong, well maintained steel that refused to even slightly budge despite Kerrigan's straining efforts.

Kerrigan's attention was drawn to the mirror that covered the wall to one side. It gave a reflected viewing upon the same consoles, walling etc, yet the person suspended by the shackles in the mirror appeared different than himself.

Before his still waking mind could determine what was different, the doors that gave access to the room opened and Director Durrant strode in. He was accompanied by the same guards who had escorted him aboard Chimera.

As he entered the room, he addressed Kerrigan, "Welcome, Mr Kerrigan." He stood in front of Kerrigan and addressed him with his hands clasped behind his back. He had to turn his head up slightly to view his prisoner.

Thrusting his chest out boldly, he continued, "I apologise for the restraints that we have placed upon yourself, but, as I'm sure you understand, we felt it better to err on the side of caution." He smiled falsely at the end of this, as if he wanted to appear more humane than his restraints perceived.

"Now" he licked his lips, "I wanted to have a little word with you about what went on at Site B."

Kerrigan scowled back at the man.

Durrant ignored it and continued, "As we both know, you were sent to Site B to locate and retrieve an item known to you as The Black Box. This you did, and on behalf of SigmaOmega I express our deepest, most gracious thanks." He looked Kerrigan direct in the eye, "You have no idea how important this item is to us.

"However," he continued "that item is now none of your concern, and I do not believe you are a man interested in anything that does not concern yourself.

"What DOES concern you however, is your freedom, am I correct?"

Kerrigan maintained his glower. Who did this guy think he was claiming he knew what he wanted????

Durrant made a small amused tone through his nose, "I thought as much." taking Kerrigan's silence as consent, "So, let us not keep you in this undignified position any longer than necessary, shall we? Explain to me exactly what happened at Site B and you shall be set free from these restraints and be allowed to resume a lifestyle completely in harmony with your inner cravings. Whether that be murder, rape, petty thievery... the choice is yours!" He made it sound like he was trying to sell the idea. Opening his arms as wide as possible, he concluded, "It's as simple as that."

After a brief pause were no one spoke, Durrant continued as if Kerrigan had agreed to the offer, "So, let's start at the start shall we?"

Durrant looked at Kerrigan as if he expected the bound man to start reciting the details. As Kerrigan's glower continued, Durrant attempted to motivate him, "You were given commands by Captain Bronco to search for, and retrieve, an item belonging to us called The Black Box. You were prepped on deck with the necessary equipment for the upcoming mission and then delivered overboard... what happened next?"

Delivered overboard? Thought Kerrigan. Was this man before him, barely old enough to shave himself without his mother's help, taking the piss out of him?

DELIVERED overboard?????

And what was it that he was wanting to know so much? There was hardly anything suspicious about what had happened. Sure, it might have been a little exciting back there for a moment or two, but surely an officer of higher distinction than Billy Bronco was not interested in hearing a childish adventure story???

When Kerrigan did not reply, Durrant's friendly exterior started to show sign's of frustration, "Come now, Mr Kerrigan, your customary silence will gain you no advantage here."

Kerrigan frowned. *Customary?*

Durrant smiled at Kerrigan's subtle, but still noticeable, response, "That's right Mr Kerrigan, I know more about you than you may think. Remember your fight with Duncan? Or perhaps your little dust up with Officer Dower?" He was referring to the large black man who Kerrigan had blocked a series of blows. It disturbed Kerrigan that he might know about his past events. "I hear you put up quite an impressive defence. And against such a large man such as he... really I'm impressed, I truly am."

Durrant smiled, "That's right, I've done my homework." Still smiling, he continued, "So, I'll ask you once again, what happened at Site B?"

Kerrigan had no idea what it was that this man wanted. They had the Black Box didn't they? What more could they want?

Taking a step closer, Durrant looked up at the suspended man in front of him, "Mr Kerrigan, we are all friends here…"

Funny way to treat your friends, thought Kerrigan, *hanging them up on a board like a piece of meat whilst you interrogate them…*

"…so just tell us what we would like to know and you can be on your way. A free man. Don't you want that?"

"You've got the Black Box. What more do you want?" growled Kerrigan, his voice as deep and as raspy as shards of broken glass being ground together.

Despite his best efforts to conceal his emotions, the breaking of Kerrigan's silence seemed to please Durrant. He saw the other man's eyes widen briefly.

"Simply to know," replied Durrant, trying to sound conversational, "exactly what happened at Site B."

"Why?"

The question hung in the air like a foul stench. There was something going on here that Durrant was not revealing.

"Because, Mr Kerrigan, I always get what I want."

It was clearly intended at a threat.

Stretching out his neck to get as close to Durrant as possible, Kerrigan replied, "Nothing happened." his voice was slow and gruff, like a caged animal's, "Now let me down."

"All in good time. What's the rush? Got an appointment you need to keep?" mocked Durrant, "You see, you're the first person to ever return from Site B alive, an admirable achievement in itself, but to return with the Black Box is…" he shook his head as if trying to shake out the missing word from his vocabulary into his throat, "…unbelievable. So as I'm sure you can understand, I have a few question's as to how you did it specifically, how you survived. So let's just hear it, what happened at Site B?"

"OK" replied Kerrigan, conceding to Durrant's questioning, "I got your Black Box, I was attacked by some kind of fucked up creature, and I returned to the ship."

Durrant smiled, "Good. Now, we're making progress! Were you attacked by any of your fellow prisoners while you were there?"

What was this guy after? Wondered Kerrigan. Did he want him to confess to killing another man? And if he did, was it so that he could revoke his freedom?

Kerrigan did not reply.

"Well? Were you?"

"Let me down" replied Kerrigan. It was not a request.

"Were you attacked by a fellow prisoner, Kerrigan?" Durrant was edging closer, as if he could draw the information out of Kerrigan with his proximity.

"Let me down."

"I asked, were you attacked?"

"I said.."

"Did you defend yourself?"

"Let…"

"Did he try and kill you?"

"…me…"

"Did you kill him Kerrigan?"

"…DOWN!" he shouted the word directly into Durrant's face making the veins in his neck and temple stand out. Bit's of spittle pelted the Director's closed eyes.

Durrant blinked away the word. He continued to stare at Kerrigan, then leaned his head slightly to address the guard who stood against the doorway that led to the room, "Officer?"

"Yes sir?" snapped the man with a smart saluted response.

"Let's see if we can persuade Mr Kerrigan to be a bit more… co-operative shall we?"

"Yes sir!" replied the guard and approached a console located on the wall adjacent to where he had been posted. As he fiddled with the console's instruments, Durrant strode a few paces backward, away from Kerrigan, "We have ways of making you talk Mr Kerrigan, whether you want to or not."

And with that said, he nodded to the awaiting officer at the console.

A huge wave of agony burst its way through Kerrigan's entire body. His back bent to an impossibly tight arch, bordering on the point of breaking. All of his muscles were strained and taut, threatening to rip themselves from the very bones they were attached to. His eyes felt like they were boiling in their sockets, ready to burst at any moment sending the hot optic liquid searing down his face, burning his cheeks. His testicles withdrew and throbbed with an excruciating pain. The world itself became an endless black void, filled with an eternal pain he had never before imagined. He knew he must have been screaming, there was no way he could have resisted even if he tried, but he neither felt nor heard himself.

His mind could not articulate any thoughts. The electricity that coursed through his body blocked out any thoughts of trying to get away. All he knew was that the pain was so immense, so all consuming, that he was about to die and he prayed that it would come quickly.

The pain lasted for an unknown, yet extremely long length of time for Kerrigan, yet just as suddenly as the pain had begun, it stopped. His entire body sagged and his chin rest upon his breast bone. If the shackles had not been wrapped around his ankles and wrists, he would have sank to the floor.

He was panting and he could smell and taste what he knew to be his own burning flesh rising up and into his nose and mouth.

Thick mucus, saliva and tears flowed freely from his face.

Distantly, as if from the other side of his own consciousness, he heard Durrant say, "What we just administered was a jolt of electricity barely below a lethal dosage. Don't make me have to be any more persuasive…

"Now," he said conversationally, trying to continue a story that had been rudely interrupted. "where were we? Oh yes, I believe you were telling me about how you got into a fight of some kind???"

Why the fuck was he so interested in his underwater fight with Fat Man's killer???

Kerrigan's head was throbbing with a sickening pulse from the electricity. The world was spinning and he knew he would vomit soon. He slowly opened his burning eyes and saw to his surprise that he already had vomited. It speckled his shirt and lay in a thick, congealing puddle below his feet.

He couldn't remember doing it.

Without thinking, or understanding why he wanted to do it, Kerrigan slowly started to raise his head. He raised it to the side first, wanting to see himself in the mirror that covered the entirety of one wall.

He saw the board to which he was attached reflected in reverse but, like before, the image seemed wrong in some way. His groggy mind took a moment to accept what he was seeing, but failed to understand it.

In the reflection he saw a man convulsing with electricity. He wondered for a second if this was himself only moments ago. Thick blue shards of electricity riddled the straining body and darted out and vanished towards the centre of the room. They almost reached Durrant who stood watch opposite...

But it wasn't Durrant, it was someone else. Some *people* else. There were more men in this reflection watching the sickening torture before them than there were in Kerrigan's own room.

No sooner had he begun to realise what was happening, did the electricity stop flowing, confirming what his mind had already begun to suspect. This wasn't a reflection. What he had at first thought was a mirror was actually a window showing the occupants of another room identical to his own.

It was only when the electricity stopped torturing the other man that Kerrigan saw that the refection was dressed, and looked entirely different, from himself. It was this that he had noticed to be wrong the first time, but he had been too sleepy from a drugged sleep to realize.

How Kerrigan had ever been confused between the distinctions between himself and the other prisoner were suddenly distressing.

The other, poor man, had a bald head with a purple looking bruise in the shape of a crescent moon behind his left ear.

Most distinctively were his clothes. He wore a long flowing gown of deep red with a blue sash that extended from one shoulder down to his opposite hip. To Kerrigan, it had a distinctly regal look.

The other man was sobbing and his mouth moved forming words that Kerrigan could not hear.

His captures did not seem pleased with whatever it was that he was saying, and signalled to recommence the torture.

Durrant spoke, "You don't want to end up like that man through there do you, Kerrigan?" Kerrigan watched as the other man convulsed silently under the deadly dosage of electricity being administered to his body.

Just who were these people?

"So, let's not continue this any further," interrupted Durrant into Kerrigan's thoughts, "how did you survive?"

Kerrigan watched the man in the adjacent room a moment longer, barely able to understand the agony that was being subjected to him.

How had he, Kerrigan, survived? What a strange question. Did they want to be regaled with his under water adventure story? With his fortunate escape? Did they want to be thrilled at the amazing tale of one man's victory over incredible odds? Did these fuckers want to be entertained???

Surely not! People did not hook one another up to torture machines to hear bed time stories.

"I don't know what your talking about" huffed Kerrigan, still panting.

Durrant looked upon the drained man before him with a mixture of disbelief and amusement. It was not the answer he had hoped for, but he had expected it none the less.

"Very well. You leave me no other choice."

He signalled to the guard at the controls and once more, the world for Kerrigan vanished and was replaced with nothing but an all enveloping agony.

His back arched until it felt like it would snap, his skin burnt as if on fire, his every muscle strained to ripping point, his brain ached as if it was being squeezed from the outside, exploding from within.

Yet, despite all this, Kerrigan knew that this time he would not be reprieved.

He was going to die.

He was going to die without ever knowing why. Without ever knowing why the Black Box was so important to these people who stood before him watching the life drain out of him so casually, why he was being subjected to such ridiculous questions.

He was going to die hung to a metallic board like a piece of meat with a thousand volts of electricity racing through his restrained body.

He was going to die pointlessly.

He would not allow it.

Watching Kerrigan's convulsing, body Durrant was almost disappointed. He'd had such high hopes for Kerrigan, especially after hearing the encouraging news from Captain Bronco… It was a shame that Kerrigan would not reveal more.

Still, he had no time for people who refused to co-operate, and those who didn't deserved whatever came to them. He watched as Kerrigan's body tried to roll back upon itself, trying to make himself into a giant human O.

He watched him die.

He realized that he must have been wrong in his earlier assumptions about Kerrigan…

He watched Kerrigan die without emotion, having ordered the death of countless men before.

Men much better than Kerrigan.

Kerrigan was merely a lowly criminal, a burden on society. In Durrant's opinion, he did not deserve the gift of life that was blessed upon him anyway.

The lethal dose of electric that coursed through his spasmming body would only take a few moments to remove him from this planet.

He watched without emotion as Kerrigan's restrained body convulsed, and then arched back upon itself. He saw him grit his

teeth and shut his eyes against the pain. He did not scream. Had he done so, it was very likely that his tongue would have been bitten off by his own teeth, and his vocal cords scorched dry.
Blue finger's of electricity scurried up and down Kerrigan's body. Soon, Kerrigan's clothes would ignite. but Durrant doubted that anyone who had previously been bound to the table had ever noticed the moment when this happened. The pain of the charge that flowed through them would dwarf out any other sensations.
*If only he had talked...*mused Durrant.

As the pain coursed through Kerrigan's body, he started to feel a lucidity below the surface of the agony he was being subjected to. His thought's suddenly cleared, emerging through the pain like a train emerging from dark tunnel.
How was it that he had come to be in this situation? And, more importantly, how was any of this his fault? He had done nothing to deliberately lead himself into this moment, and so why should he allow his death to be decided by anyone other than he????
How DARE Durrant try to kill him??
Who did he think he was???? Nobody, that's who he was. He was a mother fucking nobody and it angered Kerrigan to know that this fucking low-life, this fucking stuck up, child of a man, would be the one who would eventually kill him. He was a nobody, and Kerrigan would not be killed by a nobody.

A deep growling issued from Kerrigan, a growl that issued from deep within his chest. His back arched even more obscenely from the pain.
The end was near.
Durrant hoped that Kerrigan's clothes would at least engulf before he went. It made the scene much more entertaining.

Screaming with what might be interpreted as pain, but what was actually a strength of effort, Kerrigan arched his back even further, stretched his muscles beyond breaking point, and put all of his anger into snapping his wrists out of their restraints. He put his shoulders and heels against the metallic boarding he was imprisoned against, and pushed.

At first it appeared that his body was just reacting to the increased voltage he was being subjected to. Then, with an added grunt of effort, Kerrigan broke his arms free of the boarding.

With a loud, metallic snap, his arms snapped free along with the metal bracelets still attached to his wrists.

First his left wrist then his right.

Suddenly, Kerrigan's left arm snapped off of the restraints that held him to the board. Durrant had only a moment to accept that the impossible had happened, when it happened a second time. His other arm had also snapped free.

Speechless, Durrant backed away a step.

What was this happening????

Still attached to the boarding by his ankles, the electricity continued to flow through Kerrigan's body.

He propped his newly freed hands against the back boarding to gain extra leverage, and with a continued grunt, broke both of his ankles free also.

He fell to the ground with a dramatic thud.

There he knelt with his head bowed as a final few branches of electricity licked and crackled across his body.

The air above him shimmered like a mirage, an effect caused by the heat radiating from Kerrigan's body.

Durrant looked on in disbelief. How had this man managed to escape from his restraints? No-one had ever, EVER managed to break free from them. Men much bigger than Kerrigan had wilted within moments from the forces that were subjected to their bodies. Kerrigan was a relatively small man compared to those previous, so how had he managed to break free?

Durrant stared on. He had absolutely no idea how to even react to the situation, as it had never developed, hell, had never even been a POSSIBILITY, before.

Instinctively, he backed away to the exit.

After the final branches of electricity had snaked their way across

Kerrigan's body and crackled away into non-existence, there was a brief moment of uncomprehending silence, which somehow felt louder and more oppressive than the previous ruckus.
It seemed to last much too long.
Slowly, Kerrigan raised himself to his feet, keeping his eyes to the floor as his did so. Once at full height he raised his head to scowl at the gaping men before him.
Durrant had by this time, slowly backed away from the released man and was hammering the button that would open the door to the secured room and allow himself to escape.
With an horrid expectation of the door jamming, or to open more slowly than it should have, the door opened for Durrant and he slipped out into the awaiting corridor and ran away as quickly as he could.

Inside the room, Kerrigan was left alone with the one remaining guard. The guard had been too shocked to believe what was happening in front of him, and had also retreated. Unfortunately for him, his retreat had taken him to the corner of the room rather than to the room's only exit, as Durrant's retreat had.
Seeing the retreating man, Kerrigan turned his focus towards him, the movement done in a slow, graceful manor so that his neck muscles could almost be heard, creaking in the abandoned air.
The remaining guard was clearly terrified. His eyes had widened, his head was shaking and he seemed to be mouthing a prayer silently to himself. His hands groped the wall behind him, desperate to find an exit release button that wasn't there.
Silently, Kerrigan stalked towards the scared man with a feral, amused look in his eyes which slowly spread to his lips as he neared.
The guard spoke a few words of rejection which cascaded into a final, violent shout of rejection as Kerrigan closed upon the doomed man.
He grabbed the guard's screaming throat between his smoking hands and squeezed. He could feel the soft, flexible flesh beneath his thumbs crush and then collapse, like he were crushing a hollow

reed, as he squeezed the guard's wind pipe.

The guard's scream became a wet choke, which quickly faded into spluttering gasps.

His eyes widened and began to bulge from their sockets.

He reached up to his throat to try and remove the vice like grip that Kerrigan held.

His legs thrashed spasmodically in a vain effort to try and kick and escape from his executioner.

Kerrigan's glare never left the panic filled eyes of the dying officer.

It didn't take long for the guard's large, glassy eye balls, to loose their sparkle. Slowly, his eye lids began to droop, his thrashing legs started to relax, and his attempt at removing Kerrigan's hands became less convictive.

Kerrigan watched the man die by his own hands and felt an intense moment of serenity as he did so.

Finally, the man's movements and noises stopped altogether. His body went limp and he hung lifeless in Kerrigan's grip.

Later, Kerrigan would believe that he had taken no pleasure in the other man's death... but he had certainly felt no remorse either.

He let go of the guard's throat and watched his body fall to the floor with an ungraceful thump.

He felt over the fallen man and removed the gun that was attached to his belt. He was pleased to see that it was a proper, life stealing, hand gun, and not one of those stupid electrical stun guns.

He knew he had to be quick. Durrant had left the room and had no doubt ran for the nearest reinforcements he could find. It would not be long before they returned and he was overpowered.

He cautiously opened the door and peered out. Three men were already in the corridor running towards him.

It was the men from the adjacent room. They must have been able to see into Kerrigan's room, saw what was happening, and were now running to help out with the situation. Kerrigan had forgotten about the room next to his, and was at first startled to see reinforcements arriving so quickly.

They too appeared startled to see Kerrigan. The lead man, his uniform identifying him as a higher Officer of some degree, flinched ever so slightly in his approach.

It was all the time Kerrigan needed.

He raised his gun and fired.

Three bullets were all that were needed. His first struck the leading officer in the middle of his face. His face exploded outwards from both the point of entry and from the back of his skull as the bullet ploughed it's way through his head. Brain, bone and blood burst outwards in two spraying cones, dashing the steel walls with a gruesome splatter of gore.

Kerrigan briefly saw the remainder of the corridor stretching away behind the dead man's skull through the hole he had just punctuated, before he toppled to the floor in a broken heap.

His second shot hit the second guard above his right eyebrow. His scalp popped off his head and added it's own contribution to the blood dashed wall.

His final bullet must have hit the final guard in the eye. The entire left hand side of his skull vanished, exploding outwards sending the guard spinning to collapse atop his fallen colleagues.

Nice! Heard Kerrigan, inside his own head.

He had impressed himself with his own, deadly display of marksmanship he never knew he possessed.

Stepping over the downed men, Kerrigan ran down the corridor. His gun fire was sure to attract the attention of anybody near by.

He had no idea where he was running to. For all he knew, if he had turned and ran in the opposite direction he might well have ran headlong into the exit. However, as there were no signs or indications to suggest that either way was more favourable than the other, Kerrigan simply ran.

His foot steps echoed in the corridor as his boots thumped on the steel floor. The metal flooring and walls were a deep dark blue in colour, reminding Kerrigan of Chimera, only here things were newer or better maintained. There didn't appeared to be any rust at all as opposed to the rust that dominated on Chimera.

Had he been moved to a newer, more up to date prison ship? A model that was more sophisticated than Chimera? He hoped not.

However, with Chimera as his only basis of comparison, he could not rule the thought out completely.

Feeling incredibly exposed in the corridor, Kerrigan looked through the window of the first doorway he encountered. He did not want to just charge into the room through fear of finding himself at a dead end.

He needed somewhere to run to, or somewhere to hide. Not somewhere to be trapped.

The room he peered into was small with a large work desk filling the centre of the room. Atop the desk, lay a scattered pile of various instruments, none of which Kerrigan could identify. Glancing quickly at the three visible walls of the room, Kerrigan could see no doorways to aid in his escape. The room was a dead-end. A coffin.

Punching the door in frustration, he cursed under his breath and ran on. He could feel the claws of panic scratching away at the doorway of his sanity. It scratched and mewed, trying to break inside and wreck carnage amongst his thought's using it's long, dangerous claws. He would not allow panic to gain control. He knew that to do so would doom him as surely as if he turned the gun he had gained upon himself and pulled the trigger.

Still though… he could feel it's presence attempting to get inside… to gain control.

Scratch scratch scratch.

Onward he ran down the corridor when he was suddenly immersed in total darkness. Startled, he paused in his running, not wanting to charge head first into any obstacles in his way. He attempted to look about himself, but his eyes had not yet adjusted themselves to the darkness enough to show him his surroundings.

He felt the panic once more clawing at his sanity…

Scratch scratch scratch…

The darkness was smoothly replaced by the soft rising and falling of a glowing red light. An electronic wailing filled the air that rose and fell in time with the pulsing red light. It turned his corridor into a noisy, artificial vein as if the building itself were alive and aware of his presence. As if he were a virus in it's blood stream

that needed removing as quickly as possible.
Kerrigan understood the meaning of this sudden change in the environment. Somebody had reported his escape, or discovered the bodies he had left in his wake. They, who ever they were, were on to him. He was being hunted.
Scratch scratch scratch.
The intermittent rising and falling of artificial light which brought forth a claustrophobic effect.
Onward he ran. After turning another corner in the corridor, Kerrigan approached and then arrived at a set of double doors leading off his shrinking, vein like corridor. A quick glance through the wire grid windows showed Kerrigan a room of substantial size. With the pulse of each red glow, he could see a room filled with large smooth cylinders, and complicated machinery nestled into their base.
At the far end of the room, he could see another set of double doors leading out of the room.
With nowhere to hide should he be discovered in the bare corridor, Kerrigan rushed inside.

Desperately, he tried to absorb in as much information about his new environment as quickly and as thoroughly as possible. The room was about the same size as the mess hall had been aboard Chimera, dominated by the large cylindrical objects upon either side he had seen before entering. There were six in total, three lining each wall to Kerrigan's left and right. Each cylinder rose to twice the height of Kerrigan, yet remaining only half as tall as the roof of the room itself. The equipment that rested at the base of each of these cylinders glowed gently with a scattering of multi-coloured lights.
As the red alarm lights continued to pulse, and the siren continued to wail it's electronic distress, Kerrigan ran towards the opposite doors feeling that he had no other choice but to keep on running, and hope to reach the nearest exit.
Yet as soon as he started to cross the room, Kerrigan became aware of an immense pressure inside his head. It felt as if the air

itself had become thicker and heavier, as if the very air itself was trying to squeeze his head into a ball. He was briefly reminded of the ocean's pressure he had felt when he was so forcefully pushed over the side of Chimera to earn his 'freedom'.

Some freedom this was turning out to be.

First off he was bound and tortured by both ridiculously baffling questions and then by electricity, and now he was on the run for killing some men inside a maze like construct without knowing where he was, why he was here, or where he was going.

Further into the room he ran. He was approaching the middle of the room when the pressure he felt caused his ears to pop, filling with a natural high pitched squeal of their own. A few more steps and the pressure in his head became so great that his vision became blurry and the room swam before his eyes. As he reached the very centre of the room, his charge became a drunken stagger and it was all he could do to retain his balance and hope to break out of the foggy soup his mind had suddenly become absorbed in.

He was not aware he was still running until his head started to clear as he passed the half way point and started to reach the exiting doors.

It was like suddenly waking from a dream, but he knew he had not fallen asleep. He had a bizarre moment's thought when he realized that he did not remember passing through the middle of the room. As his mind started to return to him, he knew that he had made a stupid mistake by doing what he had done.

It was like suddenly sobering up from being drunk... not that he could remember the last time he had been drunk.

The thoughts that followed this realization scared him.

What would have happened if he would have passed out, as he knew he surely must have been very close to doing? He would have no doubt been killed upon his discovery. His only small comfort came from how he would not have even known he was dead if that should have happened.

On the bright side, he HAD managed to resist fainting and was still on the go.

On the trail of this thought came a question that was puzzling in it's honesty: just what was that weird air pressure all about anyway? Why had his mind momentarily blanked out?

Before he had time to dwell any further on the thought, a loud bang behind Kerrigan drew his attention. Without slowing, he turned his head to peer over his shoulder but knew what he was about to see before he actually saw it.

Behind him, a group of guards had slammed the same doors open by which Kerrigan himself had entered the room.

They stood poised in the doorway with their guns pointed in his direction.

"Stop right there!" someone shouted, yet the voice did not come from the guards towards which he now faced.

Kerrigan had a confusing thought that maybe his ears and mind were still suffering from some kind of after effect from the immense pressure they had recently been subjected to, and were now processing any audio input incorrectly, making it sound like any noise might be coming from a different direction…

Barely had this thought registered, when the truth exploded into knowledge, making this initial thought seem foolish and embarrassingly naïve.

Turning forward, another set of guards had filled the exiting doorway towards which Kerrigan was running. He realized upon sight that the command that he had heard had been shouted by this group, and not the first he had seen.

He came to a panting stop. He was only two thirds of the way across the room. His ears were still ringing beneath the sound of the wailing siren and from the pressure they had endured. His head pounded with a deep headache after suffering the confusion that had happened upon him with startling swiftness.

He had no where to go, and no time to think of a plan that might guarantee his escape, yet, despite his mental blockages, reason was still his prevailing attribute:

Firstly, he was clearly outnumbered, so any ideas about using the gun he had obtained were foolish. Should he attempt to use it, he would be gunned down before he could even raise the weapon against his foe.

Secondly, the fact that the two groups of guards, one each stationed at both the entrance and the exit, had not yet shot at him, implied that they did not intend to shoot him without good cause. Nor was Kerrigan inclined to offer them one willingly.

That, or they had not yet discovered the dead men he had left behind, which would surely have been enough justification to kill him upon sight.

"Good lad", sneered the front most guard, "Now, put down the gun and come with us. We don't want anyone else dying today."

Anyone else... So they had discovered the corpses. A brief wave of adrenaline swept over his body, starting from his crown and working it's way down into his extremities...

...so if they knew about the others, why had they not shot him yet???

Clearly there was a reason. Killing any Officer of the S.O. was an automatic, justifiable execution.

The guard's in the exit doorway remained where they had emerged and shouted, "I said, put the gun down arsehole. Don't make us come in there and get it!" The guard sounded threatening but made no effort to actually advance and act upon his threat.

So why was it that the guard chose not to advance? mused Kerrigan.

Presumably, they did not want to muddle their own heads by advancing into the room for themselves, thereby ruining their aim they had upon him. It made sense. But they had not yet entered the room, therefore their aim was still true... so why had they not just shot him?

Suddenly Kerrigan struck upon an idea, and without any thoughts to the contrary, he dashed to his left and behind one of the six cylinders that filled the room, putting the cylinder between himself and his pursuers.

He stood with his back against the machinery, with his eyes closed, and listened... or at least, he tried to. Being so close to this equipment yet again brought back the pressure he had felt whilst crossing the room, making him feel violently dizzy and extremely nauseous once again.

His thought's became so muddled that, like trying to filter out a diamond sinking into quicksand, he struggled to remember how he had even come to this position at all, barely able to focus his attention upon his pursuit's movements as he knew he should have been.
He fought against the muddiness in his head with all the mental strength he could muster. It was the mental equivalent of trying to catch water in his hands....
With a monumental effort to keep his mind focused upon the present and the objectives that would aid his escape, he brought his mind back to the present.
He remembered the thought process that had brought him here.
Seeing as how the guards were reluctant to enter the room he found himself trapped within, he remembered that he had figured he could stall them by immersing himself more fully in the environment. Secondly, the guards had seemed reluctant to fire their weapons upon an exposed target.
Therefore, he remembered, he had assumed that perhaps the guards were afraid of damaging this mind altering equipment, and so he had decided to use it as a form of shield.
All he knew, ignoring the pain and confusion that dominated his mind, was that he needed to believe in the instincts that edged their way into his consciousness.
Behind him, he could hear the guards shouting something, but he found himself unable to focus upon their words long enough to determine any kind of sense or logic from them.
Slowly, Kerrigan opened his eyes and turned, wanting to view this unknown equipment that he huddled against, close up. Perhaps he might determine some further knowledge that he might use upon closer inspection. Again his vision had became distorted, making everything appear to vibrate subtly, but very rapidly before him. It gave everything a soft blurry effect that was dizzying to view. Added to this was the still rising and falling of the red alarm light, and together it made Kerrigan feel sick to his stomach.
Immediately, Kerrigan knew that the computer equipment, nestled at the base of the mysterious tube was much too complicated for

him to have been able to have determined any use of, even if his head didn't feel like it had recently been used as a punch bag. A myriad of buttons, screens and dazzling lights wavered his vision.

Abandoning hope there, Kerrigan raised his head to view the cylinder the computer was attached to.

Despite his confused thoughts, the outside of the cylinder intrigued Kerrigan instantly. Instead of reflecting the pulse of the red light that fell on it, the material seemed to absorb it deep within itself and then shine it further into itself.

Believing his eyes and brain were deceiving him from the effects of his pounding headache, he moved his head forward until his nose almost touched the outside of the cylinder, wanting to get a better look at the tube, wanting to see inside… From this close, his head felt like it was going to burst, his ears felt like they would pop and pour warm blood down the sides of his head, and it was a struggle to keep his eyes open at all. Yet he could not resist. He needed to know what was inside this bizarre object.

He squinted from the pain but forced his eyes to remain open. There was some darker shape inside the cylinder and it was becoming clearer all the time.

It had started off like a barely discernible black blob floating in the very centre of the red casing, like a black smudge, but as Kerrigan focused upon it, it began to define itself into a definite shape, increasing in size. It swam closer to Kerrigan's pounding head, rising out of the gloom and taking shape like a fish rising out of thick water.

The blob was taking definition. It's blurred edges sharpened themselves into an outline.

It was taking shape.

It was…

Shocked at what he saw, Kerrigan recoiled and slammed his back against the wall behind him. As he stepped away from the machine, the fog that shrouded his mind cleared a little, yet this increase in mental clarity only served to bring the pain of the headache into sharper focus. Panting, Kerrigan suddenly realized that he felt cold all over his body and a thick layer of sweat

covered his prickled flesh.
As he gasped, he tried to clear his thoughts of the horror he had just seen.
He heard the guard's voices once more, this time much closer. He had momentarily forgotten all about them. Clearly they had risked entering the room to give pursuit after all. It was understandable. He was a fish in a barrel. Easy pickings. Even now, Kerrigan thought he heard heavy foot steps and even heavier breathing on the other side of his temporary security.
What the hell is going on here???
With no other choice, Kerrigan raised and readied his gun. He had no where left to go. He had no other choices to make. He had nothing except the gun he held in his hands. He was going to die, and he knew that this would be his time.
It was not a thought that scared him. Instead, he embraced it. He always knew that he deserved to die, in many ways he WANTED to die, but he would never allow death to take him until the very last possible moment, because he knew that he should always remain alive to suffer for as long as possible.
Because that was what he deserved.
He deserved to suffer and be punished.
Now, with death imminent, his suffering would finally come to an end.
He smiled.
A draft at his feet drew his attention.
Turning and looking down, he saw a small grid through which the draft was blowing. It was a ventilation shaft. He had not noticed it in the rising and falling of the pulsing alarm light, until it had made it's presence felt by tickling at his ankles.
The grid was approximately two feet wide square - easily large enough to fit inside, assuming the grid would allow him entrance.
Turning, Kerrigan kicked out and the shielding with surprising ease, falling down into the tunnel it had once protected.
Looks like I live to suffer another day, he thought without relief of the possible survival that might lay ahead.
As he started to clamber into the hole, the guards emerged from

around the sides of the infernal machine.

Initially, he thought that his confused mind and blurred vision were distorting reality, and that what he saw was some kind of trick that his mind and eyes had conspired against him.

The guards that he had expected to see, the guards he had seen earlier in their regulation silver triangle uniforms, were instead replaced by great hulking masses.

Some kind of protective suit, pale in colour, although the colour was impossible to determine for certain in the pulsing red light, covered the men within from head to foot. The suit puffed, bloomed and bloated outwards from every surface area making the wearer beneath appear, and move, slowly, clumsily and look extremely foolish. A black, non reflective face plate shielded the occupant's face from outside observation.

These strangely clothed men, despite their clumsy looking attire, still brandished guns that did not appear to be protected in anyway, leaving them just as deadly, but looking less threatening, in the puffy hands that held them.

Laying on his belly, with his feet dangling down the sloped passage that extended away behind him, Kerrigan fired several bullets from the gun he forgot he held. He had the satisfaction of seeing the masked man above jerk back in response to his shot. A hole had appeared in his face plate, surrounded by a widening spider web of cracks in the glass.

Despite the suddenness of the action, Kerrigan also saw a few of the rogue bullets he had fired miss the man he had been aiming at, and hit the infernal machine behind him.

A blinding flash filled his ears.

A deafening roar boomed in his ears.

And then silence.

13

With a gentle flutter of his eye lids, Kerrigan's first view of the world when he regained consciousness, was of the most dazzling blue he could possibly have imagined. In fact, for a moment or two, he had to squint his eyes shut as his pupils adjusted to the brilliant light before them. When at last he could keep his eyes open for long enough to understand what he saw, the pressure he felt against his back told him that he was facing upwards and he knew that he must be looking at the sky. It was filled with scattering of fluffy white clouds that dotted the skyscape as far as the eye could see.

Lying on his back amongst the warm, sun soaked grass, Kerrigan could hear the cry of birds chirping their mating call to prospective partners high in the branches of the gloriously blooming trees that surrounded him.

His head buzzed slightly, but the buzzing was only slight and actually helped him feel more relaxed and tranquil than irritated, as he might have expected.

He was happy to be alive, and amazed at his good fortune.

This is how Kerrigan would have awakened to the world in a better life, and how he would have liked to have awakened had he had the choice…

Instead of the sun's warm rays coating his face, Kerrigan awoke with his face plastered in a thick crusty coating of blood and vomit. His long hair had came to rest upon this ugly mixture whilst he had been out cold so that his hair was pulled taut and firmly embedded in the coating of his bodily fluids.

He was unable to determine the position he had landed in. His body lay half numbed so he could not tell which limbs lay where. Unfortunately, the numbness only extended as far as his muscles, so the pain to which his entire body was suffering was not subdued.

His headache was the worst he had ever known. With each beat of his heart, his head throbbed to bursting, feeling as if his eye balls were being pushed outward from his skull by malicious little demons within his head.

The sky was still a glorious, empty blue, but the brightness only served to add to his pain as it burned into his retinas when he looked upon it.

All he wanted to do was to drift back into unconsciousness, to sleep, where the pain that he was suffering could not follow, and that he might awaken refreshed, renewed and invigorated.

He lay there for a length of time that he could not count, willing for sleep to relieve him of his misery. He was unable to recall later whether he had actually slept or not, but he knew he had certainly lain there for a long time.

After this unknown length of time had passed, Kerrigan's mind reluctantly began to clear into rational thought once again, and he came to realize that sleep was not going to succumb to his wishes and that he would have to try and move for himself, or stay here and die.

To stay here and die was to give in.

To give in was *never* an option.

With an amazing show of strength Kerrigan righted himself. He did this without opening his eyes fearing that the dizzying movement might cause him to vomit upon himself more than he had already done.

Despite his precautions, he could feel the world spinning at an incredible rate around himself, spinning faster and faster, taking him deeper and deeper into the soil he sat in, drilling him down and down as gravity increased and pressed down upon his dizzying head.

He waited until his pounding head had stopped it's crazy spin before he opened his eyes.

Finally, his mind's crazy round-about ride, slowed and eventually stopped and he was able to open his eyes.

He did so very slowly… just in case.

He was sat in a field, that much was clear. Grass, weeds and ancient trees, whose branches looked like old men's fingers, were the only objects of note before him.

He knew it was a field, but could not remember the last time he had ever set foot upon one. His memories started and ended aboard Chimera.

No, that wasn't true, after Chimera he had been taken somewhere else…

Turning his head much too quickly than his brain would have

liked, Kerrigan turned to face what lay behind him.

In front of him, Kerrigan's vision had been filled with hundreds of leaves, a thousand shades of green, and millions of tiny blades of grass that wafted gently in the breeze that stroked them.

The view behind Kerrigan was of startling contrast.

Beyond the rise of the hill upon which he found himself, Kerrigan could see a tall building, the upper levels of which showed severe damage. The building appeared to be hundreds of metres tall and it's exterior was of a sophisticated design the likes of which Kerrigan had never seen. Sand coloured materials had been used to build the tall structure, so that the building rested contently amongst the lush landscape that surrounded it. A flowing pattern of smooth curves curled and spiralled up and down the building's exterior further adding to the building's natural appearance.

To Kerrigan, it appeared as if the building were trying to disguise itself amongst the natural formation in which it were constructed. It looked like a tree trunk.

But perhaps, he reasoned with himself, this was just his still muddled mind giving sight and reason where none should be found.

One thing was for certain: It certainly did not look like a torture chamber. But what else could it have been?

He could not see the base of the building, hidden as it was by the hill he rested upon.

The upper floors of the side of the building that faced Kerrigan were nothing but a smoking ruin that belched thick black smoke into the quiet air that rose and curled into the blue sky.

Upon observing the damage, Kerrigan came intuitively to the understanding that he himself had caused the destruction, yet he could not yet fully recall why this might be the case.

The image of the smouldering building restored part of his memory; of being inside some prison other than Chimera, but this one was equipped with torturous machines that had been used against him.

At the time, he had assumed that he must have been inside another prison ship, but now he saw the building, he knew that he had been mistaken.

How he had come to escape and end up so far away, he could not remember.

The last image he could recall was being pursued down a corridor and entering a large room through a set of double doors. Then he had an image of some kind of cylinder…that he suffered some terrible pain… and then he had awakened here on the hillside.

Knowing that no advantage could be made by sitting here in his own waste and gawking at his handy work, Kerrigan resolved to put as much distance between himself and the destruction as quickly as possible. It would not take long for the occupants of the building to pursue him when, or if, they learnt of his survival.

He made a quick check of himself, checking for anything that might be broken, before he attempted to stand.

He patted his hands down his vomit encrusted chest and a sharp pang of pain erupted in his lower left rib cage. After a couple of delicate prods and some gentle rubbing, he determined that he had not broken any bones as he had originally feared, but had instead only heavily bruised himself.

On inspecting his back he discovered a nasty gash also on his left hand side, this time below his rib cage. He attempted to twist round and observe it, but the pain that burned from the wound told him not to attempt such an endeavour any further. Touching the wound, as gently a breeze kissed the grass, he determined that the gash was at least three inches long and deeper than he would have liked. Amazingly, the wound did not seem to be bleeding hard, instead it only wept out blood like tears. After discovering the wound he also checked the part of his leather jacket that should have covered this part of his back to see the damage there. He was surprised to see that his jacket had suffered less damage than he himself had.

Patting down his legs, Kerrigan discovered no broken bones here either, but his left ankle was heavily swollen beneath his boot and both of his thighs ached as if someone had taken a shovel to them for hours on end.

Both his arms seemed OK, but again the muscles in his left

shoulder ached. Clearly it must have been his left hand side that he had fell upon when he had landed in the field.
It was with this analysis that exactly how he came to feel like a human punch back, lying in the middle of a field, came to be.
He suddenly considered himself very fortunate not to have suffered worse injuries.
Thinking back on the machine behind which he had hidden, and who's explosion had seemingly ejected him from the building before him, Kerrigan remembered the hideous sight that he had seen within that had so revolted him at the time. When he had originally seen inside the machine, he had been so shocked and his head so muddled, that he did not possess the concentration to question what he had seen. Now, reflecting on the situation, his head was still pounding but it did not feel like it was running along inside a muddy stream. Surely what he had seen must have been wrong? An image brought about by the stress, confusion and general panic of the situation? All this combined with the hideous mental pressures being exhorted to him at the time and the sure knowledge that he was about to be killed. Surely he had been wrong??? Mistaken???
Despite his best efforts to convince himself that he had somehow hallucinated the image, he could not fully accept that he had been wrong.
What had swam into his vision, as he stared inside the translucent membrane of the cylinder, had been a human face. There had been someone inside the machine. The face that had swam out of the gloom was that of a young man, bald of hair and bald of emotion. His jaw had hung loose from his skull, and his eyes had a vacant distant expression. Tubing snaked out from the man's temples and nose, back into the gloom in which he floated.
Recalling the image, Kerrigan knew that whoever had been inside the machine had not seen Kerrigan staring back at themselves from the outside. Certainly they had not responded to his staring.
Most concerning of all about the scene, was that Kerrigan knew that the man inside the machine had still been alive in some form or another. Though his emotionless face might have suggested that

he was dead, Kerrigan knew that that was simply was not the case... although what lead him to this understanding he did not know.

Whether the young man was indeed dead, or kept in a condition that seemed just as bad as death, Kerrigan was glad that he had destroyed the damn thing. For the man inside, Kerrigan considered this a mercy. Who ever was running that place had subjected Kerrigan to enough cruelties and clearly had a sick fascination with subjecting others to pain.

Now, as he sat in his own filth, Kerrigan determined that somehow the force of the expanding explosion that he had caused by destroying the machine above him, had thrust him down and out the shaft with incredible speed, expelling him out and into the field, resulting in his escape.

This, surely, was what had happened. There was no other explanation. Yet, turning to his right so as not to aggravate the gash on his back further, Kerrigan observed that if his theory was true, he had come to rest an unrealistic distance from the building, and that the force of the thrust and the resulting crash landing would surely have killed him.

Yet here he sat, battered, bruised and covered in vomit, but alive none the less.

Just what the fuck had happened in there? He wondered.

Suddenly, he felt too exposed in the glade in which he had awakened. The recollection of the recently past events told him that whoever had wanted him, had wanted him BAD and would stop at little to reclaim him.

He had to get away, far away, and as quickly as possible.

Shaking violently, his damaged thighs barely supported his weight as he rose to his feet, his back strained and ached from his new vertical posture.

Feeling like the last thing he should be doing was walking, Kerrigan set off in the direction his aching body had been flung like a rag doll, taking him as far away from the destruction he had created as possible.

His lips were cracked from thirst, and his mouth was as dry as, and had the texture of, old tree bark from thirst. His stomach grumbled from hunger to keep him company, but it was the thirst that Kerrigan would have quenched first, given the choice.

He was swelteringly hot from the sun which beat down onto his heavy leather coat. It felt like the sun.s rays were pressing down on his shoulders trying to push him down and into the earth.

His entire body ached from hundreds, thousands, of different scrapes, bruises, cuts and general muscle fatigue brought on by the brutal triple tag team of thirst, hunger and heat.

But above and beyond all this lay a sensation that was entirely new to Kerrigan, a feeling that obliterated what should have been a very depressing mood considering his current discomforts… he was free.

For the first time in as long as he could remember, he was a free man. No longer was he confined or restricted to the limited spaces of captivity. No more metal walls, no more of the same faces and routines day in and day out…. He was free to come and go as he please. To live a free life.

To live a free life.

The phrase almost daunted Kerrigan. How do you live a free life if you've never known one? Bizarrely, he actually found himself wondering how he might react and interact with other, free, human beings. Normally he would not be concerned about what others might think, but he did not want to attract unwanted attention to himself by acting suspiciously. He was quite aware that the truth was he was not a free man, but a fugitive. He may succeeded in retrieving the Black Box, but the Durrant was adamant about Kerrigan answering his questioning before his freedom was truly gained.

Plus, killing several officer's and causing an explosion was probably made him a wanted man.

Speaking of unwanted attention, his current physical appearance would certainly draw this attention to him more than any odd behaviour ever could. He walked hunched over, cradling his left arm within his right, like an old woman cradling a new born child.

Like a drunk, he stumbled and wobbled as he walked with his head hung down in front of him as if the thick strands of his hair, coated in his own dried vomit, weighed as much as stone.
He promised himself that as soon as he found some water, he would quench his thirst first and then have a wash.

For the first time as a free man, (he chose not to label himself for what he was; a fugitive) Kerrigan watched the sun drop slowly below the horizon. Instead of descending into the sea as it always had, the sun dipped it's head down into the bosom of the hills that rose subtly into the sky. Before it winked good night, the last few rays of the sun lit up the horizon in a way that Kerrigan could not possibly have imagined.
The hills to which the sun touched became a beautiful black silhouette, the fields and tress that spread out from the bottom of the hills were bathed in a magnificent golden glow, and the trees that surrounded Kerrigan extend their shadows to almost touching point with the opposite horizon. All of this was bathed in a serene, light haze that, far from obscuring the sight, added a blanket of calmness to the scene.
It was a beauty that Kerrigan recognized, but gave no sign of appreciating. Most civilized people would stop and admire the scene, letting the beauty of such a natural wonder seep inside themselves, to sooth and wash away the burdens that their life may have thrown at them throughout their day. They would bask in it's beauty like a flower tilted towards the sun's warming glow.
Kerrigan was too thirsty to waste his time staring at a sight that would happen every night for the rest of his life. Instead, he cursed the sun for taking away the light he was using to try and find even the slightest trickle of water that might alleviate his burning throat. So far, his luck had failed him.
After leaving the area where his body had been so unceremoniously flung, Kerrigan had walked in a direct line away from the smoking building, putting as much distance between himself and the destruction as possible.
The landscape that he had initially found himself in was largely

featureless; a tree here or there, the occasional cluster of shrubbery. He was on the top of a rise that led gradually down to the coast which he could see occasionally through the folds of hills on the horizon. In the distance, beyond several rolling fields, he could see a forest or wood of some kind. Assuming that this must no doubt be home to some kind of life, it was in this direction that Kerrigan headed. If there were animals, they would need water to live in which case Kerrigan too might hope to find clean water. Food and drink were without a doubt, his two primary concerns and the upcoming wood might prove to be the answer to both.
Unfortunately, the clarity of the view earlier in the day had obscured the distance that Kerrigan had assumed it would take to reach the wood. What had at first appeared to be only a short pleasant, albeit painful, walk away, had in fact turned out to have taken him the rest of the day to reach.
Now, as the sun's light faded, just when he needed it most, Kerrigan found himself on the edge of the wood.

The wood had initially seemed smaller than it actually was. Much like the clear view upon the hillside had warped the distance needed to reach the wood, the actual size of the wood was not comprehendable until it was reached.
Arriving at the outskirts of the trees, Kerrigan felt dwarfed by the collection of green leaves and brown, wooden trunks that stood before him. It was like facing a ominous army of silent, towering soldiers.
The fading light did nothing to ease the vision; the interior of the wood was swallowed by the developing darkness of the tree's lengthening shadows, giving the wood a look of infinite depth.
The wood soon swallowed him into it's belly and it was not long before Kerrigan felt completely and truly lost in it's undergrowth. The black trunks of the trees were an even darker black than that of the night, which helped prevent him from walking face first into one of the giant trees, but anything beyond the reach of his arm remained as black as anything else.
Tripping and stumbling upon unseen under growth, Kerrigan

began to think that maybe he had been foolish to enter into such harsh terrain under such poor conditions, surely it would be impossible to locate water in such poor visibility, and, crunching over unseen twigs branches and undergrowth, any hope he might have held of sneaking up or trapping an animal, was laughable. Even a deaf slug would hear his approach and have ample time to make a get away, before Kerrigan even knew it had been there.

Still though, his stomach demanded that he pressed on, insisting that he would get no sleep until both it's thirst and hunger were satisfied.

Tripping over a particularly large root, or stone, trunk, mound of mud, uneven mud, fallen branch, sleeping animal or whatever the hell it was, Kerrigan crashed ungracefully to the littered ground.

His damaged left ribs reawakened from the collision sending a stabbing pain throughout his body. He instinctively rolled onto his right side to relieve the pressure from his ribs, and let out a small whimper of discomfort.

For one small moment, the combined discomfort of his pain, blindness, disorientation, and above all, thirst and hunger, made Kerrigan feel momentarily sorry for himself. Quicker than the blink of an eye, Kerrigan dismissed this thought as weak and pathetic. Nothing advantageous could be gained from such a defeated attitude. Nor was he in any kind of predicament to warrant such self pity. He deserved everything that he got.

Renewed by his own disgust, Kerrigan righted himself to his feet.

It was at this point, now that he was not creating enough noise to awaken anything within a hundred mile radius, that Kerrigan became aware of the gentle trickle of running water.

Trying to determine the origin of the sound proved harder than he had at first thought; the sound seemed to echo and bounce off all of the trees at once, turning them from large looming giants, into large, looming, *teasing* giants as they tossed the sound to one another, like child's game.

Gauging what he hoped to be the correct general direction, Kerrigan ventured forth at a rate much greater than that which he had so far taken, his pursuit of the water providing a rush of hope.

Suddenly, the ground below him vanished and he found himself falling, then rolling down a slippery hillside, then crashing with another huge protest from his bruised ribs, into the shallow moving water of a natural stream.

It was a miracle that he had not collided with a tree on the way down, or smashed his face upon a rock, breaking his nose and bloodying his face upon his decent, but here he was, face down in an ice cold trickle of water, and Kerrigan could not care less about the fortune that fate had blessed him with, by leaving him unscathed on his tumble from hill top into the valley below.

Kerrigan lapped up the natural water with all the gusto he could.

Previously, upon waking in Chimera's isolation booth and having to suffer the sun's heat for such a prolonged period of time when Warden Ashe had delivered him a jug of room warm water, Kerrigan thought he had never tasted water so good, or ever would again.

He had thought wrong.

The water here was so clean, so cold and so pure that it was as if he were drinking a combination of liquid ice and energy itself at once.

It was like drinking the most pure, perfect, clear and innocent, rejuvenating material ever to be found anywhere in the world.

Also, after Kerrigan had drunk his fill, this water did not make his stomach convulse and throw it all back up again.

At first, the water's coolness was refreshing and invigorating as it passed over his hands and around his legs as he sat in the beck and gasped with relief after drinking his fill. He remembered that he had promised to wash himself as soon as he discovered a supply of water in preparation for the possible contact with human civilization.

Now, sat in the ice cold stream in the dark of night, Kerrigan soon began to shiver and thought better of the idea.

He did however, choose to splash the cool, midnight water over his face and felt himself awaken suddenly, as the cold water washed away the hard, congealed mounds of vomit that were still stuck to his face from earlier.

Despite the water's brittle sting, Kerrigan felt better for having washed at least his face. He expected no contact with civilization for some time yet, and so felt no compulsion to continue his bathe. After all, despite his momentary pleasure, he was still lost in a wood, in an unknown land.

After bathing and watering himself, Kerrigan's natural instinct turned to that of nutrition. The last time that he could remember having anything to eat was aboard Chimera, and even that was what?…at least two days ago certainly. He found it hard to believe that so much had happened within the last day; his underwater retrieval, his torturous interrogation…Surely all of this excitement could not have unfolded within just two short days?

His growling stomach would certainly not allow Kerrigan the sleep that his body also craved until it's appetite had also been satisfied, and so it was to food that Kerrigan turned his focus upon.

Anything vegetarian would simply not alleviate his hunger. Only meat would do, and it was meat that his stomach demanded.

It was night time and so it was unlikely that Kerrigan would hear the sound of grazing animals. Most would likely be asleep. If fortune smiled upon him, he might be lucky enough to stumble across a sleeping beast of one form or another, or perhaps he might hear something enjoying a late night snack that he might sneak up upon and kill.

Regardless of fortune, he was not going to find anything whilst he sat in the shallow river, the soft tinkle of the passing stream tickling his ears.

Rising, Kerrigan continued forward in the general direction in which he had been heading before his ungracious, yet incredibly fortuitous, fall.

After what seemed like an incredulously short distance, the sound of the running river quickly became distorted, and ultimately blanketed entirely, by the growing thicket of trees that Kerrigan put between himself and the stream. Once more, darkness enveloped him, and the only sound was that of the snapping branches that he himself was the cause of.

Attempting to choose stealth over progression, it was quickly

apparent to Kerrigan that by making such a cacophony of sound, he was not likely to find himself any kind of edible meat. Any animals that were likely to be asleep at such a late hour, would certainly be awakened by their natural animal survival instinct upon hearing such a ruckus that he was currently making.
Similarly, any roosting birds would also be startled into a squalling flight, awakening those animals too anaesthetised to awaken to Kerrigan's ungainly progress.
Proceeding with as much care as his depleted vision would allow, Kerrigan travelled through the woods at a frustratingly slow pace.
Just when he was at his patience limit, Kerrigan was surprised by his good fortune to chance upon a small group of what appeared to be sleeping deer. The deer lay in an exposed clearing, illuminated softly from above by the clear moon. No trees occupied this space, giving the sight a surreal artificial quality, as if the deer were already dead and had been laid here as a moon lit attraction for anyone who came stumbling into the middle of a forest having quenched their thirst on a nearby stream after blowing up part of an unknown, expensive looking facility of some sort.
Not one to question his good luck, Kerrigan crept upon the nearest of the sleeping deer with as much stealth as he could muster.

It was the most disgusting meal Kerrigan had ever eaten. Having successfully grabbed hold of the smallest of the sleeping deer, Kerrigan had swiftly attempted to break the beast's neck. Naturally the deer had attempted to escape it's doom and had bucked and lashed out in a panicked frenzy; prancing about and kicking it's hind legs outwards in an attempt to break free of the choke hold around it's neck.
This startling amount of movement soon awoke the pain in the bruised ribs of Kerrigan's left side. The pain bloomed like a light inside him, almost making him lose his grip. Barely gripping to consciousness caused by the pain in his chest, and even more tenuously gripping onto the bucking beast's neck, Kerrigan somehow found the resolve to break the deer's neck before it's thrashing could cause anymore pain to his ribs.

It's neck snapped beneath his grip with the sound of a broken branch.

Panting and coated in a greasy, cold sweat that was inspired more from the nauseating pain he had suffered rather than the physical endurance of killing the young deer, Kerrigan rolled off the dead animal and gazed up at the pure disc of the moon.

It hung low and huge in the sky, it's full outline was partly hidden by the trees, casting down a cool luminous glow onto the world below. A ghostly, cooling glow that should have made all who bathed in it feel chilled to the bone.

Kerrigan lay where he had rested. Panting, sweating, incredibly hot… and, despite his efforts, not in the slightest hungry anymore.

He might have dozed there for a moment, he was not sure himself, but the moon seemed to have shifted it's way across the sky, as if to get a better view of Kerrigan, to watch his suffering with a clearer view.

Rising to a sitting position, Kerrigan turned towards the dead deer. He did not seem to have taken down a particularly fine looking specimen. The deer had a bizarre looking extra leg protrusion jutting from it's rib cage.

With a slight wince caused by the pain in his side, Kerrigan leaned forward to better observe the growth.

The young deer had an extra, fifth leg growing from it's side.

Not that this made any difference to him. A feast was a feast.

A deer was a deer.

It was only now then Kerrigan realized that he had no way of cutting up the meat, and, more importantly, no way of cooking it. He had a momentary sense of deja-vu, a vaguely recalled feeling that he had had to fend for himself in the wild previously, but could not recall when this time had been. Nor could he remember any skills from this period that may have been of use to him.

Like how to make a fire for example.

He would have to eat the meat raw.

Looking at the dead animal, he considered attempting to tear the skin open with his bare hands to get at the flesh underneath.

He quickly discarded this thought. Skin was surprisingly hard to actually tear apart, and the outward movement required of his shoulders to perform such a task, would surely reawaken the pain in his ribs. Considering all of the pain that his ribs had been giving him, he conceded that the ribs might be broken after all.

Kerrigan rose and went to the base of the trees in the clearing. He found himself a sizeable rock with an impressively sharp edge, and returned to his kill. He raised the rock above his head and was instantly over come with a horrible, dizzying nausea as the pain in his ribs flared once more.

He half threw, half dropped the rock onto the deer, fell to his hands and knees, and quickly turned his head in time to heave up a burning glob of liquid vomit. There was no substance to the vomit and the bile that he regurgitated burned his throat with a harsh intensity.

Spitting away the taste, any appetite that Kerrigan might have mustered was once again lost as he gazed upon the exposed, glistening heap of bloody deer flesh. Incredibly, the rock had served the purpose he had intended and had cut neatly through the deer's tough flank.

Regaining control of himself once more, Kerrigan turned to face his meal. Without any appetite he was determined that he would none the less force himself to eat the raw meat, knowing that this would be his only guaranteed source of nutrition in the foreseeable future.

Using his hands, Kerrigan tore off a sizeable chunk of flesh, and raised the meat to his mouth.

It was still warm and glimmered subtly in the low moon's spooky glow. He looked it over slowly, twisting it and turning it as if it were a newly discovered species of animal.

He brought the meat to his mouth.

Blood oozed out of the meat as he bit into it. It flowed warmly down his chin, into his growing beard and dripped down onto his lap. The meat itself was disgustingly rubbery and tasted only of the metallic taste of the blood it contained.

He ate the whole lot and went back for more.

His stomach protested noisily from the raw meat, and clenched in upon itself. It seemed briefly to Kerrigan that his own stomach was about to turn traitor on him, and regurgitate the nutrition that it had ungratefully been forced into accepting.

His stomach quit it's rebellious phase, and Kerrigan was able to keep the meal down.

As he ate however, he became aware of just how tired he was. He had spent the whole day walking a huge distance through rolling fields in a state of near perpetual agony. Now that he was sat and had satisfied both his thirst and his hunger, his body weight seemed to double and his muscles ached with the need to shut down and rest for the day.

Kerrigan wanted nothing more that to satisfy this urge, and so he rose from the carcass of the dead deer to lean against a nearby tree. Despite his weariness, he felt incredibly exposed. The open sky above his head and the woods that stretched away in all directions, impressed upon him an openness that he had never before experienced. He was so used to his cramped cell surrounding him that the exposure he felt in the woods made him unsettled and unable to relax into the sleep his body craved.

He never thought he'd miss his tiny cubicle on Chimera, but, suddenly, he did.

Then again, he never thought he'd ever have the opportunity to miss it either.

For so many countless days, he had spent the vast majority of his life surrounded by the same four walls, ceiling and floor that suddenly he found himself feeling almost... lost without it.

His stomach clenched painfully from the unpleasant raw food it had been forced to consume.

"At least in prison you get three hots and a cot." he mumbled to no one in particular. He was surprised to hear the words come out of his mouth.

His mind started to niggle over his current, exposed position. Surely someone must be looking for him? Someone from the factory, or building, or whatever it had been. He had caused a hell of a lot of damage and killed several men along the way. He did not particularly relish the idea of falling asleep and leaving himself

defenceless to whatever search party may be out looking for him. It wasn't as if he'd be hard to find either, he had instinctively headed towards the closest and most likely destination for finding food and water, which also happened to be the most sheltered environment close by. Someone could be hiding behind any of the hundreds of trees that surrounded him, waiting for Kerrigan to fall asleep.
Yet it was also possible, that who ever was in charge back there in the ruined building, had assumed that Kerrigan had been killed in the explosion. Therefore, maybe there wasn't anybody out looking for him after all. It was possible, but just how likely it was, was hard to judge.
Also, his interrogators had clearly wanted some kind of information out of him. He had been restrained, tortured and questioned for a reason, and not just by some faceless stranger, but by a man with an important, respectful, sounding title: Regional Director Durrant.
Regional Director. Not just some cadet.
Why had someone with such a high rank felt the need not only to interrogate him, but to escort him personally from Chimera back to where he had been questioned?
Presumably whatever information they thought Kerrigan knew must be of some importance to the people who had questioned him.
Therefore, maybe they HAD sent somebody out to look for him. Just incase.
But what was it they wanted out of him?
As Kerrigan's thought's spiralled around these questions, repeatedly asking himself the same questions in a hundred different variations, he fell asleep and forgot all about his concerns about his exposure.

14

He was stood in a field of oily black grass. The grass fluttered softly in a warm breeze that danced about him, making his hair tickle his face. His coat, as red as the low hanging sky above, waved gently on the air.

The grass glistened as if it were made from a flexible polished metal. It danced collectively with it's millions of symmetrical partners, to the ever changing music of the wind. His boots stood among the grass like two immovable rocks attempting to spoil the flow of the dance with their moody motionless stance.

Raising his head from his grumpy boots, Kerrigan gazed at the horizon. The glistening black grass stretched away to as far as his eye could see until it met the blood red of the sky in a perfect horizontal line.

Continuing to raise his head, Kerrigan noticed that not a single star pricked the maroon sky, nor did a moon hang and cast it's deathly glow.

Kerrigan had the strangest thought that seemed to bubble up out of his dreaming mind, and then slip gracefully away; If there was no moon, where was the light that caused the grass to shimmer?

Although it was not possible to tell, Kerrigan knew that the sky hung lower than it should have, as if he could reach up and touch the sky above as if it were not much higher than he himself was.

CAW!

A bird called in his left ear, startling him into taking a leap to his right. Turning his head to the noise, Kerrigan saw that a black bird had became perched upon his shoulder.

Somehow, he had expected to see it there.

It did not fly off from his reflexive leap, nor did it flutter it's wings to keep it's balance. It were as if the bird were stuck to him, or were even a part of him.

The bird did not turn it's head to meet Kerrigan's stare, instead it kept it's head forward, perhaps not noticing his stare or, more likely, it was more focused on what lay ahead, in front of itself.

Curious as to what enraptured the black bird, Kerrigan turned his gaze in the same direction as that of the black birds.

A deer was grazing in the field opposite, were previously there had been none. It chomped at the grass at it's feet in blissful ignorance of it's two casual observers.

An ugly looking limp, fifth leg hung from it's flank, occasionally flapping when the perpetual wind blew particularly strong one moment.

Kerrigan's dreaming mind did not need to tell him that this was the same deer he had recently just killed and eaten.

It raised it's head to look at the horizon as it chomped on a mouth full of grass. Thick black liquid glistened from it's muzzle and dripped onto the field, as if it were chewing on a mouthful of oil. The deer had the expression of someone who admires some beautiful scenery as he eats his meal, contemplating upon it's life. It looked thoughtful, at peace with itself.

It finished it's current, oily morsel and went back for more.

The grass made a wet tearing noise, more like flesh ripping than grass, as the deer took another mouthful.

When it raised it's head this time it looked directly at Kerrigan. Where at first it had the natural dark eyes that it should, when it raised it's head this time it's eyes had been replaced with sharp green eyes that stood out in startling contrast to the murky colours of everything else.

Transfixed by these sad, yet beautiful eyes, Kerrigan became oblivious to all else. The colour of the eyes, and the sadness they projected, were morbidly fascinating in their beauty.

CAW! Said the crow, and Kerrigan dreamt no more.

15

Waking the next morning, Kerrigan felt older than the trees that surrounded him. All of his joints, muscles, bones and nerves ached with an intensity that suggested that they would rather have remained dead and lifeless forever more, rather than being rudely awoken into reanimation.

Even the very marrow within his bones seemed to ache. His head ached, his teeth ached and his heart ached as if it was tired of all the years it had ceaselessly pumped blood around his body.

He dared not touch his ribs. He was in plenty of discomfort enough without adding their flaring pain to his misery.

Staggering to his feet, Kerrigan struggled to remember which way he had been heading the previous evening. Although he had no particular destination in mind, being as how he had no idea where he COULD go, he none the less did not want to cover ground he had already traversed. It would be pointless and wasteful.

He glanced around himself, hoping to gauge roughly the direction in which he had entered the clearing. As he did so, he noticed the bloody corpse of the deer he had killed the night previous. Flies were already buzzing above it in the early morning light, thankful for the feast which had been left for them.

Kerrigan left them to it, and re-entered the woods.

Kerrigan suffered a terrible few days following his kill in the clearing. His body rejected most foods that he consumed from then on. Whether this was due to a reluctance to eat more raw meat or that the occasional fungi or berries that he ate had a toxin within that his body could not tolerate, he could not determine.

He continued his journey in what he hoped was a relatively straight line. The woods seemed to stretch on forever. His eyes began to ache from the overload of witnessing a million different shades of green and a thousand different forms of shrubbery and trees.

At one point he had believed that he had finally found signs of a settlement as a brown structure passed fleetingly amongst the trees to his left. Investigating further, he was disappointed to find only the rusting skeleton of some kind of facility.

Three thick towers rose from the ground into the air. The outer casing of the towers was a patchwork of deep rotting browns and aged red rust. The towers were clustered together in a triangle, surrounded by a collapsed concrete wall that had once contained them within. Sagging pipe work barely connected the towers together. Thick weeds and plants grew in, on and around the dead construction, suggesting that whatever purpose the towers had once served, had ceased to function, and that the towers themselves had been laid dormant for a long, long time.

Gazing upon the structure, it gave Kerrigan the impression that it might have looked better aboard Chimera's rusting deck, rather then here inside the lush, living forest.

The food that he consumed, as he passed unnoticed through the wood, was frequently the same. He dined upon either deer or pig. Anything else was too small and wiry to be caught bare handed. The deer and the pigs that he caught were often deformed in some way, much as the first deer he had caught had been. They would often have and an extra appendage, or some kind of unpleasant growth swelling out of their flesh. On Kerrigan's third night, he had thought that he had caught a prize alpha male of a small group of wild boar. It was only when he held the downed animal that he was met with the deathly stare of a lifeless skull that housed three eyes. Each eye twinkled slightly in the moonlight as if the boar wanted to cry over the loss of it's own life.

Kerrigan was not put off by this disturbing sight, and ate the pig's flesh with neither pleasure nor disgust. He simply ate to stay alive.

Throughout his time in the forest, Kerrigan spent the first couple of days cautious of the possibility of being pursued. As the days passed, he began to dismiss, and eventually forget, the possibility of this being true. The distance he was putting behind himself in this living labyrinth made any kind of pursuit more and more unlikely.

On the dawning of Kerrigan's fifth day in the forest, he was blissfully unaware of the unexpected outcome that lay up ahead.

16

It was Kerrigan's fifth day in the forest and he awoke in a warm bathe of purest sunlight. The morning sky was a startling blue that shone down upon him in with such a comforting glow, that he was momentarily blissfully ignorant of his dire situation.

The birds in the trees sung gently, celebrating the dawn of such a fine day.

Rising to a sitting position, Kerrigan remembered his predicament, and that how he was basically a wanted man in the middle of an unknown land.

This sobering thought occurred to Kerrigan, but it did little to

diffuse the calm that the new day's sunlight cast upon his person.
Rising to his feet, he was even surprised by how little pain his left ribs caused him. On previous morning's, his ribs had screamed at him with any kind of drastic movement, or shift of his body. Today however, his ribs felt almost as good as new. They had healed with surprising speed. He also inspected the gash on his lower back and was even more surprised by the rate of healing there. The gash had not only scabbed over, but most of the scabbing was now gone and only a pink line of new skin showed where the injury had been inflicted.
The ribs he could accept, for it could have been that they were broken, but if it was bruising, it had only felt worse than it actually was, but the gash should have taken weeks to heal rather than a few days.
Curious. But as it was nothing to worry over, so he dwelt no longer on the thought.
Without the need to gather his belongings, or tidy, wrap or put away any kind of temporary shelter, Kerrigan progressed in the direction that he had been travelling for the previous week.

The next day started off as sunny as the previous day had. The sun was beautifully fresh and pleasantly warm in the mornings, however the sun's heat quickly became an annoyance as it rose high into the afternoon sky. The oppressive heat would burn down upon his body, covering him in a thick, oily sweat after only a few hours of ceaseless trudging. As a consequence, Kerrigan spent much of his time seeking out water. Thankfully this did not prove as taxing as it had on his first night in the woods. A multitude of large puddles were dotted throughout his path, each of which increased in size and depth as he progressed. Clearly there had been a heavy down pouring of rain in this part of the wood recently. The grey clouds that had developed over head as the day progressed added credence to this idea.
A light pattering of rain began to fall, flicking the leaves on the trees as they fell on their way to the woods muddy floor.
As soon as the rain started, Kerrigan stopped and raised his baking

face up to the weeping clouds. The cool droplets gently fell upon his brow, kissing him coolly with a rejuvenating invigoration before rolling down his upturned face.

Shortly before what Kerrigan perceived to be mid-afternoon, the welcome drizzle progressed into light rain before fully evolving into a heavy torrent of thick droplets. The sky had darkened over so much from the thick swell of heavy clouds that, had he not known better, Kerrigan would have believed that the day was coming to an end, rather than just reaching half way.

In no time at all, Kerrigan was completely soaked and shivering. He almost wished for the sun's return, despite it's oppressive heat.

Kerrigan felt a subtle vibration through his legs. It almost tickled it was so subtle.

It sent shivers from his boots to his hips, giving his toes a momentary sense of pins and needles, although this could also have been caused by the cold wetness that had flooded into his boots.

He stopped in his tracks as soon as the shiver had occurred, but no sooner had he stopped, did it too disappear.

He stood there, as still as the trunks of the trees that surrounded him, pondering over the sensation.

His first thought was that it had been caused by thunder, but he had seen no flash of lightning and had heard no rumble.

Had he imagined it? After all, he had been alone without company for some time now and his mind was no longer as focused as it once was. In fact, now he came to think of it, he had no idea just how long he had spent in these woods. A few days certainly, but a week? A week and a half? TWO weeks?! It was hard to accept, yet the idea remained strangely plausible to him.

Over the course of this unbound time, Kerrigan increasingly found his mind wandering and dreaming over ridiculous fantasies. He would walk for long periods of time in this semi-comatose state before snapping back to reality and scolding himself for potentially putting himself at risk. He needed to stay focused at all times.

When the rumbling failed to resume, Kerrigan resolved to continue his journey, believing that he must have imagined the sensation, that the isolation of being alone in a wood for so long was finally playing tricks on his mind.

A few steps later and again, a rumble occurred which started in his feet and worked it's way up into his shins, thighs and pelvis.

Once again he stopped in his stride. This time, he was certain that he was not just imagining the feeling. He had definitely felt it this time. It had been stronger than the first, nearly audible with it's intensity.

Just what the hell had caused it?

Determined to convince himself that this second occurrence was not some kind of mental repetition of the suspicious first, Kerrigan remained completely still in hope that it might occur again.

He attempted to listen to the sounds of the forest around him, trying to listen beneath the perpetual clatter of splashing rain drops.

His heart was beating with an increased thump-thump of anticipation, and he heard every noisy inhale of breath through his dilated nostrils.

The forest, besides the clatter of falling rain, remained silent.

It took a moment for Kerrigan to realize the significance of this silence. It was only as the silence continued that he heard it's emptiness. Previously the trees had been alive with a cacophony of sound produced and sung by the myriad of unseen life forms that the trees held.

Now, the choir of voices was silenced.

Odd. Was it the rain that had silenced their voice?…

The sensation occurred once again, this time however it was a definite rumble as the increased vibration came accompanied with a deep grumble that echoed off of every tree. It was impossible to ignore as the vibration flowed not just from his feet to his pelvis, but continued on and upwards, towards and into his teeth.

Kerrigan's vision distorted slightly from the sensation and a few dead leaves from the tree tops fell smoothly from their precarious perch, to fall drenched to the forest floor. The puddle that he was standing in trembled with ripples of movement that started from the centre and fanned outward.

The combined noise and vibration led Kerrigan to the belief that he was both feeling and hearing the result of a nearby explosion or impact.
Something was causing these vibrations and, whatever it was, it was closer than it had been previously.
Standing still, Kerrigan listened. Although he had heard and felt the noise this latest time, he had not been able to determine the direction from which the noise had originated. The surrounding trees both muffled and reflected the noise making it seem as if the sound was coming from every direction at once.
Except for the heavy slapping of falling rain on tree leaves, there remained silence.
Whenever it seemed that he wanted to hear a sound, Kerrigan was met with silence.
Remaining as still and as silent as the tree trunks that surrounded him, Kerrigan awaited the next impact. He widened his nostrils so that the air he breathed made as little sound as possible. He focused upon his heart beat, forcing it to slow down, to steady itself, to decrease it's increased thumping that filled his ears so that he might fully listen upon his surroundings.
The silence continued on as if this one moment in time was but a brief picture in life's long tapestry.
Kerrigan's eyes darted from tree to tree, seeking the source of the now silent noise, hoping that he might see whatever had caused the noise, might be able to see some shadowy form dashing from tree trunk to tree trunk in an attempt to avoid his searching gaze.
BOOM!
It was clear upon hearing this third noise that he was definitely hearing and feeling the results of some nearby impact. He had been wrong in assuming that the sensation could have been generated by an explosion, the sound was too deep, too muffled compared to that of the harsh crack of an explosion.
The distinction was made when, along with the crash and vibrating, Kerrigan heard the sharp distant crackle of wood splintering. If the source of the noise had been an explosion, any wood caught up in the blast would have been burnt, destroyed or

disintegrated, not snapped.

The noise remained distant, yet Kerrigan, despite his caution, remained where he was. The traitorous trees were still hiding the location of where these noises were being made from him.

A cold sheen of sweat broke out on his forehead as he listened intently once more for the next impact. As the sweat broke out, it contributed to the rain that flowed down his skin.

It occurred to him that he could run, aware that this could finally be the S.O. having caught up to him, however this rash action led to the possibility that he might run straight into whatever was causing the impact itself. If he remained calm and attempted to find out where NOT to run, then he could possibly gain himself an advantage.

Again, time became as still as a picture.

CRASH!

He darted his head to his left rear. This time, not only was the impact felt and heard with greater intensity than before, but it was also seen.

Through the thicket of trees, Kerrigan observed a rising dust cloud and crumble of branches. Whatever was causing the impacts was very near.

At last, pinpointing the source of the disturbance, Kerrigan turned and ran as fast as he could in the opposite direction.

His silence was broken. As he fled, his sprinting feet snapped an assortment of twigs and branches beneath their soles, his breathing became a rapid rasp, and his heavy leather jacket flapped about his person like thick dead skin. It was as if his every sense had became a traitor to him and wanted to reveal his location as loudly as possible.

Their cries for attention were not in vain.

An ear splitting roar of purest anger and frustration filled the air, blurring the edges of Kerrigan's vision as the intensity of the cry vibrated the very air itself.

It was then that Kerrigan knew that whatever had been causing the impacts was not artificial, but alive, and by the sounds of it's footsteps it was BIG. Bigger than anything else he had encountered

in the wood so far, and it knew that he was here with it, that he was violating upon it's territory… and that it wanted rid of him.
Bounding over fallen tree trunks, Kerrigan sprinted away from what ever it was that was pursuing him.
He risked a glance over his shoulder and was shocked by what he saw, or more accurately, what he couldn't see.
He had expected that whatever it was that he saw could well have just been a larger sized animal from what he had seen and hunted over the last few days. Perhaps this particular creature was as deformed as it's brethren, but in size, rather than in shape. Possibly it was an abnormally large wolf or boar.
Instead, he was being chased by a shrouded, unknown entity.
A rolling cloud of dust and distortion was pursuing him, ripping up trees and discarding them from it's path as if they were mere blades of grass. The beast, whatever it was, was at least as tall as the forest's shortest trees which, this deep into the forest, were at least five times as tall as Kerrigan himself was.
This thing wasn't just big, but huge.
A longer look might have revealed some of the creature's form, but basic survival instinct returned Kerrigan's attention to avoiding the clutter of debris that coated the forest floor as he fled away from the pursuing monster. One trip would be all it might take for the beast to catch him.
Panting from exhaustion much too soon, Kerrigan pushed himself off each boulder and branch with as much effort as he could. He pushed himself off nearby trunks and stones with his arms and legs to try and gain a little bit more momentum, a little bit more speed, anything that might gain him a little bit more distance between himself and the approaching nightmare.
Another roar filled the air, mixing and adding to the already deafening crash of crushed branches and the louder snapping of entire tree trunks as the unseen behemoth charged upon him with unrelenting ferocity.
So far, it sounded like his pursuer had not gained much distance on him, but there was no way he could keep up his all out sprint for long. His legs were already tired from the previous days endless

walking, and generally it was not possible for anyone to retain a sprint for any prolonged period of time. Even with the added benefit of the pure adrenaline his body had surely supplied him with to replace the blood that normally coursed through his veins, and the guarantee of some horrifically gruesome death should he stop, these factors would not help Kerrigan maintain a sprint forever.

Although he had not seen any on any of his previous days, Kerrigan looked about him in hope of finding some kind of shelter. Perhaps a warren or animal's den that he could leap inside of, but was too small for him to be pursued through, might make itself available.

No such luck.

His mind was racing as fast as his sprinting legs.

Maybe he could find a particularly sturdy tree to climb. A tree with a truck too thick to be discarded as easily as those being destroyed even now behind him. As to how he would climb such a considerably thick tree, which might well be too great in girth to gain any kind of grip, he did not know, but he needed some kind of lucky break.

And, suddenly, here it was. Maybe.

The trees appeared to be thinning. He was coming out of the forest at last! As to how this would benefit him, Kerrigan did not know, but at least he wasn't running through repetitive, bland foliage anymore. Maybe when he was out in the clear he might find a cave, or a cluster of rocks to climb that the beast could not.

Renewed by this slim chance of hope, Kerrigan panted, wheezed, pushed, splashed, shoved and stumbled his way out of the wood, and emerged from the thicket of trees.

As the last few scattered trees petered out, at the bottom of a gentle slope, a small sea-side village lay nuzzled against the sea's shore. A thick cluster of darker black houses stood out against the blank, dark grey tapestry of land that lay out before him. The main collection of buildings hugged the coast and fanned outwards to meet the bottom of the hill Kerrigan ran down. A few lights twinkled silently like stars amongst the dark buildings of the village.

To Kerrigan's desperate mind, the village was more than just a quaint town.

It was protection, safety.

Unbelievably, now that he was clear of the trees, Kerrigan was startled to notice just how dark the day had grown. The thick black clouds, outlined with a deep green hue, had turned the day almost as dark as the night ever could. The storm filled and dominated the air with it's dark streaks. It were as if the rain were attempting to smother the world it fell upon. The noisy clatter of the rain evolved into a thunderous growl, reducing the poor visibility to a stunted snap shot that showed only the immediate area in front.

The very smell of the air seemed to thicken with the wet, ozone taste of the sky's tears.

Still not quite able to believe the salvation of the seaside village that his eyes showed him, Kerrigan bounded down the increasingly slippery slope towards the settlement. Each step became almost a leap as the gradient helped him cover more distance with the same effort.

The rolling thunder that was the beast behind him became less intense. Risking a second glance over his shoulder, hoping to see that the monster had abandoned it's pursuit, Kerrigan saw that the rolling cloud of dust had indeed become stationary. The dust that surrounded it tumbled out of the point in the woods were he had just exited, and drifting slowly up into the air, defying the rain which punctured through it.

He turned fully now, curiosity having gotten the better of him. He ran a few steps backwards before tripping and splashing clumsily onto his bottom.

He hardly noticed that his ribs did not hurt with the fall.

His pursuer had stopped just out of sight, just behind the last row of silent trees. Once the dust that still rose gently into the cold air had distilled, Kerrigan hoped that he might get a glimpse of what could well have been his final sight upon this world.

The dust continued to tumble out of the wood as if it were actually hot air radiating off the beast's incredibly large hulk. The only sound that remained in the air was the wet pattering of the heavy rain as it struck the soil.

Lightning flashed behind Kerrigan, above the seaside village, illuminating the edge of the wood in a harsh intensity which cast the trees in a startling relief against the black sky. The lightening's dance partner, thunder, followed immediately in it's wake sending a deep grumble across the landscape.

Kerrigan waited.

A stillness descended upon Kerrigan and his surroundings. The rain continued to pour, drenching Kerrigan to his very core, and coating everything else in a flowing sheath, yet the scene towards which Kerrigan observed, at the edge of the forest, remained as still as a tomb.

Finally, a deep hollow sigh escaped from the wood, pushing more dust outwards in two distinct, twin horizontal, columns. What ever was up there, at the edge of the wood, appeared to be deciding whether to pursue further or not. It was reluctant to leave the security the forest provided it with.

Kerrigan willed the beast to emerge. He wanted to put a face to where he could channel his anger, to see it's power, see it's design.

The sigh was followed by a brief, but menacing sounding, growl which was almost as deep as the thunder. The beast sounded frustrated at having lost it's meal, yet knowing it lay just a tantalizingly short distance away.

Kerrigan waited.

What was it so undecided about? Was it perhaps afraid of open spaces? Possibly, but it seemed hard to believe that such a massive creature could be afraid of open spaces - it would have the ability to move it's massive hulk around with much more freedom. Maybe it was afraid of the weather? That made more sense. Lots of animals were afraid of thunder and lightning... weren't they?

Lightning flashed, and thunder boomed again behind Kerrigan. Rain poured from the skies and splashed down onto the earth with such force that the droplets seemed to bounce back up as high as the height from which they fell. The rain water gathered together to flow down the muddy slope on which Kerrigan sat, flowing smoothly over his splayed fingers that were now well embedded in the soggy mud, and tickled around his sodden backside. The rain fell onto Kerrigan and washed down his body in such a strong flow that it verged on becoming a stream. The wind whipped violently around him making his hair lash about his face and his saturated clothes nip into his shivering flesh. His breath came in shallow pants that bloomed a small cloud of moisture before being cast off, away on the cold wind.

The beast that lay within the woods continued it's heavy breathing also, casting out much larger puffs of air, which were, more often than not, accompanied by it's frustrated growl.

Bizarrely, the dust that had rolled around the creature remained. The beast had been stationary for long enough now for the dust cloud to have settled, or blown away on the wind. However it remained, as thick and as impenetrable as ever.

If not for the movement and sensations that surrounded him, time seemed to stand still for Kerrigan as he watched and waited for the creature that had pursued him so aggressively only moments ago, to make it's decision if it would continue it's pursuit out in the open or not.

For what seemed like an absurd length of time, Kerrigan remained seated on the soaked floor of the hillside, watching the entrance, (or the exit – depending on your point of view) of the woods. Kerrigan slowly rose to his feet, convinced that the beast's conflicting animal instincts of wanting to pursue it's prey, and being afraid of the weather, or open spaces, or whatever the hell it might be afraid of, would hold the creature at bay.

Erect once again, he slowly started to walk backwards, down the slope towards the village, still keeping his eyes on where the beast lurked, making sure that it remained in place.

After only a couple of steps, Kerrigan turned his back on the trees, convinced that whatever form the beast may take, it was not going to reveal itself tonight, and so he headed down towards the dark cluster of seaside houses, confident in the knowledge that the beast would not burst from it's sanctuary to pursue him.

He even chuckled lightly to himself at the animal's stupidity. The animal was clearly driven by it's emotions. Had it any kind of intelligence, it would have made a reasonable decision by now and acted upon it.

Well too late, he thought, *I've made the decision for you now. Bye bye din dins.*

There would be no Kerrigan flavoured lunch on the menu for whatever the thing was today.

The town that Kerrigan approached could not possibly be considered large in it's size. It appeared to consist of only a hundred or so buildings of various shapes and sizes, that clustered tightly together at the coast, and fanned and spread outwards to meet the base of the hill down which Kerrigan was currently splashing.

It was clearly a fishing village, and not a particularly busy looking one from the size of it. The buildings, although varying in size, were not what one might consider large.

There was certainly no serviceable port that might accommodate a ship as large as Chimera had been.

Nor did there appear to be any kind of advanced machinery that might be used for the loading or unloading of cargo onto whatever ships, if any, may dock there.

In fact, it hardly looked capable of servicing any vessel larger than the average fishing boat.

The only building of any discernible feature that Kerrigan could see, was what appeared to be a small church or temple a little ways into the start of the village outskirts.

Kerrigan noted the building's appearance, and decided that this may be the best destination to head for upon his arrival. Although he despised churches and all faiths and religions in general, the pathetic Bishop, Father, or whatever the point of contact may be called, would presumably be good natured enough to provide even the most basic needs that Kerrigan needed at this moment in time.

Kerrigan was hardly in any kind of respectable appearance, but the religion of the holy building would no doubt compel it's followers to provide Kerrigan with, despite his appearance, the aid he required that would no doubt be refused elsewhere.

Also, the Father would not ask awkward questions about where he might have came from.

Once he had been fed and bathed, perhaps even had his filthy clothing cleaned, he could leave the church and begin his independence.

There was no one currently out and upon the streets from what he could see. This, no doubt, was a result of the awful weather. Only a few of the houses seemed to show signs of life. A couple of houses had a weak looking glow emitting from some of their windows, but those houses with illumination were certainly in the minority.

A scattering of rocks dashed around the village's outskirts.

With their heavily pregnant bellies of rain, the thick grey, green clouds continued to dominate the sky, easily thwarting even the sun's best attempts at providing light. The sun remained hidden behind the thick clouds shedding only an eerie glow past the murky edges of the dirty clouds.

It prevented Kerrigan from seeing much of the land before him in great detail but on the whole, the village appeared to be isolated and quiet.

This was all for the better. The quieter any settlement was, the easier he could sneak in, take what he wanted and get out without being noticed.

During his time in the wood, he had spent many long hours considering how he should live his new life. He had decided that in the short term, it would be best not to stay too long in any one location in case someone should discover his identity and inform the relative authorities, instead passing through one community to the next like a spirit in the night.

This was assuming that his pursuers had not believed him dead of course, and had not issued orders and mandates informing the community at large of his escape and his demanded recapture.

Perhaps in the months that followed, should he remain free and the initial pressure of his recapture had begun to subside, he might attempt to find some stability… but that would be something for later consideration.

For the immediate future, a simple plan remained his best plan: a proper meal, water, a lot of sneaking around and somewhere he could get his head down for a few hours. By the looks of the sleepy village before him, Kerrigan had no doubts that he, after an encounter with the church, might be able to break into somewhere dry enough to rest up for a day or two, allowing his body and mind to recover from the horrific days they had recently been subjected to.
He briefly realized that he had lost all sense of time and had absolutely no idea how long he had been on the run for.

On the run. The term had an unreal quality to it. He had so far experienced absolutely no signs of pursuit and so he had forgotten that he was, in fact, still a wanted man, on the run.
He approached the outskirts of the village, and began to understand that what he had at first perceived to be rocks, were actually the ruins of previously buildings. As to what had became of these building's, Kerrigan did not know, yet he pondered as to their demise. The misshapen rocks, in various sizes and shapes, hinted that the buildings had been destroyed, rather than de-constructed.
Not that this knowledge affected Kerrigan's current condition in any way.
Passing over and around the larger rocks that had once been the foundations of some long ago destroyed building, Kerrigan approached one of the still erect, outlying buildings.
Upon close inspection, he could still see no signs of life. It's windows remained black and lifeless, like the house's windows were cataract's on it's blind face.
Passing the blind structure, Kerrigan continued his soaked journey towards the church that he had seen earlier. He had attempted to memorize the route that he had needed to take, but the view had been barely discernible in the poor lighting. As he had descended the slope, the visibility had improved, but the angle had become too shallow to determine the exact route he would need to take.
Instead, he took a route that he knew led in the general direction of the church's position. Each turning took him into another thin alley

where the water flowed from the building's rooftops to splash down in the rivers that coursed through the narrow streets. The buildings were built very closely together, giving the buildings an artificial extra height. What little lighting filtered through the green clouds, was reduced further by the building's towering oppressiveness. Kerrigan had a distinct, unsettling impression of claustrophobia, as he moved amongst the buildings. The alley's felt too narrow and the buildings too tall as if the building's themselves might try to crush him before he could pillage the sleepy village of it's generous bounty of food and shelter.
After a few twists and turns, a gap in a couple of buildings emerged, allowing Kerrigan a partial view of the layout of the village.
He turned his eyes towards the horizon.
He hoped to see the church's spire cast in silhouette against the grey, green clouds. It was only when the lightning flashed that he could pin point it's direction, revealing it in profile against the dark clouds.
The lightning flashed, and thunder boomed immediately in it's wake. The nexus of the storm was clearly straight over head. The proximity of the thunder's crash sent a deep vibration humming throughout Kerrigan's skeleton. It started in the very cells of his bone marrow and continued outwards into the softer cells of his muscle tissue and buzzed his nerve endings.
His ear's rung with the vibration caused by the thunder as it's voice echoed on, across the storm.
The vibrations that he felt started off mellow, but instead of fading away with the thunder, they grew in intensity becoming a soft, then heavy, shake.
It was then, as the vibrations became a clearly defined shaking, that a terrible realization came to Kerrigan; the shrouded beast that had followed him to the village had roared at the same time as the lightning had struck. It's voice had merged with that of the thunder's, yet continued on long after the storm's voice had faded away.
It's roar made Kerrigan stop in his tracks. This roar was not like

before, and clearly indicated a different emotion from the frustrated growling that he had heard earlier; this time, it sounded pissed.

REALLY pissed.

Turning to face the roar, Kerrigan could see the outskirts of the forest he had not long since fled, crowning the top of the hill he had only just descended.

The beast that had pursued him with such enthusiasm suddenly burst from the forest in an explosion of trees and vegetation.

The beast, still shrouded in it's rolling cloud of dust and shadow, thundered towards the village. It had finally made it's decision. It was hungry for food, and either the fright of the lightning, or it's continued hunger, or a mixture of them both, had propelled the animal into action.

Previously when Kerrigan had been pursued through the wood, he had not been able to see the animal because of the cloud of destruction that rolled along with it.

Now, out in the open, Kerrigan had hoped to see the beast within, but the beast remained a rolling black blob of smoke. It was as if the cloud of dust and debris that it had created within the woods enveloped it, keeping whatever horror lay within shrouded in mystery as it charged towards the village, too monstrous it was to see.

Kerrigan observed this, yet knew that this could not be the case.

The hill down which he had descended only moments ago, and down which the animal now advanced, was devoid of any vegetation with enough substance that could be destroyed to produce such a thick shroud of smoke.

Yet here it was, rolling towards him, as he stood motionless in the falling rain. It seemed like he had gawked at the impossible for minutes, yet when he snapped back into movement, abandoning his plan of heading towards the village church and instead simply running as deep into the village as he could, he knew that only a second or two had actually passed. Whatever the beast was, it had covered a huge distance in that very short period of time.

He ran as fast as he could. After only taking a few strides, he

heard, and felt, a deep distant crash behind him.
Although the impact was not seen, Kerrigan knew that the noises were caused by the beast already smashing into the most outlying of the village's buildings. Perhaps the house with the cataract eyes.
Without stopping Kerrigan ran, hearing and feeling another violent impact, the end of which was capped with an explosive outburst of rage and frustration as the beast urged for it's prey. For Kerrigan.
Daring to look back, Kerrigan saw a rising cloud of destruction that confirmed his suspicions. What ever it was that had chased him, throughout the woods, down the hillside and now into the peaceful village, had destroyed the outlying buildings as easily as it had destroyed the trees in the forest. It was now continuing it's destructive course towards him, with perhaps more vigour than ever. Clouds of additional debris, caused by the building's destructions, were rising, combining with the beast's own tumbling shadows and coming towards him.
Life was appearing in the wet street. People were emerging from their homes to stare, point and shout at the approaching destruction.
Perhaps the village wasn't as deserted as Kerrigan had first presumed.
Ignoring their presence, and the occasional person who attempted to halt his fleet by asking stupid questions about what was going on, Kerrigan fled as fast as he could towards the only source of sanctuary that he had so far seen.
Towards the church.

He knew that he would not make it. The church had been several streets away when he had last glimpsed it between the buildings, but the beast that was hunting him down was knocking aside the buildings that stood between he and it, with such ease that the buildings may as well have been made from grass as from stone.
It would reach him before he reached the church.
Yet still he ran, in a vain hope that something, anything, might halt the animal's pursuit.
Turning right into a side street, then immediately left, Kerrigan

could see the church in all of it's magnificent glory, rising up into the dark sky. It's majesty seemed to defy the ominously low hanging of the pouring clouds, as if to say that the sky could never dampen it's spirit as it may dampen the clothes of those who were caught beneath it. As if to say that the tears that the clouds dropped may win the battle, but would never win the war. Here would remain a building, proud and dedicated to it's beliefs and nothing could wash away those virtues.
Turning his head once more, behind the dividing row of buildings, Kerrigan could see the rising wave of destruction heading towards him. It had ignored the street down which Kerrigan had crossed and had smashed it's way through the buildings that he had put between it and himself, emerging into same street as Kerrigan.
Knowing that he had no chance to reach any kind of safety, a safety that would no doubt be crushed anyway, Kerrigan planted his feet in the boggy mud of the street, and turned to face the inevitable confrontation.
From his vantage point, he was looking straight down the street that the church he had been heading towards was built upon. The end of the street was obliterated from view as the rolling wave of dust and destruction bore it's way down upon him. It was still impossible to tell just what the hell it was that was chasing him. A boiling, black cloud of liquid shadows was simply rolling towards him, crushing and obliterating everything in it's path. A glimpse of what might have been a hairy piece of black, scaly flesh was occasionally glimpsed amongst the blooming cloud of dust, but it was impossible to tell if this was indeed flesh, or just another shadow, rolling amongst the destruction.
The entire world seemed to shake with it's relentless, destructive momentum. The people who had emerged from the houses were also fleeing away from the approaching death.
A skinny middle aged man dressed in rags that hung limply off his thin body, took a quick glimpse at the oncoming destruction, appeared to utter a curse that Kerrigan could not hear above the thunderous crash of crushed buildings, and turned to run up the street in the direction of the church. He gave Kerrigan a quick

glance, and then a second, quizzical look as he ran past. Fear swam in his wide eyes.
Kerrigan couldn't help but wonder how odd it was that the thin man would take a second glance towards himself, but not towards the mysterious blooming ball of shadows that was currently rolling down his village's streets, destroying buildings as easily as a man might pass through a spider's web.
A young woman with thinning hair, emerged from a building in front of Kerrigan, saw the approaching carnage, and signalled to her child who remained within the house to come to her call. Her hair was so thin despite her apparently young age, that her scalp was clearly visible beneath. A young boy emerged, wearing clothes as shabby as her own. The balding woman briefly hugged the boy to her breast, and then also ran off in the direction of the previous villager, uttering words of comfort to the squealing boy.
Other people were also emerging from their dwellings to view the carnage and were also running past Kerrigan, all in the same direction.
Except for the old man in the rags, no one paid any attention to Kerrigan.
It were as if he were a rock, embedded in a river of flowing, scared people.
"Run man, run" shouted a man who passed by Kerrigan.
Was it possible that they knew something that he didn't? How escape from such a monstrosity could be possible was not readily apparent to Kerrigan. The village itself were being crushed as easily as Kerrigan could crush a beetle underfoot.
He turned to view the man who had shouted at him as he ran past.
In the middle of the street stood a man. Where as all the other villages seemed to be dressed in drab, faded, worn clothing, this man wore a flowing tunic of vibrant colours that stood out in startling contrast to the drab environment that surrounded him. It covered his entire body from neck, to foot. It was a tunic of the boldest reds and deepest blues that seemed oddly familiar as they shone proudly in the dire conditions. Not a single stain, blemish or crease tainted his velvet garb. He was a young man, barely out of

his teens, with a head shaved as smooth as his jaw line.

All of the residents that Kerrigan had seen passing him, including the one who had shouted at him, were now huddled behind this one, young, man. They cowered behind him as if he were made of steel, not flesh and bone, and would block the monstrosity's progress without fail. Collectively, despite their numbers, the crowd looked terribly weak and frail.

The young man stood in the middle of the street looking through, and beyond, Kerrigan towards the approaching madness. His eye's conveyed an intense look of determination, but along with it, an almost equal amount of fear. It was a look that portrayed just how young he was, despite his depiction of leadership. He was still a very young man, not a single line of age creased his firm skin, and, to Kerrigan at least, he was obviously scared of the responsibility and trust that the villagers placed upon him.

Kerrigan was being beckoned. The woman with the thinning hair and scared child was signalling him to approach the cowering group, to get behind the safety promised of the man in the flowing tunic.

With no other choice, Kerrigan ran into, and entered the offered safety of the huddled group.

"You'll be safe with us." shouted the woman over the cacophony of the looming destruction.

The rolling destruction was almost upon them. Only a few more houses blocked the monstrosity's approach, a rolling ball of shadow, dust and destruction.

Whatever it was that the bald man in the vibrant colours was about to do to save them, he had better do it soon.

The monster was now only a few houses away from them yet it's momentum did not slow.

Nearly there.

The world literally shook with it's progress. There was no other sound but the deafening crash of buildings, no other sight but the looming monstrosity.

It would be upon them in seconds.

The crowd around Kerrigan huddled and cowered even closer

together as if bracing for the impact. A collective murmur of accepted misery washed through the group as they accepted their inevitable death.
"HAAAAAAAAAALT!" shouted the bald man in the bright colours. He had raised both of his palms face out towards the beast. His voice seemed oddly loud and clear over the racket, and his voice carried clear over the town's street, hardly – if at all – dampened by the still pouring rain.
Even more bizarrely, the creature obeyed.
It stopped suddenly within throwing distance of the gathered group. The thick cloud of dust that enveloped the mysterious creature rolled forward, travelling harmlessly over the gathered villagers as it was propelled by the momentum it still contained.
The cloud momentarily blocked the villager's vision, as if dusk had descended upon them, many hours too soon. The cloud felt warm to Kerrigan as it swept over him, prickling his soaked skin.
When the dust had faded, Kerrigan expected to finally see the exposed skin and identity of the creature within. However, despite the expulsion of it's camouflage, Kerrigan saw that the creature was still wrapped in a billowing cloud of dirty dust. Despite the ever billowing cloud of shadows, the beast remained motionless in the middle of the street, presumably viewing the tasty villagers with eyes that could not be seen.
Was it possible that this was it's form? That it wasn't wrapped in dust at all, but was instead MADE of dust?
Or was it just some kind of natural defence or camouflage?
Which ever it was, it breathed heavily, shooting thin streams of dust out from itself.
After a breathless moment, the bald man continued, "R-Retreat foul beast." a nervous stutter now broke his speech, "G-g..." again, another swallow, "G-Go back from whence you came!" His voice was now less commanding that the previous halt he had shouted.
The unseen beast continued it's silent, unseen stare.
"Leave now", ordered the bald man. He turned his hands to face upon themselves as if holding an invisible orb in the air.
Impossibly, a dot of red light shone into existence between his

palms. It glowed with a small, but fierce intensity of blinding light. Other dots of light winked into existence around it, and spiralled towards the original glow as if it held it's own gravity.

A small but deep humming filled Kerrigan's head.

The beast, still holding it's distance before the cowering crowd inhaled a deep, almost impossibly long breath, as if it were trying to suck all of the air out of the street and suffocate it's intended prey.

Once it's inhale had finally finished, the air seemed to stand impossibly still and quiet, as if time itself had momentarily frozen.

Kerrigan, having closed his drying eyes involuntarily against the rapid influx of streaming air, cautiously opened his eyes. The rain that fell was hardly noticed as it fell upon his, and his fellow villager's, skin.

After a breathless heartbeat or two, the beast roared. The ground and air shook violently with the force of it's thunderous bellow. A hot wave of air brushed against and through the gathered villagers, making their shabby and dirty clothes flap about their person.

The beast's breath smelt of rotting meat and decay.

Squinting through the eye watering blast, Kerrigan thought he saw, beneath the billowing cloud of dark dust, a mouth. It was a maw of deepest, darkest red, lined with hundreds of needle sharp teeth, each of which was easily the size of a small child and each was a horrible dark, rotten green in colour.

A moist tongue that sharpened to a dull point flapped spasmodically inside.

No sooner had Kerrigan thought that he had saw the sight, did the roar end, and the dust gathered together again, to hide entirely the secret creature it held within once more.

The group that was gathered around Kerrigan whimpered and cried in fear, yet the man in the gown of flowing reds and vibrant blues remained stood where he was. His hands had turned palm outwards again, but this time in a manner of defence, rather than of command.

His head was facing slightly to one side as he instinctively flinched against the breath of the animal's roar.

After a moment, he turned his head once more to face the unseen beast.

He said, "I-I'm warning you!" and once again, he held his hands to face one another so that the small bead of light that had winked into existence before, once more glowed between them, "This is your last chance!"

His voice did not convey the intended threat with much conviction.

There was another brief moment when Kerrigan felt that the beast was watching them all very closely, deliberating and deciding upon it's next move.

This time, the beast began to rise as it inhaled, and the dust that surrounded it seemed to diffuse outwards in all directions, like a smoke filled balloon that had suddenly popped in an open field.

At this movement, the entire of the gathered group flinched at once.

As did the man in the vibrant robes.

With a small start of surprise, as if what was about to happen had shocked him as much as it did Kerrigan, a small ball of flame shot out from between the man's palms to fly towards the beast. The ball of flame was much larger than the mere dot of light it had emerged from.

It shot towards the beast and was swallowed by the dust.

As the beast roared towards the grey/green clouds, Kerrigan understood that this roar was more out of fear, rather than actual pain.

Once more the dirty maw of the animal became hazily visible through the smoke. What may have also been claws poked briefly through the edges of the cloud to disappear as quickly as they were noticed.

This was all for the better, as they had seemed to Kerrigan to be as long, and as thick, as he himself was.

After screaming it's frustrations at the clouds over head, the diffusing dust once more gravitated itself around the animal, turning it once more into a tight rolling cloud of darkness. Without appearing to turn, the cloud made it's way away from the villagers, back towards the hill that led up to the woods from which it had came.

After several silent moments of hope, the gathered crowd who were still shielding their faces behind their trembling hands, slowly began to move from their rigid, foetal position, and accept that the monster had indeed retreated.

The man in the robes was the first to speak. Muttering to his open palms in disbelief he said, "I… did it." Then a moment later he turned to his protectee's, a look of marvellous achievement spread across his smooth face as he declared, "I did it!"

With this comment, the group broke into cheer and launched themselves upon their saviour. Cries of "I knew you could do it!", "I knew you wouldn't let us down", and "GET IN THERE!" were shouted by all. Every last man, woman and child wanted to express their gratitude. They crowded round to thank, pat, congratulate, and shake the hand of the young man.

Kerrigan allowed the villagers to flow around him, becoming lost in the flood of well-wishers. He himself did not wish to pass on any thanks.

Instead, he stood looking at the young man with the bald head, who absorbed and welcomed his praise.

Just what the hell had happened here? What the hell was that thing? Who was that young man?

These, and other questions filled Kerrigan's mind until a sharp blow to the back of his head made his vision a sudden, blinding white and his body dropped to the floor.

Not again, was his last thought before his mind stopped thinking, and was drowned in a wave of unconsciousness.

17

Kerrigan awoke slowly, a little bit at a time. As always, it took him some moments to realize that he was actually conscious again and that he had been for sometime. He tried to remember just how long he had been awake, but he could remember when he had first awoken. The exact moment was a blur that refused to be pinpointed.

He was tied to a chair, that much was apparent. He sat with his head down, his chin resting against his chest and his arms bound tightly at his wrists behind the back of his chair. He gave a tug at the restraints which resulted only in a nasty scrape of tough rope which scratched viciously at his wrists.
The muscles on the back of his neck ached from were his head had hung for so long, resting against his breast bone.
With a monumental effort he never knew he possessed, Kerrigan raised his head which seemed to have grown in size and now seemed to weigh as much as a boulder.
It felt like his head was going to burst as he raised it to survey his surroundings, the pain was so excruciating. But not from the point where he had received the blow that had knocked him out, but from deep within, where a headache rocked every brain cell with a heavy fist.
A weak laugh, barely audible and only expressed through his nostrils, escaped Kerrigan. A faint trace of a smile might have been seen beneath the thick curtain covering his face that his greasy hair created, had anyone been present in the room to see it.
It was amazing how many times he had been knocked unconscious of late. The small laugh was brought about by the understanding that his brain must by now have surely suffered some kind of irreversible damage and that maybe even the slightest knock to the head might put him down and out forever. Yet here he was; alive and, for the most part, well. If he was lucky, maybe an insect might bump into his head sometime soon and make his head pop.
It would be about time.
The first thing that was clear to him, was that he was not in any kind of surroundings similar to which he had previously awoken. He was bound to a chair in the middle of a small, empty room, the walls of which were a dark grey of old stone and a thick layer of dust covered the floor. A rectangular grate, placed at the top of one wall, told Kerrigan that he was being held in a room below street level. A ghostly dark light shone through the window barely removing the darkness that lurked in the corners, awaiting it's time to reclaim the basement.

A closed door was situated at Kerrigan's back.

The air smelt thick and heavy with the tickling dust that floated lazily in the beams that cast through the grate's window.

Noticing that there was no way to escape, Kerrigan hung his heavy head, silencing his protesting neck muscles, and allowed sleep to reclaim him once more. He was simply too tired and hungry to attempt to break free even if he had thought of a plan that he might be able to act upon. Straining at his bonds was simply too tiresome to try, even if he had believed that he had a chance of snapping them.

He didn't try again.

Instead, he waited to see what suffering would happen to him next.

A rattling of keys awoke Kerrigan, startling him out of his sleep. The noise was shortly followed by the ancient creak of an opening door that swelled in volume and pitch. It fell, and was snapped to an end as the door slammed back into it's frame.

Kerrigan, although awake, kept his head down in pretence of sleep and watched through the black bars of his hair as a pair of legs walked calmly around him to stand directly in front of him, toes from the unknown entrant pointed in his direction.

They were female feet... and legs.

For a moment he waited, wondering what would happen next, when a sharp hand smacked him with incredible force on the side of his face, snapping his head violently to one side.

"Don't pretend to be asleep you ugly piece of shit!" barked a female voice.

Leaving his head resting against the shoulder it had fell against, Kerrigan opened his eyes to his captor.

Before him stood a slim woman, not much older than he himself. Her features were as sharp as the blow she had delivered to his face. Her brows were low and her jaw was set with anger.

Her eye's blazed upon him.

At first, Kerrigan thought that it was the anger that she felt that made her eyes shine and shimmer so much in the basement's poor lighting. Although this was true, he then came to realize, that it

was her anger was amplified by the striking bold green, of her irises. The startling, vibrant colour, added extra intensity into the powerful emotions she was already behaving.
Her fists were placed upon her shapely hips that were easily outlined beneath her tight trousers.
A small grey jacket hugged her slender frame, her small breasts protruded gently from her chest.
Including her emerald eyes, the other of her most striking features, so bold against the drab interior of the basement, was her fiery red hair. It capped her skull, pulled so tightly into a pony tail that it tried to raise the scowl she wore.
The thick pony tail had come to rest over her left shoulder. Like her eyes, it seemed to glow and shimmer with an internal light.
Had Kerrigan not been restrained, dehydrated, hungry, dizzy, nauseous, in pain and down right exhausted, he might have considered her attractive.
"You are a fucking cunt and I hate you!" she snapped after their eyes met, and she slapped him sharply.
They were harsh words, and harsh actions, considering he had never met this woman before in his life. As to how she could hate him so passionately - and by the look in her eyes, Kerrigan could not possibly doubt her sincerity - he had no idea.
No chance of romance then.
She leaned forward placing her hands on her knee caps, "I wish I could kill you myself." and she spat upon his face.
With this done, she then began to pace around his chair, her eyes never leaving Kerrigan as she strode, her breath coming in sharp shallow intakes through her flared nostrils.

Completing her circuit, she stopped, placed her hands on her knees again, and said, "I really hope you die slowly you mother fucking arsehole."
Once more, her furious intensity could not be denied. Every word was spoken with a sneer, with an undeniable disgust, that was not even attempted to be restrained.
Again Kerrigan wondered just how this woman could hate him so

much, so completely. Surely it must be a case of mistaken identity. He had had no form of communication or relationship with anyone other than his fellow shipmates aboard Chimera... guards included, for the many, many forgotten years he had been imprisoned. There was no way this woman could possibly know who he, Kerrigan, was. Anyone from the mainland wishing to visit inmates aboard Chimera was simply not allowed.

So how could this woman know him to hate him so?

She screamed in frustration and raised her fists in the air. "Is that all you can do you bastard? Sit there and not say a fucking word!! GOD!" The last word's vowel began a growl in her throat as she shouted it, making the word sound more like Gaaawd!

She glared at him again one more. "Say something you fucking cunt!" her voice finally broke and she slapped him once more across the face.

Panting, she stood looking down at Kerrigan's defenceless form, his dirty hair covering his face completely now.

He did not move and did not speak, his chest barely rising and falling with each breathe.

Her frustration rose as Kerrigan refused to react to her words or blows.

She screamed, "FUCKING SAY SOMETHING!" her voice breaking into a higher decibel at the end of the command.

Once more there was a brief, almost palpable, silence. Then, quietly, almost inaudible compared to the ginger haired woman's barrage, Kerrigan said, "Listen lady, I don't know who you are..." the sentence was intoned so that she knew there was more to come and not to interrupt. He took a shallow gasp, "...but your clearly fucked up." he concluded.

Kerrigan had expected, and perhaps even hoped, that the woman would loose what little self control she still had upon hearing this declaration. Instead, she let out a short maniacal laugh.

There was no humour behind it.

"What!?" she was still half laughing. A bemused, crazy smile filled her features, "So you *can* talk huh? Well Mr Kerrigan, your not as stupid as you look, I'll give you that. Your right on both accounts; you don't know me, in fact you've probably never seen me before in your miserable, little life... and I most certainly *am* fucked up..." Her body language had become as erratic as her smile. She raised her arms in the air and spun gently with her success at making Kerrigan talk, and when she referred to either Kerrigan or herself, she pointed at each of them with an accusing finger or thumb.

Her expression changed as rapidly as the wind might change direction, from a maniacal smile back to the filthy leer of her previous anger.

She leaned on her knees once more, "...Right-mother-fucking-royally-fucked-up" she growled. She grabbed the arm rests of Kerrigan's chair and brought her face to within touching distance of Kerrigan's own, "Don't give me any more of your smart arse remarks you fucking prick," she snarled. Her spittle flecked Kerrigan's face, "you know what the fuck you did and now, your gonna pay!"

She withdrew from Kerrigan and began to pace backwards and forwards in front of him, like how a predator might eye up it's prey before an attack.

Groggy and dizzy from hunger and exhaustion, Kerrigan could not find the strength to muster the anger he knew he should be feeling at this point. The woman was clearly crazy and had absolutely no right to restrain him, and accuse him of things he had no idea what she was referring to.

"Tell me one thing before..." she didn't complete the sentence, took a short breath to compose herself, and continued, "just one...fucking...thing". Her voice quivered and she waved her finger maddeningly at him, as if he didn't know how many the number one was, "Considering you've taken so much from me... from us all," she raised her arms so that she became the same shape as the letter Y. She did a twirl of the room, "how the fuck did you get out alive? You must be one lucky son of a bitch that's all I can say."

Without meeting her green eyes, Kerrigan said, "What the fuck is your problem lady?"

As soon as he said it, she darted towards him and grabbed hold of his jacket's lapels. Her fingers nipped into his flesh underneath, and she pulled his face up to meet hers.

"I'll tell you what the fuck my problem is you mother fucking piece of shit!" her anger once more causing her voice to crack with strain. Spittle speckled Kerrigan's face once more, "You killed my fucking brother you arsehole and now I want answers!"

Had Kerrigan's senses been completely focused, he would have head butted her square in the face at the first opportunity. It would not have necessarily have helped him to escape, but it would have certainly made him feel a lot better to feel her teeth snap backwards beneath her delicate soft lips, inside her pretty little mouth, spraying blood onto his face.

Unfortunately, Kerrigan's mind was still muddled and by the time he saw his opportunity, she released him from her grip with a shove that nearly sent him toppling over backwards.

His chair rocked back into stability.

"Listen," he replied slowly, each word being delivered as if his vocal chords were made from grinding gravel, "I have no idea who you are or who the fuck your brother is. So why don't you just let me go, huh?"

"STOP FUCKING LYING!" she brought her fists down in an arc to propel her shout away from her small frame. Her eye's shone with fresh tears ready to spill and flow down her cheeks, ready to catch up with the others that had gone before.

Her anger was turning to hysteria, "What the fuck do you think I am, thick or something? Or is it you? Are you fucking thick? Maybe I hit you too hard on the back of the head and it's muddled up your mind?" she stabbed at her temple with her forefinger, "No, I can't believe a someone so thick could have killed my brother. Or have you killed so many that you can't remember one from the next, you sick freak?" Her hands had turned into fists once more, which she flung about her person in direct relation with her increasing anger, "Let me jog your memory, arsehole. Ames??? Remember Ames? Ames, the Chosen One of this God-forsaken-hellhole? You remember him right? Short, bald with a crescent

moon mark behind his left ear. Remember him dickhead, remember?"
The brief description did sound familiar.
He grasped at his memory, willing the nag in his mind to present itself. He knew that he should know this, that he DID know it, but he couldn't quite hold onto the knowledge as it flirted in his recollections....
It took a moment.
"Yeah I remember him...", a small smile broke out on Kerrigan's dirty face. He remembered the man on the opposite side of the glassed wall who was in the cell that was adjacent to Kerrigan's own when he had been brutally interrogated many days ago. He, Ames, had also been subjected to an electrical torture at the hands of Durrant and his men. He had personally seen him writhing in pain.
But now, this distressed woman clearly believed that he had somehow been the cause of her brother's death.
Obviously she was mistaken, but how she had came by such a conclusion remained a mystery to Kerrigan.
"Oh you fucking shit!" screamed Ames's sister, seeing the smile as a look of fond nostalgia.
"...but I didn't kill him."
"Yeah? well whatever you say you fucking coward. I KNOW you killed him."
"Really?" Bizarrely, despite the danger he was obviously in at the mercy of this psychotic woman, Kerrigan felt exhausted by the conversation. He actually couldn't be bothered to argue with her. All he wanted to do was to tell her to fuck off and go back to sleep. Obviously this would do him no good, and so the survival instinct within him prevailed, "And how do you know I killed him?"
"For fuck's sake!" she raised her arms in exaggerated disbelief, "Did you really think you'd get away with it? There's fucking Wanted sign's all over town with your face on it. Of course it was you!"
So, despite his earlier optimism of being presumed dead, he was indeed wanted by the authorities. Obviously who ever it was who

had captured him, and this woman's brother, Ames, had made no risky presumptions in assuming his death. If he were to be recaptured it would be the death sentence for sure because although he had not killed Ames himself, as was claimed, he had killed a lot of other people upon his escape.

"Listen, the men who want me captured are the same ones who killed your brother. Not me."

"Oh fuck off" she replied horrified, "Can't you come up with something better than that? You killed my brother, and now your gonna die too. I'd do it now, but I owe it to the Gods to do this the right way."

"Fine. But the last time I saw your brother, he was still alive. Maybe he still is. But if they're doing to him what they did to me, I doubt he will be for much longer." He remembered how he had wanted to die rather than be subjected to anymore of the electricity that had flowed through his body. If Ames had co-operated however, perhaps there was a chance that he was still alive.

"Fuck you, you prick. He's as dead as you will be in the next couple of hours and YOU killed him. I'm gonna enjoy watching you die."

"Whatever." He replied nonchalantly. An idea had occurred to him that just might get him out of this hopeless situation, "But maybe I'm telling the truth. I broke out of where ever he is… I could get back in there… help you find him."

HA!, thought Kerrigan, *like fuck will I. Fucker's gotta be dead even if it is the same person we're talking about. Stupid ginger bitch might just be dumb enough to fall for it though…*

"You think I'm gonna fall for that?" she raised her arms questioningly, turned, and walked away, "Come on…" she uttered.

"Are you willing to take that risk?"

For the first time in their conversation, there was a moment's hesitation on her part. Her pacing stopped briefly and she turned to face him.

"Why should I trust you?"

"Because whoever it is that want me are the same people torturing your brother. If he's not dead, he soon will be. Can you live with the guilt of knowing you could have saved your brother's life but didn't?"

It was a cheap attack and Kerrigan knew it. Not that he cared. He'd do whatever it took to get himself out of this situation.

"Tortured?" she repeated, momentarily the constant anger she had displayed faltered. "Let me get this straight," replied the female captor before him, "your saying that if I set you free, you'll take me to my brother?"

He looked her straight in the eye, those vibrant, emerald eyes, and replied, "You have my word."

She didn't move. Nor did he. Their eyes remained locked. She chewed upon her bottom lip as she weighed up her options.

Suddenly, her decision clearly made, she darted towards Kerrigan, and once more took two fistfuls of his leather jacket, "If your fucking lying to me you piece of shit, I'll fucking kill you myself, quicker than a sick bastard like you would fuck his own mother, reward or not, religion or not." She shook him as best as she could, which was surprisingly strong despite her petite frame, "You understand me?"

He met her torrent of abuse without flinching. Taking a moment to reply to show her that she had not startled him into a sudden agreement, he said, "Sure."

She let go of his lapels and went behind his chair. A moment later, the harsh bonding that had bound his wrists together suddenly relented, and his restraints fell to the floor with a wet flop like a dead snake, cut rather than untied. As to where the cutting implement had came from, remained a mystery, but it had returned to the ether as quickly and as smoothly as it's appearance and use.

Deep red rivulets criss-crossed Kerrigan's wrists from where his bonds had been so securely fastened. He rubbed at them a moment and flexed his wrists to loosen the stiffness that had seeped within. A warm tingling sensation filled his fingers as the blood rushed back into them.

"OK dickhead don't get any smart ideas. Let's get some provisions together and then we're outta here." Declared the red haired woman as she returned from behind him to face Kerrigan once more.

Taking immediate advantage of his freedom, Kerrigan charged his captor and pinned her against the wall, his right forearm pressed against her throat, his left pinning her right arm to the wall above her head. A few strands of auburn hair came loose and hung gently over her startled face.

"OK bitch, listen up. I don't fucking take orders from anyone, least of all a stuck up bitch like you", the sharp exhales of breath from either of them, caused her hair to flutter about her face as Kerrigan spoke, "Now *your* gonna answer *me* a few questions, and if you answer honestly, I might decide to kill you quickly. Now, where am I?"

He released the pressure on her wind pipe slightly so that she could answer him.

"I wouldn't do that if I were you" she rasped beneath his arm. Her eyes fluttered downwards.

Following her gaze Kerrigan saw that her left hand was wielding the dagger that must have been used to cut his restraints so easily only moments ago. Once more it had been conjured from no where, the tip of which was now pressed against Kerrigan's stomach.

She twisted it slowly to show her intent, and Kerrigan could almost feel it puncture his flesh.

"Now," she rasped slowly, "Let ME go, and I might let YOU live."

After considering his options, Kerrigan very slowly backed away from the red head until he was out of lunging distance from the blade. He then turned his back on her and headed towards the only exit out of the room.

"And where the fuck do you think your going?" she shouted.

"Anywhere away from you." He did not stop his advance toward the door.

"Oh yeah? Well good fucking luck. In case you didn't know, there are a hundred different posters and signs with your face on it scattered all over this town. Every last man, woman and child is out there searching for you! How long do you think it'll take to report you here? If they haven't already? There's nowhere you can hide."

He stopped, thinking about his options.

"Listen," her voice had returned from a shout to a more civilised volume of normality. "We can help each other."

Keeping his back to her, Kerrigan replied "I don't need your help."

"Oh no? and where do you plan on going? I've told you everyone in town is out there looking for you, and you clearly don't know your way around this town. Also, you look like the shit you are... how far do you plan on getting by without food and water?"

"I've survived so far."

"Yeah? but for how much longer? There ain't nothing around here but woods on all sides. You think you can survive in your condition with that... THING out there hunting you down?" She was referring to the monster beneath the smoke.

He did not reply.

"Look," she continued. She took a few steps towards Kerrigan's back that faced her, "I can help you, I can keep you hidden. All you have to do is take me to my brother. What do ya say?"

He thought it over. If what she was saying about him being a wanted man, and the volume of interest in him were true, then he had no chance of surviving within the town itself. His only option would be to leave the town and venture forth into the woods with that THING, what ever it was, still out there. Combined with his weakened physique from a diet of raw meat and vomit, he did not stand much chance of any prolonged quality life.

But to return to the lion's den, back to the building he had escaped from... There would be armed guards; security would be certain to have been increased. He'd also have the burden of this deranged woman tagging along with him, placing them at further risk of exposure. Surely that option would be suicide just as much as the others.

Every choice he had, seemed to ultimately result in death.

Without much further thought, Kerrigan made his decision. If he was going to have to die, at least he might cause some shit along the way. Maybe even get a few questions answered along the way too.

"Last time I saw your brother, he was being tortured. Chances are he's dead."

"But maybe not!", she replied, a pleading to her voice, "Like you said, I couldn't live with myself if there was a chance I could save him and I didn't take it."

Still thinking it through, Kerrigan replied, "No. I don't owe you anything."

"Then at least tell me where he is!"

Kerrigan sighed deeply. He was too weary to put up any kind of resistance. All he wanted was sleep, peace, "Beyond the woods. There's a tall prison or factory of some kind…"

"The S.O. Refinery?? What the hell was he doing there?"

"I don't know the answer to either of those questions" he replied, "But that's where he is."

"Wait…. wait…" she patted her palms against the air in front of her, pushing back the answers Kerrigan was providing her with, "This is unbelievable." She paced the room a moment as she processed the information she had been provided with. "I used to work there a little while ago… I cannot believe they would do such a thing…" yet her vocal tone implied that maybe she *did* believe they would do such a thing as if she were questioning her own beliefs.

Her pacing stopped. She turned to Kerrigan, her decision made, "If you take me there, if you help me find my brother, I can remove the warrant on your head. I don't know what you did, and frankly I don't want to know, but I can make you a free man. You'll not have to keep looking over your shoulder everywhere you go."

It was a tempting offer…

"No. It's too risky." He started towards the door again.

"No! you can't leave!" Her voice was rising once more with desperation.

Behind him, Kerrigan heard her feet scraping across the dusty floor as she darted towards him. He turned and before she knew what had happened, Kerrigan had hold of her by the throat. Her knife had materialised once again. This time Kerrigan had been expecting it and he knocked it from her grasp with a sharp blow to

her wrist, sending the knife tumbling across the floor with a clatter of metallic pangs.
He drew her face towards his so that their faces were nearly touching. His fingers crushed tightly into her throat.
"I said …no" he growled and gripped even harder.
She clawed at his iron grip, her finger nails digging deep grooves into his steely hand. Her head started to turn a hot red as the blood that pumped into it could not find passage to return to her thudding heart. She could feel her head pulsing, inflating with each gush of warm blood. A headache begun instantly and her vision became filled with a scattering of dancing, flashing lights. All too soon, the lights began to fade and her vision began to fade into a numbing, milky white. Her shocking green eyes swelled out from their sockets, as if they wanted to escape from their pretty home before the pop that threatened to burst her head at any moment.
Kerrigan stared into her wide green eyes, watching, studying, observing as the life faded from her.
Her wide, pitying green eyes…
Suddenly disgusted by her, Kerrigan released his grip and flung the nearly unconscious red head's body sprawling into the corner of the room.
Before turning and leaving, he stared at her limp body a moment to make sure she would not rise any time soon and raise an alarm.
She panted lightly and moaned almost soundlessly.
She would not be in any fit shape to cause him any trouble any time soon.
He turned his back upon his captive, and exited through the basement's wooden door.

Upon leaving the confines of the basement, Kerrigan found himself in a small kitchen of sparse furnishings. There was only one small window that barely provided enough light to illuminate the interior. The filthy window shimmered with the pour of the rain that cascaded down it's exterior, making the light that entered the room ebb and flow.
A small wooden door that led to the storm outside was upon one

wall, and a door that led to further interior rooms was upon another.

A small stove, and basic cupboards were the only furnishings of note. The oven was made of a dark, thick heavy duty metal that had obviously seen many hours of intense heat. A thick pipe issued from it's back which bent into the wall it climbed, through, and onto the exterior wall of the property.

The floor, much like the basement, was covered in a fine layer of silt that sparkled in the dingy light that filtered through the dirty, shimmering window, as if the floor itself were actually covered in a delicate layer of thin ice.

The cupboards were made of a wood which was not polished or protected in any way from the elements. The corners were softened and decaying from over exposure to the damp.

Opening the nearest cupboard, Kerrigan was pleased to discover a selection of cooked meats which lay atop one another in an organised pile.

He grabbed the top layer and consumed it with ravenous relish. It's salty taste made his mouth water all the more, and drool drizzled down his chin as he consumed the delicious meat.

After eating another slice, his mind and taste buds turned to the inclination of liquid.

After opening another few cupboards, which contained nothing more appetising than an assortment of kitchen utensils, Kerrigan chanced upon a cupboard filled with crudely corked bottles.

Removing the corks, and smelling the odourless contents, Kerrigan took a tentative swig and was pleased to have discovered freshly bottled water.

He drained nearly all of a bottle in one go, until his stomach ached with consumption.

He wiped his lips and burped a salty burp in satisfaction.

Checking through the remaining unexamined cupboards, Kerrigan found and took, a long sharp knife, presumably used for the slicing and preparing of the meats he had discovered.

He took the knife and slipped it in his trousers waist band. His unkempt shirt kept the handle hidden from view.

Scanning the rest of the barren room, Kerrigan determined that little else could be gained from further investigation. Besides, the little bitch that he had nearly killed might begin screaming for help at any minute. He did not intend to be around when this happened. With a satisfied stomach and the stolen knife safely secured in his waist band, Kerrigan opened the door that led onto the street, and slipped silently out into the pouring rain.

Upon exiting the house, Kerrigan became immediately annoyed at the rain. It had not stopped since he entered the sea side village, and showed no signs of stopping or relenting. The sky was covered in a thick blanket of grey green clouds that remained as condensed and as full of water as they had been previously.
It was not long before Kerrigan's clothes were completely saturated once more.
Thankfully, the streets appeared to be deserted.
He had no idea as to where he might head. He was alone in a town that apparently wanted him dead, or at the very least, captured. The town was also, if the crazy red head was to be believed, surrounded by woodland on the three sides that did not meet the sea.
The only course of action that he could foresee was to head towards the church as he had previously decided upon. There at least, he might find shelter and rest until his mind was rested enough to think of a more productive course of action, and whoever ran the place would surely honour their fellow man rather than betray them.
Unfortunately, Kerrigan could not see the church's spire as he had before and so he had no idea in which direction he might head.
Looking up and down the street upon which he stood, neither direction offered a guaranteed success. To his right, the street seemed to stretch onwards, vanishing into the thick, grey gloom cast by the pouring rain. To his left however, he could see the looming dark outline of a hill that was topped with what must have been a crown of woodland. The diminished light that filtered through the heavy clouds made it impossible to be certain for sure.

Accepting what he thought he saw, Kerrigan instead turned to his right and hoped to vanish, unnoticed into the gloom.

The street flowed with a steady stream of muddy rain water. The ground beneath this was not paved. Instead, the street was entirely made of mud that might have been tough enough and firm enough to withstand the bustling villager's travels in finer weather.
In the torrent of rain that fell however, the muddy street became a sticky sludge that threatened to suck Kerrigan's boots off his feet with each cumbersome stride.
It took a matter of minutes before Kerrigan understood that he was concentrating more on looking at his feet, rather than looking to where he might be heading.
Not quite able to accept his luck, Kerrigan raised his head in time to see the spire of the church, to which he had originally been heading, poke briefly through a gap between two houses.
Increasing his pace and stride and walking with exaggerated steps to try and reduce the number of instances where by he had to pull his foot free from the bog that was formally a street, Kerrigan headed in the direction of where he might find refuge.

Kerrigan hated churches.
He hated everything they stood for and represented.
A church was built to worship and honour a God. Different religions had different beliefs, rules, traditions… but they all worshipped a God, or Gods in some cases.
Each religion's God's name was as varied as the traditions that the faiths themselves chose to follow, but ultimately it was the one thing that all faiths had in common: a higher being, or beings, who they dedicated their love to.
The buildings where believers worshipped their individual Gods, also went by a myriad of different names. Churches, Temples, Holy Houses…
What ever the God's name, and what ever the sanctuary where follower's prayed to their Gods, it all boiled down to the same thing.

Worship.
It sickened him.
To worship a God, or Gods, that offered no empirical evidence as to their own supposed existence was a notion that baffled Kerrigan. People spent their entire lives worshipping and dedicating their existence, to some thing that may or may not even exist.
Often, these worshippers had suffered terrible experiences in their lives, experiences that would lead any rational person to question why an omnipotent, benevolent God might allow such cruelties, such heartache, to befall them. Some people were STILL suffering, yet they believed. And did their God, to which these sufferers dedicated their lives to, give them a helping hand to help them cope with their suffering? Or even offer so little as a few words of comfort to help them along in return for their YEARS of selfless devotion?
No. They didn't.
Sure, some of these believers said that their devotion would be rewarded to them AFTER they had died, in some kind of better afterlife. Fine. But how did they know this to be true? Hell, how COULD they know? What possible reason did they have for believing, and accepting, this idea so unconditionally? Had anyone ever returned from these supposed paradises to affirm their existence upon the masses. No, of course they hadn't.
It was absurd.
Dedicating your entire life to an idea.
He scoffed at his own ruminations. He seemed to be inadvertently enraging himself with his mental tirade.
To Kerrigan, anyone who believed in a God, or followed any religious beliefs, was a fucking arsehole.
A FUCKING arsehole.
You get one life, and only one life, so what was the point in possibly wasting it on some ridiculous idea or notion?? These believers must be so pissed off when they died and discovered that they had totally wasted their entire lives on some stupid notion of an after life... That's if they were able to be pissed off because, after all, there was no after life to be pissed off in.

Arseholes.
Stupid fucking arseholes.
In a deep, primal way that went to the very core of his being, Kerrigan found religions to be more than foolish, he found them to be disgusting.
Yet they had their uses. In their preached compassion, most religions were compelled to help those in need. Especially in times of crisis.
And there was no one in more of a need of help, than Kerrigan.
Surely whoever resided at the church must help him. Their God and beliefs TOLD THEM to help needy people out.
And this is why Kerrigan headed towards the church that he hated upon sight. Despite the dire weather conditions, his dirty wet clothes, his weakened body and his self created disgust, he headed there with a smile on his face.
Arseholes.

The road down which Kerrigan splashed was as depressing as any that could be imagined.
The road was nothing more that a slowly running river of mud and sludge that absorbed Kerrigan's feet with a glutinous consumption.
The walls of the buildings that contained the street were of a dark grey granite that was crumbling apart from erosion at every edge and corner. Algae grew and spread across the walls giving the buildings an organic skin, as if they were hulking beasts, curled up for warmth amongst one another waiting for the bad weather to pass.
Above all, the oppressive grey clouds, with their eerier green outline, blotted out the sun and drenched the town with their ceaseless downpour of rain.
As Kerrigan headed in the direction of the church, one building's wall in particular caught his interest.
The wall was large and flat and covering most of it, was what appeared to be a newly appointed decoration. He knew it was a recent addition to the decorum as if it had been on this wall for any prolonged period, it's corner's and edges would have peeled and

softened under the pummelling of the rain.
Instead, the decoration was in perfect condition, all corner's and edges firmly attached to the rough wall.
The image upon the decoration stared back at Kerrigan with a dark scowl.
It took a moment for him to realise what it was that he was seeing, and his hunched stride through the pouring rain came to a steady stop as he stood to stare at the image that stared back at him.
What Kerrigan saw, was an image of himself printed upon a square poster that stood at least three times as tall as he did.
His head and shoulders loomed over him. His chin length black hair, his half goatee that covered just his chin and his blood red leather jacket, towered above him in sharp definition.
It was an image that must have been taken when he was first imprisoned upon Chimera; his expression was of fierce rebellion and revolt as he stared directly back at the camera that had snapped his image, forever capturing his frown.
Above Kerrigan's image, the word "HEATHEN" was declared, printed in bold white lettering.
Directly below this, in writing not so large or bold, were the words "Wanted for the murder of Father Ames Tellingos, Chosen One, Trendid."
Kerrigan pondered at the phrase "Chosen One". The crazy red head had used the same term earlier but he had been too dazed to dwell upon what the title might mean. Now, having encountered it for a second time, Kerrigan wondered what it meant. He had never heard the term until recently, but the phrasing held religious connotations leading him to believe that this must be the term used to describe the Father, the leader, of this town's church.
So, apparently, he had killed Trendid's religious leader, the red head's brother.
It came as no surprise that such a large campaign would be orchestrated for his capture. In his opinion, religion was held in too high a regard, religious belief being one of the few things that bound communities together. Even aboard Chimera, the prisoners were forced into masses to pray to their Gods and to beg

forgiveness for their crimes in either this life or the next.

Despite his scepticism, Kerrigan had been forced to attend these masses also but refused to join in the collective prayers that the guards and prisoners alike conducted with such passion, often mouthing along to the prayers to keep the guards attention off himself, yet feeling thoroughly stupid throughout.

On the poster, below his twenty foot tall face, was a figure of money that would allow even the poorest of families, along with several generations of grand children, to live out their lives in lavish comfort.

Below the money were conditions that the reward money would only be paid for his safe return.

Alive.

Well that was something at least.

A logo of some sort was positioned in the lower right corner of the bill which Kerrigan assumed to be the image of whoever it was that wanted him returned so badly. It looked like the letter E constructed entirely of straight lines followed by the letter O with the bottom chopped off ... Whoever they were.

So the red head had not been lying. Although the poster branded him a "HEATHEN" and not a "MURDERER" as she had accused him, the intention of the poster remained clear.

Kerrigan, was a Wanted Man.

He stood there transfixed by the image of his own face, blown up to multiple times it's actual dimensions. Everyone in the village must have seen this. The reward money would have gotten people's mouths talking quicker than any other incentive, and those that had not seen the poster would soon come to view the advertisement, forever branding his image into their retinas.

Every man, woman, and child would be looking for him with a promise of such wealth.

The enormity of his own infamy slowly seeped into Kerrigan's exhausted mind.

As Kerrigan stared at his Wanted poster, he slowly became aware of a sound hidden beneath the noisy splash of the rain.

At first, the noise remained subtle, barely audible at all, but as it grew in volume Kerrigan realised that he had unconsciously been hearing the noise for some time.

Like the noise of the rain, this secondary noise was also a permanent din that seemed to rise and fall as the wind pushed it to and from his ears.

As such, he was unable to determine exactly what the noise was, however it appeared to becoming from an alley further up the street. The sound, impossible to pinpoint in the thrashing of the wild rain, could be emanating from around the next turn.

He approached the turning in the road, keeping his back hugged against the wall.

Suddenly, just at the new road that intersected Kerrigan's loomed upon him, voices became clear within the dull noise he had been hearing.

The noise was a crowd. Somewhere nearby, there was a whole host of people.

For one horrible moment, he imagined a horde of angry villagers waving flaming torches and sharp farming equipment in the air, demanding he hand himself over to them.

However, the din did not sound menacing or threatening in any way. The crowd's noise consisted of the up beat sounds of rhythmic clapping, cheering, laughing, singing and general upbeat conversations.

Under different circumstances, hearing the party above the rain, the sound might have been inviting.

For Kerrigan however, having just appreciated the gravity of his own jeopardy, the origin of the ruckus was to be avoided at all costs.

Approaching the corner of the building that stood on the junction of the two streets, Kerrigan stole a glance around the corner.

Through the shaking haze of the rain, Kerrigan saw yet another street much like his own. Grey granite walls on both sides kept the flowing road trapped in a straight line.

Unlike his own flowing alley however, there glowed a small patch of light. This light originated from the interior of a building only one down from the corner structure at which Kerrigan was currently hiding.

No sign hung from the exterior of the building to signify it's purpose, but what Kerrigan observed was the welcoming glow of a pub that spilling out onto the liquid street.

He withdrew his head, and considered his options.

He could have turned around and attempted to find a different street to follow in order to reach his goal, but he had not passed any other streets that might cut across, and lead him to a road parallel to his own. No doubt such a crossing would exist, yet he would have to travel in completely the opposite direction, away from the church, and risk encountering random people who might be foolish enough to be out for a stroll in the abysmal weather.

The road ahead still looked clear.

Risking what he knew over the dangers of the unknown, Kerrigan raised the collars on his leather jacket, and hunched his shoulders in an effort to hide his profile from those who may see him as he quickly crossed the intersecting street, and continued on his way.

Even if he was observed, he hoped he would look like he was simply huddling up from the rain.

No sooner had Kerrigan taken a couple of steps into the open, did he hear the drunken singing of a couple of nearby males.

Peeking to his left, around his collar, Kerrigan was alarmed to see how close these intoxicated men were to himself. They must have left the pub as soon as he had finished observing the alley.

The two men had their arms about each other's shoulders, and each held aloft a glass of liquid which was rapidly being refilled and diluted from the heavens. They were singing, yet what they were singing about remained a mystery as their drunken slurring was drowned and washed away by the pouring rain.

A myriad of sores pocked both their faces.

Despite their drunkenness, one of the men noticed Kerrigan and immediately stopped his good natured, yet off key duet, to shout, "Hey, hey, hey" he pointed his watery glass at Kerrigan, "… why ya not joinin' in the cele'bray'shun man?"

Kerrigan did not reply, stop or look in the drunkard's direction. Why the fuck did this drunken idiot have to talk to him????? It was best to simply continue, and vanish from view. In his delicate predicament, social etiquette was not a priority.

Remaining hidden, however, was.

"OI!" shouted the drunkard, clearly annoyed at being ignored, "Don't fuckin' ignore me!"

"Yeah" slurred his drunken friend who was leaning ungainly on the first drunk's shoulders. Had he not had his friend there to support him, he would have fell to the ground and possibly drowned in the street, his lungs filled with thick, flowing mud.

Refusing to slow down for the two bothersome men who had now turned the corner to enter in the same street as himself, Kerrigan hoped for another street to appear off his own so that he might turn down it and escape the shouting and gaze of the two men.

Why the fuck are these guys taking such an interest in me?

They were obviously drunk, surely they couldn't have recognised him? Didn't they have better things to do? Like return to their "cele'bray'shun"? Or was it just the alcohol that made them become annoying, pesky little fuckers?

"EE looksss like that fuckin' 'ethen guy!" laughed the second man, his words barely discernible from the liquor, induced giggle that coated the words, as if he had just cracked the world's funniest joke.

Kerrigan's heart quickened as he heard these words.

Oh ha fucking ha!

"Yeaeeah..." said the first - Offended At Being Ignored - drunk. He said the syllable with unnatural length as his drunken mind struggled to recall the image of the valuable refugee. Where as drunk who had made the comment, clearly thought he was being amusing, his companion was giving it serious consideration. "Ee does doesn't ee?"

Unfortunately for Kerrigan, luck graced the drunks at this point. Offended At Being Ignored looked to his right and saw a twenty foot tall replica of Kerrigan staring down at him.

He looked at the back of the rapidly retreating Kerrigan, his bright red jacket shimmering in the rain.

A look back at the poster, with the larger than life red coat.

Kerrigan with his chin length black hair, plastered to his scalp.
Kerrigan with ten foot long, chin length hair…
"Fuuuuck" whispered the insulted man, his soaked mind slowly absorbing the truth, his words inaudible even to Kerrigan as he escaped through the rain.

Behind him, Kerrigan heard the words that he hoped he had avoided.
The loudest of the two men shouted, "It's 'im! It's the fookin' HEATHEN!".
His partner in crime still held onto his shoulder for fear of falling down. He seemed disappointed that his drinking buddy had put an end to their drunken fun.
The first man's shouts continued on in this urgent manner, bringing to the attention of the inn's occupants Kerrigan's presence in their town.
Snapping another look over his shoulder, Kerrigan could hardly believe the speed that further attention was being brought to the situation. Already two extra people were in the street. They looked at the two drunks with desperate hope who pointed their wobbly arms at Kerrigan's back.
With only a moment's wide eyed comprehension, the two new arrivals, clearly more sober then their friends as they stood rigid in the rain, shouted their affirmation of the drunk's claim bringing even more unwanted attention to Kerrigan.
The image of rioting villager's with burning stakes dashed across Kerrigan's mind again.
Not waiting around to watch the growing mass of people, Kerrigan ran.

Splashing through the running stream that was once a street, Kerrigan headed away from the pursuing crowd as fast as he could. His feet seemed to want to slow him down; the weight of the rain water that had collected in his boots, and soaked into his trousers, made his leg's feel as solid and inflexible as heavy iron bars.
Without looking where it may lead, Kerrigan turned into the first

street he encountered coming to the conclusion that he would not be able to out run his pursuers. He was at a major disadvantage of being totally disorientated in unfamiliar territory, and immensely weak from days of poor nutrition and sleeping rough.
Somehow, he would have to try and lose them instead.
In the street he had left, he could hear the voices of those who had collected behind him, egging one another to increase their pace, to attract more numbers to their group and, most of all, not to let him get away again.
Turning right at the nearest exit of his current street, he broke into a sprint, knowing that he was now out of sight of those that followed him and his rapid escape could not be seen to be falsely interpreted as a sign of guilt. He took the next left, followed by an immediate right, left, another left and so on until he felt even more lost than he had previously.
Taking the next right turn, he was startled into stopping as he ran straight into a group of angry looking villagers not twenty feet in front of him. Their faces turned from frowns to surprise as their prey found them, instead of the other way around.
The wide eyed, slack jawed looks did not remain for long, and they soon found their feet and voices, to continue their pursuit.
Turning one hundred and eighty degrees, Kerrigan bolted in the opposite direction of the villagers. He did not risk returning into the alley he had just so recently left, just in-case his pursuers had somehow managed to follow him throughout his twisting and turning escape.
No sooner had he returned to full sprint when Kerrigan noticed another group directly in front of him.
Somehow another group had been fortunate enough to chance upon him also.
With villagers closing in on him from both directions, Kerrigan backed onto one side of the street and found himself trapped.
There was no way he could rush through either group without being resisted and caught.
The two groups were closing in fast.
He looked about himself. Surely there must be somewhere he

could go, or something he could use to gain altitude and leap nimbly up and onto a ledge. Maybe then onto the roof tops where he would be free of the hungry eyes, hands and wallets of the villages.

There was nothing of any usefulness about him. Only the running river of the street and the flowing walls of the surrounding buildings as rainwater poured down them, were present.

Stepping away from the building he had backed to, Kerrigan turned in desperate hope of finding one final escape route.

He turned, and in front of him was a door.

The door to the church.

He could hardly believe his eyes. The chances of him ending up exactly where he had been heading after all the twisting and turning he had made through the unknown streets, were incredible.

Finally, a bit of good luck.

With only a moment's hesitation as he recalled all of his moral's about church's and the religion's they represented, Kerrigan took a firm grip of the wooden door's metal handle, pushed the door of the church open, and stepped inside.

Once inside, Kerrigan felt a huge wave of nausea that started from his stomach and rose up his larynx, to fester unsettlingly at the back of his throat.

God he hated churches.

The interior was vast and cold. A huge space had been allocated to the interior of the building, yet it contained little of any note. Uncomfortable looking pews ran the length of the central chamber, facing towards a raised altar of simple, yet elegant design. The flooring was decorated with an intricate design of interloping marble tiles. The thick pillars that ran the length of the room were decorated with an elaborate gothic twining, binding them to the roof they supported like an exotic spider web.

Glowing torches of naked flames were scattered sparingly throughout the interior, giving the room spot light illumination but no warmth.

Using his back as leverage, Kerrigan slammed the door behind him and took a moment to breath in the rancid air of the churches interior.

It did not help his nausea.

Knowing that standing with his back against the temporary protection the door offered and concentrating on his own unease, was only going to result in a knife in his back, Kerrigan stepped away from the door.

Running down the aisle that ran like a spine down the centre of the building, Kerrigan headed to the far end of the room where a statue of the God the villager's worshipped hung from the ceiling, suspended over a central pedestal used to issue sermons.

It looked like a giant fish. There was certainly nothing special about the fish, nothing God-Like; it had the long thin body of a fish, the scales of a fish, the beady little eyes that stuck out on opposite sides of it's head like a fish... Just a fish.

These people worshipped a fucking fish?

He was amused at the thought, that an entire community could dedicate their lives to such a mundane creature, but he was not entirely surprised. It was a fishing village after all. The sea was what supplied them with their food and business, what allowed them to prosper. Was it really so ridiculous to accept that these people therefore worshipped an entity from the sea?

Despite his initial amusement, Kerrigan was also revolted by the image of village's dedication. Not because of it's aesthetics, but by what it represented. How people dedicated their lives to a being that thought it could tell other people how they should live their life. By imposing rules that he or she must follow throughout their life.

It was like a dictatorship.

And for what?

A possible afterlife in paradise of which there has never been any proof?!

Kerrigan was unsure what disgusted him more: the God that sought to rule all, or the people who believed in that shit.

To Kerrigan's left, a door led out of the central chamber.

He ran for it and reached it just as the door to the outside world, the one he had only moment's ago closed behind himself, slammed open.

Angry villagers spewed into the church's interior, as if they were afraid of the terrible storm that raged in the streets outside.

Once inside, they didn't stop like a sodden crowd might, but headed straight towards Kerrigan.

While this happened, he had reached the door that led out of the chamber and had tried the handle. He was horrified to discover the door was locked.

Twisting the old metal ring that acted as a handle with increased vigour, Kerrigan tried once more to open the door.

This time he pulled, instead of pushing.

The door stubbornly remained embedded in it's door frame.

Desperate to leave, Kerrigan thrust his shoulder into the door.

It didn't even shudder. It was as if it were made of stone rather than wood.

The villager's had rapidly closed the distance, and were now only feet away from him. From this distance, the soft globes of light cast by the churches torches illuminated their emancipated frames, giving them a sickening appearance.

They would be upon him any second, too large in number for him to fight back or struggle through.

He had his back against the door.

His options had run out. There was no where else to go, and nothing left but to stand and fight.

If he was going to die, he would meet it face on and embrace it.

It was almost a tranquil thought as he understood the death he deserved had finally come to take him away.

As the realisation came, all the anxiety and emotion he felt drained away from the moment, like colour fading from the world, leaving him with a drab, black and white acceptance of his fate.

Smiling, he raised his fists.

He would take as many lives as possible with him before he went.

"STOOOOOOOOOP!"

A female screamed at the top of her voice, high above the din the bloodthirsty crowd made. The cry rang out in the cold air, silencing the rabble of the crowd, repeating itself in multiple echoes before fading away into silence.

Like a flock of birds changing direction mid-flight, the crowd suddenly stopped as one and turned to face the source of the command.

Annoyance and outrage filled the faces of those closest to Kerrigan, as they strained to see over the heads of their neighbours, to see who had delayed their lust for blood.

Equally as baffled as those who seemed to want him dead, despite the substantial reward for his capture alive, Kerrigan also wondered who had put a temporary hold on his death, yet he turned his furious glare off the man in front of him, several moments after everyone else.

He was startled to see that it was the woman who had held him temporarily hostage in the basement of her house.

The red head.

Standing on one of the church's pews, she held her arms raised in the air, commanding the attention that she had gained.

"LEAVE HIM BE!" Once more her shrill voice echoed around the stone chamber, amplifying it beyond it's natural quality, giving it a majestic overtone, as if she were a queen addressing her subjects.

Certainly her words were respected as royalty; the crowd mumbled in disappointment amongst themselves, but not one person singled themselves out by voicing their objection openly.

"WE ALL KNOW WHAT THIS MAN DID, AND YES HE DESERVES THE DEATH THAT YOU ALL SO RIGHTLY WISH TO BRING TO HIM," she looked around the condensed cluster of dripping wet villagers. The crowd, with their thinning hair and torn clothes, looked at their shoes or at one another from the corner of their eyes as if they were naughty children being reprimanded by their mother who had caught them eating sweets before a meal, "BUT HERE, IN THIS HOUSE OF OUR LORD, IS NOT THE PLACE FOR BLOODSHED. LEAVE HIM BE WITH ME AND I SHALL DELIVER UPON HIM HIS PUNISHMENT!"

"But my lady," begged a hunched man close to the red head. He wrung his sodden hat nervously in his hands. His balding head added years to his apparent age, "He... He is The Heathen." He risked.

"GOOD SIR, I KNOW WHO HE IS, AND WHAT IT IS THAT HE HAS DONE. BUT THAT IS ALL THE MORE REASON TO LEAVE HIM WITH ME, TO DEAL WITH HIM IN THE APPROPRIATE MANNER. THE S.O. WANT HIM ALIVE, BUT WE ALL KNOW THAT THIS IS TOO GOOD FOR THE DESPICABLE CRIME THAT HE HAS COMMITED - A CRIME UPON MY OWN BROTHER NO LESS! THAT IS WH I REQUEST YOU LEAVE HIM WITH ME - IT IS WHAT MY BROTHER WOULD HAVE WANTED."

Another chunter rippled it's way through the subdued crowd. Some agreed with the speech while others seemed reluctant and uncomfortable to stall the inevitable any longer.

"NOW GO," boomed the red head before any more arguments could be raised, "LEAVE IN THE SAFE KNOWLEDGE THAT EACH AND EVERYONE OF YOU HAS HELPED BRING THIS MONSTER TO JUSTICE. YOU ARE ALL HEROES."

With the short congratulatory speech completed, the red head stepped down from the pew, observing the flow of villagers as they left the church and went back into the pouring rain.

"ONE MORE THING," she asked as the villagers streamed past her, "NO ONE HERE IS TO INFORM THE AUTHORITIES OF WHAT HAS HAPPENED ... I WANT THIS MAN FOR MYSELF". She smiled wickedly. An old woman, who passed next to her, patted her on the shoulder in affirmation of her unveiled threat.

The procession was conducted at a slow respectable pace. Every other villager seemed to thank the red head, bless her and her strength, courage, beauty, wisdom, compassion, faith, future and leadership in an assortment of overly flourished sentiments.

Once the last villager had finally left the church, the red head closed the door behind them and turned to face Kerrigan across the expanse of the empty chamber.

There was only the briefest of silences between them.

The red head raised her voice again so that she could be heard, but this time she spoke, rather than commanded, "I could have let them kill you, you know. In fact, I still could. All I need do is open this door again and shout them back in here. Anyone of them would gladly rip your throat out with their bare hands."
Kerrigan did not respond.
"It's lucky for you that I'm kind hearted by nature."
Walking slowly towards Kerrigan, she continued. "Surely now you see that there's nowhere for you to go, nowhere for you to hide? As long as you remain a Heathen, your blood will be sought from now until the day you die. There really is no escaping from this."
The only response was the soft clicking of her shoes echoing throughout the empty chamber.
"So here's my offer, you either help me by taking me to my brother as I asked earlier, or I open that door and watch you die. Your choice."
When Kerrigan remained silent, the red head prompted, "Well?"
"It doesn't seem like I have much of an option," growled Kerrigan behind clenched teeth, his voice full of menace.
"Oh you have a choice alright", she mocked, "Die now at the hands of these poor people, or not. What do ya say?" her smile was patronising.
What the fuck??? Was this woman blackmailing him!?!?!
After much musing, he replied, "Fine. I'll take you to your death."
Her smile widened to show the white of her teeth, "Good choice." she replied happily.

"So, let's get down to business", she continued. She walked forward and sat down upon the end of one of the pews closest to the altar, her foot steps echoing around the elaborate chamber as she stepped gracefully crossed the multi coloured flooring.
Once more Kerrigan noted the elaborate gothic design of the church's interior. The thick pillar's curved like twisted tree trunks to hold the decorated ceiling high above the church's occupants. The ceiling was designed with layers of over lapping circles, giving the roof a natural, canopy effect.

The upper flooring of the church that circled, but did not cover, the pews below, connected to the support balusters with the same exotic spider web design that decorated all of the interiors connecting right angles.

It's beauty and calming atmosphere stood as a stark contrast to the outside world. It was like a being inside a large geode.

She crossed her curvy legs and placed the palms of her hands in her lap, "Feel free to sit down Kerrigan, I don't bite." Despite their earlier confrontation, she was amazingly confident in his presence.

The use of his name sounded strange coming from the stranger's lips, yet no doubt everyone in the village knew his name just as well as they could recognise his face. It was plastered in lettering as high as he himself was upon the poster he had seen. Presumably there were countless more scattered throughout the town.

Ignoring her invitation, Kerrigan remained stood in the shadows at the far end of the cold room that only they now shared. He leant his back on the door that had stubbornly refused him exit and had forced him into servitude with this cocky bitch.

No, not servitude. He would never allow himself to be the slave of anyone.

Partnership. Yes partnership better described their current arrangement. After all, she had promised him freedom in return for his help.

That's if the bitch could be trusted to honour her promise.

"How can I trust you?" Asked Kerrigan, ignoring the woman's control of the conversation, attempting to gain it for himself.

Although she would not have been able to see it as he stood in the shadows, she met his scowl with a look of pure determination, "My name is Nina Ann Tellingos and I was -am- " she corrected herself, "the sister of Father Ames Tellingos, the leader and Chosen One of this village… until recently."

This explained why the villagers had so willingly accepted and obeyed her orders; clearly there was a well established and respected hierarchy within the community. Being the sister of such a well honoured member of the community gave Nina a status almost equal to that of her brother's.

She brushed some unseen dust of her thigh offhandedly, then continued, "Twenty three days ago, Ames left this village on the Holy Pilgrimage. Seven days ago, officers from the S.O. unexpectedly showed up and started plastering posters and fliers up about the town showing that he had been murdered and that you were the one who had killed him." She pointed a finger accusingly at him, "Initially, I couldn't believe what I saw, thought that there must have been a mistake or that it was some kind of sick joke… although the S.O is not in the habit of doing either. When the truth finally sunk in, before my tears had even dried, I swore to myself that I would never, ever forget your face and that I would hunt you down from then until the day I die to avenge my brother." Despite the poor lighting that filtered through the church's small windows set high into the wall, her eyes rippled with unshed tears as she reminisced. The corners of her mouth twitched and quivered as they tried to pull themselves down. With even more effort than it took to withhold her tears, she continued with her story, her voice a barely suppressed scream, "I just stopped an entire town from killing you. Better yet, I prevented anyone of them from bringing in the entire fucking army of the S.O. on your arse." She stabbed her fingers at the closed door behind her, "Do you have any idea how much your life is worth to these people?!?! Personally, I don't give a fuck about how much your life is worth, what I want is my brother back, even if it is a fool's chance of success."

She rose to her feet, "I just saved your fucking life, so don't you dare ask how the fuck you can trust me, you fucking piece of shit!" Despite having clearly offended her, Kerrigan offered no words of conciliation.

He folded his arms across his chest, the crackling of leather rebelliously loud in the echoing chamber of the church's interior.

Nina's rippling eye's never left Kerrigan's shadowy face, his own never backing down either.

Nina's eyes were the first to look away as she tried to regain a little composure. Bizarrely, she almost felt foolish for her outburst when it was he, Kerrigan, who should have felt something. Guilt, maybe, at the heartless lack of gratitude or sympathy he refused to offer.

Clearing her throat, Nina continued on, but in a lower voice, "Don't worry I'll still do what I promised, I'll make it so that the warrant on your head's removed and you can go on and live your life as a free man." Almost as an after thought, she then said, "Oh, and don't even think about killing me you prick. If you think your hunted now, you've got another thing coming. This is bliss compared to what would happen then. You wouldn't be able to have a shit without someone there to smell it and take you down." The menace in her voice was proof alone that this statement was the truth.

"So, where is he?"

Resigned to his fate of teaming up with this desperate woman, to embark upon a suicidal mission to possibly save an already dead man, Kerrigan repeated what he had previously stated, "He's in a large building beyond the woods."

"The S.O. Refinery?" she shook her head, "No, you must be mistaken."

"Fine, whatever" He pushed off out of the shadows and headed towards the exit. If she refused to believe him then she could go fuck herself.

"No, wait" She took a step in his direction, "I'm sorry okay, it's just that it's a little hard to believe, you know?"

Kerrigan didn't know, but did not voice his ignorance. These people had abducted him, Ames, and presumably others, for who knows what reasons and had subjected them to tortures worse than anyone should suffer. Why would it be so hard to believe that these cruel people would hold Nina's brother, Ames?

"After every thing they've done for us... why?" she muttered to herself.

After a brief contemplation, she visibly shook herself from her thoughts, "Okay, let's get going"

"No."

"No? What do you mean 'no'? Listen you shit we had a d..."

"Before we go anywhere, I need rest and food. It's a long journey."

"I know how fucking far it is but..."

She wanted to object, knowing that with each moment that passed,

it put her brother's life into further jeopardy.
Time was something that they simply didn't have enough of to waste.
Yet, if Kerrigan did not have the strength to make the trip, she would be putting her own life in further danger. She was pretty handy with the knife she wore in the belt of her trousers, but it wouldn't be enough alone to guarantee her safety.
She needed this man who had seemingly survived against all odds, through the Forbidden Forest and, even more infeasibly, from the offices of the S.O. Refinery itself, and she needed his skills to survive.
"Okay", she conceded, "But not for long."

Five hours later, Kerrigan awoke, alert and ready to go.
Checking the Chronometer on Nina's wall, he was surprised by how well he felt having slept for such a relatively short period of time. When he had first went to bed, having gorged himself on the fresh food Nina had provided him with, he had felt like he could, and fully intended to, sleep for at least twelve hours. His body had ached everywhere, yet despite this, he awoke feeling completely anew, as if he had awoke in a brand new copy of himself, free of all the injuries and pain he had suffered.
He raised his head off the bed in Nina's house.
Rain continued to beat against the dirty window as hard and as heavy as it had from the moment he had entered the village.
The bulbous grey clouds above gave no indication that their full bodies were going to dry up anytime soon.
Just then, Nina walked past the open door of the bedroom and noticed that Kerrigan was awake.
"Feel better Your Majesty?" Her sarcasm was as heavy as the rain soaked clouds that miraculously stayed afloat in the sky.
"Doesn't it ever stop raining here?"
"What?" she asked, "Shut the fuck up you prat, and get the fuck off my bed."
Her ability to switch her emotions from one to the next so rapidly was impressive. One moment she was angry, then desperate and

pleading, and now cocky and insulting.
"I've packed us some supplies and I want to get going straight away." She held a shoulder bag aloft. She read out the contents of the bag, more as a verbal check list for herself, than to actually list them for Kerrigan's benefit. As she named each item she lifted the respective item out of the bag, "OK I've got us plenty of food, mainly cans of stuff that wont go off or get crushed. Bottled water, and of course plenty of vaccines..."
Upon naming the last item, she held up a collection of small vials, syringes and pills.
"What the fuck do we need vaccinating against?" He had raised himself up onto his elbows so that he could watch what she was doing.
She turned to him, "Oh ha ha, we're really fucking funny this evening aren't we? First with the rain comments and now with the vaccine. You're a real fucking comedian you know that? You should do a show, you'd make a fortune."
Suddenly, the vigour that she had displayed vanished, expelled in a deep sigh as she stared beyond the interior of her bag as if she were looking at something embedded below the foundations of the house itself.
"What the fuck am I doing?" she asked quietly to no one in particular, "What am I doing?"
She tore her gaze away from her satchel to look at Kerrigan, "What am I doing trusting you? I must be fucking nuts." She shook her head as she spoke as if she herself were refusing to believe her own compliance.
Kerrigan met her shimmering gaze, but did not reply.
"What if your right?" she asked, "What if Ames really is dead? I'm risking everything, EVERYTHING on the slim hope that he might still be alive."
She sighed deeply once more. Clearly she had further things that she wanted to voice and so Kerrigan remained silent, giving her the opportunity to do so, "I was born in Trendid Kerrigan, and I was lucky enough to be born into the Tellingos family. For generations my parents, and my parent's parents and so on have

been fortunate enough to be blessed by the ever gratifying Gods with their almighty gifts. Although I myself have never been blessed with their powers, the males in my family always have, and it is those men, my father, his father and my brother who have served and led the poor, suffering villagers of this town." As she spoke, her eyes shifted from his own to focus on the corner of the room. She gasped lightly as if she were out of breath, although Kerrigan got the impression that she was finally giving credence to the musings that had always floated at the back of her mind.

"I've been lucky Kerrigan," she continued, "Very lucky. Because I'm the sister of The Chosen One, I'm blessed with the privileges and respect that those in the church are given… I've had a very easy life in many ways.

But my brother, Ames, he gave something to this village that I could never give." Suddenly her focus sharpened and she looked at Kerrigan with eyes filled with restrained pools of tears, "Hope. That's what he gave those people out there, hope that one day they'll be able to live a normal life, free of all the struggles they live with everyday. Without hope they really have nothing. None of them. Not even me. What will I do after we infiltrate the S.O. Refinery only to find he really is dead? They'd place a bounty on my head for such treason."

Kerrigan stared at her shimmering eyes. She was giving voice to thoughts and feeling that had clearly long been suppressed.

Almost mockingly, he replied, "You could always go on the run."

"On the run?!" she scoffed, "Like you huh? and where would I go? There's either here, the S.O Refinery, or one of the two other villages, both of which are within only a few days travel of each other. If I go against the S.O. my face would be plastered all over Trendid, Kallingos and Ferralin as much as yours is!" Her sorrow was rapidly turning into anger.

"What do you mean?" asked Kerrigan. Only two more villages???

"For fuck's sake Kerrigan, how long where you out there on that God damn ship?" she spat, "There's only here, Kallingo, Ferralin and the S.O. Refinery. That's it. One block of land with four locations. There is no where else!"

Kerrigan took a moment to accept what he had just been told. Only three villages and a mysterious central leadership? In the entire world? What the hell? How could that be possible? He had spent so long on board a floating prison ship, how was it possible that no other land had ever been discovered?

He voiced his thought's to Nina.

"You really have been out of it for too long. It's quite simple", she replied, "Out there, on the sea, is Forbidden. It is not a Holy Land. Out there, in the sea, is where Heathen's like you are sent for committing crimes against the civilised world, for defying the God's Laws." She had risen to her feet now, unable to contain the anger that swelled within, she seemed to be in a trance as she preached to Kerrigan, "No body ventures out to sea, at least not those who follow the teachings of The Gods." She looked Kerrigan up and down with this comment, "The sea is Forbidden, and no one here, or anywhere else for that matter, is willing to give up what little life they have by questioning it."

She had slowly crossed the distance between herself and Kerrigan as she gave the impromptu speech. She loomed over Kerrigan as he sat upright on Nina's bed.

"If your wrong, or you have lied to me, I have no where else to go, or to hide." She leaned towards him, "I might as well be fucking dead."

The tears that she had fought so hard to restrain spilled silently down her cheeks.

After a moment she collected herself once more, not feeling ashamed for her sudden emotional outburst, "Now," she rose once more to her full five foot three inches height, "when I said I wanted to get going I meant it…As in now shitface!"

She turned to walk away from Kerrigan.

"Hey Nina, you know what?" he called out to her back.

She turned her head to look over at him as he rose to a seated position on the edge of the bed, "No Your Majesty, believe it or not I'm not a fucking psychic. What?"

"You've got a real dirty mouth for such a pretty face."

For the first time since they'd met, Kerrigan saw Nina genuinely

lost for words. Her mouth hung loose and open.
"You're a real arsehole you know that?" She walked away from Kerrigan's sight and so missed the look of pleasure that dawned upon his face.

They stepped out into the evening rain and both became instantly soaked.
Moments after becoming engulfed in the torrent, Kerrigan began to shiver from the cold rain that coursed down the centre of his spine, seeping into areas that should have remained dry.
The water quickly turned his once comfortable attire, into a heavy bulk that weighed against his body and caused his skin to chaff as his body rubbed against it.
Following Nina's lead, Kerrigan was quickly led from her property to the outskirts of the village without encountering anyone who was inquisitive to their business. They glimpsed the occasional villager who was foolish enough to risk the terrible weather, but only from a distance far enough to leave Kerrigan feeling that their passage had been unnoticed and un-scrutinised.
Once they had reached the outskirts of the town, they immediately climbed the rise that took them back into the woods that Kerrigan had barely escaped alive. He did not relish the idea of entering the woods where that thing lurked.
How could they know that it was not waiting for them? It was a question that Kerrigan had raised as the pair had traversed the sodden street.
"Trust me, I know" had replied Nina, "That thing that attacked us, that attacked you, has attacked before. That attack upon your life was not, and will not be, the last." Nina had to raise her voice in order to be heard above the crash of endless pouring rain, "When it has been defeated in the past, it runs back into the Forbidden Forest as far as it can go, and as deep as the woods have to offer, trying to put as much distance between itself and the Chosen One".
How the Chosen One might have influence over a wild beast was of little interest to Kerrigan at the time. As long as the beast that hid itself in a perpetual cloud of dust remained at a safe distance

away from them, was all that Kerrigan was concerned about.

Once the duo reached the top of the rise, just as they were about to enter the Forbidden Forest, Nina turned her back on the woods to stare back at the village that lay below and before them.

It looked pretty much as how it had looked to Kerrigan the first time he had seen it.

Dead.

Empty.

He knew that Nina saw the village in a way that he himself could never see it.

The village appeared dark, with only the occasional, flickering light of a flame lantern peeking it's way forth from the gloom that tried to envelope it. No activity or movement gave sign to any life that may have inhabited the seemingly deserted town.

Yet here was Nina's village. A village that she was revered in due to her religious heritage. Her brother had previously been a figure of some importance, which naturally gave her a status of great authority also.

She was leaving behind a world, albeit a very small one, where she had complete freedom, control. A world in which she knew and understood every eventuality, no matter what that may have been.

She could resolve any situation that was hostile, threatening or dangerous with only a few words which would have been honoured, respected and above all, obeyed, without question.

As Nina gazed upon her village, she knew that she was leaving behind everything that she loved and treasured. A world she could control.

Behind her lay a forest where her social status would not be respected and her words would not have the controlling affect they once did.

A world of unpredictability.

Of chaos.

Tears rose to her eyes and pooled there. She would not allow them to flow as she wished a silent prayer of goodbye upon her beloved village. If the tears were to fall accidentally, she hoped that they might mingle with the rain that already coursed down her face, and

hide her grief in their flow.
She would not allow Kerrigan to see her weakness.
Kerrigan observed her sorrow in silence, and wondered if she had ever left the village behind before.

As they observed the flowing rooftops, walls and streets of the shadow black village before them, a vehicle appeared from around the corner of the hill to Kerrigan and Nina's right. The vehicle illuminated it's path with two bright cones of light that stabbed through the rain, bouncing as the vehicle traversed the lumpy field. The two observers watched the vehicle descend the hill and approach the village. As it was about to disappear behind the right most building, Nina said, "I've got an idea."

Kerrigan looked across to Nina in the poor grey lighting. Whether she saw his stare or not, she continued, "Let's infiltrate the S.O. directly. Let's use their own tools against them."
It was apparent to Kerrigan that she was referring to the vehicle that they were still currently observing. It would remain in sight for only a few more seconds before it vanished.
Still Nina had not finished, "Let's steal some S.O. uniforms and infiltrate their base from within."
She turned to Kerrigan silently asking for his cohesion in her scheme.
Kerrigan looked blankly back, between strands of shiny wet hair, "Whatever you say" he said, barely audible above the crash of rain.
A moment later a flash of lightning, followed immediately by the harsh crack of thunder seemed to end their deliberation with an ethereal full stop, deciding for the pair that the conversation was at a close, and that their plan had been decided.

They ran back down the bank that they had only so recently climbed. The incline of the hill aided their descent, turning each step into a bound, were once it had been reduced to a struggling shuffle.
With each extended bound, Kerrigan was aware of the ever present

threat of tumbling face first into the hill's liquid mud. It was an exercise in balance just to remain upright during their descent.

Within what seemed like only moments, they reached the town once more.

Following Nina's lead, it became quickly apparent to Kerrigan that they were skirting around the outside of the village, once again reducing the possibility that they might encounter any wandering villagers to a minimum.

Following in Nina's wake, Kerrigan passed through streets and sideways that he had not previously traversed, and, judging by their appearance, had not been travelled and had remained empty and abandoned for a long time.

The places that he had previously seen on his short visit of Trendid, had been poorly maintained by even the most basic of human standards. Nothing that he had previously seen could be considered homely, welcoming or inviting, with the possible exception of the church, however his ingrained disgust of all churches denied him the appreciation that the church should have deserved.

These streets, even compared to the dilapidated paths he had already traversed, were in a state of complete disrepair.

Where previously the walls of the buildings that flanked the streets were damaged with pockets of missing concrete, where the walls themselves had crumbled from natural erosion, these building's walls were simply falling apart. The clear square shape of a building's exterior wall was not apparent in these streets. The top horizontal definition which would normally indicate were the wall ended and the roof started, was not in existence. Instead, the top horizontal bar was replaced with a ragged delve, where the now missing roof had been ripped off. The walls were still pocked with holes of missing stone, but at a much increased rate. Where previously the outer walls had been marked with the occasional spot, these walls were covered like that of an spotty adolescent child.

The streets were like an obstacle course of debris and potential accidents. The remains of the destroyed walls were strewn across the roads, making progress down the streets all but impossible to the most nimble and flexible of travellers.

Together, Nina and Kerrigan, ran, climbed, walked, jumped, bounded, hopped, stumbled, and sidled their way down the ever flowing streets of the outer village.

Kerrigan noticed that during this exhaustive trip, Nina never seemed to show any signs of physical exhaustion herself. She hardly seemed to draw a single deep breath as they continued their traversing of the obstructive terrain.

He was not impressed, but at least appreciative of her fitness. She certainly kept herself in shape. At least he would not have to wait for her to regain her composure before their plans could continue should she fall behind… IF she fell behind.

Kerrigan climbed over the boulders that often blocked their passage, focusing only on preventing himself from injury upon the metal poles that protruded from the fallen chunks of wall. Previously, the poles had been used for the supportive frame work of the buildings they had once been a part of. Now, the sharp edges that protruded from the fallen poles only served to provide dangerous edges for him and Nina to hurt themselves upon.

As such, he hardly noticed how much distance they must have covered, it must have been considerable, as before long, Nina signalled that Kerrigan should stop, as she peered around the corner of a building ahead of them both, that she was huddled up against.

After a moment or two, she turned back to Kerrigan and whispered just loud enough to be heard above the torrential rain, "That vehicle we saw is parked just around the corner, about thirty feet away in the middle of Angler's Square. It's a Class D model which means that there's only two crew members, one of which is standing guard outside of the Chosen One's door on the far side of the Square. I dunno where the other crew member is but I guess they must be inside if their crew mate is guarding the entrance."

Kerrigan peeped over her shoulder and saw both the vehicle and the guard to which she was referring. Although both were completely still, the rain that fell upon them, and flowed down and

away from them, gave them a strangely moving, living quality.
"Here's what we'll do…"
Although he did not protest, Kerrigan became instantly, although only mildly, annoyed at Nina's attempt to tell him what to do. Admittedly, she lived in this village and therefore had much more knowledge and experience of the town itself than he did, but that hardly gave her the right to tell him what to do, to take charge of the situation.
However, without hearing out her proposal – or orders – he had not yet thought of a strategy that was potentially more successful than the one she was about to suggest – order. As such, he held his tongue.
"Or more accurately, here's what I'M going to do."
Better, and interesting…
"Those guards over there are outside of The Chosen One's quarters. Being as how I'm the sister of the previous Chosen One, the guards will not suspect my approach. If they do decide to ask about my business, I'll tell them that I'm here to discuss religious philosophies and demand that they let me through. Given my grieving status, I highly doubt that they will ask anything of me, never mind object. Once inside, I'm going to find out just what the hell it is that they want. In the mean time, you stay here and do nothing. We don't want to go stealing their truck until we've distracted them, or gotten rid of them somehow. These guys mean business when they've got you in their sights… You got all that?"
Kerrigan had assumed that she had intended their steal the truck, as well as their uniforms, but this was the first time she had voiced her plan.
Nina had not expected a response, so she was not disappointed when none came.
Turning away from Kerrigan, she slipped around the building's corner and strode casually across Angler's Square.

With Nina out the way, Kerrigan was finally able to scrutinise the square for himself.
The square was large enough to have several, large faced buildings

glare down upon it from all four of it's sides. Each of the buildings on the circumference of the square, peered down upon the square with dark, blackened windows that looked a little too much like blind eyes.

In the centre of the square stood a stone statue twice the size of Kerrigan. The statue was of a coiled serpent that rose from the street to point it's arrow shaped head at the sky above. It's mouth were open as if it were screaming in pain or frustration. The rain that splashed down it's flanked sides gave the statue a wet, flowing quality that no doubt increased the beauty of the stone creature, rather than if it were dry.

The statue did not appear to have suffered the erosion that the buildings surrounding it had.

Of more interest, parked up next to the statue, was the transport that Kerrigan and Nina had seen entering the village from high upon the hill side.

When they had first seen the vehicle, it had appeared to be large enough to hold a couple of men at best; a small transport.

Now that he was closer, Kerrigan re-evaluated the size of the machine, estimating that it could hold up to twenty or more.

Upon paired wheels that were almost as large as Kerrigan himself, the rectangular block that was the main body of the vehicle itself, was plonked on top. A large dark window covered what must have been the front of the vehicle, but other than that, the vehicle was practically featureless. It did not display any kind of weaponry, and only a relatively small antenna, given the vehicle's size, protruded from it's rear.

It was not a combat vehicle, but it looked thick and sturdy. Certainly, it was highly reinforced.

It's metallic skin glittered in stark relief to the smooth graceful contours of the square's statue.

Other than these two objects, the Square was empty save for Nina who was walking diagonally across the square towards the man that stood guard outside of the building that Nina had referred to as the Chosen One's Quarters. The guard was certainly in a state of discomfort as he stood in his soaked uniform with his rifle held across his chest, yet his stance remained as still as that of the building he stood in front of.

He did not turn to acknowledge Nina until she stood directly in front of him.

It was impossible for Kerrigan to hear what Nina said to the guard, but he moved aside without any resistance, taking a side step to his right.

Nina entered the building and vanished from sight.

Kerrigan remained focused on the Square in front of him. Nina had been correct in her predictions so far, but he wondered just what might be taking place inside the building. It occurred to him that Nina could at this very second be informing the people within of Kerrigan's location and half expected to see a sudden flow of armed men flood out of the building to capture him.

After some time, when this did not happen, Kerrigan started to accept that perhaps Nina was being honest with him in her need to help save her brother, and perhaps she could be trusted.

However, after watching the motionless scene for what seemed like weeks, Kerrigan became anxious and concerned by the length of time that Nina was taking. What was she up to in there?

He decided that he had been foolish to trust her so quickly after all. Hating the feeling of powerlessness that had crept into him, Kerrigan decided that despite Nina's request to the contrary, he would take action.

Sulking down an alley that ran parallel to the Square, Kerrigan arrived at another corner that also looked out onto the square. Instead of being opposite the guard posted outside of the Chosen One's housing, he was now positioned to the man's immediate right and viewed the guard in profile.

Remaining in the shadows cast by the looming buildings, Kerrigan picked up a small stone and rolled it into the Square, towards the guard.

The guard turned in the direction of the soft clatter caused by the rolling pebble, but did not move from his station. The buildings of the village were in a constant state of ruin, and bits and pieces were often falling and crumbling from the walls. He no doubt considered the pebble that Kerrigan had tossed to be just another piece of crumbling masonry.

Picking, up a larger stone, Kerrigan also rolled this stone towards the guard. The stone tumbled it's way out of the shadows with such deliberation that it clearly had not just fallen from the roof tops.

It aroused the guard's suspicions were the previous attempt had not. The guard lowered his weapon to his hip, and advanced upon the darkened alley, the tip of his rifle ahead of him.

Just as Kerrigan had wanted.

As the guard approached, he shouted advice and warnings to whoever may be hidden in the shadows, "Whoever's hiding in there, come out into the open where I can see your face before you get hurt!"

Kerrigan remained hugged to the alley wall, becoming one with the shadows. His breathing had not increased, and his heart rate remained as slow and as steady as it would when at rest.

All the while, the rain beat down upon the world with unrelenting ferocity, making the air heavy and the growing dusk darker than it should have been.

There was no other sound to be heard other than the continual hiss and crackle of the rain. It sounded as if a million pieces of paper were being torn apart in unison.

As soon as the guard entered the shadows of the alley, Kerrigan made his move. He twisted away from the wall, grabbed the muzzle of the guard's gun, pointing it away from himself, and punched the man in the throat with the taught flesh between his thumb and forefinger.

The guards windpipe was instantly crushed preventing him from breathing and, more importantly, screaming.

The guard dropped his weapon and brought both of his hands to his throat as if invisible hands were strangling him and he might be able to remove their grip.

He fell to his knees as he struggled to draw a breath through his ruined larynx.

Kerrigan stood above the guard and looked directly into his wide,

gleaming eyes, watching the life drain out of him.
The guard's eyes met Kerrigan's with a look of disbelief and horror. A moment later his arms stopped scratching at his broken throat, and fell to his sides. He tumbled to the ground, dead having not made a single noise.
His dead eye's continued to stare at his murderer.
Looking at the dead man lying before him, Kerrigan noticed something he had not at first seen.
Although it was different in it's markings, the badge that was pressed onto the man's breast showed Kerrigan that he had been a member of the same group of people who had boarded Chimera and taken him away…
Who the fuck were these people?

Picking up the guard's weapon, a rifle of some sort, Kerrigan ran to the motionless vehicle that was parked in the square.
He had already determined that the truck must be empty of it's occupants as no movement had came from the truck, and no one had exited the vehicle to investigate why one of their colleagues had left his post, entered the alley, and had not returned.
Arriving at the side of the truck that did not face The Chosen One's Quarter's, Kerrigan found the handle that slid open the side door of the vehicle.
Sliding on smooth runners, Kerrigan whipped the door aside and swept the interior of the truck with his rifle, just incase the truck did indeed house additional men.
As he had predicted, the truck's interior was empty.
The truck's interior remained mostly hidden in shadows as the light of the obscured sun reached only the parts that were exposed to it's rays; the front seats from the front windows, and the flooring of the area Kerrigan had just revealed.
A closer look showed a few rows of chairs and, towards the rear of the vehicle, some sort of equipment that looked as lifeless as the rest of the truck.
Jumping inside, Kerrigan slid the door shut behind him.
As soon as the door was shut, an interior light came on over head,

illuminating the seating area that Kerrigan now sat in. The electronic equipment that was previously dead and lifeless, also whirled into life. A multitude of lights flashed into existence and a bank of monitors glowed with information.
Curious, but not of immediate concern.
More interested in watching the Chosen One's now unguarded door, Kerrigan could easily see through the truck's front windscreen knowing that his presence could not be seen from outside observers much as he had not been able to see within when he himself was outside. Although it had appeared made of black steel, the windscreen was completely clear from within. Clearly some kind of technology was at use whereby he could see out, but others could not see in.
Despite such reasoning, Kerrigan remained reluctant to expose himself, preferring to peer out the window with as little of himself showing as possible.
The rain trickled down the windscreen in erratic cascades.
If only he knew how to drive the damn thing, he might have stolen it for himself and went on the run, bounty or no bounty on his head.
Unfortunately he could not, and was left with no option but to wait until one of the other officers within The Chosen One's Quarters returned. He would then use the element of surprise to swiftly overpower and abduct the guard, and then force them to drive himself out of Trendid.
With this idea, came a brief regret of having killed the previous guard so hastily, but regrets would serve him no use now.
Fuck Nina, he thought.

It was some time later before anyone emerged from the building, back into the pouring rain, but Kerrigan waited with infinite patience, a skill he had been forced to learn whilst imprisoned upon Chimera.
When the door finally did open, it was opened by another of the guards who had arrived in the truck. He walked out ahead of Nina who was clearly in a state of agitation. Her face was scowling and

she was waving her arms furiously at his turned back.

The guard walked patiently away, oblivious to the insults that Nina was shouting to his back.

He was on his own.

It would seem only two guards had entered the village via the vehicle in total.

Good. Kerrigan would make quick work of this other officer.

As the other officer and Nina crossed the courtyard towards the vehicle in which Kerrigan hid, another figure emerged in the shadow of the building's doorway and stood watching the retreating couple.

It was the bald man in the bold robes who had saved Kerrigan, and the rest of the villagers, only hours ago. He stood in the door way and folded his arms across his chest, impassive to the outrage that Nina was exhibiting.

With a burst of insight, Kerrigan knew who this man was.

A Chosen One.

The guard was approaching the truck now. He approached around the front windscreen so that Kerrigan was looking down upon the top of his capped head as he passed below.

Raising himself from the driver's seat, Kerrigan repositioned himself in the chair that was closest to the sliding door through which he had entered. He braced himself for when it slid open.

Just as he had expected, there was a clank of metal as the locking mechanism was disengaged, and the door slid open on it's runners. As it did so, the internal light and electronic computers also blinked out.

Kerrigan had decided against using the gun he had acquired from the guard in the alley almost as suddenly as he had gained it... unless it came to an emergency. It's noise would draw too much attention.

As Nina was continuing her objections to the guard's back, Kerrigan thrust his open palm directly upwards and into the guard's shocked face, just below his nose.

The heel of his palm hit exactly where he had hoped it would. He felt the satisfying crunch of the man's front teeth snap against his

crushed upper lip. This was then followed by a slight resistance and then crack as the nose bone snapped free of his skull and was thrust unnaturally upwards into his soft brain tissue.
Withdrawing his hand as quickly as he had thrust it, the guard's face had taken on a surreal concave quality.
Slowly, blood oozed out of his broken mouth and flattened nose and as it did so, his knees buckled and he fell half slumped in and half slumped out of the truck's doorway so that only his legs were being saturated by the falling rain.
Nina stood where she had been. The vocal protests at whatever she had been upset over remained stuck and unvoiced in her throat.
She watched the dead man crumble before her with a look of disbelief.
Grabbing hold of the dead guard's collar and belt loop, Kerrigan heaved up the dead weight of the guard's body and tossed him unceremoniously into the rear of the truck.
"Can you drive this thing?" Kerrigan asked turning back to Nina who remained rooted to the spot where she was stood in the pouring rain.
"Fuck…" she mouthed, but the word was lost in the rain. Her gaze had followed the dead man's body to the back of the truck, where he lie in a jumble of scattered limbs.
Grabbing her by the spare material that hugged taught at her chest, Kerrigan dragged Nina out of the rain and inside the truck. If she would not move herself, he would have to do it for her.
"Hey" she protested as she fell ungracefully into one of the many chairs that filled the interior.
Kerrigan closed the door behind her, reducing the roar of the falling rain to a muffled din. The reduction in volume was startling in it's own, subdued, way.
The interior once more bloomed into light.
The light seemed to bring Nina back to her senses, "Just what the fuck are you doing?! Didn't I tell you to stay the fuck out of this and leave everything to me?"
It was clear to Kerrigan that Nina was too hysterical at the moment to focus on their current goal - to get the hell out of here - and

judging by her previous episodes, her rage would continue to rise before it settled back down.

"What the fuck have you done? Do you have any idea what this could mean to us? To Trendid?"

He climbed over her and sat down in what appeared to be the driver's seat. A myriad of confusing dials, lights, knobs, buttons, displays, readings and gauges stared up at him expectantly.

He looked over the controls hoping to find something that was clearly labelled to it's function. Possibly a button labelled "Start" or "Go" would be helpful, but he doubted he would find anything so obvious.

"Are you listening to me?" screamed Nina. She had risen from her chair and placed a hand on his shoulder, attempting to draw his attention back to herself.

He grabbed her fingers in a tight grip that sent needles of pain rocketing up the back of her hand, into her forearm and beyond.

Before she had a chance to scream, Kerrigan threw her hand back at her without saying a word… but the message was clear.

Still, she would not be ignored. Rubbing her crushed hand, she said, "Just who the fuck do you think you are?!? Do you have any idea what you've just done?!? Who he works for?!" she pointed at the jumbled heap of the still cooling guard, "SHIT!" she was almost panicking now, "What if his mate comes back looking for him?"

"He wont. He's dead"

"How the fuck do you know?"

Kerrigan had given up looking for anything that was labelled with a function. Maybe a big green button…?

"FUCK!" she screamed, understanding Kerrigan's silence, "I've never met anyone so reckless in my entire life! Fuck me! You wanna just fucking shoot yourself now buddy before they get their hands on you? You fucking dick."

"Instead of crying like a baby," replied Kerrigan, still examining the instruments before him, "why don't you make yourself useful and drive us the hell outta here? We'd planned on stealing this thing anyway, what's the big deal?"

"What's the big deal?!" Nina replied uncomprehendingly, "are you fucking joking me?! Fuck you!" She wasn't listening. She would continue her rant until she had vented all of her frustration on Kerrigan.
It might take a while.
"I should never have trusted you in the first place. I knew you couldn't be trusted. Fuck me, I'm such a silly cow…"
"You got that right."
"…Why the fuck did I allow myself to be sucked in by you? FUCK!" She raised her hands in the air and dropped them with exasperation.
"Listen," Kerrigan turned in his seat to look at Nina. She was slumped lazily in one of the chairs behind the driver's seat as if she were exhausted from her own anger, "I can't drive this thing, and if you remember, this was your idea, not mine."
"It wasn't my idea to kill two S.O. Officers!" she sat forward once more. Apparently she still had more anger in her. "Now we'll both be executed for sure. Wait there, what do I mean, WE?" she laughed heartlessly at her comprehension, "*I haven't done anything, it was all YOU!* HA!" She rose to her feet. "So long Kerrigan you fucking loser, this is where I bail out." She headed towards the doorway.
So fuck, Kerrigan thought, *I don't need you.* Immediately following this came the realisation that he could not allow her to leave. She might, in her delirious frame of mind, decide to alert the local authorities to his location after all; Stuck here in the useless van he couldn't drive like a fish in a barrel.
No, she could not be allowed to leave, or live.
Kerrigan began to rise from his seat.
"How the fuck do I get out of here?" she asked.
Although there was a handle to thrust the doorway closed, a switch or button was needed to disengage the automatic locking mechanism from within.
Nina scanned the door frame for it's release.
Abandoning his futile efforts to start the vehicle, Kerrigan left the controls and began his silent advance towards Nina.

Nina went to the row of monitors that stood to the side of the exit. She looked over the instruments, continuing to curse her own stupidity.
Kerrigan was only a few steps behind her now.
And then Nina's monotonous self-deprivation stopped.
Her jaw hung loose as she leaned in to peer closer at one of the monitors.
A pale green glow touched her face as it reflected the green writing on the screen.
She mouthed a single word – Fuck – but no noise escaped her.
Kerrigan, unprepared for the sudden change in Nina's mood, stopped to watch her a moment.
After viewing the monitors, Nina walked shakily over to one of the many chairs that filled the interior of the truck, and plonked herself down in the nearest seat, her attempt at leaving momentarily forgotten. Her gaze was focused somewhere beyond the confines of the S.O truck.
She did not notice how close Kerrigan had silently sneaked upon her.
Curious at observing her sudden and uncharacteristic actions, Kerrigan approached the monitors for himself.
There were two monitors, both black and filled with glowing letters.
On the left hand monitor was a list of names:

Hammond, Illnes
Avery, James
Duoro, Iain
Gettersby, Lia
Tellingos, Ames
Foroq, Janbar
Chrisforth, Dree
Verany, North
Blanke, Ni
Tridale, Westler

Each name glowed with an ethereal, green glow except for one.
Ames's name was flashing from green to red.
On the right hand monitor stood a document. A list of information:

Ames Tellingos: Ref: 23914

Age: 32
Height: 5'10
Weight: 162 lbs
Address: Anglers Square, Trendid.
Religion: Leviathan

Status: Amateur progressing to Professional.

Additional Notes: Suggest that Ames is contacted and processed for Extraction.

Progress: Complete. Pending further developments.

Results: Pending.

Photos: Click HERE

So it was true, Ames had indeed been abducted by the same people that had abducted Kerrigan himself.
He did not need to click, or touch, the link to the photos to know that it was the same man who he had seen tortured in the cell adjacent to his own, back in the S.O Refinery, who was also Nina's brother.
He looked from the monitor back to Nina.
She was rocking slightly as she held her face in the palms of her hands.
She cried silently.
Kerrigan walked away from the monitors, stepped over Nina's outstretched legs, and returned to the driving seat from which he had came.

He took advantage of the silence that Nina unwittingly gave to concentrate more fully on the confusing instruments before him.

Unfortunately, despite the reprieve that Nina's grief gave him, Kerrigan could still not understand the function of the various instruments in front of him.

If he did not hurry, the bald man, Trendid's current Chosen One, would become suspicious to why the truck of the officers who had came to visit him, and who had left some time ago, had not yet left the village and gone on their way. He may come investigating.

It was something Kerrigan could do without.

He turned to Nina, "Can you drive this?"

She did not raise her head from her hands.

Instead, she wept for a moment longer, took a deep breath, steadied herself and then raised her head, turning her bloodshot eyes towards Kerrigan, "I'm sorry I doubted you. You were right."

Never one to be comfortable with the heart's true voice, Kerrigan heard the apology but without feeling any gratitude. Awkward of the moment, he felt that it was in his own best interests to acknowledge the apology but then to use it to his own advantage.

He replied "I know. But we have to get out of here. Now. Can you drive this thing?" He put as much compassion as he could muster into the statement, although he felt an inner disgust at himself for the display of false emotion. It was a disgust that hardly stuck, understanding that it was merely a charade, a display that would hopefully lead both of them towards escape.

He desperately hoped that Nina would not see through his deceit. Without her co-operation, they were both as good as dead, "Nina, we have to get out of here. It's the only way to save Ames." The words sounded false even to his own ears, but Kerrigan hoped that Nina's grief would deafen her to his poor acting, and accept the words themselves, rather than listen to the unnatural intonation in which they were delivered.

She met his eyes; his cold and deep, her's shimmering even in the artificial illumination.

She nodded her head, "Yeah. Your right" and she rose from her chair. Repeating her motion, Kerrigan vacated the driver's chair for Nina.

However, instead of heading to the front of the vehicle as Kerrigan had expected, she headed back to the row of computers and flicked a switch that opened the sliding door to the pouring rain. As she did so, she asked, "Where's the other guard's body?"

"In the alley." He twitched his head, indicating the direction he meant.

Without another word to explain her actions, Nina jumped out of the van, into the rain, and ran with her shoulders hunched to where Kerrigan had hidden the first guard's body. A moment later, she was dragging the guard's limp form across the soaking Square by his ankles. She soon reached the open door of the truck and, panting heavily, heaved the dead man inside and tossed him unceremoniously into the corner to land sprawled across his dead comrade in a macabre embrace.

Brushing her soaked hair away from her face Nina explained, "We can't leave any bodies behind."

With a wet squeak, she sat down in the driver's seat and with a quick flurry of her nimble fingers, she started up the truck's engine and headed out and away from Angler's Square, and out of Trendid itself.

During their escape, Kerrigan watched Nina from the corner of his eye. Her face became streaked with tears as the truth of her brother's abduction, from these people she thought she knew and had clearly trusted became first reasonable, and then uncomfortably real.

Once they left Trendid, Nina plotted a course through the lavish wood that surrounded her village by route of a worn path that, for the most part, was clear of any obstacle that might hinder their progress. Despite the truck's size, it was well designed to travel through and amongst the growth of bushes, roots and vines that criss-crossed their path.

The path they followed was a used roadway that Kerrigan had been unfortunate enough to miss as he crossed the woods, approaching the village directly. Curious, he asked Nina about it, "I used to work for the S.O. It was along this road that I was taken to and from my work for them. It's also the same path they use to visit our village."

Despite their rapid and clear journey, Nina explained how it would still take them more than a day to reach the S.O Refinery. The route was not direct, but it was the only passage that their truck could follow in order to reach it.

When night fell, the beams cast from the truck's head lights were pathetic cones of light that hardly pushed back the night at all. Their progress would have needed to come to a halt for the day if it had not been for the ghostly glow of the moon illuminating their way.

It cast a pale bleached glow over the tree tops and on the worn, muddy path down which they rode. The world was transformed once more into the bright black and white gloom he remembered from a few nights previous.

A ghost of a taste of animal blood crept into Kerrigan's mind and swept briefly across his tongue.

Oddly, his mouth started to salivate.

"I'm gonna pull over here for the night" announced Nina to Kerrigan after travelling awhile in both darkness and silence.

She pulled off the muddy path to nestle the truck amongst a couple of particularly thick looking trees. Their branches arched and hung down over the top of the truck providing a natural canopy.

Once stationary, Nina stretched and yawned at the controls, "I dunno about you but I'm fucked." She rose from the driver's seat to walk down the alley that ran between the passenger seats that Kerrigan himself was sat amongst. He had chosen not to sit next to her during their travel, preferring to sit on his own, with only his thoughts as company, rather than to sit up front with Nina and possibly become engaged in a conversation that he did not want to become involved in.

She passed by him without giving him a glance, and headed towards the supply bag she had packed for them both.

She withdrew two small vials of clear liquid and two syringes. She offered one of each to Kerrigan with her left hand, while she looked and rummaged further in the bag with her right, "Now what do I fancy to eat...?" She asked herself.

"I told you," Kerrigan replied, "I'm not taking your fucking drugs"

"Listen" replied Nina, her patience already worn thin from the hours she had spent in the driver's seat, "I'm tired and I'm hungry, and I don't have the patience for your shit, OK? Just fucking inject yourself as normal and we'll have something to eat. I can't be arsed with you fucking around. I just want my bed." She resumed her rummaging for food in the pack.

Slowly, Kerrigan took the vial and syringe off Nina. She tossed him some food preserved in a reflective wrapping and sat in a chair opposite his own, her feet perched upon the seat adjacent to it.

Casually, she unwrapped her own syringe from it's plastic sheath, and stuck it into the vial she held upside down. Filling the syringe, she then inserted the needle into the hollow of her left elbow and injected the clear liquid.

She caught Kerrigan watching her. "Well? You just gonna sit there and watch me while you fucking die or what?"

He looked back at her and put the equipment she had given him aside, "What the fuck's your problem? Are you really gonna keep up this pretence in front of me?"

He did not respond, and it was then that she finally understood what she had mistakenly taken for arrogance, to be what it was: Misunderstanding.

"Your really not gonna vaccinate yourself are you?"

Again he did not reply, but she understood the silence and the truth it tried to hide.

"You do know what we have to do this for, don't you?"

"I don't care for your addictions."

"Addictions?" she spat, "Oh no hunny, you got it all wrong. Yes I'm addicted, but not in the fucked up drug sense you mean. I'm addicted to this" she shook the now empty vial, "because I'm addicted to life. Kerrigan," she sat forward and addressed him directly, for the first time striving to send home a message of absolute sincerity, "Kerrigan, without this I'll die. And so will you."

Kerrigan met her gaze. She was either one of the best liars of all time, or somehow she believed what she was saying.

Die? She'll die without it? And so will he? How could that be? He had not ever been given, or taken, any kind of drug on Chimera that was meant to preserve his life, yet here he was in, relatively, perfect health. Hell, PERFECT health. So what the fuck was this drug she was obsessing over?

Their gazes remained locked on one another for a few moments. He was reluctant to admit his ignorance to the drug if what she was saying was true, yet he knew that what she was saying was so baffling, so ridiculous that it surely could not be true.

Nina was reluctant to accept his naivety, and also equally reluctant to fall into his stubborn little game. If that's what it was. If he was just playing with her, then it was a stupid, foolish game to play.

Finally, it was Nina who took the risk, "Where have you been for so long Kerrigan?"

"Locked up."

"I know that, but fuck me, for how long? Are you seriously saying that you don't take this stuff?" She waved the empty vial at him.

His mind noted that he had never said any such thing, yet she had understood him none the less.

Although he had not told her so, she had interpreted his silence and lack of responses to her questioning to determine that he had never taken the vaccine before.

"Leave me alone" he answered and turned away from her. He was uncomfortable with the line of questioning. He felt stupid although he knew he shouldn't. Of course he had never taken any drugs, how could he? He had been trapped aboard a prison ship for who knew how long, and then had spent most of recent memory trying to survive in the middle of a forest. How could he have gotten hold of any drugs even if he had wanted to? Part of his mind screamed that Nina must be mocking him in her own perverse way, but another, smaller part of his mind insisted that her eyes showed she believed in what she was saying.

He did not want to appear either foolish or stupid and so he chose to turn away, hoping she would leave him to sleep rather than him having to face more uncomfortable questioning.

"For fuck's sake Kerrigan, stop fucking around for all our sakes and take the God Damn vaccine!" she had risen from her seat and was waving the vial that he had discarded at him.

He swiped the vaccine out of her hand, knocking it into the corner of the truck with a subtle twinkle, and grabbed her by the throat. He thrust her back onto the seat she had risen from. She lay there, staring defensively up into his shouting face, "GET THE FUCK AWAY FROM ME YOU CRAZY BITCH!" he shouted. Spit speckled Nina's face. His voice boomed at her in the close confines of the trucks interior, "I DON'T GIVE A FUCK ABOUT YOUR DRUGS AND I DON'T GIVE A FUCK WHAT YOU DO TO YOURSELF, BUT YOU DO NOT, DO NOT TRY AND LAY THAT SHIT ON ME! OTHERWISE I WILL BREAK YOUR FUCKING NECK!" with each sentence his grip upon her neck seemed to increase in tandem with his anger, "IF I COULD FUCKING OPERATE THIS THING FOR MYSELF I WOULD HAVE KILLED YOU A LONG TIME AGO, BUT LUCKILY FOR YOU, YOUR NO GOOD TO ME DEAD. SO WHILE YOUR ALIVE, YOU WILL NOT TRY AND FORCE YOUR CRAZY DRUG ADDICTION UPON ME. DO YOU UNDERSTAND?" At first she did not reply - Perhaps too shocked to perform the movements that speech would require. So he repeated himself, shaking her so hard her teeth rattled, "DO YOU UNDERSTAND ME?"

"Y-Yes" she choked.

He remained atop her for a moment longer to push home the message of his conviction.

Once risen, he left her sprawled on the chairs, panting for breath. He went to the supply pack that Nina herself had brought aboard, and withdrew himself some food.

Nina rose from where she had been thrust, and tossed her hair back over her head, attempting to regain a little dignity. She would never admit it, and was just as keen not to show it, but Kerrigan's outburst had startled her.

She hoped that her shock did not show.

"Fine" she said with an air of authority, as if Kerrigan's demand was still under discussion.

She rose from where she was and went back to the driver's seat and flicked a switch. The internal lights snapped off, and the monitors of the computers faded into darkness.

Kerrigan finished eating his food in the dark.

For hours after the small cabin's lights had been turned off, Kerrigan remained awake, staring at the low ceiling.

He was not tired and so could not sleep. He could hear the soft, sleep-filled breathing of Nina nearby.

After their argument, and after she had stubbornly turned the light off, Nina had tossed and turned for awhile, clearly still too frustrated at their exchange to rest comfortably.

Slowly, her fidgeting had eventually subsided and she remained still. Not long afterwards, her breathing changed to that of the shallow breathing of one who is entirely wrapped in the healing comfort of deep sleep's heavy blanket.

Kerrigan took advantage of the quiet to dwell upon his thoughts. He was at his most comfortable with his surroundings when he could take stock of what had taken place, and analyse what information he had gained to better understand his situation, hopefully learning something new from his reflections that had gone unnoticed at the time.

Focusing upon Nina's breathing, Kerrigan's first thoughts naturally flowed to her. Again he wondered just how far she might be trusted. She was emotionally involved in their endeavour in a way that Kerrigan could never be. She believed her brother was still alive inside the S.O Refinery - a thought that Kerrigan still did not agree with - which drove her to risk her life against staggering odds. Was her love for her brother so great? Could she not live without him?... or was there something more? How might she fare further down the line should they encounter hostilities? He had already witnessed first hand her wild and erratic behaviour. If she fed on her emotions so easily when she was frustrated, the

possibility was there that she might do the same in other emotional situations. The last thing that he needed was for her to abandon her logic and succumb to the primal panic that would arise within. It would only conclude in her death and no doubt his own would follow soon after.
Thinking of the risk that she was taking, that they were both taking, his mind bent and flowed to his own motivation; his freedom.
He had already seen for himself the level of attention and determination that had been focused towards his capture. Even in such a relatively small town as Trendid was, walls were covered in his image with the promise of a bountiful reward for his capture.
Was he to be captured alive or dead? He could not remember the warrants specifying either way... he thought it was alive. Did it even matter?
All that mattered was that everyone he might here forth come into contact with could potentially know his face, and that, potentially, everyone he met was hoping to be the lucky one to find him, turn him in, and claim the substantial reward his capture represented.
He could not live in any normal, civilized fashion with such a never ending fear looming over his head. He would always be looking over his shoulder, waiting and expecting the knife in his back that would finally end his existence.
Even life aboard Chimera had not been so fearful. Could he live like that? Maybe, but there was a better future out there for him. If Nina could be trusted, if she could wipe away his records, he might have a chance at peace.
Yet this too came with the contradiction that he knew he deserved to be punished.
He swore to himself that he would continue to repent for his crimes, despite his freedom.
And so it was that he found himself trusting his future, his freedom, even his life to the skills of this one woman. Their goals and motivations were intertwined with one another leading from Trendid, back into the very heart of the S.O Refinery.
He did not remember much of his experience within the S.O

Refinery, but what he could remember was enough to convince Kerrigan that what they were attempting to do was suicide.

He *and* this strange, emotional, drug addicted woman.

What was it with her and those drugs? Surely her reactions, although proven to be as quick as a felines, would become hampered by the use of her narcotics? What with the dangers of the hell hole down which they were freely entering, surely they needed all their wits about them at all times?

And those comments she made about dying if the drugs weren't taken? What the hell was that all about? Nina herself certainly seemed to believe it when she had spoken about it at the time. Surely it couldn't be true…could it?

"Nina" spoke Kerrigan aloud into the twilight. His voice sounded incredibly loud in the dead silence of the deep night.

"Nina" he repeated, "wake up."

She groaned groggily.

"What is it?" she slurred still rousing from her sleep.

"We have to talk."

"Can't it wait till morning?" her usual cocky attitude had not yet awakened. She was still much too asleep to work up the energy her arrogance needed.

"No. We have to talk about your addiction."

"What are you on about?" She had risen to a sitting position now. Kerrigan could see her silhouette rubbing sleep from her eyes; she was a darker black against the black interior of the truck.

He too rose, "Your drug addiction Nina. The one you tried to force on me."

Although he could not see her eye's directly, they appeared as pin pricks of light in the dark, reflecting the moon light that partially illuminated the front of the cabin.

Perhaps it was still her sleep grogged mind that prevented another torrent of verbal abuse, but this time Nina accepted his tone not for sarcasm, as she had previously, but as the genuine concern it was.

"Your serious aren't you?"

Kerrigan felt no need to reply. He was always serious.

"Fuckin hell,,," She kneaded a knot from the back of her neck.

"Kerrigan, *I* need to take that vaccine, we *ALL* need to take that vaccine, or else *we will die*. Me, all the people back in Trendid... even you."
She met Kerrigan's eyes once more. They sparkled like the stars in the night sky.
"You really don't remember this do you?"
Again he chose not to reply. His naivety to the free world would make him appear stupid to anyone who really knew just how little he actually understood...
How long had he been out of touch?
"For as long as anyone can remember, we have all needed to take this drug, every single day, for our entire lives. If we don't, we die, it's as simple as that."
"Why would you die?"
"Because the air is poisoned, Kerrigan. Because every time you breathe in your inhaling millions upon millions of tiny little air borne pieces of poison that get absorbed into your lungs and into your blood stream. Because every time you eat, your eating little tiny bits of poison that lay inside the animals that you eat - Animals don't take the vaccine Kerrigan." She said this last as if he were stupid, as if what she said was basic knowledge that any stubborn child would know.
Nina seemed to be on a roll, and so Kerrigan let her continue her story without interruption, "Or maybe the poison's in the water. We all have to drink right? There's no way around that. And even if we tried to filter the rain water, the animals that we eat also have to drink, and so we'll absorb the poison from eating them anyway. To be totally honest with you Kerrigan, no one really knows for definite. Maybe it is in the rain water, or the air that we breathe. But maybe it's in the suns rays and somehow it permeates our skin, or even from the light of the moon... who knows!? Maybe we're all just fucking born to die that way, I don't know!... but what I do know is that if you don't hurry up and take your vaccine too, it's gonna quickly become one lonely trip for me... if you catch my drift?"
Kerrigan heard her tirade but found it hard to accept what it was

that she was saying. Poison? In the air? Or the water or food? How could that be possible? And even if it were, without taking the medication for so long, by now he must surely have been feeling the effects.

"I don't feel like I'm dying." He replied.

"Well of course you don't... yet." She took a moment, as if the next revelation caused her an inner pain, "It doesn't happen suddenly. You don't just fall over dead, flat on your face like a tree that's been felled. No, it takes time. Your hair will fall out, your skin will sag and hang off your bones like your wearing clothing that are too big for you. Boils will sprout and burst. Gaping wounds as your flesh tears and rips itself apart will all start to appear on your skin, making you wish that you could just hurry up and die. Fuck, didn't you see all the sick people back there?" She pointed in what might have been the general direction of Trendid, "Didn't you see all those sick, dying fuckers walking around back there like the living dead? Or did you walk around with your eyes closed?" During her speech, Kerrigan had noticed that Nina's attitude had become increasingly more and more agitated as her mind slowly awakened from her sleep. Her language was returning to it's former colourful theme.

"Why would a twenty year old woman look like she was a frail seventy year old if she had taken the vaccine, Kerrigan?" she asked. He recalled the thin haired woman, and the skeletal frames of the villagers who had chased him. When Kerrigan didn't reply, she continued, "Because they, like you, mustn't have taken the vaccine on time. So if you don't want to spend your last few moments alive walking around with a crooked spine, with your cheek muscles trailing the floor in front of you while you try to avoid tripping over them, ripping the skin off your face then you better hurry up and take the fucking vaccine."

She glared at him menacingly, daring him to question her.

"You seem awfully passionate about this whole thing." He couldn't help but feel that Nina was inappropriately upset by this virus, this poison that had been in her life and the lives of others for so long.

If the virus was really so wide spread, so strong and had really been around for such a long period of time, how was it that he had not heard of it before?

"Of course I am! Do you have any idea what it's like growing up watching those around you, your friends and family, become as old… no OLDER, and weaker than a geriatric? To watch children dying from conditions that should not have afflicted them till they were grandparents? To watch women give birth to deformed babies? If they're lucky it might just be an extra toe or finger, something not so noticeable, but maybe it'll be an extra arm or leg. Some babies are born too disfigured to live outside of their mother's womb, Kerrigan!" The pinpoints of light that were her eyes, now shimmered as if they were sparkles of light reflected in a pond's rippling surface, Her words were beginning to warble with emotion, "I'm sorry if you think I should be as relaxed and as calm about these things like you are Kerrigan, but I've had to live with these.. these… abominations! I have a heart. I have feelings. And I cannot accept the way things are in this world so complacently like you do, even if I know I have no way of changing them."

She lay back upon the truck's chairs with a heavy thud. She was too overcome with sorrow to continue the conversation further. Her breath came in rapid, wavered breaths as if she had ran a marathon rather then vent her frustration. After a moment or two of silence, she regained control of her breathing.

Remaining on her back, aiming the question at the ceiling, but meaning it for Kerrigan, Nina asked, "You really don't know any of this stuff, do you?"

Although Kerrigan did not reply, Nina understood his response. She had begun to understand his silence as reluctance to admit his ignorance. It was his weakness.

Despite her emotions, she chose not to address his silent admission of confusion with confrontation. For the first time she regarded his silence with a soft pity, "I hope you understand me more now Kerrigan, and why I need to find out for myself if Ames really is still alive."

With that said, she rolled over and went to sleep.

Kerrigan remained awake long after Nina had eventually returned to sleep, musing on the revelations she had made to him.

Morning came with a smooth and golden start. Warm beams of light flowed through the front windshield of Kerrigan and Nina's renegade transport, to warm the interior gently. The rays of light were filtered as they shone through the one way glass, reducing their glare from an intense focus to a softer hue, yet retaining their original warmth as they did so. Fuzzy dust particles drifted lazily in the gentle light, aloft upon an unfelt breeze.

As Kerrigan stirred into consciousness, he had never felt such tranquillity before. No more was he awakening to the sharp creek of aged iron welding, straining to hold themselves together upon the open seas. No more was he emerging to the sound of unseen creatures hiding among branches of giant trees that hung and swayed overhead. Instead, he awoke to the warm silence and welcoming glow of a fresh new morning. He felt welcomed by the day, feeling instantly rejuvenated by the warm welcome.

Nina was already awake. She was rummaging through their back pack once more.

She noticed him looking at her. "Good morning sleepy head" she tossed a wrapped morsel of food at him which landed upon his chest.

It took him only a few moments to gather his senses and become fully awake. His body had become used to the sudden revival needed when returning from the black abyss of unconsciousness, however it was initiated, during his time in the Forbidden Forest.

Nina plucked her own breakfast out of the satchel and sat in the chair that faced the bank of computer monitors.

She ate her food while she worked.

"What are you doing?" asked Kerrigan, obtaining a sitting position so as not to choke on his breakfast. It was a dried piece of salted meat.

"Yesterday I noticed my brother's name on this computer. It confirmed to me what you had already said; that Ames is being held at the S.O Refinery."

She took a bite out of her breakfast and continued, "What it also showed me, is that Ames IS definitely still alive... but unfortunately little else."
She switched off the computer and strode over to the truck's driving seat and sat down.
Within a few moments, Nina then reawakened the truck's engine with a disgruntled metallic growl as if it were offended by it's premature awakening. She was prepared to depart, "If we set off now we can be at the Refinery by nightfall. The less time we waste the better."
She said this as if she felt the need to justify their uncivilly, early departure.
Once said, the truck lurched forward taking Kerrigan and Nina closer from where they had slept, to where Kerrigan believed they would die.

The remainder of the journey passed without consequence. In fact, it seemed to both Kerrigan and Nina, although both would dare not voice it, that the journey itself passed in a boring, anti-climatic fashion. Both had expected from the start that their journey would be rife with an assortment of various discoveries and attacks from unexpected disasters, sentient foliage and wild creatures. They had both particularly expected an ambush from the beast that remained shrouded in it's own dark cloud... but nothing had taken place.
Perhaps it was the combined knowledge that they both shared, and had both experienced, of the hostile environment into which they were both willingly headed that made their minds expect them to encounter a series of escalating hostilities upon their journey.
The only thing of any significance that occurred throughout the day's voyage was when the rain that had pounded upon them ever since they had left Trendid slowly petered away. First it faded into a shower, then into a fine drizzle that barely obscured their stolen truck's windscreen, and then finally it stopped completely. Peering upwards at the sky that lay behind them, Kerrigan could see the green outlined clouds remained above the village they had left, presumably continuing their heavy discharge upon the pitiful

villagers below.

Nina saw Kerrigan's observations and commented upon them, "Well, we're finally out of Trendid's broken umbrella."

"What do you mean?"

"The eternal rain, of course." She had kept her eye's on the winding path ahead.

"Eternal? You mean it never stops?"

She glanced across at Kerrigan, "No," she replied, finally acknowledging his ignorance for what it was… naivety. He wasn't, Nina understood, just being the pig headed prick she had mistaken him for. He genuinely had no understanding of the natural order of the world. "Never. It never has, and never will. It's just one of those things you learn to accept as you grow up in life. Like the rising of the sun or the virus."

Their expectation of hostilities remained unfulfilled as the bright, cloud filtered, sunlight gradually gave way to the glowing purple of twilight. It bloomed over the horizon, staining the sky with a deepening, violet stain. It was at this same time that the pairing finally emerged from the woods, rising up the steep gradient of a barren hillside.

"We're here." Nina announced to Kerrigan

Although nothing could yet be seen, Kerrigan did not doubt Nina's word. The woods had faded along with the sun's light, and the lush green grass of the rising hillside was a dark black growth that was silhouetted against the darkening purple sky.

A sense of anticipation gnawed at Kerrigan's mind as they neared the peak of the rise, and he too knew that they had finally reached their destination.

The hill's gradient reduced, and they topped the blackened hillside. As Nina brought their vehicle to a halt, Kerrigan had not expected to see the sight that lay before them both.

Below them, a hugely complex structure, many times larger than he had remembered upon his awakening many days ago, stretched out in a large concentric circle that almost touched the horizon.

What appeared to be a small industrialised city was laid before

him. Each building, chimney and structure was connected by a confusing myriad of complex intertwining pipe-work and cables. It looked as if every building was connected to every other building.
The thick chimneys that dotted the city vomited think clouds of dark smoke into the air that drifted lazily upwards, despite their impossibly heavy appearance.
Standing tall in the centre of the city, lay the tall, main structure that Kerrigan had seen many days ago.
 It still bared the scar of the explosion that had expelled him from it so violently.
Instead of the mated yellow colour that he had seen the first time in the bright sunshine of daylight, the building was a black shadow against the violet sky, the base of which was illuminated by pale blue lighting cast by a ring of high intensity flood lights. Above this, a stuttering line of the same, light blue, pocketed the outline of the building's exterior.
Kerrigan did not remember ever having seen the surrounding network of structures that bloomed outwards from the central building's base upon his expulsion, but soon came to understand why. When he had first came to, the lower half of the building, and therefore also the structures that radiated from it, had been blocked from his sight by the hillside that had rose and blocked his view.
He had always remembered the Refinery as just a solitary building, not as the huge system of interconnected buildings and structures that emanated and fed to and from it.
Several thick looking pipes at the edge of the complex snaked away from the complex, towards the horizon and disappeared beyond sight. Other's extended beyond the city and fed down and into the soil of the land, beyond the boundaries of the city they had originated from.
To Kerrigan, the entire interconnected structure looked like a giant metallic scab upon the natural landscape of the countryside.
"Well, this is it" remarked Nina. Her voice gave off a subtle indication of the trepidation she felt, but tried unsuccessfully to hide, "you ready for this?"
Kerrigan met her eyes, and then returned his eyes to the metallic

maze that filled the land below, "I'm always ready"
Nina flicked a few switches, and with a lurch, they slowly trundled forwards.

18

Earlier that day, during their trip to the Refinery, Kerrigan and Nina spent a long time discussing the Refinery itself, or rather Nina spent a long time discussing it – Kerrigan for the most part remained silent listening carefully to everything that Nina told him. What she told him could potentially make the difference between life and death. Nina, having worked at the Refinery previously, lead the conversation, "The S.O Refinery is basically the local base for all of the S.O officers, and it's certainly the largest that I know of.
It's here that the research is conducted to try and solve all of the problems in our lives. Not least of which, is a permanent cure to the virus that plagues us all.
It's a beautiful, spiritual place, blessed by the Gods Themselves."
In Kerrigan's opinion, it was odd that Nina would hold such compassionate feelings about a place from which he had been so brutally tortured and had only narrowly escaped death.
He scoffed at her compassion.
"What?" she stole a glance across at him, "Are you saying it isn't?"
"Not last time I checked."
"Of course it is! How can you say it isn't? It's the God's blessing of the S.O. that allow them to live in such extravagant comforts. Why else would the Gods allow them to use the forbidden power?"
"What 'forbidden power'?"
"Electricity, of course."
Growing increasingly more confused by Nina's explanations, Kerrigan interrupted Nina. She either had forgotten Kerrigan's ignorance to the world, or presumed it to be false, and so he forced a reminder upon her, "Wait a second, back up. If we're gonna do this, I need some answers. Let's start at the start. Who are the S.O?

What the fuck is the Refinery? And what's all this shit about being allowed to use electricity?" His questions sounded foolish to his own ears. There was no such things as 'Gods' after all, "Are you saying Trendid doesn't have electricity?" he felt like a fool for even asking, but that was what her explanation had suggested.
"Of course it doesn't!" replied Nina. She sounded almost offended at the question. Once again she stole a look to her side at him. This time, however, her look was full of concerned pity. "OK, let me start at the beginning for you…"

"…The S.O. – The SigmaOmega - is the collective name given to all the people and buildings that serve the Gods purpose. They are the God's servants upon Earth. They are both our spiritual guides, and our law enforcers. Through their leadership and by obeying their laws that the Gods have decreed, we can all achieve a better afterlife when we die. There is no higher power. Every man, woman and child, regardless of their occupation or social status, must obey whatever the S.O tells us to do because that is what the Gods themselves want us to do. There is no exception to this rule.
The S.O. have bases set up throughout the land with a representative based within each town: The Chosen One… but they're a little different from the S.O. themselves.
Now don't get me wrong, the S.O. are not some kind of ruthless dictatorship bossing us about all day, every day, no, no, no far from it. The vast majority of the time they leave us be to live out our lives completely as normal. In fact, they are in many ways our carers, because it's they who supply us with all of the vaccine that we need to live out our lives.
Without the vaccine, Kerrigan, without the S.O, we would all be dead. Every man, woman and child, every disfigured person that you saw back there in Trendid would have ceased to exist a long time ago.
The S.O have been around for as long as records hold. No one, and no piece of documentation, recalls a time prior to when the S.O were in existence. They have always been and always will be, just

like the Gods themselves."

Nina took a moment to collect her thoughts. Her stare remained vacant and she took a slow, deep breath that seemed to penetrate, and shiver through her entire core. After a moment, she continued, "As you already know, there is a great pestilence that covers all of our lives. The virus. It too has been around as long as anyone can remember, but much, much longer than the S.O. has. The virus has been in existence forever, where as the S.O has only been around for as long as the history books record. Because the S.O is a human made creation, there must have been a point where it began, but as for the virus…. That's been around forever.

It is this plaque that the S.O are trying to eradicate. The Refinery where we are headed is the biggest research facility into the virus that there is. Once a cure is discovered, we will be free to live our lives free of the burden of having to inject ourselves everyday with that bloody vaccine..." Her focused stare began to fade, "Can you imagine what a sense of freedom that would be?!"

Having previously been confined to the limitations of Chimera, Kerrigan could relate with Nina's desire. However he chose to hold back his empathy.

Nina continued, "As such, to aid them in their endeavour, the Gods have granted upon them the awesome power of electricity. They need this power to activate and control the phenomenally powerful machines that they use in order to try and understand, prevent and then ultimately destroy, the virus.

Electricity does not work all over the world of course, it only works in those places where the S.O themselves are, for only they are worthy enough to use such a destructive force."

Nina turned the truck around a particularly tight turn in the road and continued, "Obviously the S.O. use the electricity in other ways too, such as this truck for instance, but again this is all in aid of enforcing the laws that the Gods have also assigned to them.

So, as you can imagine, it is best not to piss these guys off, because if we do, if for example two of their officers were discovered to have been killed in Trendid, the vaccine that the entire town depends upon could be in jeopardy. The wrath of the God's could

be unleashed upon us all."
She cast a brief look in Kerrigan's direction, but maintained her focus upon the road ahead.
"You don't really believe in all that God crap do you?" asked Kerrigan.
"Of course I fucking do!" she replied offended, "There's evidence all around us, just look around. The virus, electricity, the weather… how can you not believe in the Gods?"
It was a philosophical argument that Kerrigan cared not to entertain. Especially when more important questions needed to be discussed and answered.
"So, electricity doesn't work in Trendid?" asked Kerrigan avoiding Nina's question.
"No. Nor anywhere else outside of an S.O. base."
"So what about this truck? Those computers back there aren't running themselves"
"Your forgetting something. As I mentioned before, the S.O have been blessed with the power of electricity. This is an S.O transport. It's been blessed and therefore, accepted by the Gods. Electricity will work here"
"OK. What about Chimera?"
"Chimera?"
"The ship I was imprisoned upon."
"Well again that's a part of the S.O. They're here to enforce laws, not just to find a cure for us all."
Kerrigan thought back to Bronco and Durrant… were they part of the S.O?
Durrant sure, as it was he who had interrogated him inside the S.O Refinery, but Bronco? Blessed by the Gods?
He couldn't see it, but if that was his job…
"OK, fine" replied Kerrigan, still defiant to Nina's claims, "But I still haven't taken the vaccine in my entire life. So why aren't I dead?"
Nina stole another glance over at him. Her answer did not come as quickly as they had previously.
"IF I accept what your telling me is true and IF you really say you

haven't taken the vaccine like you say, then they must have found another way of administrating it to you aboard Chimera. Can't really have mass murderers running amok with syringes in their hands after all can they?" She smiled craftily at him, "Maybe they injected you in your sleep or put it in your food or something. The vaccine doesn't just have to be injected directly into your vein Kerrigan, but believe me this stuff makes your food taste foul which is why most people choose to inject themselves."

It was possible, Kerrigan had to concede, that the Grey Snot that he and his other prisoners aboard Chimera were forced to eat everyday could have contained any chemical makeup that the guards chose to put in there, maybe even the vaccine - it wasn't as if the Grey Snot was a culinary delight.

Kerrigan mused upon these revelations. "Tell me about these Chosen Ones you've mentioned. You said they were different."

"The Chosen Ones work alongside the S.O, though are somewhat of a different entity. They are so called because they're chosen specifically by the Gods to be unique. Special. They are individuals, blessed at birth, who at some point in their life will start to develop and display divine qualities. Special powers that me and you could never perform."

"Like what?"

"Well, like you have already seen for yourself. Remember how you nearly killed us all when the beast from the Forbidden Forest followed you into town? How it was sent fleeing away from a a fireball made by the man in robes? That man who saved us was Ames's replacement Chosen One."

"Ames was a Chosen One?"

"That's right." She replied with pride. She straightened in the driver's seat, "One of the greatest there has ever been. All of Trendid loved him."

It occurred to Kerrigan that this was why Nina had commanded such respect from the mob who had tried to kill him in Trendid's church. Nina was the sister of one of Trendid's most beloved and powerful religious leaders. Although he was no longer the resident leader, it was a testament to his respect that the town folk would still honour and respect his family.

A sudden jolt shot through Kerrigan; If Ames was a Chosen One, and therefore part of the S.O. by extension, that would mean that Nina was also a part of the S.O.

Was it possible that she actually delivering Kerrigan back into the hands of her superiors? Instead of pursuing the life of her lost brother?

No, Kerrigan thought feeling foolish about himself for rushing into such an idea, this could not be the case. Nina had already had multiple instances where her trust had been tested. She could have let the mob in the church tear him apart limb from limb as they had so clearly wanted to. He had been vastly outnumbered and, although he might have prevented the initial few, he would have been unable to stop the entire crowd... Nina had been the one to stop them.

Nina had also spent a long time in the presence of an S.O officer inside the Chosen One's Quarters. During this time, Kerrigan had been unable to see or hear any treacherous plans she might have made with the guard. She could have simply told the officer where he was there and then. Like a fish in a barrel he could have been shot from the window of the house without ever knowing that he had been targeted.

No, Kerrigan knew Nina could be trusted. But still...

"So as I was saying, The Chosen Ones are selected by the Gods themselves and because of this blessing, they work alongside the S.O. Eventually, when their powers become great enough, or another Chosen One is blessed within the same town, The Chosen One will go with the S.O. to their base where they will be closer to God. They go there to pray for civilisation's salvation. It is the ultimate goal and privilege for the Chosen Ones."

She paused for a moment collecting her thoughts, "When Phon, Trendid's latest Chosen One, the one with the fireball, showed signs of the blessing, the entire town was in celebration. Especially Ames. He was so happy, like a child with a new toy. He was so, so..."

Her voice rose and nearly broke. She paused and took a moment to gather her thoughts. She tried again, "He was so... enthusiastic." She concluded.

"He could now go with the S.O to be next to God, to try and bring peace and happiness back to all those he knew and loved. Of course he knew that he would not be coming back from his pilgrimage, but he would never allow something like that to blight the town's celebrations. It was the happiest day of his life." Her eyes had glazed over.

"To think that the S.O would harm him in anyway is almost inconceivable. If your right, then everything that I have known and believed in since I was a child would be wrong."

She turned her shimmering eye's towards Kerrigan, "It would change the face of the world if you're right Kerrigan."

The rain continued to beat with as much intensity as it always As their journey continued, Kerrigan and Nina began to discuss their strategy for infiltrating the S.O Refinery when they eventually reached it, "The entire Refinery is one huge security system." Nina explained, "Every entrance to and from the central buildings, especially the H.Q. building itself, which is the large central building where you were held, are manned by armed guards day and night who will check your credentials every step of the way.

"The compound itself is like a set of ever increasing rings, with the smallest most protected areas at the centre and the larger, less sensitive areas on the outside. Like the layers of an onion or the rings of a tree trunk. Each concentric ring is protected by an elaborate security system and armed guards. Assuming that you have the relevant clearance to grant you access beyond each barricade, then you may pass. If you don't, you wont. No arguments. While I worked there I had first hand experience of this for myself. A truck not too dissimilar to this one once tried to get past a particular barricade to which it did not have clearance. The driver challenged the guards who gave him a couple of opportunities to turn around or he would be shot, regardless of who he claimed to be or what he claimed to need entrance for. The guard's attitude is; if you work there, you should know the rules.

Anyway the driver continued to rant on at them about how much he was needed within the compound, and before he knew what had happened, the guard closest to him shoved the muzzle of his gun in his face and shot him. His brains exploded all over the inside of the windshield and the truck was taken away by internal reinforcements. The driver was never publicised as being missing or dead. His identity was completely erased by the S.O's might, as if he had never existed at all… What I'm trying to say is that these guys are not to be fucked with."
"I thought you said these guys were some kind of religious groupies… That doesn't sound very holy to me."
"The God's have granted these people with the knowledge and technology to save the human race, Kerrigan" replied Nina with utter sincerity, "If they choose to be a little heavy handed at times, so be it. If what they were doing was wrong, then the Gods would step in and take away what privileges they have, but they don't. So yeah, maybe it can seem a little harsh at times… but who are we to stop them?"
Nina heaved hard on the large steering wheel, putting her entire, yet slender, weight behind the motion as the truck approached a tight turn in the road.
"So", continued Nina putting into words the unspoken questions that hung between herself and Kerrigan, "How do we get into this fort without credentials? Well, this is why I suggested we take this damn truck in the first place." The truck finished it's dizzying swerve around the bend and regained a stable, forward momentum, "The outer defences of the Refinery are merely scanning machines that read the I.D of each vehicle that passes between them. As this truck is one of their own, it'll have no problem passing through. The scanners are manned by guards, granted, but their role is to stop and speak to the drivers who are highlighted by the scanners as not having the appropriate I.D. Therefore, having the appropriate I.D signatures, we'll be fine."
The rain that had fallen continuously was starting to fade away. The constant drumming of the rain that pounded against the roof of their transport was slowly fading away to a steady beating.

Kerrigan looked out of the truck's windshield and up at the clouds above. He couldn't be certain, but it looked like the clouds looked less burdened with water than the clouds that had smothered the sky above Trendid.

"We're coming out of the rain now, so it's not too much further." remarked Nina, as if the weather were an indication of distance, "So here's what I'm thinking: Those two passengers back there that have been travelling with us..." she hooked a thumb to the back of the truck where the two bodies of the dead guards remained crumpled atop one another. Occasionally the limp hand of one of the men would bounce in tandem with the bumps in the road, "...could still be of use to us. What we should do is take their credentials that should be attached to their belts someplace, disguise ourselves in their uniforms and use that to gain as much entry into the Refinery as possible. Once inside we'll have to improvise, but that should at least be enough to get us inside the H.Q itself which is where we wanna be anyway."

"No." replied Kerrigan without a moment's hesitation, "that's a bad idea."

"Oh really?" Nina glanced a look over at him, "Well if your so fucking clever, you tell me why not Mr Smarty Pants. I don't hear you coming up with any better plans."

"Because one uniform is covered in blood from where I broke his face, and the other is covered in filth from where you dragged him through the streets."

She couldn't argue with that. They wouldn't pass even the most casual of inspections, always assuming that the uniforms would fit anyway, and the chances of that were pretty slim. She and Kerrigan differed in height by over a foot. She could not recall such a height difference between the guards when she had seen them stood together outside of the Chosen One's Residence.

"Well we should still use their I.D.s" replied Nina with as much pride as she could muster, "We'll just have to sneak around a bit more that's all. At this rate we'll be approaching at night and the majority of people that work there will be either asleep or off duty. Only the security staff will still be on guard and we'll at least have

the cover of darkness to help us out."
Outside their truck, the rain had finally stopped and the sun poked it's rays through the clouds and warmed the interior of the cabin. If Kerrigan had been an optimist, or read into nature's face and saw omens, he might have felt that the suns re-emergence was a positive sign of things to come.
However he wasn't an optimist, and did not believe in portents.
For Kerrigan, Nina's plan was the stupidest, most foolish plan he had ever heard.

19

Later that evening, the truck rolled forward to meet the glittering light's of the S.O. Refinery below, reminding Kerrigan of the night sky, but laid out below and before him, instead of above.
As their ride grumbled it's way across the distance between themselves and the citadel below, nestled within the rise of the hills that surrounded it, Kerrigan felt the awaiting doom that lay before them in the Refinery. Yet instead of feeling scared or anxious about his and Nina's impending doom as one might have expected, Kerrigan remained calm and focused, his heart not beating any quicker than normal.
Panic would entertain failure, and he felt the need to be calm enough for both himself and Nina.
The distance that they needed to cover to reach the S.O Refinery seemed to elongate itself out in front of them. What had seemed like a relatively short journey was extending itself further and further out of their reach, as if the Refinery itself was trying to outrun them.
Suddenly, the glittering artificial lights of the S.O Refinery that had previously seemed so far away, exploded out from their condensed cluster to flow out and fill the windshield of the truck.
It was only upon viewing the industrial citadel so close that Kerrigan understood that his first observations of the size of the Refinery had been greatly underestimated. The entire compound

was easily larger than Trendid had been, and significantly more technologically advanced. Movement that Kerrigan had first seen from a distance soon resolved itself into a marvel of technology. Monorails criss crossed the entire complex, providing quick, efficient transportation from one side of the complex to the other. Most of the mono-rails either entered or exited the base of the central H.Q building which stood as a lynch-pin to the entire complex. It's exterior was illuminated from the base in a ghostly, artificial blue that was provided by a series of high intensity flood lights that surrounded the building.

It was clear that the electricity that 'The Gods' had 'blessed' upon the S.O. had been put to full use in ways that Kerrigan could not possibly have imagined.

Gradually, an archway appeared in the chain link fence that encompassed the entire complex, it was one of the entrances into the Refinery that Nina had mentioned earlier. The archway was made of solid metal and was easily large enough to allow admittance to vehicles much larger than their own. A small hut stood to one side of the archway where a small light fluttered within.

"OK here we go" muttered Nina as the archway loomed. A small sheen of sweat on her forehead glistened in the moonlight.

She approached the archway, and slowed the truck to walking speed. With this done, she walked the vehicle through the archway allowing the scanners to search, detect, and authorize the I.D that was stored within the truck's computer system.

Kerrigan had half expected their arrival to trigger some kind of alarm, as if somehow the scanner knew that the two living occupants within the truck were not the S.O officers that had taken the vehicle out of the compound, yet their entrance into the Refinery was met with no alarm, fanfare or signal of any kind. They emerged on the other side of the archway without incident and Nina increased their speed once more.

Kerrigan heard Nina exhale loudly next to him. The sheen of sweat he had noticed upon her brow earlier seemed to have doubled in it's intensity.

"OK, since this is a military truck, we can also pass through the next security barrier." Explained Nina, "After that, we're on foot."
"Why?"
"Because we don't have the clearance to progress any deeper."
Passing other stationary vehicles much smaller than their own, Kerrigan determined that the majority of the outer ring was designed to be a parking bay for the multitude of vehicles that would pass to, from and into the huge complex.
There were buildings scattered amongst the vehicles, but they were merely the size of a house back in Trendid, much smaller and less impressive than those Kerrigan could see looming beyond the next ring of defences.
One of the buildings that he could see, was a monorail station that was connected to the end of one of the massive rail tracks that criss-crossed the entire Refinery.
Without pausing to take in anymore of the outer rings contents, Nina drove their stolen vehicle directly across the parking lot towards the next defensive archway. It did not take them long, and the HQ grew marginally larger in their windshield.
Slowing once more to a walking pace so that the scanners could once again confirm the class of vehicle and the authorization codes it held deep within it's belly, they passed through the second archway without incident.
Once more Nina exhaled loudly in the driver's seat, having felt just as much nervous pressure as previously. Perhaps more so.
"OK, lets park this thing up."
The inside of the second ring was much larger than the first. It was as if when they had passed through the second archway they had somehow passed through a doorway that opened up directly onto the very outskirts of a large, advanced city. Huge buildings rose in all directions blocking from view those buildings that were smaller and stood next to them. The streets were significantly wider and paved with level concrete. The roads on the outer ring had also been cemented over, but were strewn with pot holes of ill-maintenance. Thick monorail beams crossed over head, stretching ever onwards until they reached, and penetrated, the HQ which

stood as a looming, oppressive monument on the horizon.

Although the city was clearly much more advanced, in every sense, than Trendid, Kerrigan felt a discomforting feeling of clutter. There was just so much stuff everywhere; illuminated signs, cables that hung from building to building, wires that crossed the streets overhead crossing over the night sky like thick spider silks, thick pipes that snaked up the sides of buildings and stuck out as smouldering chimneys at the top, the thick metallic pillars that held aloft the monorail, the steam that rose gently from an assortment of vents, grilles, grates, chimneys, and from various points in the concrete streets... all this gave Kerrigan the feeling that the city was much more untidy, cluttered and... dirty, than Trendid had ever been.

Yet most notable of all, standing out in contrast to everything that Kerrigan had experienced before or could ever remember... everywhere there was the glittering of light bulbs. The city shone with an artificial light the likes of which Kerrigan had never experienced before. He had never previously thought of Trendid as being dark. In fact he had hardly noticed the darkness at all, yet now he was inside the Refinery, the city seemed to glow with it's own artificial light.

For Kerrigan, the entire atmosphere seemed unnaturally bright and alive for a city that should have been enshrouded in the blackness of night.

It made him feel uncomfortably vulnerable.

Shadows still remained of course, but the rays of artificial light that were generated shone upon, and illuminated, all of the surfaces nearby giving every surface an unnatural luminescent.

Nina eased their vehicle into a nearby parking space, in-between two other vehicles of the same style.

When she powered down the engine she said, "OK, we're here." Her voice sounded strangely loud in the silence given by the quietened engine, as if her very voice might give away their position.

They looked at each other a moment in the gloom. Nina's face was creased up with nervous anxiety.

It was Kerrigan who broke the tension by rising from his chair and going to the glowing computers behind them both that would open up the doorway, "Let's go, before you change your mind." he grumbled.
"Right" she replied. In her nervous frame of mind she had not picked up on Kerrigan's subtle inflection.
She rose from her chair, the stolen I.D.s that she had taken from the two dead S.O. officers, jiggling at her belt.
She stood staring at the blank face of the still closed exit. She inhaled a deep breath and let it out slowly. She closed her eyes and muttered a wordless prayer. Once done, she turned to Kerrigan, and with a quick nod of her head, Kerrigan flicked the appropriate switch. The computers winked out and with a snap of decompressing air, the doorway popped outwards and slid back upon it's runners.

As the open sky stretched out to infinity above them, both Kerrigan and Nina felt incredibly exposed as soon as they stepped out of their truck and into the cool night air of the open, hostile environment that they had infiltrated.
A sense of urgency ignited within them both. It was foolish to remain amongst the vehicles. They were well illuminated by the flood lights that shone down upon them and it was entirely possible that someone could come by to use one of them.
Having both circled around their vehicle, trying to absorb as much information about their surroundings as quickly and as effectively as possible, they both agreed that an alleyway, a quick dash across an open street, would be their first and best destination. No street lights shone inside the dark alley and so, having looked up and down the street to make sure it was empty, the pairing darted across the street.
Once inside the alley, they hugged their backs tightly against the buildings, further reducing any potential visibility.
Although it had only been a quick dash, Nina panted as if she had ran a marathon.
"You need to calm down." advised Kerrigan, turning towards, but

unable to see, Nina in the alley.

She did not respond, but knew that he was right. Should either of them succumb to the panic that threatened to enshroud them both, they would both be as good as dead.

While Nina caught her breath, Kerrigan peeked around the corner. The street was deserted, which wasn't surprising considering it was the dead of the night.

Towards the end of the street, nestled amongst a larger condensation of vehicles, was another hut that gave access to the monorail above.

"We'll use the monorail."

"What?" hissed Nina.

"We'll use the monorail."

Nina peaked in the direction that Kerrigan was looking and then hid back amongst the shadows.

"You've got to be kidding me. How are we supposed to get in that thing without being noticed? The streets may look empty but you can bet your ass that there'll be people getting on and off that thing. The S.O. doesn't ever stop working. And incase you'd forgotten, your still a wanted man, Kerrigan. Anyone in this entire Refinery WILL recognize you."

"We're getting on it, not in it."

"What are you talking about."

"We're gonna get on the roof."

"Your kidding me, right?"

Silence.

"Of course not, I should have known." Said Nina, "You never kid."

As soon as she had accepted Kerrigan's plan, but before she could question it, Kerrigan said, "Come on." and slipped out into the street.

Taking advantage of the abandoned streets, Kerrigan dashed towards the monorail station with only a casual indication to Nina of his intentions.

Keeping his right side as close to the buildings as he could so as to minimize his exposure to the street lamps, Kerrigan arrived at the base of the mono station within a few seconds.

He hugged his back against the wall and strained his neck upwards to see if there was anyone present on the platform above.

The building was essentially nothing more than a concrete staircase that led up to a paved platform that would allow the boarding and unloading of passengers. A transparent roof capped the platform to keep commuters dry in poor weather.

Squinting his eyes against a light that not only lit up the platform, but also spilled out onto the stair way and street below, Kerrigan was pleased to see that the platform was as deserted as it had been when he had scouted it out from the alleyway.

"What the fuck are you doing?" hissed Nina from his left. She was panting again, and clearly pissed off with him, "Fucking tell me next time you go to pull a stunt like that."

Kerrigan dismissed her attitude as quickly as it had surfaced. His next concern was how they should board the monorail when it arrived. They couldn't board the train in the conventional sense incase commuters would recognize him.

Kerrigan had an idea. But how….?

"Are you listening to me?" Nina had stepped out of the shadows and away from the station's wall to confront Kerrigan face to face, "I've had just about enough of your silent treatment Kerrigan. We're supposed to be a fucking team remember…?"

Kerrigan cut her off from saying anything more by covering her mouth with his left hand and placing the index finger of his right against his lips.

"Shhhh" he whispered into the night, "You don't wanna go waking up your friends now do you?"

He removed his hand slowly. Nina's mouth hung open aghast, as if she were still mid-sentence.

After a moment, she pouted, "They're not my friends you arsehole."

The terminal at which they stood was the first, or last, stop on the monorail track. The thick metal railing ended with a bumper on the end of the platform.

"Just fucking work with me here" Nina continued to grumble, although a lot quieter than before.

Kerrigan remained focused upon the track above. Maybe he could use the bumper....

"What happens when the train stops at this end station?" asked Kerrigan, ignoring Nina's rant.

"Oh so NOW you wanna work with me?"

"We don't have time for your social inadequacies, Nina." Retorted Kerrigan, "What happens when the train terminates here?"

Taking a controlled breath, and letting it out in an exasperated sigh, Nina answered. "Normally during the day, passengers disembark and new personnel get onboard. Obviously the train can't be turned around, so the drivers swap engines to the one at the opposite end. Maybe have a little cigarette break while he's at it."

"How many drivers?"

"Two usually. Although I can imagine that working this time of night there might only be need for one, but I couldn't say for sure."

"Might only be one"... Great.

A metallic whining was starting to fill the air. The monorail train was making it's approach.

"OK, here's what we'll do." Said Kerrigan, having decided upon their course of action. "When the train gets here and when the driver is swapping carriages, we're gonna climb up and on top of the train using the bumper at this end of the station. Then, we hold on tight and hitch a ride right into the HQ."

"Your joking right?"

Kerrigan didn't answer. He stared at the receding line of the monorail, extending away from the platform above. The metallic whining was growing steadily into a screech. The train could now be seen emerging out of the darkness, gliding along on it's metal runner.

"Get ready." he answered.

"Fuck."

The train ground to a squeaky stop on the platform above them. The sound seemed absurdly loud in the quiet of the night.

Automated doors opened but no passengers emerged.
Both Kerrigan and Nina watched and waited for the driver to emerge from the carriage closest to them. After what seemed like a very long and tense time, but may well have only been a few minutes, the driver emerged, cupping his hands to his mouth. He lit a cigarette and slowly strolled down the platform, away from Kerrigan and Nina.
"Now." hissed Kerrigan.
While the driver's back was turned, they ran as stealthily as possible up the paved stairway onto the platform. Kerrigan immediately climbed onto the waist high bumper with ease, and used his arms to pull himself up and on top of the top of the train, trying not to bang his feet or knees against the metal carriage in the process.
Shuffling forward to make room for Nina, Kerrigan turned to see her nimbly climb onto the train's roof with a graceful, feline agility that made his own quiet efforts look ungainly.
Once they were both aboard, they lay as flat as possible, squashing their bodies tight against the cold steel of the roof, and found the best hand holds they could.
Moments later, the carriage shuddered beneath them as the engines were wound up in preparation for departure.
With a violent lurch, the train left the station and began it's trip that would lead Kerrigan and Nina directly into the very heart of the HQ.

The train accelerated at a pace that seemed almost impossible, yet Kerrigan knew that the effect was greatly enhanced because of his predicament: He was desperately clinging to the roof of the train, instead of being sat comfortably within. The cables that criss-crossed overhead, connecting the buildings on either side of the monorail, shot past overhead with blurring speed. The wind whipped at his hair and flapped his coat about his ankles as if the wind itself had taken hold of his coat and were shaking it like a child having a tantrum.
His ears pounded from the wind's heavy drumming.

Unable to look straight ahead, the wind instantly drying his eyes otherwise, Kerrigan turned his face and pressed his cheek against the metallic roofing. He squinted against the passing wind that, none the less, attempted to dry his eyes. He saw building after building dashing by along side him, street after street whipping past in a flurry, briefly revealing roads that stretched away and curved in an arc that reflected the circumference of the Refinery's inner rings. He thought he saw the thin boundary of another security ring flashing by between gaps in the buildings, but could not be certain.

Each breath that he took chilled his lungs and froze his throat, so that each new breath both burned and tickled.

The acceleration of the train kept increasing, increasing, propelling Kerrigan and Nina farther and farther, faster and faster into the heart of the S.O. Refinery.

Towards the H.Q.

Kerrigan did not know how far they had travelled upon their hijacked journey, but it was already much further than he had expected. What had happened to the other stops?

Surely, he thought, they must already be arriving at the H.Q. at any second...

As these thoughts crossed Kerrigan's mind, the ever increasing speed of the train hit an impossible crescendo. The passing air whipped itself over his flattened body. It clawed at his face and back with sharp nailed talons, tearing away at his fingers, desperately trying to remove him from the roof of the train he should not have been travelling upon.

Then, as soon as it had reached it's terrifying peak, it immediately started to drop.

As rapidly as they had accelerated, the train was decelerating. Kerrigan could feel his hand holds digging painfully into the soft flesh of his palms, were as previously the acceleration had ached his fingers.

Eventually, with another violent shudder, the train came to rest.

Kerrigan tore open his eyes. They seemed to have frozen shut from the chilling wind that had buffeted against him. He could almost hear the crack as his frozen eye lids reluctantly parted company with one another. He opened his eyes to see that he and Nina were still outside in the open night air. They had not yet reached the H.Q. as he had assumed they must have.

Another stations flood light bathed the train's roof in a cold artificial glow.

Lifting his head, peering through his tangled mass of wind swept hair, the H.Q. was significantly closer than it had been previously, yet it was still a great distance away. Still too far to be covered by risking the trip on foot.

Below, he heard the automated doors of the carriages open once again to allow the admittance of passengers. He could not tell if anyone boarded.

He wondered if Nina was behind him and had not been blown off of the train during their brief, but incredibly fast, journey from one station to the next.

He wondered... but did not really care. It was her own stupid fault if she had ended up loosing her grip.

In fact, Kerrigan mused, it might be more humane for her to die this way, rather than to fall into the S.O.'s clutches.

He had experienced for himself just how cruel they could be.

After only a few, silent moments the doors of the monorail's carriages slid shut once more and Kerrigan braced himself for the next hop of his stowaway journey.

Although having experienced the rapid acceleration of the train only moments ago, Kerrigan was once more astonished at the train's rapid increase in speed. In fact, he could swear that it had not been this impressive the first time, although he knew that surely it must have been just the same.

Arriving at the next stop upon the train's route, Kerrigan once more looked to see how much their journey had progressed.

The H.Q. was now only a short distance away. It's impressive cream fascade that appeared to be made of matt stone, rather than the dull, grey metal of the buildings that nestled all around it, towered into the night sky. It was illuminated from below by an assortment of light blue floodlights.

This close, the building's majesty was even more impressive. It did not just reach towards the sky, it pierced it.

Halfway up the structure, Kerrigan noticed an emblem that he had not been able to see from a distance. It looked vaguely familiar. It looked like a reversed numeral 3 and the letter O with the bottom chopped off.

It took a moment before the recollection presented itself. It was the same symbol that he had seen emblazoned upon his own Wanted poster.

SigmaOmega.

With another lurch, Kerrigan prepared for the trip as he had before; tightening his grip upon his uncomfortable handholds, and pressing his face into the train's corrugated rooftop.

This time however, he also prepared himself for his own ultimate arrival at the H.Q. station.

The arrival at the H.Q. station happened suddenly. One moment he and Nina, assuming she was still attached to the train's roof, were screaming across the inner levels of the Refinery and then, with a deep thump of altered air pressure that pressed down violently upon them from above, the train entered the H.Q. station.

Kerrigan could feel and hear the framework of the building's structure whipping by over head with deadly speed.

He opened his eyes and was alarmed to see just how close the steel beams and pipe work flashed by above, probably only a foot or two. If he had even tried to raise himself to a kneeling position, not that that would have been possible travelling at such break neck speeds, he would have been decapitated before he knew what had happened.

He help on, gripping for life, and just hoped that his erratically flailing jacket didn't get snagged upon one of the beams that whipped by above.

When the train finally came to rest, Kerrigan took no time in waiting. He raised himself up and nimbly climbed up and into the maze of framework that canopied the interior. Nina took her queue from Kerrigan and did likewise. He was momentarily surprised to even see her, having previously suspected her demise. There were no lights in the rafters directly above the rail track so they could hide within the dark web of pipes and support beams quite comfortably for the time being.

As soon as he was within the rafters, perched upon a thick beam and feeling very much like a bird trapped within a cage, Kerrigan took the opportunity to observe and understand his, and Nina's, new surroundings.

The H.Q. station was vastly different from the outlying stations.

Firstly, the H.Q. station was internal and huge. The room itself was as large as any building Kerrigan had seen in Trendid, and could quite easily have housed even the most majestic of Trendid's property with plenty of room to spare. The railing that the train ran along could be seen entering and exiting from the station via a dark tunnel at each end of the station. A large waiting platform was placed on each side of the monorail and was accessed from above by a wide stone staircase on each side. The internal lighting was provided by internal floodlights that cast off the same eerier blue lighting that illuminated the exterior base of the H.Q. building itself, giving the station it's own artificial night. The station had a cold, lifeless feel to it, like being outside, inside.

The train left as suddenly as it had arrived, leaving Kerrigan and Nina perched in the rafters above.

The train's departure made the station feel even larger and emptier than it had initially. Nothing stirred or moved in the cold, lifeless blue of the station below.

Silently pointing to a staircase to which they should head, Kerrigan and Nina crawled, scuttled and crept their way amongst the dirty rafters as quietly as was possible. Although there was no one about, it would be foolish to risk making any noise that might attract some unwanted attention.

Once they had crossed over the monorail and platform, they reached a pipe that led down from the upper rafters to the platform below. It looked sturdy enough to hold their individual weights should they choose to use it in their descent.

It was either that, Kerrigan concluded, or free-falling down to the platform below and risk breaking their ankles in the process.
The choice was clear: They would descend using the pipe.
Before doing so, Kerrigan turned to Nina and asked in a voice that was too quiet to be heard by anyone else, "Where does that staircase lead?"
"To a hallway that's got loads of stair wells and elevators branching off from it." She hissed in reply. "It's basically the central column to the entire complex. All the major areas are directly accessed from there, and those others that don't have a direct route are accessed *through* one of the connecting areas. We should be able to take one of those routes to the floors above. Which floor was it you were held on?"
Good question. A one he had not thought to dwell upon previously. Which floor had it been?
Nina saw his hesitation, "Kerrigan, which floor were you held on?" Her face twisted up with disbelief, looking ghoulishly ugly as it reflected the eerie blue glow that shone from below.
"I'll recognize it when we get there."
And with that said he turned and shimmied down the pipe.

He hit the empty platform with a soft thump. The noise echoed painfully loud in the cold, blue twilight, and returned after completing a lap of the station back to Kerrigan.
He watched the stairway in expectation of a guard coming to investigate the noise.
No one came, and so he moved out of the way to allow Nina to descend also. Unlike Kerrigan, she hit the floor with barely a sound and took the lead up the wide staircase, taking them up and out of the station.
Despite now being indoors, Kerrigan felt as exposed as he had in Refinery's streets, possibly more so, knowing that should they be discovered, it would mean capture for them both. Should she be accused and found guilty of co-operating with a Wanted Man – a Heathen – she too would no doubt meet the same fate as Kerrigan, whatever that turned out to be. As Nina had explained to him

during their arrival, the S.O would enforce and judge their own laws with a brutal stringency, regardless of the social status of the accused.

Arriving at the top of the staircase, they once again hugged the walls as Nina scouted out the path ahead.

Satisfied the way ahead was clear, Nina indicated for Kerrigan to follow with a quick jerk of her head.

Kerrigan followed. The featureless corridor was as silent as the station platform had been, and bathed in the same ghostly blue light.

They dashed past a collection of closed sliding doors with little green buttons glowing on either side. They reminded Kerrigan of cats eyes glimpsed in the darkness.

A sign above the doorways identified their purpose. Elevators.

Before the row of elevators had completely passed, Nina stopped them both in front of a billboard that was attached to the wall opposite the elevators.

Without needing to explain to one another what they were looking at, Nina and Kerrigan studied the map of the inner levels of the HQ.

Above the basement levels, were three floors dedicated the monorails. Every monorail led into and out of the H.Q. in a straight line, and so to avoid collisions, each monorail was erected above or below one another, resulting in several floors of the H.Q being dedicated to the sole purpose of monorail stations alone.

Knowing that he had definitely been in one of the upper levels of the H.Q., Kerrigan directed their attention to those upper floors.

Judging from the sights that he had seen, most of the departments that they saw labelled were definitely not what they were looking for: Ferralin Administration, Kallingo Administration, Trendid Administration, S.O. Administration, Archiving, Communications... Other's had suspicious sounding connotations but did not sound right either: Land Control????

An entire 5 floors at the very top of the building were labelled suspiciously as "Private".

"This is where I used to work when I worked here", advised Nina.

She tapped the floor marked with all of the Administration offices, "The S.O like to keep records of everything that takes place in their land. Population, names, addresses, crops, money, the lot. Even criminal records." She turned to Kerrigan, "This is where we'll need to go to clear your name, Kerrigan." she turned back to the floor plan, "AFTER we find my brother."
Kerrigan turned to her as she made this final statement, but she ignored his glare and continued to scan the floor plan. It was Nina who eventually found what they were looking for, "Testing and Experimentation." She tapped the point on the map that she was referring to, "This has got to be it. Testing and Experimentation huh?" she repeated, "Well it certainly sounds like it could be a euphemism for torture I suppose…"
A quivering bolt shot through Kerrigan's spine as he remembered the brutal torturing he had endured, or was it a ghost of the pain he had endured that ran through his backbone as his mind recalled the scene?
"Come on, let's go."
Nina turned to use one of the elevators, but Kerrigan grabbed her upper arm and instead led her to a set of windowed double doors. A sign above read "STAIRWELL".
Peaking inside to check that this too was clear, Kerrigan dragged Nina inside.
"The stairs? Your joking right? We've got a shit load of floors to go up and you expect us to use THE FUCKING STAIRS?! Let's just use the fucking lifts, that's what they're there for. We've got the I.D's that'll let us use em." She held up the two dead guards I.D's.
"No, it's too risky. I don't wanna use those I.D's unless we absolutely have to. If those dead guards have been discovered by now, then using their I.D's will flag up our position straight away. Besides," he took another look back into the corridor from which they had just fled. It was still empty, "I sense a trap."
"A trap?"
"It's too quiet."
She thought it over.

True, it was the middle of the night so most people would have left their jobs hours ago and gone home to bed. But, thinking about it, surely there would be some late night workers on shift manning the computers? Someone running late?, someone on a night shift?, or even someone desperate enough to be working overtime? Certainly there should have been guards on duty.
Yet the H.Q, even the out skirts of the Refinery itself, had remained practically devoid of life. Not even a single security guard or insomniac had been seen by herself or Kerrigan, save for the monorail driver.
"Your just being paranoid." replied Nina. "It's the fucking dead of the night for fuck's sake, what do you expect? Every one with half a brain is tucked up in bed at this hour. Besides, what you've got to understand is this; Although this place may look like some kind of crazy factory, with all of it's metal buildings, cables and smoking chimneys, this here is sacred ground. This is the home of the S.O. remember? The God's workers? They have no need to feel threatened because they have no one to fear, hence, no guards."
She had a point. But still…
"You listening to me Kerrigan?"
"Yeah. But no elevators."
"Wha….?" She looked at Kerrigan incredulously, but his stern face told her that it was not up for debate. "OK, OK whatever you say big guy. Come on let's get going, we've got a lot of stairs to climb."

Their ascent up the inside of the S.O H.Q was long and tiring… for Nina. After topping the first ten floors she started to breath heavily. Another three, she was visibly out of breath, and another three after that she was panting and leaning on the banister as if she were ready to fall flat on her face.
Kerrigan suggested that they stop for awhile, but Nina's pride prevented her from accepting his offer, although it was clear to Kerrigan that she wanted to, that she needed to.
Another floor later, and Nina finally suggested that they stop, making the suggestion sound as if it had not already been offered

by Kerrigan, and that it was a novel thought entirely conjured up from deep within herself. Despite not being out of breath himself, Kerrigan agreed, knowing that Nina would be of no use in her current state of near exhaustion. They stopped half way between the seventeenth and eighteenth floor so that they could flee to either exit should someone enter the stairwell.
Once her breath had begun to return, Nina asked Kerrigan how it was that he too, was not out of breath, "I mean, you must be a bit fucking tired."
"I like to keep fit." he replied, thinking of all the hours he had spent in his cell doing endless push ups, sit up and crunches, honing his defined body into a sinewy perfection.
Continuing on up, and stopping twice more for Nina, Kerrigan was pleased to see that his internal count of what floor they were on was correct. A sign posted on the inside of one set of double doors confirmed that they were on the Administration floor. Only another five floors remained above them before they reached the floor that the foyer map had named as 'Testing and Experimenting'.
They were still to meet anyone on the stairwell, and every floor that they checked for guards proved to be as deserted as the previous.
Nina did not seemed worried by this fact.
Neither was Kerrigan… but he remained extremely cautious.

Arriving at the floor labelled 'Testing and Experimentation', Kerrigan and Nina followed the same routine that they had on all of the previous floors. They attempted to steal a peek through the doorway to see if the way ahead was clear.
They pushed against the double doors and were mildly surprised when the doors refused to budge.
"I think we need a key." said Nina.
Next to the doors, was a small keypad. The keypad had a small readout screen and a slot for the insertion of keys in the top.
Nina withdrew the I.D's that they had stolen from the two dead guards and chose one.

She went to slide it into the keypad when Kerrigan asked, "What are you doing?"

"What does it look like I'm doing?" she replied, "I'm opening the door."

"But if the guards have been discovered..."

"I know, I know" she interrupted, "Then using the keys will disclose our position, but what else do you suggest? We can't go breaking the door down for fuck's sake, we'd be heard a mile off! And no, before you ask, there's no other access to this floor. Unless you wanna take a lift, which incidentally, we would have to use the I.D's for anyway. So it's your choice, I can use the I.D here and now, or we can use it in the lifts, what do you say?"

Fucking bitch, thought Kerrigan.

Without waiting for a reply, Nina slid the I.D into the keypad where it momentarily locked in place.

The readout lit up and informed Kerrigan and Nina that it was currently validating and authorizing their I.D, and to please be patient whilst it did so.

As this authorisation was performed, Nina checked over both her shoulders, fearful that the computer knew that they were imposters and had already sent word to the guards on duty to come and collect them while it delayed them with it's validity checks.

The screen blinked out.

Nina held her breath. Had something gone wrong?

It winked back into existence with approval of their I.D. and a polite "Thank You" for their patience.

She let out the breath that she had not realised she had been holding.

No sound indicated that the 'Testing and Experimenting' doors had become unlocked, but this time when they were pressed against, they swung smoothly inwards.

They peeked inside to check the coast was clear.

As usual, it was.

Kerrigan led them inside.

The corridor did not seem any different from those on previous floors, and it certainly did not immediately leap out at Kerrigan as being the correct floor.

"OK, we're here." Whispered Nina, despite the floors apparent desertion, "You're sure this is the right floor?"

He could not recall ever affirming his opinion that this was the correct floor earlier as they had studied the H.Q map, but he none the less scanned the level for anything that might confirm their suspicions.

It did not look familiar. This was not surprising however, as the last time he had been here he had only just escaped from a mind-altering electrical torture and was fleeing desperately for his life. It had not been the appropriate time for him to admire the architecture of his surroundings.

The main difference was the lighting. As with all the previous levels, this floor was filled with the cold blue light provided by artificial lighting. However, the only images that Kerrigan could recall during his escape were smothered in the rising and falling of the red alarm beacon that had pulsed around him.

"I think so..." replied Kerrigan.

Despite his lack of conviction, Nina seemed inspired by his response and excitedly set off to scan the interior of the nearest room that branched off from their own corridor. She peered through the wire frame mesh of the small windows set into the double doorway that granted entrance to the room within. She needed to rise briefly upon her toes to get a better view.

Kerrigan observed her do this, wondering if she had really heard him at all... or was she only motivated by the thought that her brother may lay nearby? It was concerning to think that her emotions may be controlling her actions.

After a quick, cursory glance, Nina opened the door and stepped inside.

Kerrigan followed.

The room appeared to be the 'Testing and Experimenting' floor's reception. Large computer stations were situated along three sides of the room, the fourth containing the doors through which they had just stepped, which were flanked on either side by identical sets of metal filling cabinets. In the centre of the room was a large welcome desk, with it's own, yet considerably smaller, computer, chair and name plaque with the word "Receptionist" emblazed upon it.

Yup, this was definitely the reception.

Nina crossed the room and sat in the chair that was nestled behind the wooden desk. The glow of the computer's monitor reflected upon her face.

After a moment's typing at the keyboard, her face melted into a disappointment that was extenuated by the cold glow of the monitor.

"It's locked." she announced.

She cast her eyes around the room. All of the monitors showed that they too were securely locked from prying eyes.

Turning from her, Kerrigan approached the filing cabinets. He grabbed hold of the top most draw and pulled. No good. It too remained as locked as the computer terminals.

He considered attempting to open the drawer by sheer brute force, but he quickly discarded it as foolish. The noise of trying to force the drawer with his bare hands would surely make enough noise to attract a guard who might be unlucky enough to work such an unsociably late shift.

Nina was already up and moving away from the computer, "Come on, this'll get us no where. Let's keep looking."

With that said, they left the reception with all of it's secured information behind, and continued on down the corridor.

The next set of double doors that they reached were conveniently labelled with their content's purpose. A small sign next to the doors declared the room to be a "Compatibility Room".

They stepped inside. The room was hardly any bigger that that of the Reception's, but the size of the equipment it contained filled the room, giving it the presence of a room much smaller. Along one side of the room, were three transparent cylinders, ten feet tall and three feet in diameter. At this moment in time, the cylinders were empty, but their design was clearly intended so that outsiders could easily observe whatever may be held within. Cables

connected the cylinders to the individual computers that stood facing each cylinder in the middle of the room. The eerie blue light, that smothered all of the previous floors, remained alight here also. It made Kerrigan wonder if the H.Q had entered a kind of sleep mode, a setting that provided enough light to see by, but still impressed upon those within that the sun had gone down.
The wall opposite the empty cylinders had a number of notice boards which were covered in squiggly writing with untidy bundles of paper and memos pinned to them.
Once more, the computer monitors showed that they were secure from prying eyes.
For anyone entering the room, it was clear by the rooms layout what it's intention was for.
Analysis, and reading. Something would be placed in the tanks, and the computers that were connected to them would show the results.
It gave Kerrigan a sharp bolt of recall. Instantly, he was reminded of the final room he had seen of this building before his violent expulsion.
It was similar, yet less intimidating. Less oppressive somehow.
Intrigued by the cylinders, Kerrigan stepped towards the one closest to him, while Nina studied the information on the notice boards.
As Kerrigan stepped towards the nearest cylinder, he felt a wave of warmth sweep over him. The cylinder was radiating out a strong, yet soft heat into the surrounding air.
As he stepped closer, feeling himself gently warmed, he looked through the thick looking glass to try and see what may be placed inside the cylinder. It was empty, and displayed no evidence to suggest what it might have previously held within it's glassy confides.
"Kerrigan". It was Nina.
Halting his stride, Kerrigan heard Nina but did not turn to acknowledge her..
"Kerrigan." She repeated, "Here."
The urgency that sharpened her tone told Kerrigan more than the

short, chopped words had: She had found something.
Turning from where he was, Kerrigan stepped out from cylinder's light, and headed towards Nina. He had a fleeting thought as he backed away, that he missed the warmth that the tank's light had radiated upon him.
He reached Nina's side. She was staring at one of the cluttered notice boards that adorned the wall opposite the empty cylinders. He scanned the confusing scatter of information before him that had so enraptured Nina.
Upon the notice board immediately in front of her, a large map had been posted with a tumble of multiple additional documents framed around it. Some of these additional documents had colourful lines of cotton connecting them to various, scattered points upon the map.
Initially, Kerrigan was bewildered by the haphazard, yet strangely complicated display of information before him, but as he took a moment to comprehend the display, the overall message became clear.
"This... this cannot be" uttered Nina beside him. Kerrigan looked towards her and saw that her face had slackened. Her jaw hung low, her eyes looked dark and tired, and the flesh that enshrouded her skull seemed to hang as if it barely fit her skull.
It was a look of pure shock...
...of disbelief.

Nina's world had literally shook apart as she looked upon the map before her. She literally could not comprehend the revelation that confronted her.
All through her life, Nina had been brought up with a strict religious belief. Her parents, who were respected leaders amongst the community, had always imposed upon their daughter a strict, but fair, upbringing. She would abide by The Gods Laws and adhere to all of Trendid's traditions, beliefs, etiquette, superstitions and religious celebrations with gusto.
Among her many lessons, Nina had been taught that the sea was for those who had betrayed the Gods, and that the land was for

those who remained true to Their Teachings. Pure.

From an early age, Nina had vowed to adhere to the God's Laws, with the threat of being sent to one of the Prison Ships afloat aboard the fearful sea, aboard one of the dedicated ships designed to hold those who could not behave themselves amongst society.

During her education, in preparation for her respected role as the sister of one of Trendid's religious figureheads, Nina was also taught about the shape and reality of the world...

"The world is really very small, Nina" her mother had said, "Just one small blot of land that contains within it three small villages and our leader, the S.O. In regards to the villages, there is of course here, Trendid, and two other villages – Kallingo and Ferralin. They're very much like our own, surviving on what little we can provide for ourselves and what ever might be spared is delivered to the prison ships that anchor off shore. Other than that there's not much to tell.

And of course you already know about the S.O...."

The recollection of her childhood lessons faded, and Nina stared at the map before her, upon the S.O's wall.

She barely realised what she had done, but she had unwittingly called Kerrigan to her side.

The map contained the familiar shape of the island that Trendid, Kallingo, Ferralin and the S.O Refinery were contained within. The same shape that she had been taught as a child, was the entire world.

However, this shape only constituted a small portion of the overall map before her. Surrounding their island was an ocean, and within that ocean was a huge collection of further islands, many of which doubled her own island many, many times over.

There were entire continents that's dwarfed her world. Their solitary island, which was all she had ever known and all she had ever been taught to believe in, was not alone. There was suddenly a whole host of undiscovered islands out there, other continents, that had never even been conceived of.

Not by her, not by her friends... not by anyone.

Nina, Kerrigan, her village...they were not alone.

With this revelation, everything that she had been brought up to believe in was suddenly in doubt.
Suddenly, everything that she had been taught, her beliefs, her heritage, her perceptions and expectations… suddenly, they all seemed so… so... false.
Upon viewing the map and it's revelations, Nina knew with certainty that what Kerrigan had told her about her brother's punishments was correct.
Her knees give way.

Staring at the map of the entire world portraying Trendid, Kallingos, Ferralin and the island they were based upon to be but only a small part of the greater world, Kerrigan noticed that Nina was about to fall a moment before she had time to react.
She stumbled backwards from the map, barely keeping her balance.
Kerrigan wrapped an arm around her waist for support. Clearly, the revelation of the expanded world had paid a heavy toll upon her.
"I'm okay" she gasped as she leaned into his embrace, "It's just a little… unexpected is all." After a moment, she composed herself and regained enough self control to analyse the wall before her once more.
For Kerrigan, he had always known that the world was larger that the solitary island that contained the four named institutions and so the revelation came as no real surprise. More, it came as a comforting confirmation of his beliefs.
Yet for Nina, the information had clearly paid a heavier toll, and she stared with wide, wet eyed mystery upon the unexpected.
Finally, she noticed that surrounding the map, connected by high-lighted threads, was a confusing assortment of further information.
Kerrigan had no idea what the additional information might mean, never mind what he was looking for.
All he had to go on was a name: Ames Tellingos, Nina's brother.
"Look. Here." She said.
And there it was, AMES, wrote in sloppy capital letters in a

marker pen upon a sheath of paper that portrayed the world map.
It was the third name down on a list, and was followed by a series of random numbers and confusing words that Kerrigan took to be scientific lingo for things he did not care to understand.
At least not yet.
"Any idea what this means?" Asked Nina.
"No."
"Me neither…"
They could have spent hours reading through the various dog eared documents that hung from the wall, in hope of finding out what was taking place in here, assuming they could interpret the scientific terms.
Clearly, something was taking place , something that involved the S.O Refinery… but more.
Much more.
Despite the questions, revelations and mysteries that the map provided, none of which would provide Ames with the freedom to which Nina and Kerrigan diligently sought.
They did not need to debate their next course of action.
They left the 'Testing and Compatibility' room and continued further down the corridor.

The next set of double doors was also clearly and conveniently labelled with it's contents. In the cool blue lighting, the top, and boldest, line was engraved "Detection:", Below, written upon a reusable noticeboard, was written "Blanke", and then below this, in even smaller writing, "Tridale"
"Those names… it's the same ones we saw on the computer in the truck."
Kerrigan stared at the names with only the vaguest feeling of recognition.
"Definitely. Yes definitely. They're the same names."
She seemed to be convincing herself more than Kerrigan.
Looking into the room, there was another corridor, although much shorter than the one they were currently travelling down.
The corridor down which she peered had two large, blackened

windows on one side of the hall with two closed doors set next to each of the darkened windows. The short corridor seemed only to serve as an access route to the two additional rooms that branched off from it.
Seeing recognition in the sign, Nina stepped into the room and Kerrigan followed. She seemed keen to pursue any familiarities that they found, even if they were not leads that lead directly to her brother.
The corridor was illuminated, but the two rooms that the windows gave sight into, were not. As such the windows remained as dark as the night sky and gave no hint as to their contents.
Nina held her face next to one of the dark panes, cupping her hands around her face, hoping to see within.
It did not help.
With an exasperated sigh of frustration, she removed herself from the glass and peered about herself, hoping to find something that might illuminate the room within.
In her desperation, she had forgotten about the doors, and had went straight to the windows.
A small control pad was positioned next to each of the doorways; the buttons upon the keypad labelled with their functions.
As Nina held her cupped face against the mirror, Kerrigan pressed the button upon the relevant keypad marked "lights".
Kerrigan watched with a slight thread of amusement as Nina leapt back from the window in surprise as the room that had previously been but a black slate, blazed into existence. As he looked into the room himself however, his mind brought forth an unpleasant memory from the past that shook out the amusement of Nina's reaction from within him...
The newly illuminated room was identical to one that he himself had found himself within a long time ago. At least it seemed like a long time ago, but in reality it was possibly only around a week.
The newly revealed room was identical to the room he had been in when he had been strapped, bound, interrogated and eventually, tortured by Durrant and his officers.
A huge metallic table with wrist and ankle restraints dominated the

majority of the room. Although it could not be seen from this side of the wall, Kerrigan knew that hidden within the corner closest to himself, was a computer that controlled the deadly electricity that had coursed through his body as he lay strapped to the table beyond.

Before he had chance to restrain it, a shiver broke out from the base of Kerrigan's spine, tickling up his backbone, down his shoulders and arms, and out into the very tips of his splayed fingers.

Nina saw his reaction, "What's up?"

With only the briefest delay, Kerrigan replied, "This room. It's the same as the one I was in."

Upon sight of the room, his treacherous mind brought forth the horrible memories of the time he had spent bound to one of those tables. He quickly discarded the memories. He did not want to dwell upon them any more than he had to. He could feel his extremities tingling with the unwanted recollection...

Nina returned her attention once more to the room, but then immediately looked back at Kerrigan, only realising that she had done so the moment she opened her mouth and asked the question, "Is this the room that you were tortured in?" She had seen the table's restraints and understood the room's function.

"I don't think it's the exact one, no. But it's the same type of room. There may be more than one." he replied, but would elaborate no further.

Nor did Nina try to force any further explanation from him. She took her gaze away from Kerrigan and looked back into the room.

Her head was filled with more questions, mysteries and revelations than she thought was possible. She worried that her mind might hurt or explode as it tried to comprehend all of her thoughts at the same time.

So it was true. The men and women of the S.O., the same men and women who were meant to be trying to find a solution to the world's problems, who were chosen by the Gods themselves, were torturing people behind closed doors.

The people that she had trusted, the people she had been brought

up to love and respect beyond question, were TORTURING people!
Why? For what? How many people knew about this? And if they did, what did they make of it? What would the people back in Trendid make of this? Did they somehow know, and it was just she who had somehow been left in the dark, ignorant to their tortures?
Was there an alternate explanation? A benign one that would cast aside all the doubts that now dominated her mind?
But also, apart from the S.O., what did this mean about her faith? About her faith in The Gods? Were they too phoney and not to be believed?
Were they too, also made up?!
No no, her mind objected, *that cannot be true! Look at the blessing of electricity, the power of The Chosen Ones. That's not fake. No, No the Gods are real, but all this must all be a mistake, a misunderstanding. It must be* The Gods *will for this to happen. There must be a reasonable explanation!*
Whatever the reason, here before her were instruments of torture. It shook her faith in the S.O. to her very foundations.
They were not the people she thought they once were.
She felt sick to the very pit of her stomach. She had lived and dedicated her life to the teachings of the S.O. Never before had she felt the reason to question their wisdom or guidance.
Nor should she, for they had always been.
For as long as Nina's family tree could remember, the S.O had been connected to the lives of the Tellingos. They (for they were more a collection of individuals rather than single religious entity) had always remained connected to the histories of hers, her parents, her grand parents and their parents before them, in an unquestionably benevolent light.
But now all that turned out to be a lie. They were savages who tortured people with instruments that used the power that The Gods themselves had gifted upon them.
No wonder there is no cure for the virus, mused Nina, *The Gods must feel betrayed that their own disciples are using their own, blessed powers to hurt people...*

No, no that cannot be right. Her own mind contradicted, *The Gods would take away the electricity if that was the case.*
What the hell was going on here!?
This time it was Kerrigan who spurred Nina on, "Let's go. Ames must be here somewhere."
He was right. The room beyond was empty, except for the revelations that it had contained.
They removed themselves from the empty room and searched the final, adjacent room.
It too revealed itself to be empty.
Returning to the main corridor, each new set of doors that they came across all held a sign that displayed the dreaded word, "Detection", below which were the crudely written names of previous occupants.
Finally, they came across one such label that displayed Nina's brother's name.
Ames. The name seemed to radiate outwards at them, emblazoning itself upon their minds as the previous names had not. Finally, here was what they had been looking for.
With much relief, excitement and trepidation, Nina entered the corridor beyond.

Familiar with the layout, Nina dashed to the light switch. She flicked it on and was disappointed to see the room beyond empty.
Disappointed, but not discouraged.
She must have flicked the wrong switch, or had the wrong room. Without delay, she dashed further along the hall to flick the only other switch. Finally, she would see her brother. She could free him, and they could all go home together…
The lights in the room beyond stuttered into life and revealed the room to be as empty as all of those that had gone before.
There was no brother. No Ames.
"Nooooooo!" she cried out. Nina fell to her knees with despair, forgetting about the potential security that might be near by to hear her. She screamed and howled as if her brother had been killed before her very eyes.

Kerrigan did not try to console her. He stared at the empty room beyond and wondered where Ames might be. The empty room was not a guarantee that the man was dead. Infact… was there a memory that he held, deep within, that maybe told him that Ames had been moved from here…?
He grasped at the memory, but it fled his prying mind like a leaf on the breeze.
Fuck it, he must be mistaken.
Nina continued to cry in anguish at Kerrigan's feet. She seemed to take the empty room as a sign that her brother was already dead. Her sobs came in big, thick inhales as she hid her face in her hands.
"Let's go Nina" said Kerrigan with as much compassion as he could muster. His voice still grated with it's usual intensity.
Despite her grief, they could not remain here for long. They had to keep moving.
Besides, Nina had her end of the deal still yet to honour…
He placed a hand on her shuddering shoulder, not in comfort, but as a form of connection. A link back to reality.
"Nina."
She continued to sob, but she nodded in acknowledgement. It would do no good to grieve here.
She rose to her feet and wiped her eyes. The tears that remained turned the striking green of her irises into glimmering jewels in her face.
"OK", she stammered, "let's go."
They turned and left the room where Ames had once been held. It felt to Nina as if she were somehow leaving his dead body behind her. She felt as if she should somehow take something with her, some memento of the place where he had died.
IF he had died, she tried to remind herself, but the empty room's disappointment was still too fresh in her mind to take much conciliation in the thought.
Still…
Searching the remainder of the floor, they found no more clues to suggest that Ames was still here or any clues as to where he might

be found.

Disappointed, yet satisfied that this floor held no more information, they returned to the stairwell. Kerrigan began to head down to the Administration level.

"Wait", Nina said. He turned to see her stood at the top of the stairs, "We're not done yet."

"Yes we are."

"No, we're not. I want to see what's above."

"Why?" barked Kerrigan in reply. Her incessant naivety at her brother's survival was finally taking it's toll upon his patience. "Your brothers gone Nina, like I said he would be. Now, it's time to clear my name and get the hell outta here before we both get killed!"

His sharp tones echoed back at them from below within the stairwell.

"No," she repeated. "We're going up. And without me, you'll never clear your own name."

Kerrigan looked up the stairwell to the floor above, "Why? What's up there?"

"I don't know..." she too turned her attention to the levels above, "It's the floors that were labelled 'Private' on the map below. But, you were right Kerrigan, my brother WAS here and I owe it to myself and to my people to find out just what the hell is going on here." She looked Kerrigan straight in the eye. Her own eyes glimmered with barely suppressed tears, "Just what the hell were those machines, Kerrigan?"

Kerrigan rose back up the steps he had descended, meeting Nina's glare back upon the Testing and Experimenting landing, "Exactly what I said; They're torture machines. I was nearly tortured to death when I was attached to them, and your brother was most likely killed by them." He took a step forwards so that he stood directly in front of her, leering down, "He's not upstairs Nina."

"Maybe, maybe not." Her eyes swam as she battled her own inner turmoil, "But there's a chance he might be… either way, I must know the truth about the S.O. These people have lied to us all Kerrigan."

Her eye's sparkled with the barely repressed tears. Why couldn't he understand the impact all this was having upon her once organised, controlled life?

"Don't you want to know why they wanted you back so much, Kerrigan? Why they put so much time, effort and expense into recapturing you?"

"No."

"Well I do, Kerrigan. I want to know who these people really are, who the S.O really are... I want to know why The Gods would allow them to conduct such heinous things."

"THE GODS"?! For fucks sake! He could hardly believe they were having this conversation. There was absolutely no way he was going to be drawn into a religious debate here and now upon the upper levels of the S.O. Refinery stairwell.

Talk about wrong time and place...

"Get over it Nina. Your brother's gone. That's what we came here for, and that's all there is to it."

"No!" she cried vehemently, "there's more here than meets the eye... More here than anyone ever suspected. We're going up Kerrigan, and we're going to find out what happened to Ames and whatever else is going on here too." Her eyes did not flicker.

Kerrigan's eyes did not flicker also, "Do you really want to die that much?" he replied.

"Without him, I'm already dead!" Finally the tears that had quivered with delicate fragility upon her green eyes, broke free and slid down her checks, "He's all I have, Kerrigan."

Her gaze, despite the show of tears, remained as fixed and as determined as ever. Perhaps more so.

A short moment later, Kerrigan turned from her and started up the flight of stairs.

After another moment of miscomprehension, Nina caught up with him.

Although the floor plan had indicated that there were five floors exclusively dedicated to the 'Private' section above, Kerrigan and Nina reached the top of the stairwell after only one flight of stairs.

The stairwell ended in a set of old fashioned, sturdy looking wooden doors. The doors were meticulously well maintained and highly polished. They reflected back the subdued lighting that glowed within the stairwell, deflecting the artificial light like a knight's shield. When the light touched upon it's smooth contours, it sparkled back like sunlight upon a shimmering lake, dazzling the eye.

A small, golden plaque, also exquisitely polished, was stamped to the middle of each wooden door, merely labelled, "Private".

On the corner of the wall adjacent to the impressive doorway, was a small control unit suitable for a key to be inserted, not unlike those on the previous floors.

"I don't know if these I.D's will give us access to this floor," confessed Nina. It sounded as though she were admitting this more to herself than for Kerrigan. "only one way to find out I suppose."

She withdrew the I.D's from her belt and slid one of them into the keypad.

As before, the display politely asked for their patience.

It blinked out and then a moment later, winked back into existence. Denied.

Nina cursed under her breath and withdrew the I.D. She swapped it for the other one and tried again.

She held her breath for what seemed like an inappropriately long length of time.

She had the sudden impulse that the lock was deliberately taking longer than it normally would to complete it's checks, deliberately keeping Nina and Kerrigan where they where whilst it contacted, and informed, the active security services to their presence.

Just as Nina was about to voice her concerns and declare a hasty retreat, 'Cleared' suddenly appeared on the small security screen and was accompanied by an audible click as the locks holding the doors were disengaged.

"Guess this guy was higher ranked" said Nina as she studied the card she'd removed from the keypad.

Kerrigan pushed on the golden pad that opened the heavy wooden door, and stepped inside.

The inside of the 'Private' floor was in stark contrast to the previous levels. Gone were the cold painted walls, the concrete flooring, exposed piping and cables, and gone was the cold blue light that smothered everything and seemed to cool the very air.
In their place were lavishly decorated, luxurious cream wall paper, plush red carpets that remained as fluffy as the day they were created, and lighting that shone with a naturally hued, subdued glow from delicate, but not overly elaborate, wall mounted fixtures. It looked more like the inside of a wealthy home, rather than the inside of a formal building, nor was it in anyway apparently holy or religious as might have been expected in the private area of the S.O HQ. The doors of each room were opened by the traditional manner of handle and keyhole.
Bizarrely, Nina suddenly felt herself becoming extremely conscientious of her appearance, not wanting to dirty the plush carpet or the elaborate wallpaper with her clothes that suddenly seemed all too dirty in the lush environment. She felt like a burglar inside a mansion… which was only half true.
Despite the lavish furnishings, they were still just inside another corridor, on another floor of the HQ… albeit a much nicer corridor and floor.
As such, they continued their search in the same fashion as they had previously. They headed down the corridor as silently as possible (made much more easy thanks to the soft carpet) and peered around corners and into each room as they chanced upon them.
The problem with this floor, was that there were no windows through which to peek inside. Every door that granted, and prevented, access to the individual rooms, was made of solid oak, polished to an immaculate, glistening finish.
The floor seemed to honour the 'Private' branding which had been disposed upon it.
However, like the previous floors, each room was labelled with a polite, polished golden plaque labelling what the room's function served. It helped decide if they should enter and investigate

further.

The first few rooms were marked with such mundane functions as 'Reception Area', 'Lounge' and even 'Ladies' and 'Gentlemen'.

As they crept down the sound dampened corridor, Kerrigan snapped out his arm across Nina's chest bringing both himself and Nina to a sudden halt.

"What is it?" hissed Nina.

"Voices."

Nina strained her ears, but could not hear anything over the sound of her own controlled breathing.

"I don't hear anything…"

"Ahead somewhere." He listened some more, "They don't sound like they're moving."

"They?"

"There's more than one." Again he listened to the inaudible, "come on, let's see who it is."

They crept further down the corridor.

Gradually, the voices that Kerrigan had heard became audible to Nina also. He was right, there was more than one voice speaking. They appeared to be coming from behind one of the polished closed doors further down the corridor.

As they neared the source of the sound, they were able to definitely establish that the voices were coming from within the next room.

The plaque on the doors told them that the voices were coming from within the "Dining Room".

Although the voices could be heard, the words remained too muffled to be defined from the outside.

Having reached the doorway, Kerrigan crouched down and peeked through the keyhole at the occupants within.

"Well?" asked Nina in a barely audible hiss.

Kerrigan's expression turned into a fierce scowl. He rose without turning to Nina and without removing his face of hate.

He stared angrily at the closed doors.

"It's Durrant."

"Who?"

"Durrant. The man who brought me here," replied Kerrigan, "the

man who took me off of Chimera and brought me here… to torture me. He's in there having dinner with his family."
He turned towards Nina with a cold, hard stare, "He's the one who ordered the torture of Ames too."
The significance of what Kerrigan was saying dawned upon Nina, "By the Gods!" she muttered in disbelief, the realisation finally striking home…
The man beyond the doorway could be responsible for what might have happened to Ames since Kerrigan had last seen him alive…
Nina's blood began to boil.
"OK, let's do it" said Nina, although she had not voiced what it was that she wanted to do, she could tell by Kerrigan's mannerisms that he thought the same: Time to make this fucker pay.
He turned to her, still scowling, and asked, "Ready?"
"Of course."
The fact that he had to ask her co-operation reinforced her suspicions.
With that said, Kerrigan retreated to the wall opposite and ran at the Dining Room doors, shoulder first.
He struck it with a thud that sent splinters scattering in the air, and with only a slight break in his momentum, continued onwards and into the room.

Durrant and a small child remained seated at the large polished table at which they sat, and looked up from their meals. Durrant himself looked up with an expression of disapproval, as if his meal were being rudely interrupted rather than invaded.
The small child who he dined with was startled and squeaked with surprise.
The room was incredibly large, large enough to comfortably accommodate an entire family and all of their belongings, but the table at which the two sole occupants sat, dominated the interior. It sat comfortably amid the many paintings that hung upon the walls surrounding it. Upon one wall, was a long sword with a thick blade and ornamental hilt that sparkled magnificently in the artificial, yet

natural looking lighting provided by the room's lamps.

The sword was suspended upon a pair of golden brackets, surrounded by a decorative frame. It looked incredibly heavy.

The pair of diners looked up in tandem to gape at the intruders that had so rudely interrupted their meal.

Taking advantage of the scene, and having seen the layout of the room through the keyhole, Kerrigan kept up his initial momentum and headed straight towards the smallest occupant of the dining table.

Too overcome with the shock of the invasion, neither Durrant, nor his smaller companion, rose from their seats to take action against the intruders that had disturbed their meal. They merely sat and gaped with disbelief.

As they sat immobile, Kerrigan dashed through the torrent of splinters that rained from the destroyed doorway and immediately grabbed hold of the small boy dressed in a suit that was tailored to fit his small frame.

Wrapping his arm around the young man's throat, Kerrigan raised the boy from his chair whilst cupping his mouth with his large, calloused hand.

Once immobilised and under Kerrigan's will, the pair retreated away from the table.

"Don't move" said Kerrigan as Durrant finally started to rise from his chair.

"I said, don't move!" shouted Kerrigan with intense ferocity.

Durrant froze mid-rise. His mouth hung slightly agape.

Kerrigan dragged the restrained boy back towards Nina who had now also entered the room. She seemed as confused by the sudden invasion as Durrant and his newly restrained company, yet she kept her composure and did her best not to show her surprise.

"Don't hurt him!" shouted Durrant, stretching out an arm towards the captured child.

"Shut up!" snapped Kerrigan retreating as far as he could towards the door frame, to stand next to Nina, "Clear my name." he barked.

"What?" replied Durrant, "I - I don't know what your talking about"

"Fuck you!" replied Kerrigan, seeing through his bluff, "of course you do! You were the one who took me off of Chimera in the first place!" Referring to his previous experience, he continued, "You were the one who tortured me with those machines down below and who put the bounty on my head. Clear my fucking name."

"Really?" laughed Durrant lightly, as if this were all a simple case of mistaken identity, "I don't know what your talking about. If we just sit and talk about..."

Kerrigan withdrew his hand from the child's mouth and punched him as hard as he could, square in the face.

The boy's nose cartilage crushed beneath his fist, making a satisfying crunch that was both heard and felt by those surrounding him. Kerrigan's fist warmed as the boy's blood burst forth from his shattered airways, and spread over his hand.

The boy barely had time to shout out in pain and shock when Kerrigan covered his mouth once more, "Lie to me again and he'll drown in his own blood."

Blood poured out of the young man's nostrils in large thick rivers that coursed between and spilled over Kerrigan's fingers. As the boy attempted to breathe in, his breath was restricted by his own blood. He started to cough as his own blood entered his lungs, the coughs blocked by Kerrigan's hand. As a result, the coughing came out of the boys nose instead, sending more blood scattering in front of him. The blood exploded outward and hung in the air like dust particles before falling onto, and staining, the carpet below.

Durrant looked upon the scene with wide eyed disbelief.

"OK, OK" beckoned Durrant, raising his palms outwards to Kerrigan, "Take it easy, take it easy. I'm sure we can all co-operate here."

Seeing the hurt in Durrant's eyes, Kerrigan opened up a gap between his fingers to allow the boy to breath. As he did so, a large, wet intake of breath was heard from the boy as he sucked in the air he desperately needed. A bubble of blood bloomed from his nostrils as he exhaled.

"OK, now we're co-operating." Replied Kerrigan, "You claim that

I killed a Chosen One. I want that bounty removed."

"I… I don't know what you mean."

Again, Kerrigan removed his hand covering the child's mouth and smashed it as hard as he could into the boy's face. He felt more cartilage succumb to his aggression, but not as much as the first time. Blood gushed from the child's nostril's in even greater quantities.

"OK, OK" beckoned Durrant once more, his open palms patted the air, "Whatever you want. Just, please, release my son."

"No" replied Kerrigan. He strode over to the wall were the decorative sword he had seen earlier was displayed. Keeping one hand covering the boy's mouth, he raised his free arm to grasp the handle of the weapon. The sword was a formidable size, clearly intended to be used with two hands but, as Kerrigan released it from it's brackets, he was surprised by just how light the weapon was. Not only that, but it was not just a single blade. Two blades were embedded into the hilt, the second blade an inch apart from the first, running in direct parallel to it's twin. Elaborate looking additional decoration that looked mechanical in it's design held the blades together at the hilt.

Kerrigan held the released blades to the boy's neck and returned to Nina's side, "You do exactly as I say, or your son dies."

Durrant saw the fire in Kerrigan's eyes, "OK, OK, whatever you say." He replied, still patting the open air with his open palms, "Please, just let the boy go…."

"No" replied Kerrigan once more, "We do this my way."

The child began to choke.

Durrant stuttered with his response as he viewed the life threatening grip being inflicted upon his son…

"Remove the bounty from my head!" bellowed Kerrigan, breaking Durrant from his mournful trance.

"OK, OK" replied Durrant again. He pressed his palm's even further forward to try and reinforce his compliance, "OK…." This time, the gesture was made with final reluctance.

After another moments contemplation, Kerrigan accepted Durrant's pleases as being true, and released his son enough for him to breathe.

Durrant let out a heavy sigh of relief. He looked Kerrigan straight in the eye and said, "The computers I need are on one of the floors below us. I can remove your bounty from there."

A stillness froze over the scene, "Alright" replied Kerrigan, approaching the door that led out of the room, "Lead the way."

Together, Durrant, Nina, Kerrigan and Durrant's son left the dining room, ventured down the plush hallway, and descending to the floor below. Durrant had suggested that they use the elevator; he had the clearance that would allow them to descend, but Kerrigan disagreed, concerned about the close confines that the elevator would provide.

Besides, they would not all fit in there at once.

Descending the cold stairwell, Durrant kept up a tirade of comforting statements to his captive son. "It's gonna be OK Phillip" or "Don't worry son, everything's gonna be OK" seemed to spurt from Durrant's lips with annoying frequency.

They arrived at the Administration level and Durrant led them inside. It was much more formally decorated than the cold, bland interior of the Testing and Experimentation level but less luxuriously furnished than Durrant's Private levels: Carpeting was laid out before them, but it much less plush and was severely worn. Wall paper decorated the walls much like it had in Durrant's 'Private' floors, but it was clearly cheaper in it's design.

Durrant advised the group that they need travel no further than the Reception room that lay directly infront of both the stairwell, and the elevator exit.

"In there," he indicated, pointing towards the room's entrance, "I only need one of the computers in there."

The Reception was laid out in exactly the same formation as the reception on the Testing and Experimentation level.

Without being prompted, Durrant headed straight towards one of the computer terminals that lay against the wall.

Pulling up one of the wheeled chairs that adorned the room, Durrant sat in-front of the illuminated monitor. He raised his finger's, but paused before he continued, "You will release my son if I do as you ask?" he asked Kerrigan over his shoulder.

"Maybe, but I'll kill him if you don't" replied Kerrigan, once more tightening his grip around the young man's neck, making his adolescent eye's bulge with pressure.

Durrant hesitated, then logged onto the computer.

"OK I'm just logging in," explained Durrant as his finger's fluttered across the keyboard.

The room was uncomfortably silent a moment as Durrant did what he was told.

When the silence had dragged onwards for an obscene length of time, the computer at which Durrant was sat issued a fanfare of acknowledgement and Durrant was granted access to the computer programmes within.

The monitor displayed a myriad of various logos and other baffling information.

As Kerrigan watched the slow log-on of the computer terminal, he kept his strong hold upon Phillip's throat. He did not want the child to believe that he might escape during his father's co-operation.

The screen upon the computer monitor turned from that of authentication, to that of acknowledgement.

The computer screen flickered black for a moment, then reawakened, changing it's image to display several icons that would allow further access to the information the terminal held.

"OK, we're in," acknowledged Durrant, explaining his actions as he went along, "I'm accessing your Warrant files now, Kerrigan."

Watching the computer screen, Kerrigan observed Durrant access the necessary files and wipe the records that branded him a Heathen.

"There," said Durrant, leaning back in the reclining computer chair, "all done." He swivelled to face Kerrigan in the glow of the active monitors, "Now release my son."

A huge weight lifted off of Kerrigan's shoulders as he watched Durrant delete the files pertaining to his arrest. He was almost free… assuming he could get out of here alive to enjoy it.

"It's done, Kerrigan. You're a free man. Now," said Durrant still reclining in the chair in which he sat, "let him go." Kerrigan still held his son, Phillip, in a deadly embrace.

"Not just yet," replied Nina, stepping forward in front of the pair as if to block Durrant's demands, "Where the fuck is my brother?"

Durrant turned his fixed gaze towards Nina, "I have no idea what you're talking about young lady."

"Don't you lie to us you son of a bitch," replied Nina, her voice hardening with anger and frustration, "We want to know what sick experiments you've got going on here. All those machines with the wrist straps and the electric cables? What the fuck are you doing to people here?"

"I don't know what you mean" replied Durrant coolly, confidently.

Nina slapped him hard across the face. The slap echoed in the empty room like a thunder crack, startling Nina as much as it must have startled Durrant.

"Now listen here, you fucking shit" spat Nina, thrusting her index finger in Durrant's face as she spoke, "I don't know who you are and quite frankly I don't give a fuck, but you better tell us what we want to know or your gonna wish you'd never been born!"

A hint of a smile rose in the corner of Durrant's mouth, "Your threats don't scare me."

"You better answer her." this time it was Kerrigan. As he spoke, he pinched the bloody nose of Durrant's son. Phillip's eyes bulged as he tried to squirm his way out of Kerrigan's grip.

"What…what are you doing?" asked Durrant, uncertainty finally hinting upon his emotions.

"Tell us what we want to know," demanded Kerrigan. Phillip's struggles were becoming increasingly frantic as his restricted breathing became apparent to him, "Or your son dies."

Durrant's eyes darted from Phillip to Kerrigan.

Phillip's eyes bulged with an urgent desperation to breathe. With a silent prayer to his father, they urged him to co-operate with the two strangers who were slowly, but surely, killing him.

Kerrigan's eyes remained dark and hidden beneath his furrowed brow.

Durrant visibly gulped. "You wouldn't." he replied, attempting to call Nina and, especially, Kerrigan's bluff. But even he was not convinced by his reply. His voice had wavered as he spoke,

Kerrigan didn't reply but Phillip continued to resist. His struggling had escalated into a desperate thrashing, lunging out and striking at any part of Kerrigan that he could reach.

He would be dead in less than a minute.

A silence hung in the air: Kerrigan and Nina letting Phillip's struggles convey their seriousness without them having to say a word, Durrant still not believing their threat.

"Are you just gonna watch your son die?" asked Nina with disbelief.

Phillip's resistance was becoming notably weaker, his previous thrashings had lost it's initial gusto and had faded to the weak struggling of someone suffering from a bad dream.

Yet still, despite Phillip's demise clearly being only a few moments away, Durrant refused to believe that Nina and Kerrigan would follow through with their threats.

The sparkle in Phillip's eyes was also fading…

Not long now.

"OK OK!" spat Durrant, his eyes portraying that the words from his mouth had defied the ill-logic of his brain.

Kerrigan released his pinch upon Phillip's nose.

The young man inhaled several long, wet, breaths of much needed air, sucking the much needed oxygen into his starved lungs.

"OK, you win" gasped Durrant, almost as much out of breath as his son. Durrant had not realised himself that he too had been holding his breath.

Leaning forward, taking hold of the arms of the chair that Durrant sat within, Nina said, "OK you fucker, you better start telling us some answers! Now, I'm not really one for small talk, so let's get straight down to business shall we? Where's Ames?"

"Who?"

"AMES!" she bellowed, her instant fury exploding out from within her like a volcanic explosion. Her voice cracked as it expressed the undiluted anger she felt, "AMES, you miserable fucker, AMES!

My fucking brother. I've seen his name all over this place and I want to know where he is. I swear by the Gods that if you've hurt him, I'll rip your fucking balls off and shove them so far up your ass that the next time you shit, you'll shit all over your balls. You got that?"
Despite Nina's aggression towards him, Durrant did not seem particularly frightened. At least, not for himself. He cast his eye's over Nina's shoulder to stare at his son who remained gasping within Kerrigan's grip.
He didn't look well.
"I'll take you to him" he replied.

Nina persisted in her enquiries as Durrant led them down the empty, blue tinged corridors of the Testing and Experimentation level. First Durrant, followed closely by Nina, who held one of their stolen guns to the rear of his head, and lastly Kerrigan, holding Phillip in an iron vice grip.
"So who the fuck are you exactly?" asked Nina.
"My name is Regional Director Alexander Durrant of The Northern Sector of the SigmaOmega and I…"
"I know who the fuck you are, what I mean is who the fuck are you REALLY? The S.O.? We all grow up in this world admiring and respecting you, the ones… "Chosen by the Gods themselves" She deliberately quoted the term that had been used in her upbringing, "But your meant to be helping us, leading us towards salvation, towards a future without deprivation, without the virus… not fucking kidnapping people and torturing them."
"We are the enlightened ones, yes." Replied Durrant. His voice and posture - chin and chest thrust out in front of him – were both full of pride, "But don't be mistaken by what you think you have seen here today." He looked both Nina and Kerrigan square in the eye, "We *are* the saviours of man kind."
"Like fuck you are." Replied Nina.
"Of course we are. Why else would the Gods allow us, the S.O., and only us, the use of electricity?"
"Maybe they made a mistake."

"I doubt that very much young lady. You cannot begin to comprehend the work that we do here."
"Try me."
"As much as I would like to, I fear that my efforts would be wasted on someone such as yourself."
"And just who the fuck do you think am I?"
"Like everybody else out there, just a sheep," replied Durrant calmly, "and we, the S.O, are your shepherds."
"For fuck's sake, you really are full of horse shit you know that?"
Durrant did not reply. They turned a corner leading them further to the rear of the 'Testing and Experimenting level'.
"So if the S.O.'s so good, so benevolent, why the fuck are you kidnapping people?"
"We haven't kidnapped anyone, they come of their own accord."
"And then you torture them."
"No."
"I've seen the machines, you idiot. Of course you do."
"No," replied Durrant offended at the accusation, "We don't."
Another turn in the corridor. At the end, a closed door blocked any further progress down the hall. An 'Authorised Personnel Only' sign was fastened to the front of the restricted doorway.
"So if you don't torture them, what do you do?" enquired Nina further.
"We… help them realise their inner potential."
"What the fuck do you mean?"
"We're here." announced Durrant stopping infront of the closed door. Avoiding her question. He turned to face Nina, Kerrigan and Phillip. He looked in his son's eyes to make sure that he was still alive.
Phillip's mouth was still wrapped in Kerrigan's arms, his face was smothered in congealed blood… but he was still alive and he was still breathing.
That was all that concerned Durrant.
"If I show you the answers to your questions… you will let my son and I go." It was not a question. Durrant was not asking if they agreed upon his terms, he was telling them how the situation was.

"Fine," said Nina, without consulting Kerrigan, "We're not savages like you."
After a moments hesitation, as if he were still considering his options, Durrant turned to the keypad that hung next to the door, and swiped his I.D. card through.
With a soft ping the reader accepted his card and the thick locks that secured the door were removed with a heavy thunk.

The heavy door swung inwards into a room totally absorbed in darkness. The rectangle where the door had previous been snuggled, was replaced with a blackness so deep it made their current, dimly lit corridor look bright in comparison.
Durrant stepped inside, with Nina following quickly at his heels.
It occurred to Kerrigan that this could perhaps be some kind of trap, that Durrant may use the darkness that now concealed him to spring upon Nina and over power her. Perhaps even try and use her as a hostage against Kerrigan.
He had no time to discover if this would work as, just before he was about to voice his concerns, the darkness was replaced by a powerful light that momentarily stung Kerrigan's retinas.
Durrant had switched on the overhead light's within. Now, fully lit, Kerrigan stepped inside the room, bringing Phillip, who's previous restraints had subsided into a reluctant acceptance, with him.
The room was huge, much bigger than Kerrigan had expected it to be, much bigger than he had thought had remained unexplored on this floor.
However, despite it's impressive size, the room was largely empty. The floor, walls and ceiling were covered in a soft, padded material which was both creamy in colour and texture. It looked like the flooring in particular would squash beneath their footsteps, yet the flooring held their weight comfortably as Kerrigan's group progressed inside. Only a slight cushioning was felt beneath their feet as they walked across the padded surface.
Against all the walls, without leaving a gap, were tens, perhaps as many as fifty, of the glowing cylinders that they had seen in an

earlier room. Like before, they stood motionless and silent, like sentinels on guard, however these cylinders were not clear, but had a dark, yellowish, shield concealing their contents. Each cylinder was connected to the next by cables and piping that expelled from the top of each container.

The cylinders gave off an oppressive atmosphere to the room, as if they were faceless, sleeping warriors who's hallowed ground was being violated.

It made both Kerrigan and Nina felt as if they were being watched.

Having been in the darkened corridors for so long, Kerrigan's head immediately started to ache as he viewed the scene through the intensity of the reignited lights.

Confident of his newly revealed surroundings, Durrant strode over to the only other piece of equipment in the room; a large semi circular computer console that stood in the centre of the room, before the blind cylinders.

Arriving at it he addressed Nina, "Ames, wasn't it?"

His voice conveyed that he had not forgotten, yet he asked it anyway. It added to the atmosphere that something here was not quite right, and that Durrant knew what it was. He was teasing them, teasing them to reveal his secret.

"What are these things?" asked Nina, ignoring Durrant's question, turning towards the silent, cylinders that lined three of the room's four walls.

Durrant smiled, although Nina was not facing him to see it, "I'm glad you asked. Allow me to show you."

With a flutter of his hands, Durrant typed proficiently at the console's controls.

A deep humming filled the air.

Movement caught Kerrigan's eye. He turned.

One of the cylinders was suddenly moving, the mucky yellow cover was sliding away, revealing the contents it held secret from the top down.

It was only now, as the shielding slid slowly away, that he understood that the yellow shrouding was not a casing at all. Instead, the yellow was actually the colour of the liquid that filled

the entire of the cylinder's interior.
As the liquid drained out, it revealed cabling running from the inside of it's roof down to something further within...
The cylinder to the right of this one clicked and also started to drain away, following the same course that the first cylinder had started.
A moment later the next container in line also followed suit, all three of them now draining slowly away to reveal their contents one after the other.
The original cylinder won the race.
Kerrigan could hardly believe what it was that he saw. The rational part of his mind tried to reject the sight, but his eyes and the part of his brain that processed the images refused to be ignored.
The cables within the tube snaked slowly down from their roots within the tubes lid…
As the thick yellow liquid drained away, it revealed the destination of the snake-like cables decent…
They were attached to the wet glistening globe of a bald man's head. His eye's were so wide that the entirety of his blue irises could be seen, his jaw hung down in an expression of dumb disbelief.
The cables plunged deep into his naked scalp. A small mound of flesh ringed each location where the cables punctuated his exposed skull.
As the liquid continued to drain away, revealing his naked and shrivelled torso, the next body in the second tank also came into view, revealed by the flow of it's own inner cables…
This time it was a woman. Her hair was also absent, allowing the intake of the cylinder's cables.
She also wore the same shocked expression as the first man.
Finally, the third tank revealed it's contents. First off the glistening bald head was exposed neither revealing whether it's contents were male or female.
Next came the moon shaped birth mark….
"NOOOOOOO!" screamed Nina, she flung the gun she held to the floor and ran to her brother's tank.

"NO, NO, NO!" she shouted, repeatedly beating her fists against the cylinder's thick glass in rhythm with her protests.

Kerrigan stared at the three lifeless figures that hung suspended within the tanks. It was impossible to tell if they were still alive or not:

Their chests did not rise or fall,

Their eyes did not blink,

Infact, they showed no signs of seeing the people infront of them at all. Ames in particular should have been expected to react to the arrival of his sister, but he remained as motionless as the others.

What the fuck?, thought Kerrigan. *Was this what they had intended for me also?... Why?*

What was their purpose?

"You fucking bastard!" spat Nina twisting to face Durrant, "You fucking, fucking bastard!" She strode towards him, fists clenched and swinging like pendulums at her side, "What the fuck are you doing here?"

Durrant hardly seemed to notice Nina any longer. He was staring with awe at the lifeless forms before him. Looking upon them like an artist may admire his own work.

His head moved languidly towards Nina, "You couldn't possibly understand." He replied.

"Oh I understand alright," she replied, "You killed my brother and now, your gonna pay." She was rapidly covering the distance between them both.

"Oh he's not dead. Far from it infact." replied Durrant, dreamily. "He's in a much better place now."

"Better place?! Does he look like he's in a better place to you!?" She stopped directly in front of Durrant and pointed at Ames's without turning her face away from Durrant. Her brother's form, Trendid's saviour, hung shrivelled and limp, like dead meat upon a hook, inside an artificial cylinder.

"NO," she continued, "he's fucking dead. You killed my brother! And now..." she punched Durrant so quickly he could not even reflexively raise his arms in defence. He went sprawling to the floor, "...I'm gonna kill you."

She took a stride towards his defenceless form, her fists raised with purposeful intent.

A secret door opened within the egg white room. At first only it's outline was discernible, but as it withdrew itself deeper into it's own recess, the outline became more prominent, revealing it's true form as it slid away upon unseen runners.
Neither Kerrigan nor Nina had noticed it previously as it had blended itself so seamlessly into the perfect white surroundings that it was encased within.
It froze Nina in her lust for blood.
Within the newly formed doorway, a tightly crowded bunch of S.O guards appeared, each seeming to try and enter the room ahead of their fellow officers.
"Hold it!" shouted the closest guard who filled the doorway.
"Get behind me." This time it was Kerrigan who spoke. His voice grating together like broken glass, cool and confident.
Nina turned around to look at him. He still held Phillip in a hug across his chest. The boy's eyes looked less frightened now that his father's cavalry had arrived.
Understanding the situation, Nina dashed behind Kerrigan, putting him and Phillip between her and the guards still within the doorway.
All of a sudden, despite the seriousness of the situation, she was shocked by the amusing thought that rose up within her mind: *Bet the kid doesn't look quite as relieved now...*
She could smell the warm leather of Kerrigan's jacket as she pressed her face against his back. The leather coat creaked as she hugged herself as close as possible to the taller man. His back felt hard as the sharp angles of his muscles pressed into her cheek.
"It's about bloody time." Said Durrant, wiping away a tear of blood that wept from the corner of his mouth.
Durrant, thought Nina. *Shit! He must have alerted the guards when he was at the console...*
"Back away from the Director and let the boy go." Commanded the lead guard who had stepped into the room. The other guards

fanned out to flank him.

Nina doubted that they would risk shooting while Kerrigan still held Durrant's son through fear of hitting the boy himself, or fearful of Kerrigan's actions.

Durrant laughed obnoxiously, "Oh my, I thought you two might have proved a little cleverer than this. Didn't you think it odd that the Refinery was so quiet?"

Nina couldn't see Durrant, but she could imagine the triumphant grin that no doubt smothered his face, "Unlike you two, some people remain faithful to the S.O. and our teachings. Your devout leader from Trendid, Phon I think his name was? Remains true to The Gods and kindly informed us of your little plan."

SHIT! Thought Nina, *he betrayed us.*

She felt sickened that one of her closest friends had stabbed her in the back.

Although Phon was Ames's replacement, and was not blood related to Nina, she had accepted his guidance, wisdom... and friendship.

She felt betrayed. She had always thought that they were so close, despite him replacing what she had lost, what Trendid had lost, in their lives.

Yet at the same time she knew that she shouldn't feel so personally offended. Phon must have recognised Kerrigan back in Trendid and informed the S.O, honouring his devotion and allegiance. He was one of The God's representative's. She was foolish to consider that their friendship might mean more than his life long devotion to the world's religion.

Unfortunately, this was not the time or place to dwell upon the loyalties of those that she had trusted.

As she was crouched behind Kerrigan, he took a slow step backwards and nearly stood upon Nina's feet. Knowing that he intended to retreat across the room, she accompanied his retreating steps.

Slowly, they withdrew across the room. Although she had thought that the room was large upon first entering it, Nina knew that they would cross it all too soon and they would be trapped with no

where to go.
She turned to see just how far they had left.
Not far, much less than she had expected. In another five or six steps they would reach the wall.
Just what was his plan? To back up into a corner? What type of plan was that? Surely he must have something in mind…
It was then that she noticed it.
The door.
The door they had entered by was only a step or two to their left.
Suddenly, she knew all to well what Kerrigan's plan was.
"Kerrigan, the door…" she hissed
She twisted his waist so that they were now backing up directly towards the exit.
She heard the snapping of guns as the guards readied their weapons, "This is your last warning." It was the same voice as before and Nina assumed that it must have been the same guard, although she could not see anyone anymore from behind Kerrigan's back.
It sounded uncomfortably as if they too, had realised Kerrigan's plan, "Stop or we WILL shoot!"
"Careful not to kill him." Spoke Durrant, afraid for his son.
"Careful not to kill him" so you don't mind if they HARM him? Great father you are. Thought Nina
"Get ready." she hissed.
Just a couple more steps.
"No, don't!" it was Durrant. He blurted out the command before the guards could honour their threat. "Don't shoot! He's too precious."
Aww isn't that sweet?
Despite the guards readied stance, Kerrigan and Nina knew that the guard's would not betray their superior's orders and so it was that they passed out of the white room and were once again enveloped in the ghostly blue of the corridor. They continued to face forward, keeping their hostage between themselves and the guards.
Nina stopped their little train, "If any of you tries to follow us, we will kill him."

With that said she reached up and pressed a button on the keypass reader that hung beside the door. The door that they had just passed beyond slowly closed putting itself between themselves and the S.O guards.
Just before it swung shut, Nina peeked around Kerrigan and saw the look of loss upon Durrant's face.
And then he was gone.

20

"How do we get out of here?" Kerrigan asked.
"I don't know." Admitted Nina, flustered, "We can't go back out the way we came in, there'll be hundreds of guards." She turned towards Phillip, "Is there another way out of here besides the stairs or elevators?"
Kerrigan released the smothering hold he had on his mouth. Too small and frightened to attempt to defy his captures in anyway, Phillip replied, "There…There's a service elevator…". He wiped the tears from his eyes and cheeks as he spoke, careful not to touch the shattered cartilage of his broken nose.
"Where's that?"
He pointing the way with one bloody finger in the general direction that the service elevator lay.
"Let's go." Nodded Nina towards Kerrigan.
Together they ran towards the service elevator following Phillip's directions whenever they came to more than one direction to choose from. His continued cries echoed throughout the deserted corridors and bounced back in sharp accents that stabbed into Kerrigan and Nina's ears.
The service elevator might not be ideal for their escape, but it would surely prove better than taking the normal elevators or stairwell which would surely be infected with hundreds of alerted guards by now.
Of course, no doubt the service elevator would also prove to be secured - the S.O had no doubt stationed guards at every entrance and exit point in the entire building.

Still, thought Nina, *who said anything about* using *the lift?*
Following Phillip's directions, Nina, Kerrigan and Phillip soon arrived at the service elevator doorway. Without using the buttons to call for the elevator carriage, Nina forced her fingers between the slim slit of the currently sealed, sliding doors. With all of her might, she attempted to pry the doors apart. Her muscles strained, and she groaned with the effort she exhorted... but no matter how hard she tried, the doors refused to budge.
She turned and asked Kerrigan, in a panting voice, if he might try, taking hold of Phillip's hand before the larger man could reply.
Kerrigan approached the sealed doorway and stood there, facing the challenge before him.
After a moment's pause, he forced his fingers in the tiny gap where the two doors connected, and braced himself.
After another moment's pause where all the sounds of the Refinery dimmed into silence... he pulled.
With a reluctant squeal of protest, the doors grated slowly apart.
"Great!" exclaimed Nina.
Kerrigan looked down the elevator shaft that he had exposed. The darkness extended away to a point beyond his sight. The shaft was hundreds of feet deep.
Nina also peered over the abyss.
They both understood the unspoken plan.
They would descend the shaft using the ladders that were embedded in the side of the shaft. The ladders were intended for use in emergencies should the lift ever malfunction and trap it's occupants between floors.
Hopefully, the guards that would be expecting them to use the lifts as normal would not be expecting them to use these, usually overlooked, ladders.
They both also knew the unvoiced problem: Phillip. Nina looked at the boy. He was still crying softly to himself, although his tears had mostly dried up and his wailing had reduced to muffled sobs. He was a pathetic sight, but could still prove a danger to them if he revealed their escape route to anyone of the S.O. officers.
Kerrigan stepped forward, raising his newly acquired sword...

"Kerrigan, no!"
...and hit Phillip with hilt of the sword on top of his head.
The boy fell unconscious onto his face with a soft smack.
Once upon the floor, he did not move and Nina at first feared that he may be dead... but a slight gasping could be heard from his open mouth.
"For fuck's sake!, was that really necessary?" She could hardly believe that she had seen such cruelty.
"Would you prefer me to slit his throat?" replied Kerrigan, admiring the long blade he had taken from Durrant's dining room. The sword sparkled from multiple pints in the soft lighting, as if it were embedded with tiny, blue stars.
"NO! of course not!" she said horrified, " but... come on!..." She didn't put up much more of an argument. What was done, was done.
Besides, it did the job. Phillip wouldn't be telling anyone where they had gone anytime soon.
She stood over the small, sleeping boy. He looked like a child's doll that had been cast aside when the child had grown tired of playing with it.
Kerrigan had already gone to the elevator shaft and had crawled his way over the lip. He stood with his feet on the first few rungs.
Only his head and shoulders were visible to Nina now, and they too disappeared below the floor.
Nina followed.

Being in the service elevator shaft reminded Nina of the corridors that they had only just left behind, only this was vertical instead of horizontal. Pipes and cables slithered their way across and around every surface of every wall as if they were in a serpent's liar. The blue lights were still here, shining their sickly glow, although they were fewer and farther between so that their descent would occasionally become enveloped in darkness only to re-emerge into the icy blue light a few rungs further down.
The air was noticeably cooler in the shaft. A slight draft fluttered from below to tickle Nina's ankles and occasionally flutter an

irritatingly loose strand of hair in front of her face.

They descended in silence, Nina catching the odd glimpse of the top of Kerrigan's head as she tried to watch her footing. She wondered what he was thinking but she felt too exposed in the empty shaft and unable to ask. Their voices would surely travel in the hollow trunk down which they descended; potentially alerting the guards positioned upon multiple floors should they be heard.

She just prayed and hoped that he knew what he was doing.

The silence that reigned their downwards progress filled Nina with an ominous anticipation, filling her head with unwanted observations...

Surely, it would not take long for the guards to figure out where they had gone? A quick examination of the "Testing and Experimenting" floor would turn up the unconscious body of Phillip next to the open service elevator... It wouldn't take a genius to figure out where they had gone next.

Nina cursed herself for being so stupid.

Although they had now descended sufficiently not to be seen by anyone looking through the doorway they had entered the elevator shaft by, it would only be moments later that the guards contacted their colleagues on the floors below and made them open the service doors on those levels. It would then only take one lucky group to open a set of doors that was near them and they would be easy pickings. They did not have Phillip as a human shield anymore.

It could happen at any moment.

It could be happening right now.

"Kerrigan" she whispered, her voice a loud hiss in the hollow shaft, "We need to get out of here."

He did not reply but she hoped that he had heard her above the flutter of the breeze.

A moment later he stopped in his descent.

Nina did likewise.

Kerrigan fiddled with something on the wall.

She couldn't see what it was that he was doing. Now motionless, her paranoia grew even worse than it was before and she kept looking above and below herself, expecting to hear doors sliding apart and the heads of the S.O guards peeking out peering upon them both like nosey birds.

A loud, but distant crash from below startled her. She tightened her grip on the ladder and inhaled sharply.

They had found them! The S.O had found them and were throwing explosives at them!

She looked below and saw Kerrigan had half crawled inside a tunnel that ran off from the elevator shaft. He was still angling his large frame inside the narrow tunnel.

The crash had came from the fallen cover that had protected the tunnel. Even now the protective plating tumbled downwards, sending echoing splashes up and down the shaft as it knocked against the metallic walling.

She exhaled her held breath wishing that Kerrigan hadn't made such a racket. Not only had it startled her, but it must surely have been heard on the floors below.

It could work as a distraction, making which ever officers heard the crash believe that Kerrigan and Nina were actually further down from where they where, as they peered out and observed the covering's continued descent.

However, it would definitely direct their attention to the shaft from where it had came.

As soon as Kerrigan vanished into the elevator shaft wall, Nina descended down to enter the new route for herself.

The narrow tunnel led away from the elevator shaft. It was claustrophobic even for Nina, making her wonder just how snugly Kerrigan was fitting through the tunnel.

Although she had never been in this tunnel - she was not in the habit of escaping corrupt religious H.Q's - it was clear to her that the tunnel was some kind of air ventilation tunnel. The silver segmented tunnel had a warm draft of wind that pushed gently against their progress.

It was no doubt this tunnel, in collaboration with a series of others, that had provided the breeze that had tickled her from below in the main elevator shaft.

Once again, Nina could not see where they were going. The only thing she could see was the shuffling rear end of Kerrigan as he progressed through the narrow shaft in front of her. Once more, she found herself trusting in Kerrigan, hoping that he knew what he was doing, but unfortunately knowing that Kerrigan could not know where they were going any more than she did.
Turning blind corner after blind corner, Kerrigan finally stopped without warning in front of Nina.
"What is it?" she hissed. Her voice sounding horribly loud in the confines of the tunnel, despite her restraint.
"Nothing." He hissed back, his voice seeming to come from his bottom as his body filled the shaft.
It might have almost been comical under other circumstances, "Just a headache. Come on"
They continued further into the intestines of the H.Q, taking more twists and turns until Nina felt that they must surely be covering old ground if not for the tunnel occasionally bending at a right angle directly up or down, causing Kerrigan and Nina to bend and twist their bodies respectively as they progressed to higher or lower levels.
Kerrigan stopped in front of Nina once more. She could hear him fiddling with something metallic in front of him, at knew at once what it was.
Another covering for the ventilation shaft.
She hoped he had scouted the way ahead before removing the cover and that he would be more delicate when removing it than he had previously.
A loud crash exploded from in front of her as the cover for the tunnel smashed loudly onto the concrete floor of the corridor it led to.
Panic threatened to erupt in Nina. Now they would surely be discovered in no time at all.
FUCKING HELL KERRIGAN! She thought, *Why aren't you being more careful??*
She watched him flop ungainly out of the tunnel ahead of her.
What the fuck? Something was wrong.

She scurried out of the tunnel herself and found Kerrigan leaning against the wall of the corridor. His bone-white face was twisted in pain, his skin was oily with sweat and he was panted like an old, dying dog.

"Kerrigan... What's the matter with you?" she asked, rushing towards him.

"My... head" he replied, twisting his head deliriously from side to side, as if trying to deny the pain that tortured him.

A migraine... thought Nina. Just their fucking luck for him to suddenly get a migraine. Of all the times and places! She would have to take the lead.

Wrapping his arm over her shoulder, she lifted Kerrigan and half carried him along the corridor as fast as she could... which was only half as fast as she'd have liked.

His taller frame leaned heavily upon her, making her stoop with effort. Every step soon became a struggle. He was incredibly heavy.

They had taken only a few steps when she heard running footsteps approaching from off one of the corridors that branched off from their own.

They were going to be discovered!

With no other option, Nina pushed open the nearest set of doors that she chanced upon, and dragged herself and Kerrigan inside.

At first, the room reminded Nina of the cylinder chamber from the floors above. It was large in size and the only contents of the room were six cylinders spaced evenly throughout the room: three on either side. These cylinders however, were allowed to stand freely, rather than against a wall.

The cylinders, standing silently independent, were a deep, blood red in colour rather than the sickly yellow of those in the levels above.

Perhaps it was the way they were aligned or the different colouring, but to Nina, these cylinders were instantly much more imposing than those before...

... until she noticed that only one of them appeared to be in full working order. The other five varied in damage or were destroyed entirely.

Only the reinforced bases that held the shattered glass bases of the man-sized tubes they once contained, remained on two of them.

The other three had had their glass casings smashed or cracked, allowing the contents of which to drain out, leaving only the dead, hollow shell of the glass tube behind.

It was not only the cylinders within the room that were damaged. The room itself had also suffered some harm.

The wall immediately to Nina's left was completely blown out, exposing herself and her silent companions to the vast night sky.

Outside she could see the glittering pinpricks of infinitely distant stars piercing the darkness above the glowing rooftops of the disturbingly close buildings that surrounded and encircled around the H.Q.

The cool night air drifted in through the missing wall, caressing her skin so gently as to be almost deliberately delicate, a sensation that she might have relished had she had the opportunity.

She took all of these tranquil observations in while still carrying Kerrigan further into the room, desperately attempting to put as much distance between themselves and the approaching S.O officers as possible.

This room, Nina knew instinctively, was the same room that Kerrigan had made his escape from the last time he had been here.

Had he led them both here deliberately?

"Kerrigan...?" she said, not knowing what it was she had been about to ask.

"The.... wall" he muttered, his voice barely audible. "Go... to the wall"

Although he didn't say which wall, it was obvious that he meant the only wall out of the four with a hole in it. None of the other walls had anything significant about them.

Go to the wall? What the fuck?

"Kerrigan, it's just a hole."

She knew that they were about to die. They had no where left to run, no where else to hide, and no one to save them. As soon as the pursuing guards opened the door, they would tear their bodies apart with their gunfire.

Perhaps it was through sheer desperation that Nina found herself doing as she was asked. She aimed both herself and Kerrigan towards the gaping night scape.

Was his plan to scale down the outside of the building? If so, she herself might have been OK. Providing Kerrigan had the relevant equipment to do so secreted about his person.

Kerrigan however… he in his current state… he would certainly fall to his death. She had not the strength to support his decent.

"Kerrigan, you've got to wake up," panted Nina, her strength already failing her. "I can't do this alone!"

Kerrigan's breathing was coming in hollow rasps.

They were only a few more steps from the deadly outcropping. Whatever it was that Kerrigan was thinking, if he was even thinking coherently at all in his current muddled state of mind, Nina wished that he'd hurry up and explain himself.

"The wall….. hold me."

"I've got you Kerrigan." Nina reassured him. He seemed about to fall at any second. What ever it was that he had had in mind, was gone.

"No…", he was barely able to mutter.

One more step.

Nina could see the glowing city below them staring up with twinkling artificial eyes. It seemed terrifyingly close.

"HOLD me" he uttered.

"I am…"

He turned his sagging head up to face hers. His eyes, beneath the sweaty hair that flopped over his face, were rimmed bright red as if he had spent several days rubbing them with grit, but the intensity with which he met her eyes was more powerful, more certain, than anything she had ever seen before.

Tears streaked down his twisted face.

"HOLD ME!" he growled between clenched teeth as if his initial instructions had been ignored.

Standing on the very edge of the destroyed flooring, Nina wrapped her arms around Kerrigan's waist, pulling him tightly against herself.

The night air whipped about them, now filling her ears with it's sighing, threatening to spill them over the edge at any moment.

We're going to die and the last thing this man wants is a hug...

Unfortunately, Nina had absolutely no other ideas remaining to her. Despite his arrogance, selfishness, rudeness and all of his other flaws, she couldn't leave Kerrigan behind to die alone anymore than she could have allowed her brother to be harmed.

Ames, she thought, *I'm so sorry I couldn't help you.*

She clenched her eyes shut.

She heard the doors spring open as the S.O guards entered their chamber.

They fell.

21

The fall from the H.Q Refinery was peaceful. Nina did not feel any panic and was not frightened by her own, and Kerrigan's, head first plummet to the deserted ground below.

Soon...

Her faith had been shattered. Those that she had respected, that her community had respected, had betrayed her trust. Her family particularly, had worked in conjunction with the S.O for generations. She had no direction anymore.

She wished that she had been able to save her brother, but she was content in knowing that she had tried her best.

Soon...

Bizarrely, she felt quite peaceful. Everything she had ever believed in was gone, or had changed. Perhaps it was all these revelations that provided her sanguine at this time.

She kept her eyes shut throughout the fall as if she were only resting her head, about to fall asleep.

Soon...

The wind that gushed past them both was her blanket, Kerrigan's chest, her pillow.

Her fall happened in slow motion. She knew that they had been falling awhile and that soon, very soon, their journey would come to a brief sudden stop.
Very soon...
Suddenly, a great pressure filled her head from one side. It felt as if they were turning, no longer falling straight down.
Spinning... she thought.
The pressure eased and the wind continued it's cascade across her body.
Surely, soon...
Bizarrely, she felt herself almost becoming impatient.
Impatient, for the impact that should have happened by now.
She cast these thoughts aside almost as quickly as they occurred with the understanding that it was just her brain's way of dealing with the impending doom.
A doom that most definitely should have happened by now.
Morbid fascination made her open her eyes.
"Wha....?"
The glowing blue roof tops and glittering concrete of the city that she had seen from the broken wall of the S.O Refinery, that SHOULD have been spinning towards them both was, instead, zooming past below them, in a disorientating blue blur.
They were somehow, Nina understood, moving over the rooftops at an incredible speed...
"Kerrigan..." she gasped against his chest.
"Hang on, Nina" said Kerrigan, his voice once again resurrected with strength. He clutched the back of her head with a reassuring hand.
What the fuck's going on?
Too stunned to articulate her thought's, Nina remained silent as the outer ring of the Refinery's security went zooming past below them. They had covered the entire length of the Refinery in almost no time at all, although, Nina would later reflect, it could have been much longer. Her sense of time and recollection had become confused during the disorientation of the moment.
Soft, moonlit trees and fields replaced the harsh angles and sharp

edges of the Refinery's buildings below her. Nina thought she even saw a small herd of deer dashing below them in the gloom, startled by the nameless animal that soared over heads.

Before long, the ground was rushing up to meet them.

"Hold tight." Said Kerrigan.

She clenched her eye's tightly shut, knowing that their flight was coming to an end.

With a stomach churning flip, they decelerated with dizzying speed and righted to a standing position.

She felt a light thump course through Kerrigan's body as his feet touched upon the solid ground.

She tenuously lowered her legs and also felt the reassuring comfort of the grass beneath her feet.

Although she knew that they were now standing on solid ground once more, she found that she couldn't release her grip on Kerrigan.

She felt his hand on the back of her skull again, petting her.

With a controlled effort, she opened her eyes. In the far, far distance, she could see the glittering light's of the Refinery sparkling upon the horizon. The cool cream of the H.Q building stood proudly in the centre.

It looked tiny.

She released her grip on Kerrigan. Her finger's ached with the movement, having gripped so tightly around him..

Without warning, her legs buckled and she fell on her rear before Kerrigan.

She looked up at him.

He stood, silhouetted by the light of the moon which filled the night sky behind him. He stood with his fists clenched tightly by his sides, his leather jacket fluttering gently at his ankles. His head was turned towards the opposite horizon from the S.O Refinery and behind him…

…Behind him, silhouetted against the white moonlight, as if the moon itself were a spotlight focusing upon Kerrigan, were a pair of huge, black wings, twice as tall as Kerrigan himself was. With a soft flick, the wings stretched themselves outwards, each and every plume of feather fanning outwards in a strained stretch. With a soft *thwick* of fanned air, they then started to fold in upon themselves, folding and twisting until they disappeared again behind Kerrigan, hiding themselves once more beneath his ankle-length leather jacket.

"Kerrigan…" whispered Nina, hardly finding her voice.

"Come on, we have to go." He started to walk away from her.

She wasn't sure if her legs were ready to support her yet. She rolled onto her elbow, facing his direction.

"Kerrigan, what was that?" she whispered.

"Nothing. Let's go" He did not stop to offer her a helping hand up. Desperate for answers, she stumbled to her feet and ran after him.

"Kerrigan. What happened back there?"

He did not reply or slow down. Nina had to jog just to keep up with him.

"Kerrigan…"

"IT WAS NOTHING!" He stopped. His face was filled with anger. "Nothing happened back there! Now come on, before they come after us!" He turned and started off without her again.

The virus…thought Nina, *he's been affected by the virus…*

"What the fuck? You expect me to just ignore what happened back there? Kerrigan, you saved our lives. You've got wings…."

"SHUT UP!" he bellowed, turning towards her. "SHUT THE FUCK UP!" he punctuated each word. His face was consumed with an anger like Nina had never before seen… but beneath it, behind his eyes, Nina thought that she could see other emotions too. Emotions she had not seen within Kerrigan before.

Was it shame that she could see?

Shocked more by his pain, than by his anger, Nina dropped the subject and, with a moment's choice, Kerrigan strode silently away.

They continued their way on foot. Kerrigan's pace never slowed, and Nina was forced to jog on occasion just to keep up with him. Occasionally Nina would look at Kerrigan and see a profile of pure anger. He did not look in her direction even once.

She had so many questions in her mind that she needed to know, that she needed to voice, to discuss and possibly make some sense of, but she remained silent, respecting Kerrigan's clear portrayal that he did not want to talk to her.

She could not keep her mind focused on one particular area. So many were her questions, that her mind floated gently and easily, from one subject to the next.

Her entire perception of the world had changed in so many ways. Kerrigan...

Who was he really? She knew absolutely nothing about him. He had been framed, that much she was sure of now... But where had he come from? What was his story?

He was still very much a stranger to her.

And his wings...

It was clear that he was embarrassed by them, but Nina had tried to warn him. He had not taken the vaccine as Nina had advised. She had warned him of the mutations that it would inflict, so what had he expected to happen? Did he think she had been joking him?

Still though, she had never seen such a bizarre mutation. Normally the virus was harmful; premature ageing, additional dead limbs, deformed babies... but in a way, Kerrigan's mutation seemed almost advantageous... almost... beautiful.

Who am I kidding?, she thought, *They* are *beautiful!*

Her mind turned gently away from Kerrigan, back towards herself and towards her brother. He heart ached for him.

Tortured and subjected to experiments beyond her comprehension, Ames was even now still wired up to the infernal machine within the Refinery.

What was that machine doing to him? What did the S.O want with him? And why?

From thoughts of her brother, her mind drifted smoothly, yet naturally, to the most horrific subject of all: her brother's captors.

The S.O.

Some of the most respected and honoured collection of people in Nina's life. In EVERYONE'S lives. But now they had turned out to be nothing more than twisted, mad scientists, preying upon the very people that it was meant to be helping, performing twisted experiments upon human beings for reasons that remained beyond Nina's comprehension.

Were they trying to accomplish something? Durrant's mannerism certainly seemed to suggest that they were aiming for something… but what? Or was Durrant simply as twisted as his own experiments, and they really had no goal other than to cause misery and suffering upon those who trusted them?

Speaking (or indeed, thinking) of trust, Nina's next thoughts were of Phon, Trendid's current Chosen One and leader.

He had betrayed her, and by extension, her brother.

Bizarrely, she found it hard to muster the same amount of anger she felt towards the S.O, towards him.

After all he was as brainwashed as she had been herself by the S.O's teachings and therefore believed his own actions in the best interests of all those whom he gave leadership to…

…and finally…

…finally…

… she reflected upon the final revelation, a one that should have been life changing in it's own regard, yet her feelings had become numb due to the sheer volume of shocks she had experienced of late.

They were not alone.

The general civilised understanding that Trendid, Kallingo, Ferralin and the S.O. Refinery, were the only… ONLY… settlements in the entire world, was wrong. They were all PLACES certainly, but only places contained within an ISLAND…. An island that they were all based upon.

Yet that one island was just one small, singular piece of an over all, much larger picture.

Again, the S.O. had betrayed and lied to them all!

Her next action's were obvious. When they got back to Trendid, she had to make everyone aware of the true nature of the S.O. and the lies that they inflicted upon society.

They were traitors and they had to be exposed.

With what Kerrigan and herself had seen, along with her

established position within Trendid's society, she ought to be able to muster together a group large enough to confront the S.O. and question it's authority.
She had no idea how the S.O would react to such a confrontation but she had to try…
For herself…
For Ames…
For Trendid and the entire world, she had to try.
She had to try.
As she was pondering all this, she once again fell behind Kerrigan a couple of steps.
She jogged to catch back up to him.

To Be Continued…

Printed in Great Britain
by Amazon